DEN OF LIARS

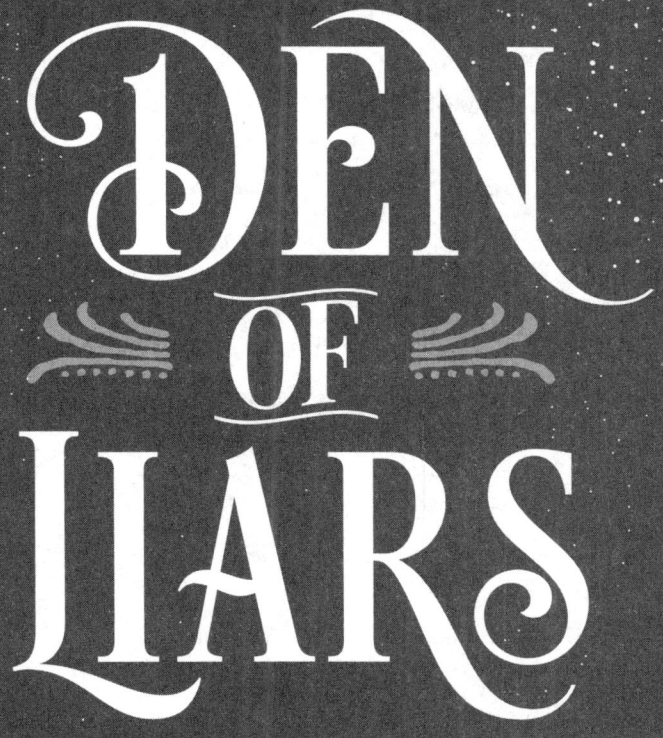

DEN OF LIARS

JESSICA S. OLSON

FEIWEL AND FRIENDS
New York

CONTENT WARNING:
depictions of child abuse, trauma, kidnapping, violence, loss of caretakers, and mild language

A FEIWEL AND FRIENDS BOOK
An imprint of Macmillan Publishing Group, LLC
120 Broadway, New York, NY 10271 • fiercereads.com

Eu representative: Macmillan Publishers Ireland Ltd, 1st Floor, The Liffey Trust Centre, 117–126 Sheriff Street Upper, Dublin 1, DO1 YC43

Copyright © 2025 by Jessica S. Olson. All rights reserved.

Our books may be purchased in bulk for promotional, educational, or business use. Please contact your local bookseller or the Macmillan Corporate and Premium Sales Department at (800) 221-7945 ext. 5442 or by email at MacmillanSpecialMarkets@macmillan.com.

The publisher of this book does not authorize the use or reproduction of any part of this book in any manner for the purpose of training artificial intelligence technologies or systems. The publisher of this book expressly reserves this book from the Text and Data Mining exception in accordance with Article 4(3) of the European Union Digital Single Market Directive 2019/790.

Library of Congress Cataloging-in-Publication Data

Names: Olson, Jessica S. author
Title: Den of liars / Jessica S. Olson.
Description: First edition. | New York : Feiwel and Friends, 2025. | Series: The devious ; 1 | Audience term: Teenagers | Audience: Ages 13 and up | Audience: Grades 10–12 | Summary: "A young thief attempting a daring casino heist during a high-stakes tournament is torn between two warring brothers" — Provided by publisher.
Identifiers: LCCN 2024041901 | ISBN 9781250329721 hardback
Subjects: CYAC: Robbers and outlaws—Fiction | Blessing and cursing—Fiction. | Brothers—Fiction | Fantasy | Romance stories | LCGFT: Fantasy fiction | Romance fiction | Novels
Classification: LCC PZ7.1.O4862 De 2025 | DDC [Fic] —dc23/eng/20250320
LC record available at https://lccn.loc.gov/2024041901

First edition, 2025
Book design by Aurora Parlagreco and Abby Granata
Feiwel and Friends logo designed by Filomena Tuosto
Printed in the United States of America

ISBN 978-1-250-32972-1
10 9 8 7 6 5 4 3 2 1

To anyone who has ever loved a lie

"THE DEVIOUS"

Devious Liar, devious Thief,
Devious pair of sin,
Who lied and stole a moonshard whole
And let corruption in.
Devious brothers, you cannot hide
The powers you have seized.
The skies, they watch your devious deeds;
They'll claim devious reprise.

—Aetheran nursery rhyme
Author unknown

PROLOGUE

The Thief came for her heart in the night.

He rippled through the wall of that windowless basement and found Magnolia St. James exactly where he expected. Huddled in the corner, lit only by a sliver of light from the bottom of a locked door. She blinked up at him through swollen, bruised eyes. Blood crusted her pale cheeks, caked in her gold-spun hair, dripped from her chin.

He expected her to be afraid, but she did not shrink back. Her gaze trailed along the glowing voratium hoops in his eyebrows, dropped to the matching studs in his nose and lips, traced the rings cuffing his ears, and finally settled on the glittering black octopus wrapped around his left wrist like a bracelet.

She did not ask who he was. Instead, she cocked her head toward the door. "They'll be back soon, so whatever you intend to steal, you'd better make it quick."

A murmur of gruff voices argued in the other room. Apparently, Magnus St. James, the girl's father, hadn't taken the bait and come to rescue her. The Thief couldn't entirely hide his satisfied smile.

Everything was going according to plan.

"I say we put a bullet through her brain," one man barked. "Send a message."

"And bring the wrath of the St. James empire down on our heads?" another shot back.

"Snatching her in the first place should have done that," the first retorted. "The other families are as finished with St. James as we are. This move would win Salazar every ally we'd need to finally take him down."

The Thief met her eyes. Blood accentuated their azure color, a blue as vivid as the heart of a flame. And how they blazed. A whipping icefire that burned past the fear that kept her cowering in the corner.

Perhaps she was just as lethal as he hoped.

"They're going to kill me." Her voice did not waver, but her hands quivered like the wings of a butterfly skewered to a wall.

"Not if you come with me," the Thief said softly.

"You're one of the Devious," she said. "You don't help people."

"I might. Many believe me starblessed, that my power was a gift from the gods."

She jutted out her chin. "I believe you want something."

"Clever girl."

"Last time I checked, thieves weren't in the business of making trades."

He almost laughed. "Quite true. But what I want is not something I can steal. It must be given willingly."

"And what do you want?"

"Your heart."

The corners of the girl's eyes tightened. "My heart?"

"Not your physical heart, of course; I'm not a monster." He cocked his head, smiled at his own joke. If this girl had truly been raised by the most infamous street lord Aethera had ever known, then she had seen her fair share of monstrosity.

"I've heard you steal the starlight in people's souls," she whispered. "Is that what you mean?"

"Yes. I want the soullight of your heart. Its capacity to feel. To love. To care." He dropped his voice to a whisper. "To hurt."

There. Quick as lightning, he saw it. A flash of agony so acute it spat sparks in her gaze. He had her.

She opened her mouth, but before she could ask him how or why or what, the doorknob rattled.

"Do we have a deal?" the Thief asked, extending a hand.

The lock mechanism in the door clicked. The sound of the second bolt being thrown back resounded like a punch.

She stared at the Thief's outstretched fingers. "What do I get in return?"

"Rescue," he said. "And, as long as your heart is mine, protection."

"Take it." She grasped his hand so hard his knuckles cracked. "I don't want it anymore."

So as the door swung open, he lifted the only voratium pendant hanging from his neck that did not yet glow and pressed it to the bare skin above her collar. It vibrated as he called forth his power.

"Hey! How'd you get in here?" A burly man with a thick mustache raised his pistol.

The Thief grinned. "Magic."

By the time the gun fired, the Thief and the girl had already vanished.

Nothing but a pair of shadows, they prowled like wraiths through the city. The voratium fragment between their fingers pulsed violet blue, and the Thief sighed as it thrummed a steady *thump-thump, thump-thump* against his skin.

One heart, two souls, for as long as the girl would live.

He only prayed he wouldn't need it that long.

CHAPTER ONE

LOLA

Damn, if I don't love a good police chase.

"Halt!" the cop behind us barks.

Enzo snorts next to me. "'Halt'? Do they ever realize how ridiculous they sound?"

I laugh as our feet slap in tandem across the slippery roof tiles of Aethera's factory district. Our heart thunders in my chest, and adrenaline sparks in my pulse as sharp as the electricity rumbling in the clouds overhead. "Wholly unoriginal," I agree as we leap across an alleyway and land midstride on the next roof, never breaking our pace.

We haven't been chased in at least a year, and I can't help grinning as the constable falls farther and farther behind. With Enzo's magical ability to render us both incorporeal, we're always long gone by the time the police show up to the scene of our thefts. Which means our heists are usually uneventful.

But six minutes ago, when dancer Louelle Martine returned home early to get ready for her performance tonight at the Liar's Den Casino, she caught a glimpse of us vanishing through the wall with the four-thousand-plat tutu she was supposed to wear. Unluckily for us, a constable was just next door managing a domestic disturbance. Her cries of "It's the Thief! The *Thief*!" had him hot on our trail in seconds.

The tutu is valuable, sure, but the Thief? His capture would be worth far more.

Since he and his brother, the Liar, rose to infamy five years ago for their magical powers, Enzo has become something of a myth. Most believe him dead thanks to a slew of rumors he started soon after he met me, but those who have recognized him during one of his cons whisper stories of a bejeweled specter who haunts the streets, seeking revenge for his ruination.

Not entirely incorrect, if you ask me.

Rain mists above our heads, and my breath fogs up the lenses of my glasses as we dodge chimneys and radio antennas, dislodged shingles and electrical wires. Enzo and I have done a thousand heists together, and we move like a pair of dancers across a stage. When he turns, so do I. When I leap, he does, too. We may only share a heart, but after four years of heists and training, we may as well share a body, a mind, a soul.

We angle west toward where the iron-gray sea churns in the distance. We just have to get to the last apartment building four roofs away, and then he'll magic us through to the ground floor, where our getaway motorcar waits on the street.

Leap, roll, dash. Grasp arms, swing a pirouette around a smokestack, launch in an arc to the next roof. My poor depth perception, courtesy of the severe nearsightedness in my lazy eye, was a difficulty early on in my training, but now my body instinctively tracks Enzo in a way that ensures I always land on my feet. In turn, his typical rigidity bleeds away when he works with me, his body mimicking the lethal grace mine learned from a childhood of ballet training.

Together, we are unstoppable.

"Halt!" The police officer's voice is a gasp, so far behind us it's almost lost in the intensifying roar of the sea.

We finally reach the last roof. The ocean slams against the cliff mere yards from the base of this sixteen-floor structure, which trembles in the angry wind. Enzo jams his hand into his pocket, pulling out a lump of raw voratium so dark it seems to suck in the light of the streetlamps below, and presses the metal between our palms.

I wait for the familiar sensation of my body rippling into nothing, the weightlessness like a balloon inflating in my chest, the bubbling tingle of my limbs turning to air.

But only Enzo vanishes. My body barely flickers.

With a growl, Enzo reappears, chucking the voratium off the roof. "Damn it, this better not all be bum voratium." He digs into his pocket again, retrieving a whole handful of the pitch-dark metal and gripping my palm.

Once more, when his body mists into nothing, mine stays firmly corporeal.

"Magnus St. James, you bastard!" He reappears, hurling the lot of metal as far as he can and letting out a string of curses I feel like bursts of rage in my own chest.

My father's name, a dirty word on his lips, makes shame simmer under my skin. It's becoming harder and harder to get our hands on good voratium these days with the way St. James has monopolized the entire industry. We steal what we can, and this lot came directly from one of his top lackeys, so we assumed it would be pure.

But it seems my father doesn't do even his own staff favors.

Memories of him teaching me all about voratium ripple across my mind. The business of mining it, polishing it, driving up its price. All over again, I see the textbooks he had me study, their pages full of diagrams of the precise angles lumenors use to direct starlight into the metal. I glimpse his cunning smile, hear his sawdust voice describing how I will one day inherit his illicit network of families and businesses, all loyal to our name because of the power we wield with our voratium and our corruption.

All my life, I was his little secret. A weapon, stored away for her own protection until the day she would take her father's place as the most infamous crime boss in history.

But that future died four years ago. To keep my father's enemies from hunting us after Enzo whisked me away from them, we went to great lengths to convince the world I'd been killed. A corpse wearing a face doctored to look like mine was dumped on the street outside the warehouse I'd been locked in, and my father never knew the difference.

Every time I think of him, my chest constricts. Dust like glass in my lungs, hurt like ice in my veins, sting like poison at the corners of my eyes.

Because when he thought Magnolia St. James had been kidnapped, he did not come for her. And when he thought she had died, he did not cry, did not care.

That was when I learned the difference between the lies told to protect the ones you love and the lies told to make a person think that's what you're doing. Lies that last a whole childhood, lies that tell you they love you and that you matter and that you have a place, lies that slice through bone and muscle and tendon when they surface and leave you with a pain that hurts everywhere.

So I let Magnolia St. James die, and now I'm nothing more than her ghost, rippling through shadows with Enzo in the night. In the four years since I was kidnapped, I haven't befriended anyone besides him, haven't shown my face in daylight, haven't even met Enzo's gang of thieves he lovingly calls his Tentacles. Because I am too valuable, my heritage too dangerous, my existence a live wire ready to catch flame.

But tonight, as long as we make it through this heist and the one that comes after it at the Liar's Den, I will finally prove to Enzo that I

DEN OF LIARS

don't need to stay in the shadows. That I'm enough of a con artist to manage the baggage of my history and my parentage. And when we finish this heist and break the curse that requires us to share a heart, my freedom will no longer be a liability.

Enzo stalks to the edge of the roof, his panic slicing like a knife through our shared heart. "How do we get you down, damn it?!"

The police officer's cries grow. He's only two roofs behind us now. We need to act fast.

I search our surroundings. None of the other buildings besides the one we just came from is close enough to reach by leaping. I lean over to survey the wall below. I'm an excellent climber, but the walls are lacquered in a glossy finish popular in this part of town that's impossible to climb without a rope, and I don't have one.

Whirling, I scan the area, cursing the smudges on my glasses that make it difficult to see. My gaze snags on an abandoned laundry line waving in the breeze, connecting this building to the one the police officer just leaped onto. Yanking out one of the two daggers strapped to my belt, I sprint toward the rope, hurling my blade toward the other end of the line. It slices through easily, bouncing off the opposing building and flipping to the street below as the rope drops, hanging only by the end connected to the window directly beneath my feet. Dropping to my stomach, I stretch my arms over the edge to detach the knot, then scramble back toward Enzo, dragging the rope behind me and shoving it at him, pointing at the massive smokestack at the apex of the roof.

"That rope isn't long enough to even go around the whole chimney, let alone reach the street," he protests.

"Good thing it doesn't need to go *around* the chimney." I raise my brow.

His eyes glint as he gathers the rope. "Knew I kept you around for something." He vanishes, and the rope does with him, reappearing with its end through the brick of the chimney as Enzo coalesces on the other side.

I grasp it with both fists. "I'll meet you at the car," I call, swinging over the side of the roof.

A massive thud tells me the police officer just leaped to our building. I keep my eyes on the cobbled street below, feeling the burn of friction through my leather gloves as I slide down, feet skidding along the slick wall.

"Hey!" the constable shouts, and I launch myself the final twelve feet to the ground, rolling through the landing as our getaway automobile comes screeching around the corner.

I salute the officer with a cocky grin, yanking the passenger door open as the motorcar passes, and leap inside. We peel onto the main road, cackling like crows.

Stars, I love this.

CHAPTER TWO

LOLA

Sirens wail ahead—likely the police officer's backup—and Enzo jerks the steering wheel, sending us into an alleyway. Flashing lights reflect in the rearview mirror as he pulls onto the next street and angles north toward Waterside, the entertainment district that gives our city, Aethera, its worldwide nickname: the City of Indulgence.

"Want one?" Enzo digs under his seat for a paper bag and hands it to me.

I open it and let out a squeal. It's full of raspberry tarts from Enzo's favorite pastry shop downtown. "You brilliant devil, you stocked our getaway car," I declare, handing one to him before shoving another in my mouth.

He grins, turning the wheel with one hand as he takes a bite. The sleeve on his left arm rides up, revealing Septavia, the seven-armed pet octopus who spends most of her time wrapped around his wrist. She wriggles forward, climbing off his arm and onto the steering wheel, her glossy black skin reflecting stoplights in shards like diamonds.

My eyes stray to the marks on his wrist where she was, a series of circular bruises from her suckers, so crisp and dark they're black as ink on his skin. Because of his magical curse, he heals quickly, but she'll be back in place on his arm before they fade. He told me once about how his Tentacles all have an identical tattoo twirling around their hands and forearms, marking them as his team. I try not to glance down at my own wrist, where the skin is distinctly mark-free.

Soon, I reassure myself. If the Liar's Den job goes off without a hitch, Enzo will have no choice but to admit I'm good enough to manage a false identity so I can finally join his gang.

And if we succeed tonight, he won't need my heart anymore. He'll have his own.

I dust crumbs from my knees as Enzo turns on the radio. "Love Me Like a Lie," the most popular song of the summer, fills the cab.

The grin fades from Enzo's lips as we enter the Waterside District, where music blares from every direction and signs flash like candied lightning. Theaters, casinos, and resorts twinkle on both sides, and people spangled in diamonds and pearls crowd the sidewalks. Even the air in our motorcar thickens with the scent of expensive colognes.

Enzo's fingers rattle on the steering wheel. Septavia slicks a single tentacle against his thumb, as though to steady him, but her touch brings him little comfort tonight. Our heart rate thrums like an accelerating drum, and I know what he's going to say before he opens his mouth.

"I'm not so sure this is a good idea anymore, Lola."

"You never thought it was a good idea," I say, trying not to let my irritation flare enough for him to notice. The last thing I need is for him to feel defensive alongside his fear. "But it's our only lead left."

Five years ago, Enzo and his brother, the Liar, stole an extra-

DEN OF LIARS

ordinarily powerful hunk of magicked voratium called a moonshard from Aethera's holy zenithic temple. That same night, his brother turned on him, wielding the moonshard to curse Enzo. Since then, Enzo's been trying to get his hands on the moonshard, following lead after lead, searching for the secret location where his brother has stowed it.

And our only lead left has just checked into the Liar's casino.

Enzo grips the steering wheel so tightly his knuckles blanch white.

"Maybe I could go in."

"We've been over this at least forty-two times." I sigh. "You can't go in there, and neither can any of your Tentacles. You said yourself he's magicked the place to keep you out."

He grits his teeth, glaring hard at the street in front of us. The traffic lights reflect reds and yellows against the deep green of his irises.

Enzo's curse, which the rest of the world believes to be as free and powerful as the Liar's sprawling magic, came at a steep cost. Though that curse gave Enzo the ability to walk through any wall and enter any safe, it also took away his capacity to feel, to speak, to be. In order to say words, he must first steal them from someone else's mouth. In order to have emotions, he must first take them from someone else's heart. In order to be corporeal, he must first pilfer physical form from someone else's existence.

Since the night the Liar cursed him, he's had to plunder people's homes and bodies, drawing out this soullight and capturing it in shards of voratium. Unfortunately, that power runs out quickly. To have some semblance of a life, Enzo must spend every waking moment searching, stealing, siphoning.

Thankfully, his ability to see soullight makes it possible for him to glean intimate details about the lives of the people he steals from. Details that tell us whether they're connected to the moonshard. Details we've been following in order to find and destroy it to free him of its curse.

We're closer than we've ever been, but our last remaining target is in his brother's casino, the one place he cannot go.

But because no one knows about me, I can.

"Spin me like a tale, one where I'm the one you need. Spare me the truth and just let me belieeeeeeeve . . ." The song fades into static, and the radio host cries, "That was Celestia's own Shirley LaCour, who is due to perform tonight at the Liar's Den Casino Resort in Aethera for the grand opening of the Liar's Dice Tournament!" Adrenaline flares hot in my stomach. "Your very own LERA hosts will be covering the event live, so make sure not to miss it! The tournament kicks off at midnight. Fifty contestants will gamble their most dangerous secrets over several rounds of challenges for the chance to win a single die with the power to sow one untraceable deception . . ."

I snap the radio off. My stomach churns, and I try to tell myself it's Enzo's worry making it feel like the world is closing in on me.

But I know that's a lie as surely as my heart does.

Four years ago, my father entered that Liar's Dice Tournament, and the dirty little secret he bargained was the fact that he had a daughter hidden away. When he lost, his biggest rival, Moratin Salazar, snatched me to use me as leverage to dismantle the St. James monopoly on voratium.

A monopoly that, it turns out, mattered more to Magnus St. James than I did.

The Liar's little tournament tore my childhood to shreds. Exposed that my father did not love me like I thought he did. Broke me and left me abandoned.

I have just as much reason to hate the Liar as Enzo does.

It's a satisfying irony that the tournament is going to be our way back to the moonshard. Once Enzo's curse is broken, I fully intend to use the shard to destroy the Liar and his precious casino. Destroy it like it destroyed me.

A muscle twitches in Enzo's clenched jaw, and I press my hand to his arm as his anxiety churns in my chest.

DEN OF LIARS

He's not only worried about my safety because he cares about me, though that is a concern. The fact that he's able to *share* my heart, rather than stealing pieces of soullight the way he does with everyone else, has loosened his leash immensely over the past four years. With me around, he only needs to siphon speech and corporeality from others, and that small reprieve has given him the time to track down the moonshard. If I'm hurt or killed, he'll go right back to grasping for soullight every moment of every day like he was before.

The Liar's Den Casino Resort blazes into view, and Enzo pulls to a stop just before a blockade guarded by several police officers. A massive crowd pushes toward the entrance.

"What an eyesore," Enzo mutters, and though I'm staring at the casino, I know exactly the expression he's wearing. It's his I-want-to-set-my-brother-on-fire-and-maybe-his-casino-too-while-I'm-at-it face, complete with a scrunched nose and a scowl.

"I don't know, I think it's kind of impressive," I tease.

He shoots me a glare. "You obviously have no taste."

The Liar's Den towers in front of the sea like a glittering dragon, a massive campus complete with high-end hotel accommodations, a luxury spa, and an array of theaters boasting cabarets and acrobat shows alike. The main casino scrapes the clouds with its twenty-six levels studded with multicolor lights that dance like tiny fairies. Marble arcs twist out into the air in decorative loops that seem to defy gravity—which, considering the stories about the Liar's magic, is probably exactly what they do. A massive lion emblazoned in a rainbow of neon at the center of it all spreads its jaw wide in a silent roar. Jagged flippers protrude from its ribs, and the lower half of its body scintillates with scales like a fish.

A symbol of the Zenithic Church's goddess of truth, Ivara the Lionness, taken over by Ivian, the god of lies, and his underwater wickedness. If I wasn't so disgusted with the Liar for what he did to my father, to my life, and to my best friend, I might actually be impressed by his bravery in being this openly sacrilegious in a city so steeped in zenithic belief.

"Remember," Enzo whispers, voice urgent. "Get to the roof by eleven-thirty. I'm only going to be able to have that skylight open for you for ten minutes."

"I know."

"Don't draw any attention to yourself."

"I know, Enz."

"And—"

"Funny enough, I *have* done a heist before." I push my glasses up my nose to scowl at him.

"Not like this one."

"This is not a complicated job. I won't even have to interact with anyone, which means the odds of me being recognized, especially with the way we've dyed my hair, are next to zero. I'm going to waltz in there, snatch Legrand's watch, and get out through the skylight, just like we planned. I'm not going to be seen, and I'm not going to get caught. Take a breath."

The pocket watch, according to our research, is an extraordinary treasure. Usually, Enzo needs to press raw voratium against a person's skin to access their soullight. However, in rare cases, if a person wears raw voratium long enough—typically in the form of a trinket the owner never takes off—the metal begins to siphon some of the person's soullight on its own. The pocket watch is one such item, which means that we won't need to interact with Legrand at all if we can get our hands on it.

Enzo winds his thumb around the pendant that houses our heart. "Don't let him discover you."

I don't need to ask who he's talking about. The loathing in our heart is a specific sort of hatred he feels only for his brother.

"I am more than capable of handling *you*; how much worse can the Liar be?" I try to tease.

"A lot worse." He blows a slow stream of air through clenched teeth.

"You always said his power was nothing more than magic tricks and misdirection."

"I oversimplified."

I raise a brow. "Care to under-simplify, then? I'm about to go in there."

"My brother can sense lies, which means you cannot deceive him. And his illusions are so powerful you will lose all sense of reality if he wants you to." Enzo's mouth twists. "While you're in there, you cannot believe anything you see, hear, taste . . . and especially not anything you feel."

"What do you mean?"

"I mean," he says, "that if he discovers you work with me, there is nothing he won't make you see or hear or feel in order to get what he wants out of you. The Liar is more treacherous than any god, Above or Below. Your life and mine depend on you never losing sight of that."

"I won't."

"If you get caught and by some grace of the stars you're not dead by the end of it," he says, jabbing a finger at me, traces of mirth flickering through the unease in his voice, "I'll filet you myself. I've worked too hard to keep you a secret."

"Fair enough." I hold out my hand. "And *when* I succeed, you owe me a bag of those fizzy candies they sell at the pier when this is all over. What are they called again?"

"Snazzatazzles." A ghost of a smile flits across his mouth as he shakes my hand. "Get me that watch, and you have yourself a deal."

"You'd think I'd have learned by now not to make bargains with you."

"You'd think I'd have learned by now that you're more trouble than you're worth."

"Tough love, my boy." I wink and yank off my leathers, revealing a dancer's leotard and stockings. I pull on Louelle Martine's tutu, and the prickle of the tulle against my legs sends my mind back to golden afternoons spent leaping across the private dance studio in the isolated home where I grew up. Grunting, I push the memories away. That was the life of a naive dancer. I'm a thief now, and I need to focus.

"Here," Enzo says softly, handing over a coil of rope from beneath his seat, which I wind around my waist several times and tuck under the tulle before adding lockpicks, a dagger, a pair of gloves, a vial of putty, and a screwdriver. "And this, too." He holds out a voratium bracelet glowing faintly green. "Filled this with strength just for you, Lollipop."

I raise a brow. "Lollipop?"

"It's a nickname. A charming one."

"Charming according to who, exactly?"

He scowls. "I could have called you Locust. Or maybe Lobster. Would you have preferred that?"

"I suppose Lollipop is just fine, Enema."

"Enema?" he deadpans. "Really?"

I give him my most innocent smile. "It's a nickname. A charming one."

"Just take the damn bracelet." He chucks it at my face.

Smirking, I catch it and run my fingers over the glowing shards of metal. With the way my father has ratcheted up the price of voratium in the city—particularly when it's infused with starlight—this trinket's worth several thousand plats at least. Tucking it into my cleavage where it won't be seen, I say, "See you in an hour."

Then I jump out of the motorcar and dart across the street before he can change his mind.

CHAPTER THREE

LOLA

I have only fifty-two minutes to complete this heist, and the massive crowd is *not* helping.

People press in on all sides, most chatting animatedly about the tournament in colorful evening gowns and crisp tuxedos. Others seem to be fans of the celebrities the Liar has commissioned for the event, dressing in imitations of Shirley LaCour's iconic scarlet dress from the cover of her most recent record. A whole bank of worshippers from the Zenithic Church wave signs decrying the Liar as a charlatan who's fooled the public into thinking he's harnessed divine power. They hurl the title he and Enzo assumed when they were the most infamous pair of thieves in the country like a curse through their teeth. "Down with the Devious!" they shout. "Who make a mockery of the gods!"

One of the believers waves a leather-bound copy of the Odelion, the zenithic holy book of scripture, in my face as I plow through them toward Louelle's troupe. The nearest dancer raises an eyebrow as I join the line filing through the side door. "Who are you?"

"Understudy," I say. "Louelle broke her ankle."

She purses her lips, looking me up and down.

"What's going on back there?" I jab a thumb over my shoulder to redirect her attention.

"I think they're feeling smug," she muses, her narrowed gaze following my gesture. "You saw the news, right? The Thief's dead; they proved it last week. Starblessed people aren't supposed to be able to die, so I guess he and his brother have been charlatans all along, just like zenithics have claimed."

"They proved the Thief's death?" I ask, trailing her to the door. I wonder which medical examiners he paid off this time and how much it cost.

"Apparently his body washed up onshore three and a half years ago, but it was all covered up. A whistleblower leaked the undertaker records," she says. "The newspaper article I read even had photographs of his corpse. It was disgusting."

"How did that stay secret for three and a half years?" I try to keep from snorting. People come up with theories about Enzo and what he's up to every single day. I learned long ago not to listen to anything anyone says about him. *If you want to know the truth about the Thief, don't talk to a zenithic or a baker or a journalist. Talk to the Thief,* he always tells me. *Everyone else has an agenda. Also,* he usually adds with a smirk, *they're all imbeciles. You can quote me on that.*

The girl shrugs. "Somebody obviously paid to keep it quiet."

"Who would do that?"

She raises a brow pointedly at the casino. "If the Thief is killable, then the Liar likely is, too. And a lot of people want him dead."

"Ah, of course. The Liar. That makes sense," I say, hiding my grin. "So . . . you think his magic is a farce?"

Her eyes glitter. "No one who's been inside the Liar's Den thinks that."

DEN OF LIARS

As if on cue, we're ushered through the back entrance, and the casino's interior unfurls before me, stealing every word and every thought and every breath. Chandeliers dribble liquid light in glittering waterfalls, their firefly sparks slipping into astral mist just above our heads. Deep-blue-and-purple walls shimmer on either side, threaded with intricate veins of molten ebony. Cinnamon and ginger dance in my nose. A distant melody twines like temptation up the hallway.

"First time?" The dancer nudges my elbow.

I snap my gaping mouth shut and give a nervous laugh. "That obvious, huh?"

She chuckles. "Don't worry, everyone doubts the magic until they experience it themselves."

"Do you know how it works?" I ask, taking care not to meet her gaze so she won't notice my lazy eye. Somehow, nobody ever seems to be able to get past a pair of eyes that don't point the same direction, and the last thing I need is to be memorable tonight. "Is it illusion?"

"Most of what we see is something closer to glamour," the dancer replies as the group turns down another hallway, where the carpet gives way to white floors polished dewy like ice. Gilded archways twist overhead, giving off a rosy dawn light, and servers in crisp black-and-violet uniforms speed past bearing golden platters of food. A bellhop rushes across our path pushing a trolley laden with luggage.

"Everything you see or hear or touch is actually there," the girl explains, "but the Liar's magic transforms the way you experience it into however is most appealing to you. No two people see anything here in exactly the same way."

I glance down at my costume and gasp. Instead of tulle, ribbons of violet-black smoke swirl around me like fragments of midnight sky. What were once sequins are now stars, scintillating with shocks of rainbow light.

A murmur of voices rumbles nearby, and I peer through a door into one of the main gambling halls. White lights droop like willow branches overhead, illuminating a crowd with their eyes trained on a stage. I follow their gazes to the young man there, and the air shoots out of my lungs.

No one needs to tell me who he is. He stands with the effortless grace of a god, his broad shoulders accentuated by a deep ebony tuxedo. A purple fedora with shimmering silver stitching along the brim sits cocked low over his forehead. In its shadow, a square jaw frames an aquiline nose, thick black eyebrows, and long eyelashes.

But his scar . . .

All the tales I've heard about the Liar seem to revolve around the scar he supposedly got the night he claimed the magic of the moonshard. Iridescent purple-white marks swirl like the tails of a galaxy out of his collar, snaking over his ivory cheekbone and through his brow. Where it meets his ebony hairline, a brilliant-white-blue lock of hair spills across his forehead.

His eyes glitter a violet as luxurious as sin, and the right one where the scar crosses it catches light like the facets of a polished amethyst.

"Welcome," he says, his voice silken dark chocolate edged in smoke, "to the opening ceremony of this year's Liar's Dice Tournament!"

Cheers reverberate from all sides, and the hairs rise on the back of my neck as I watch the crowd track his every move with wonder, salivate over each word he speaks. Cheeks flush and eyes widen and hands extend.

He is a predator, luring them in with his pretty eyes and his pretty lies.

It's disgusting. And yet I cannot look away.

"Midnight," the Liar continues, "is in less than an hour. Who here is brave enough to claim the chance to win an Unbreakable Lie?"

Another murmur ripples through the crowd, one of awe and hunger, of curiosity and fear, and I try not to wonder for the thousandth time which lie my father wanted so desperately to tell he was willing to gamble my life for it.

As that thought crosses my mind, the Liar's mystical eyes catch mine. He holds my gaze for a heartbeat. Two. A devil's smile curls his lips.

Every nerve in my body pulls taut as I meet that stare. I do not try to mimic the way the admiring crowd looks at him. Do not blush, do not fawn. He may be beautiful, but I know what he is at his core, and I will not give him the satisfaction of thinking he can fool me, too.

When his gaze finally breaks away, I back into the hall and trail after the last of the dancers into the elevators. In silence, we ascend to the exclusive upper levels where the troupe is meant to perform, and I try to focus all my attention on the job, on the watch, on Enzo.

But no matter how firmly I shove the Liar's curious stare from my mind, I cannot seem to still the panicked thudding of my heart.

CHAPTER FOUR

LOLA

Ten minutes later, we stop at a green door labeled DRESSING ROOM. I follow the girls inside, and once everyone is distracted with cosmetics and hair, I begin my search. According to a blueprint of the casino's ventilation system we nabbed from the Aethera City Architecture Records Office, there should be a vent I can use as an access point. I locate it above a mirror in a room where a group of young women are busy lacing one another's corsets.

Adrenaline pounds like acid in my veins as I hide in a wardrobe full of feather boas and fishnet stockings until the dancers are ushered to the stage. Once the room is empty, I push a chair over to reach the vent and remove the bolts one by one with my screwdriver. Prying the grate free from the wall, I peer into the shaft. It's a straight vertical drop. Uncoiling my rope, I knot one end around the slats of the grate, then hoist myself inside. My weight yanks the grate back into place as I descend into the swallowing dark.

DEN OF LIARS

I've crawled through dozens of spaces like this—chimneys, pipes, sewers—seeking Enzo's prizes. Where my thicker thighs and arms were always criticized by my dance tutor growing up, they have proved some of my best assets as a thief. My body is strong and capable, and more than once, Enzo's had me scale my way into places his Tentacles could not breach.

Soon, I come to the end of the rope, but the shaft that will take me horizontally along the fifteenth floor is just out of reach. Lodging my feet against the wall, I launch myself toward the opening, letting go of the rope at the last moment. I sail for several heart-stopping milliseconds until, thanks to my poor depth perception, I slam into the corner, banging my face on the jutting metal so hard my glasses fracture.

Gasping at the sudden pain in my right cheekbone, I hoist myself over the ledge. My eye waters where it was struck, but thankfully the lenses of my glasses didn't cut me when they broke. Gritting my teeth, I pull them off and drop them down the shaft. Enzo usually carries a spare pair for me, so I'll just have to make do until I meet up with him.

Squeezing my throbbing eyelid shut and switching to use my weaker left eye to see, I scrabble forward on all fours, squinting as though that might somehow make up for its nearsightedness, limited peripheral vision, and reduced muscle function.

Gentle light streams through the vents of the luxury suites beneath me, and I count them as I pass, taking extra care not to disturb the guests below. When I get to the twenty-seventh one, I stop, peering through the slats.

The suite is resplendent, featuring a massive bed overflowing with cloudy duvets, marble-and-gold pillars, and dainty glass chandeliers that tinkle faintly in a breeze from the open balcony doors. I wait several moments, listening intently, but I see and hear no one, so I push the grate free. It drops with a plop onto a plush, satin couch, and I swing down after it, landing like a cat on the carpet.

Recalling the description Enzo pulled from a socialite who spent two weeks in this very suite, I prowl over to an exquisite oil painting framed in gilded finery and swing it open like a door, revealing a nondescript panel. I then dig in my leotard for a small vial.

One of Enzo's favorite tricks of the trade is to use putty to plant fingerprints at crime scenes to keep the constabulary off our trail, so when we found out about the casino's magical handprint-detecting security spell, I knew instantly what to do.

Turning to survey the room, I look for places Legrand might have touched with her whole hand. The breeze from the balcony ruffles my hair, and I glance at the door. It's difficult to tell without my glasses, but a few smudges on the windows look promising. Squinting, I approach until my nose is nearly pressed to the glass, scrutinizing the cloudy marks on its surface.

"Aha," I breathe when I catch sight of a full handprint near the doorknob. I pull on a pair of gloves and spread the putty over the print, shaping it to match the contours of Legrand's palm and fingers. Peeling it away carefully so as not to damage it, I return to the exposed panel.

Pulse skittering, I situate the putty against the wall and wait for several heart-rending seconds.

The panel ripples.

"Yes, that's it," I murmur as a safe door with a combination lock flickers into view. A Cavendish & Coppell model, my specialty. "It's just me, Dr. Legrand, here to fetch my pocket watch."

The wall goes solid. A screeching alarm shreds the air.

Cursing, I toss the putty aside and run my palms over the panel, feeling for the dial I saw beneath the glamour. Footsteps pound in the corridor outside as I press my ear to the wall and twist the dial, straining to hear the lock mechanisms over the wail of the sirens and the thunder of my heart.

I've cracked a thousand safes, but never by feel alone, and it takes far longer than I'd like. The ticking of the latch inside counts down the seconds as the stomping in the hall grows ever closer.

Precious moments later, I step back, take a deep breath, and pull. The glamour of the panel disintegrates as the door heaves open, revealing a glittering platinum pocket watch adorned with black voratium polished to look like diamonds the size of my knuckles. I snatch it and stuff it into my waistband alongside my dagger, climbing the armoire to reach the vent as the door to the suite slams open.

"Stop!" a man barks as I hoist myself into the vent.

Gunshots fire as I crawl at full speed the way I came.

Shouts echo through the walls, rattling the metal beneath my hands and knees. I stop at the end of the line where it meets up with the vertical shaft and search out the end of my rope dangling five feet above me in the dark. A gunshot explodes behind me, and I duck as the bullet ricochets past.

With a cry, I throw myself at the rope and slam against the wall, managing to grasp the end by the tips of my fingers. Gritting my teeth, I pull myself up hand over hand, but as I approach the dressing room opening, someone heavy swings onto the rope below me, sending me spinning.

Shrieking, I dig in my tutu for my dagger. Hanging by one hand, I saw at the rope. Another gunshot fires, and the sound rings in my ears at a fever pitch.

A terrible creaking noise whines from above. I look up.

My chest constricts.

The slats of the vent bow inward, pulled down by the weight on the rope.

"Bleeding—"

My curse is drowned out by an earsplitting shriek of metal as the rope tears through the grate.

Air screams past, and I slam my dagger into the wall. It shreds through for several feet, shards of aluminum ripping gashes into my forearms. The man below howls until a terrible crunching sound cuts everything to silence.

I gasp, clinging to the hilt, arms trembling. Then, with a cry, I crunch my knees to my chest and kick until my feet hit the other wall. Wedging my back against the opposing side, I stow my dagger between my teeth and push my spine upward with my feet. My whole body is vibrating with strain by the time I reach the broken grate, shove it in, and spill into the dressing room.

The cries of dancers mid-costume-change ring around me as I jam the dagger back into my belt, yank on a glittery jacket to cover the wounds on my arms, and steal a glance at a clock on the wall. Five minutes until I'm supposed to be on the roof, but it's at least ten floors up. I'm never going to make it through the labyrinthine hallways or endless stairwells with security stationed at every corridor.

As I dash past a washroom, I nearly choke on cigarette smoke. I halt, turning back to the door.

People don't smoke in enclosed spaces. Which means there's got to be a window in there.

Yanking out my screwdriver, I fiddle with the lock until it snaps open. The woman inside screams, but I slip the screwdriver into my sleeve and throw myself past her out the open window, latching onto the sill.

I climb.

Wind whips my hair and clothes, and my already-aching body quivers with fatigue as I draw magic out of the voratium bracelet Enzo gave me. The familiar prickle of ice fills my veins, giving me just enough energy to drag myself upward, floor after floor after floor. My hands grow slick. My head pounds. My injured eye is swollen shut and the other one's vision has gone even blurrier than normal from exhaustion. Still, I force myself onward until finally, once my arms have gone numb and the bracelet's magic trickles to nothing, I pull myself onto the roof.

I roll onto my back, gasping for air, grinning even as my limbs spasm.

I did it.

Enzo and I are going to be free.

CHAPTER FIVE

NIC

Depths, I hate people.

I don't *want* to hate them, but their secrets and their greed and their betrayal cloud my nose with a stench so noxious I nearly choke on it every time.

But their adoration? That shit is delicious. And here onstage, costumed in finery, surrounded by magic, and set apart from them enough to breathe, I can gorge myself on their slack-jawed worship and pretend for a moment that I deserve it.

"Welcome," I say, flashing my most charming smile, "to the opening ceremony of this year's Liar's Dice Tournament!" The crowd cheers, and I pull at the icy magic in my veins to infuse my gaze with charm, to soften my features in just the way that will endear me to every patron. It's an art, a dance, and they salivate after it.

Anywhere else in the world, a lie is a sin. But in a casino? It's a performance. A spectacle. A game. And these folks have traveled across oceans and paid exorbitant prices for the privilege of my deception.

So I give the people what they want.

"Midnight," I remind them, "is in less than an hour. Who here is brave enough to claim the chance to win an Unbreakable Lie?"

The torrent of ice in my chest tilts, pulling me suddenly toward the back of the room as though the earth has been knocked off its gravitational axis. I resist, keeping my feet planted on the stage, but look to where the sensation is pulling me to a doorway in the dark.

A girl watches from the shadows, head high, jaw tight. Thick brown curls frizz to the waistband of her tutu. Butterfly-frame glasses accentuate expressive blue eyes above freckled cheekbones and a slightly crooked nose. Her body is muscular, the lines of her arms sharp in the gentle light, her physique thicker than that of a typical dancer.

But it's not her musculature nor even her beauty that piques my attention. It's her glare.

I'm no stranger to hate. Work in my line of business for long enough, and anyone is bound to make a few enemies. Typically, however, people make an effort to disguise their loathing.

Not this girl. Her eyes are as cold as the Deep where my soul will rot if I ever manage to die.

A thrill rolls through me, a spark that reminds me of the old days when my brother would get into trouble and I had to save his sorry ass. I've always loved a good challenge.

I send a tidal wave of magic toward her. *Love me*, it says. *Whatever you want me to be, that is what I am.*

Her pupils do not dilate. Her jaw does not soften. Her loathing goes deep.

Interesting.

My magic yearns toward her, pressing against the inside of my skin like a tide. I want to let it free, see what it'll do, but the crowd between us roars their enthusiasm.

DEN OF LIARS

I've got a tournament to prepare for. I don't have time for pretty dancers, no matter how scathing their glares.

I drag my attention away from her.

It doesn't matter who she is or why she hates me. I am a liar, after all.

My gaze snags on Dr. Olivia Legrand, who sits at the bar on the right side of the room, nursing a gin as she watches the spectacle. Her hand lifts to her chest, fingers dipping into the inner pocket of her silver tuxedo jacket where she usually keeps her pocket watch. But when she remembers she left it in the safe in her room like I suggested, her face falls.

Guilt surges alongside my magic. How will she react when my brother's Tentacles steal it?

I'll make sure she gets it back. Maybe not right away, but soon.

Lights flash, music flares, and soon my part in the show has reached its end. With a grin, I gesture singer-songwriter Shirley LaCour to my side and toss a farewell wave to the crowd. They scream and stamp their feet so hard the walls vibrate.

"I love you!" one young woman cries from the front row, makeup running in tears down her cheeks.

"I love you, too," I say with a wink, and her friends swarm her, squealing.

As Shirley croons into the microphone, I head backstage, pausing to cast a final glance to the doorway where the dancer stood before.

But of course she is gone. As she should be. Her troupe, if I'm not mistaken, is due to perform upstairs shortly. Shaking my head, I let the illusions on my face fade and step into the back hallway.

The radio on my belt crackles, and the voice of Paol Chen, my head of security and the closest thing I have to a friend, breaks through. I unlatch the radio as I navigate to a private elevator up to my floor.

"Talk to me, Chen."

"I think the Tentacle is here, sir. There was a loud bang in one of the vents."

"The vents." I grin. "He's getting creative now; how cute. Any idea which Tentacle he's sent us?"

"No, sir. Haven't seen them yet."

"Get me their identity as soon as you know."

"Yes, sir."

"And you've verified the roof is where they're aiming?"

"Whoever forged new schedules for our security team created a break in the watch up there from eleven thirty until eleven forty. My bet is it was the Thief, sir, crafting a getaway point for his guy. It was so well done, I wouldn't have noticed it if you hadn't had me specifically looking."

I groan, mopping a hand over my face. Enzo *would* choose the roof. The magic from the voratium in the casino's construction doesn't penetrate the walls well enough to supply me with magic if I go outside, which means I'll need to remember to grab some voratium chips on my way up. I hate doing so, as it leaves me susceptible to having my power literally pickpocketed.

"Thank you, Paol. Remember, I need that bastard alive."

"Of course, sir."

I clip the radio back to my belt, exiting the elevator and stalking down the hallway to my office.

My brother is a *problem*. Four years ago, when he was first cursed, it was easy for me to stay ahead of him. He was so burdened with keeping himself functional that it took little effort to plant false clues to lead him away from the moonshard. But over the past few years, he's gotten faster, sharper. Now it's like I'm holding on to things by my fingernails.

I'm getting tired, so *tired* of it all. Of the guilt for what my actions have turned Enzo into, the shame for what the moonshard has done to the girl I once loved, the horror of becoming what I swore I never would.

All I need to do is figure out Enzo's secret, what has made him so efficient. Then I'll be able to knock him out at the knees. Slam him solidly back in the dark so I can breathe.

Suddenly, an alarm cuts through the air, shrill bells ringing throughout the casino, and I grin.

It appears there's a thief who needs apprehending.

Dressed in an illusion of invisibility, I watch the Tentacle hoist herself over the lip of the roof and roll onto her back. Brown curls spill out in a fan around her face as she gasps for air, a triumphant light in her eyes.

I recognize her instantly. Not because of her face, for it is shrouded in shadow from this angle, but because of the way my magic spools toward her, a tug on the ice in my chest that sets my teeth on edge.

The dancer from downstairs.

I frown, twirling a voratium chip in my pocket. I know Enzo's gang inside and out. Their weaknesses, their aliases, their pedigrees, their health history. Even what brand of toothpaste they prefer.

So who the depths is she? And why is my magic having a conniption trying to get to her?

I move to the open skylight—likely the exit point she planned to use before she tripped my alarm and had to improvise. I kick it closed, and it slams like a clap of thunder.

She leaps to her feet, raising her hands in self-defense. "Hello?"

I draw in a bit more magic to muffle my footsteps as I move across the roof to a chimney, which I scrape against purposely.

She spins. "Who's there?"

She's well trained, judging by the careful placement of her feet and the practiced grace of her raised fists. And she's got good instincts, it seems, because when I prowl behind her, she swivels toward the sound of my breath.

After five years among the worst of society, I have good instincts, too, but when she whirls to slam me against a marble pillar and digs a dagger against my throat, I let her, just to see what she'll do.

Call it morbid curiosity. It's not like she can kill me, anyway.

"I'm not afraid to hurt you," she growls as thunder rumbles over the sea.

I cock my head as the secret behind her lie tinges the air soft and sweet, a delicious contrast to the vast majority of the secrets that assault my nose on the daily. I laugh, a sound I render silky and musical with a touch of the ice in my veins. Give her a bit of healthy fear, this mysterious dancer who somehow slipped into my brother's clutches without a trace.

Lightning flashes, and her eyes widen in horrified recognition.

"What a delicious lie," I breathe, and then I wrench the dagger from her grasp and toss it aside, whipping her around and yanking both hands behind her back. In one swift movement, she's on the edge of the roof, toes jutting out over a twenty-six-story drop.

"Careful, little thief," I purr as rain begins to fall like stars from the sky. "One wrong move, and it might be your last."

Sea-salt wind whips her faint fragrance of orange blossoms against my face. I glance down at her wrists, where blood trickles from the fresh lacerations visible beneath her sleeves, but other than that, her skin is clear.

Enzo never lets anyone into his inner circle without first performing his tattoo-and-branding ritual. Pain breeds loyalty, though he'd never admit that's why he does it.

Whoever she is, she is not a Tentacle.

Interesting.

"Tell me, how am I supposed to do business with the most powerful people in the world," I breathe, watching the downy hairs on her neck rise, "if thieves run off with their valuables while they're in my care?"

She tries to wrench away, but I tighten my grip.

"Are you going to have me arrested?" she asks.

DEN OF LIARS

"That's one possibility. But the constabulary tend to be fairly . . . unimaginative in their methods of interrogation."

I do not intend to torture her. I don't have to. Sometimes all people need is a little push, and they'll create illusions terrifying enough on their own.

I spin her to face me, and she keeps her balance just like the dancer she's pretending to be. She studies me, lit only by the glare from the neon below. Raindrops catch on her lashes like tiny diamonds. Her left eye squints, as though she's having difficulty focusing, and her right one is swollen shut. But though strained, her glare is full of the same ferocity I sensed downstairs.

"Who are you?" I ask.

"Nobody."

I can't help myself. I laugh. Most people at least try to charm me, but she radiates a disgust as sharp as the dagger she jabbed against my throat.

"Fine." I give her a cocky grin sure to rankle her and consider my options. Perhaps she's not working for my brother. But if she is, the last thing I need is for her to know I set them up. So I raise a curious brow and ask an innocent "Who sent you?"

She rewards my grin with the scowl I was hoping for. "No one."

Though she's happy to lie with her mouth, it's almost like she wants me to know *exactly* how she feels. Exactly what she thinks of me.

Perhaps that is what makes her secrets taste so different.

"Give me a name, little thief," I say quietly. "Yours or your employer's."

"I'm Astra Tremaine." Another lie from her lips shadowed by a truth in her glower.

I cock my head. "But that's not true, either, is it?"

She pauses, and I watch her realization that I can sense lies in the gentle flex of her jaw. "I'm sort of a freelance artist. Anyone could technically hire me."

Her words are ambiguous enough that my magic senses no secrets. She's cunning. And defiant.

"A vague nonanswer, how very clever." I play her game with a coy quirk of my brow. "Let me be more precise, then. Who hired you to steal that watch?"

"What kind of thief would I be if I gave up my clients' identities?" she hedges.

"One who wishes to remain alive." I am not a killer nor a sadist who thrills in violence, but if fear will motivate her to give up her secrets, I will gladly play that card.

She does not quail, does not shiver. The damn girl *smirks*.

"Ah," she says. "Threats. I expected we'd get to that, though I hoped you'd take a more creative route there." She gives me a sweet smile. "Unfortunately, I'm afraid this particular threat is not all that effective. You see, sir, if I give you my client's name, he just might kill me to make a point."

"If that's the case, then you'll have to make a choice." I raise a brow. "Option one: You keep your client's identity secret and die by my hand, or . . ." I pause for dramatic effect. "Option two: You tell me what I want to know and risk dying by his. At least with option two you'll have the chance to run."

"Or . . . there's always option three," she says. She jerks her wrist, and something sharp jams straight through my palm and out the back of my hand.

A screwdriver.

My shock is enough for her to wrench free and ram me back onto the rain-spattered roof where she can reach her dagger. She digs it against my throat again, and we glare at each other, chests heaving as rain sluices from her nose to mine.

That's when I sense it. A secret in her, flitting behind her eyes like a whisper, brewing like a cataclysm. Something big, something devastating, something delicious. Dusted with the scent of orange blossoms,

DEN OF LIARS

tinged in spice and danger and . . . yes. The slightest trace of an aroma as familiar to me as my own.

Enzo.

Whatever she's hiding, it's got my brother all tangled up in it. Could she be the key to finally understanding how he has gotten so powerful, to finally gaining enough of an upper hand to keep him away from the moonshard once and for all?

I lick my lips, let her glimpse a razor smile.

That secret is as good as mine.

CHAPTER SIX

LOLA

"Do keep in mind," the Liar says as I bear down over him, teasing his skin with my knife, "attempted murder would be a waste of your time. Pesky immortality and all that." A single silver raindrop slides down his scar, and light refracts through the water, blue, then violet, then white.

I bat my eyelashes. "Judging by the way you reacted to being stabbed through the hand, your immortality doesn't make you immune to pain."

"You don't want to make me your enemy, little thief."

"I think I'd like nothing better."

"So you're going to stab me?" he muses. "Claw my eyes out? Gut me from throat to navel?"

"All excellent ideas."

"Your pulse is quick and your arms are trembling. You are spent." His mouth curls. "If there is to be a fight between us, you will not win it."

"Then why," I ask, "haven't you taken back the watch?"

"Priorities change when circumstances do."

"If you're going to speak in riddles, let me put us both out of our misery and slice this artery already."

The hunger, amusement, and curiosity in his expression fuse into something sharp enough to draw blood. "At the Liar's Den," he murmurs, a bass pianissimo in the rain, "secrets are power."

"What are you talking about?"

"Some secrets are simple knots," he says. "A man does not like his wife's new blouse, but he loves her, so he pretends. A harmless lie told, an innocuous truth hidden." His right eye sparkles as his gaze traces my features. "But a weapon manufacturer's classified blueprints, for example? The lies necessary to keep that secret are like a spider's web. Tug one corner, and the whole thing trembles."

My hair hangs around our faces, cocooning us so the crackle of thunder and the roar of ocean waves seem from another world. I dig my knees into his arms, but his whispers crack open my sternum and probe at the heart pumping double-time inside.

"And some secrets," he whispers, still holding my gaze, "are intricate tapestries impossible to disentangle. But when you do, the world unravels."

"Can you see people's secrets as well as you see their lies?" If he can see mine, it doesn't matter who holds the dagger. I'm already dead.

"Secrets are only *revealed* when given freely," he says, gaze darting to my lips for a heartbeat, "but the one you carry, little thief . . . What a tantalizing thing it is."

"So you can see that I have secrets, but you can't see what they are?"

His lips curl. "Tell me your name."

"A name is not an identity."

"Ah, but yours is. Otherwise, you would not be so afraid of it."

His words claw at the raw place where the memories of my father live. "I tire of your riddles, Liar. Get to the point."

"Enter the Liar's Dice Tournament," he says, his voice a rumble, a whisper, a breath. "Bargain your secret."

I dig the dagger into his neck until a tiny bubble of crimson blossoms. "Not interested."

"Are you aware how valuable an Unbreakable Lie is?" he asks softly. "A lie like that, one so valuable it must be kept alongside the most dangerous secrets I have won, could save you from whatever secret you keep. Make it as though it never happened."

My eyes sharpen on his. "I don't need saving."

"Of course you don't, darling," he says, and the words paint his lips in a smile so wicked I want to slap him.

He raises his bleeding hand, still stabbed through with the screwdriver, to graze the bruise beneath my right eye. I stiffen, but his touch is soft as the rain. "Let whatever you are hiding be the thing that saves you, little thief."

Sparks trail through me, and I nudge the blade deeper. "No."

He laughs. A sound like midnight steeped in scotch.

His body ripples into nothing. I still feel him beneath me, but the sudden disappearance surprises me enough for him to wrench from my grasp, sending me skidding onto my hip. I scramble to my feet, whirling, brandishing my dagger at empty air.

"Option one." The Liar's whisper sends chills over every inch of me. "You join the tournament. If you prevail, you'll keep your secret, win a lie that could buy you a future, and I'll leave you alone. Or . . ." His breath tickles my ear. "Option two, refuse, and I'll show you just how terrible my glamours can be."

"How about option three again?" I jab my blade where his body would be if he were really whispering in my ear.

Laughter echoes from every side. "Midnight is in twenty minutes."

And then, like the guttering out of a candle, his presence whips away, and I am left alone and trembling in the dark.

CHAPTER SEVEN

LOLA

Noise blares suddenly loud in my ears. The rush of the ocean and the pound of the rain, the honk of automobiles and the wail of distant police sirens engulf me from every side, as though the Liar's presence kept us in a bubble and his departure has popped it. I sway on my feet, blinking at my surroundings.

Enzo's anxiety sharpens. He's approaching. We planned to meet up nearby after I got to the roof, but suddenly everywhere feels too close. The last thing I need is for the Liar to see us together, so even though my body quivers with fatigue, I take off running. I leap to the neighboring roof several stories below, slamming hard enough to see stars, but I channel my stumble into a dash to the next one, and the next, and the next.

This way, I call to Enzo silently. *Over here.*

I cannot read his thoughts, nor he mine, but sharing a heart does have benefits. I can sense how close he is by how strong his feelings are and follow them the way I might follow a sound to its source. We've also learned to manipulate our emotions to send each other signals, so if I hold my breath until my adrenaline spikes, Enzo will sense it and know I need help.

Once I'm sufficiently far away from the Liar's Den, I swing down a fire escape and pick the lock on the back door of an empty diner. A faint multicolor glow emanates from the jukebox inside, illuminating plastic booths and checkered tile floors. I slump onto a sticky plastic stool and rest my head on the Formica counter.

Enzo's panic steadily crescendos, confirming he's following me, and I try to calm my breathing as the Liar's face swims behind my eyelids.

Let whatever you are hiding be the thing that saves you, little thief.
Little does that bastard realize, hiding is all I know.

I grew up locked away like a treasure in a curling, expansive estate tucked among the orange groves along the southern Celestia coast. The house bore no address, belonged to no town. To the world, it did not exist and neither did I. And how I longed for more.

So when I turned eight, my father hired the most accomplished ballerina in the world to train me. He custom designed a studio off the back of the estate, and I spent nearly every evening spinning and twirling, toes cracking and blisters forming in the only freedom I had. One that came in pushing my body beyond limits because limits were all I'd ever known.

When I danced, I *became* someone. I could close my eyes and see audiences I'd never glimpsed, dance on stages I'd never touched, listen to them cheer in languages I'd never heard.

But my first *real* taste of the world outside was the salt of fingers clamped over my mouth when Father's enemies came for me. My first smell the scent of fear that coated my skin like sweat when they dragged me out into the moonlight. My first sound the scream of my nursemaid when her blood spilled across the estate's marble steps.

DEN OF LIARS

My childhood, no matter how charmed, wasn't freedom. Neither was my capture. But Enzo is. And though the life I have with him still requires me to stay hidden, I can live in a typical apartment. Walk among typical people on typical streets. Buy typical bread from typical shopkeepers and pretend I'm a typical girl.

And for me, it is anything but typical.

Enzo barges through the wall, pulling me from my reverie, his fear so sharp it turns my stomach. He catches sight of me and stops short. "What happened? You're bleeding."

"I'm all right," I wheeze. But I'm not. I've been climbing chimneys and evading guards and throwing daggers for four years now, but never all three in one night, and certainly not with this much at stake.

He crosses to me, tipping my chin to look into my eyes. "You were seen."

I should tell him about the Liar's threat. Tell him I messed up.

I stare at him for several long moments as his panic vibrates in my chest. I've never lied to him before. Never once. How could I? We have shared a heart from the moment we met.

And yet . . .

Sweat slicks my palms.

I know Enzo. If he finds out his brother saw me, he'll worry to the point of making himself sick. Should I really torture him with the added fear? Especially considering we have the pocket watch—the key to the moonshard's location. As long as we destroy the shard before the Liar finds us, Enzo won't ever have to know I was caught.

The truth will only hurt him.

So I take a deep breath and, praying he'll chalk up the dread pounding through me to adrenaline, I lie.

"I ran into a couple of guards. Nothing I couldn't handle." I dig into the waistband of my sodden tutu with shaking hands, pulling out the pocket watch, which glitters in the filmy jukebox light.

He does not question my sincerity, and somehow that makes it worse. I bite down hard on my lip and shove away my guilt as he lifts the trinket from my palm and cradles it reverently, like an offering to the stars.

His eyes go distant, signaling he's sorting through its soullight, and I prop my head on the heel of my hand to wait, breathing slowly through my nose to steady my roiling stomach.

I still remember the first time I saw Enzo use his magic like this. He'd been training me for almost a year, teaching me to crack safes and pick locks, slip among shadows and scale buildings, and it was time for my first real con. We broke into a palace, and he was standing over a sleeping duchess in the dark, a shard of voratium in his palm. He pressed it gently to her temple and went still, his eyes going unfocused, his breathing slowing.

A few moments later, once we'd slipped back outside the palace, he held out the voratium for me to see, and I stilled, enthralled. It glowed, but not the way voratium infused with starlight by lumenors did. Those shone steadily, like electric light bulbs. This flickered like a tiny glowing bird fluttered within. An ethereal phantom. A fragment of soul.

"When a lumenor activates voratium trinkets like the ones sold in magic shops," Enzo explained carefully, "he does it by setting up his mirrors just so, channeling starlight at exactly the right angle to set off the chemical reaction in the metal that gives it power. From the star Vivaris, for example, he'll direct luck. From Ivara, truth."

I nodded. "I know. I've seen it."

"Well, starblessed people like me—or starcursed, as I would define it," he said with a humorless laugh, "people who, for one reason or another, can channel magic from themselves instead of the stars, are able to infuse voratium with something else."

"Soullight," I whispered.

"People carry traces of every kind of starlight in them," Enzo continued, nodding. "The moonshard's curse gave me the ability to pull tiny wisps of that starlight out of people, capture it in voratium. Emotions, speech, corporeality, stamina, things like that."

As he spoke, the calm in his part of our heart cooled my fear.

"When I press raw voratium against a person's skin, I essentially see their whole existence. Words they know, phrases they use, emotions they often feel. I experience their joys and pleasures, heartaches and pains all in the span of a few minutes."

"You see their memories?"

"Not memories exactly, though I can often guess at their pasts based on what I'm seeing in their present."

"So you just . . . choose something to take?"

He nodded. "In this case, I'm running a little low on speech, so I've bound as many words to the metal as it can hold."

"How many?"

"A few thousand. Speech runs out quick, I'm afraid."

"When you take their speech, can the person no longer talk?" I asked.

"For a time."

I glanced down to the purple voratium pendant on his chest. "Not like my heart."

He followed my gaze and said softly, "No. Your heart is different."

"How?" I asked.

He ran his thumb along that pulsing glow. "I got the idea from my brother, actually. He set up his whole casino based on the fact that while he can steal the *capability* to keep secrets without consent, he can only keep the actual secret—and see its content—if it is given willingly. Or lost in a bargain."

"That's kind of brilliant."

"The pompous ass does have a brain," he conceded. "So I figured if I could find someone from whom I didn't have to steal, someone who would *give* of their soul, the voratium would function as more of a conduit between us so we could share the soullight."

"But when he takes secrets, there's no conduit between him and his victims, is there?"

"No. Hearts are different than secrets. More . . . permanent."

"Why my heart?" I asked. "Why not speech or strength?"

"A life still can be a life without speech, without strength, without even corporeality. But I ran out of heart once, and that . . ." He shuddered, turning to stare at where the horizon glowed lavender with the dawn. "That was the torment of the Deep."

Neither of us spoke for a long time. We didn't need to. His grief and mine were the shared foundation we'd built our friendship on, stones piled over and under one another until we didn't know which belonged to whom, only that the house they built had become home.

Enzo growls, pulling me back to the present, and I blink around at the shadowed diner, dazed, until the pocket watch in his palm comes into focus, still flickering with its otherworldly light, and I remember where I am.

"There's nothing in here about the moonshard. Nothing," he says, anger flaring like fire.

The hope in my chest deflates. "Nothing at all?"

"That was the last lead," he growls, tightening his fist around the watch until his knuckles pop white. "We are officially out of options."

His words are harsh. Final. Heavy as a stone thunking into place over a grave.

It doesn't matter that I proved myself tonight. Until Enzo doesn't need my heart to function, he will never let me join the Tentacles or show my face in daylight. And it seems that the moonshard just slipped out of our fingers yet again.

Only this time, the Liar has caught our scent.

CHAPTER EIGHT

LOLA

"All right," I say, trying to stop the hopeless spiral of my thoughts. "We'll keep looking. See if we can't pick up on another lead."

"There's no more time!" He slams his fist against a countertop.

I want to argue, but he's right. We've tracked dozens of the people whom the Liar has bought favors from with his moonshard, and all of them bear traces of the same terrible truth: It has begun giving off signs of lumonic decay, a chemical reaction indicative that the starlight will soon overwhelm the atomic makeup of the voratium. When it does, any magic it has cast will remain in effect forever. Including Enzo's curse.

"Hey." I steer him around to face me. "We're going to find it. Why don't we do some more digging with that lawyer we hit for strength a week or two ago? What was his name?"

"Perez."

"Isn't he one of the Liar's top whales? Perhaps he's seen something."

He nods, but his heart roils like bubbling tar.

I pace to the front window and stare down the street to where the Liar's Den's lights reflect off the cobblestones, limning them in fuchsia and blue. The colors blur together in my poor vision, a smear of hues against the night. For a moment, I'm back on the roof, wind and rain lashing against my face as the Liar asks for my secrets.

I turn to Enzo. "What was his vault like?"

"Whose vault?" he mumbles.

"Your brother's."

He shrugs. "Never found it."

"What?"

"Before he so rudely banned me from that casino and put up all his wards to keep me out," he says, leaning against the counter and crossing his arms, "I searched it top to bottom and never saw a trace of the vault."

"But—"

"The vault isn't important, anyway." He shakes his head. "He wouldn't keep the moonshard in the same place he keeps his own secrets. That's just bad business."

I frown. "What do you mean 'his own secrets'?"

"It doesn't matter."

"By whose standard?" I stalk to him, hands planted firmly on my hips. "Tell me."

He crosses to the sink and plugs it up, then turns on the faucet and pulls out a vial of white powder from inside his jacket. "When my brother first got the moonshard, he got so caught up in his glamours he lost track of what was real." He dumps the powder into the water and swishes it around before holding out his arm. Septavia emerges from his sleeve and slinks into the basin.

"That sounds terrifying," I say, dropping onto a stool.

"We were already avoiding each other at that point." Enzo shrugs, watching Septavia play, extracting a small tin of shrimp from his pocket and upending it into the water for her to eat. "But he's my brother. I can tell when something's wrong, and things were . . . really wrong for him for a while. I almost felt bad for him."

"So he extracted his secrets to keep track of them," I muse.

Enzo nods. "And locked them in his vault."

A thought strikes me so hard I gasp. "Wait. If his secrets are tangible objects, couldn't we steal the one with the moonshard's location?"

Enzo toys with his lip rings. "Theoretically, but his vault is impossible to find. We've tried. All of us."

"All of *you*," I mutter.

Enzo's mouth tightens, but he does not reply.

I stare at Septavia, trying to detangle the knot in my stomach. Some of it is guilt from having lied to Enzo, but there's something else, too. Something sour.

"Why haven't you mentioned this before?" I whisper.

He nudges my elbow, and I know he senses the hurt in our heart. "I didn't think it mattered. It was a dead end. It honestly never occurred to me you'd want to know."

I swallow hard, trying to shake away the sting. He's right. It shouldn't matter.

But it does.

"I could enter the Liar's Dice Tournament," I say, staring at my hands clasped on the counter.

Enzo steps back. "Have you lost your mind?"

"Not to win it, just to get to the vault and steal that secret."

"I told you, that vault is not findable!"

"I can't think of a time when it will be accessed more than during the tournament. I could stake out who retrieves things from it, follow the staff around, maybe even keep tabs on the Liar."

Enzo shakes his head. "You'll get caught."

"The tournament is the time when I'm *least* likely to get caught. It's absolutely packed right now, full of celebrities and crowds . . ."

"And security."

"I'll blend in."

"Not if you're a contestant!"

"The contestants are given closer access to staff and the Liar than the general public."

"You won't last longer than two seconds in a game like that. You're the worst bluffer I know."

I glare. "Not at cards. My father was an absolute shark, and he taught me everything he knew."

"And even *he* lost the Liar's Dice Tournament." Enzo's voice rises in pitch. "No. I'm not letting you go in there."

"But—"

"You'll end up hurt. Or dead." He pinches the bridge of his nose. "Even if you win, you'll be vulnerable to my brother. It won't take long for him to learn your true identity, discover you work with me, and then it's only a matter of time before he finds out about our heart."

"The Liar thinks Magnolia St. James is dead," I say. "And I'm not a Tentacle. He won't look twice at me."

"He will if you break into his vault."

"He won't find out I've done so until we're long gone." I jab a finger at him. "You know I can do this. I'm a better con artist than all your Tentacles combined."

"Yes." His hand wraps around our voratium heart at his throat. "But you're also more valuable than all of them combined. And I cannot protect you as long as his wards keep me out."

"I am the only person alive who wants the moonshard as badly as you do, which means I am also the only person who will do absolutely everything in my power to make sure this job is successful. And," I say, stepping closer to him so he has to meet my eye, "we have no other options."

DEN OF LIARS

"That casino is crawling with St. James's minions. You'll be recognized."

I nod at my reflection in the mirrored wall behind the counter. "Magnolia St. James was a scrawny blond kid with teeny spectacles. Do you see any of that in me now?"

He stares at my face, at the freckles we've had tattooed over my cheeks, the nose that healed a different shape after my kidnapper broke it, the hair we've dyed darker and let grow nearly to my waist. I dig in his outer jacket pocket for my spare set of glasses and slide them on, completing the effect. "Let me save you the way you saved me."

He considers me for what feels like an eternity, a storm raging in our heart. Fear slamming against desperation against hope. Finally, he extends a quivering arm into the sink, and Septavia curls into her place there. "Fine," he croaks. "But you'll need to be careful. He may not be able to see your secrets until you're eliminated from the game, but he can sense them . . . whether they'd be valuable to him, and how much so. You cannot think about me, about our deal, about anything to do with your heart when he's near you."

I shake off the dread that coils in my stomach before he can sense it.

"Under no circumstances," he goes on, "will you wager any of the secrets that have to do with me." He braces both hands on my shoulders. "To get into the tournament, you'll bargain the secret of who you are."

"But . . ." I frown. "You just said—"

"That's the only secret you have that'll be valuable enough and won't compromise us."

"If people find out I'm alive, it would cause problems. Someone might try to use me as leverage against my father again."

"That bastard didn't come for you last time you were used as bait."

The words hit like blows, and I swallow the lump that rises in my throat. "Fair."

Enzo pulls me against his chest, smoothing my hair with his palm. "I don't like it."

"You don't have to. You just have to let me do it anyway."

He sighs, grinding his teeth, and glances down at the pocket watch. "Well, Loophole, I guess if you're going to do it, you'd better go quick. Only two minutes until midnight."

My mouth drops open. "Really? I can go?"

He grasps my hand and pulls me through the wall into the rain. "Please be careful."

"Thank you, Enzo," I say, squeezing his fingers. "I promise I'll get us out of this mess." Then, before he says another word, I take off at a run down the street.

Fear pulses through me. Anxiety. Anger. Guilt. And there, ever present, is an ache like a shard of glass, lodged deep where the skin has grown over and the scar has faded but the hurt never ever will.

I was the collateral my father used at this casino four years ago, and that pain will live with me forever. But tonight, I will be the one gambling a dream. A reality. A future.

And, whether I win or lose, I will get what I'm after.

CHAPTER NINE

☾

NIC

I am a man of many faces.

Tonight, I wear soft wrinkles, translucent white hair spun like spiderwebs, a long nose, and cloudy blue eyes. I call this character Gorlo, and in his skin, I imagine a lifetime of memories that might have been mine if I'd been born as him and not me.

Perhaps I would have been a fisherman, raised somewhere I'd never heard of the Gods Above or the so-called devils of the Deep that distort their light into sin. I might have grown up playing on shores without guilt, swimming in lakes without shame, watching sunrises over sea-stained horizons without fear.

Usually, I can almost convince myself I am Gorlo. I can get lost in a story far more enthralling than the one I was raised in.

But not tonight.

No, apparently tonight this disguise is only good for keeping patrons from bothering me, because no matter how hard I try, I can't seem to stop myself from searching every face for one with a black eye and a defiant glare.

I lean against the wall in the casino lobby and watch the front entrance, searching through sheets of rain for signs of her. Searching my heart for a hint that my magic has sensed her. Searching the air for the scent of secrets I need.

I glance at my wristwatch. Midnight is minutes away. I should be in the main hall, kicking off the tournament. A thousand guests await.

Instead, I watch diamond raindrops dance down the glass in the front door, resisting the urge to pray to gods who don't exist for the return of a girl who shouldn't.

In the past twenty minutes since I met her on the roof, I've combed through every file in my office cabinets—police reports, housing statements, birth and death registers—but no one called Astra Tremaine lives in Aethera. Whoever this girl is, she's more of a ghost than my brother.

What if she doesn't show?

The thought turns my stomach. Nothing makes me feel like more of a monster than manipulating secrets out of people, but if I don't find some way to slow Enzo down, it won't be long before he discovers just how far I've gone to keep him away from the moonshard. Once he does, it's only a matter of time before he figures out who really has it.

Laurel. The girl I once loved.

If I have to become a monster to protect them both, I will.

I try not to think of Laurel's heart-shaped face, her long, dark hair, or her suntanned golden skin, but the memories pull at me like a tide.

And for a moment, I'm no longer twenty-one years old and lord of a casino, but rather a terrified sixteen-year-old thief in way over his head.

It was the night Enzo and I stole the moonshard from the Aetheran temple, a heist I'd spent the previous weeks trying to convince Enzo would be a useless waste of our time. Moonshards didn't exist, I'd told him a thousand times. They *couldn't* exist. We'd been taught from the cradle that the gods would never allow such power on earth.

Enzo'd only scoffed every time I brought it up and told me I didn't have to come if I didn't want to. He wasn't scared of gods or demons or temples, and he sure as the depths wasn't going to let my convictions ruin his plans for getting his hands on the most powerful piece of voratium known to humanity.

So, desperate to keep my brother safe on what I considered a pointless mission, I donned a priest robe alongside him and snuck into the temple. We picked locks and slipped past clerics. Everything was going off without a hitch.

We ventured deep into the temple's belly. Enzo ushered me through the final door, urging me to snatch the shard while he stood guard in the hall.

Stomach churning, I slipped into the room and stopped.

There it was, a stone the size of a small melon, vibrating with a light so intense it hurt to look at, colors rippling across its surface in every hue imaginable.

The blood drained from my hands and face. My stomach dropped.

Father had told me . . . he'd *told* me moonshards were nothing more than a myth.

And yet here it was.

Father was a priest, and he'd worked in this temple for decades.

Did he know? Had he lied to me?

I approached the case, picked the final lock with shaking hands, and lifted the stone from its velvet bed. It was frigid as ice, sending shards of pain through my palms as I hoisted it, unable to tear my eyes from its mesmerizing surface.

Magic wasn't real. The Odelion had said so. The priests had said so. My own father had said so.

I stared at it. Magic. Raw and rabid.

I felt like I was going to vomit.

"Nic!" a voice cried from the opposite end of the room. A door slammed, and a shadow hurtled toward me. "Stop!"

Startled, I lurched, and the moonshard slipped from my grasp as Laurel pelted straight for me.

She dived for the shard, her hands slipping beneath it just as it smashed into the floor with a sound like a bomb detonating. She screamed. An explosion of light slammed into my chest. Everything went dark.

When I awoke moments later, she was still screaming. Magic shredded through me.

"Laurel," I wheezed. "What are you doing here?"

But she was writhing in agony. Light poured out of cracks in the moonshard, molten and hot, white and sparkling, and where it connected with her skin, steam curled.

I scrambled over to pull the shard out of her hands, but it wouldn't budge.

She met my panicked look in the dark, tears and sweat streaming down her face. Eyes wide with horror.

"How?" she gasped. "How is this real?"

"I—" I began, but shouts echoed from above.

The priests were coming. We needed to get out of there.

I shoved Laurel toward the back door she'd come in through. "Run," I croaked through my teeth. "Run!"

With the staccato of her panicked footsteps fading away, I whirled toward Enzo. The entrance he'd been guarding was a pile of rubble, and he was unconscious beneath it, flickering in and out of focus like a television set. I hoisted him over my shoulder and took off the way Laurel had gone, pelting through the back door just as the priests burst into the room behind us.

I did not stop. Not until we were outside, not until the magic coursing through me was like a thousand knives puncturing muscle and bone and sinew, not until we were far, far away from the temple blazing like an omen on the horizon.

I dumped Enzo onto the sand, and he awoke, wheezing, his body half-corporeal and fading. Blood painted his skin, and chips of wood protruded from his cheek, but he scrambled to his feet.

"Where is the shard?" he asked, staring at my empty hands, but his voice was warbled and far away, faded as though I was hearing it through water as my panic tilted the whole world sideways.

That moonshard wasn't supposed to exist.

"Someone got to it first?" Enzo's voice cracked. "Did you see who?"

I stared at him as magic coursed under my skin like icefire, raw and new and wild. I was not a monster. But I would be if it would protect Enzo from what else that moonshard might do to him. If it would protect Laurel from what he might do to get it from her. And so, with the frigid power in my veins, I became the monster I swore I never would.

And I broke my brother's heart.

Tremors rock through me as I blink away the memory. The casino swims back into focus, the echoes of screams fade. Clearing my throat, I straighten my jacket, swallow the lump in my throat, and rub my eyes so I can peer through the front entrance one last time to see if the thief girl has come.

A shadow breaks through the rain, and my magic lurches toward it. Astra yanks open the door and blows into the room with the wind, splashing puddles in her wake, and it's all I can do to not gulp at the air, so thick and delectable with the scent of her secrets. An aroma I'd bottle and devour if I could.

She's put on a pair of wire-frame glasses, but she still squints as she scans the faces around her, gathering her dripping hair over one shoulder. Her right eye is swollen entirely shut, and the multicolor lights from the fountain at the center of the lobby accentuate the deep bloom of purple beneath her skin.

She crosses to the reception desk. "Hi, I'm looking for the Liar?"

The clock in the main hall begins to toll, and I allow my features to sharpen, my hair to darken, my glamour to shift and change until it settles.

The receptionist points, and the girl whirls. When she catches sight of me, her jaw hardens as she pushes her rain-speckled glasses up her nose. "I'm here to enter the tournament."

"Welcome back, little thief." I flash a sharp smile and retrieve a parchment and pen from inside my jacket. "You'd better sign the contract quickly, then, before the clock finishes chiming."

She crosses her arms. "Not until you tell me exactly what that contract entails."

The spite, the defiance, the *fire* in her has me biting down a grin. I haven't had anyone address me like this since before I became the Liar.

"The terms of our last bargain said 'by midnight,'" I remind her.

The clock finishes its toll, and the air goes eerily silent.

"Yes, you told me to *return* by midnight," she says, eyes narrowing like she wishes she could eviscerate me with her glare alone. "You did not say I had to sign anything by then."

I sharpen my grin. "Mincing phrases with a starblessed? You're awfully brave."

She draws herself taller, throws her shoulders back. "If you want a shot at my secret, you'd better give me the terms of your game before I sign. Otherwise, I will not play, and *you* lose out, not me."

She's right. But it won't help me, my brother, or anyone else for her to know just how desperately I'd rather avoid having to manipulate the secret out of her. It wouldn't bode well for my reputation as the up-and-coming cutthroat.

So I tip my head, pretend there's an argument here, just to let her think she has to convince me. Besides, there's something addictive about sparring with her, this girl who wears her heart like a crown.

"It is not necessary for you to play," I say, "for the House to get what it desires."

DEN OF LIARS

She levels me with that delicious glare. "You underestimate just how desperate I am to keep my secrets, Liar."

"And *you* underestimate just how desperate you will be to be free of them once I'm done with you, little thief."

"You can perform as many little magic tricks as you want; we both know you can't physically extract my secret unless I allow you to. But if I compete, you'll have a forty-nine-in-fifty chance of getting my secret with no fuss. To me, that sounds like much better odds. And a heap of a lot more fun."

I trail my gaze along her blackened right eye, her sodden tangle of dark hair, and her rosebud mouth. "Many who sit at my tables," I say slowly, "put too much stock in the cards and not enough in the words they play, forgetting the game is not simply about the hand they are dealt, but the story they use that hand to tell."

I glamour the contract into invisibility. Her breath hitches when it vanishes, and I smile in spite of myself. That flicker of hard-won awe is the most decadent thing I've tasted in years.

"You find yourself incredibly impressive, don't you?" she says through her teeth.

I only smirk in response, and she rolls her eyes.

With a wave of both wrists, I draw her attention to the glimmering ring on my finger, tucking the contract into my jacket with the other hand, deft as a pickpocket, fluid as a stage magician. "You wield your tongue well. But do not make the mistake of thinking that because you are quick with words that you are clever enough to outsmart the House. You will lose, in the end." I extend my arm. "Everyone always does."

"Ooh, impossible odds." She tosses her hair over her shoulder, sending raindrops sparkling through the air as she curls her palm around my elbow. "My favorite kind."

I try to ignore the way my magic sucks from every part of my body to that exact point of contact between us as I guide her through a doorway spangled in diamonds. "Come, little thief. This way."

CHAPTER TEN

LOLA

I hate the Liar's cocky grin. I hate his irritating riddles. And I especially hate his ridiculous fedora. It takes all the self-control I possess not to knock it askew just to spite him as he leads me through the intricate diamond doorway. No longer sopping from our fight on the roof, his hair is swooped to perfection, his black tuxedo with its midnight-purple shirt crisp and dry. The brim of the hat in question sits diagonally over his brow, casting shadows across his glittering scar. A lavender orchid flutters in his lapel as we walk, its head angled toward me as though watching my every move.

He is beautiful, but dangerous things often are.

He watches me survey the illusions in every hallway, the sparkle in every room. His gaze is a caress, but I do not give him the satisfaction of my awe or my admiration. I scowl. He laughs, coming to a stop at a glossy black door, which opens to reveal a small space lit by ebony candles on platinum candelabras that seem to float in the air. Vibrant purple orchids dusted in silver spill from the walls, their vines climbing overhead, so thick and tangled I cannot see the ceiling. The floor beneath our feet is carpeted in petals.

The Liar gestures toward a cozy white chaise, and I'm seized with the urge to smear my blood-caked hands all over it, just to show him how unfazed I am by his little mind games.

"Please, sit," the Liar says, perching on a matching chair.

Swallowing a snippy retort, I sink into the cushions.

The Liar meets my gaze over a coffee table laden with silver dessert trays. Violet strawberries drizzled with indigo-tinted chocolate, fluffy cakes dusted with cream light as clouds, and miniature roses made entirely of spun pink sugar make me salivate. The Liar lifts a gold-stemmed flute from one of the plates and offers it to me, making the bubbles of the rosy drink dance.

"Thank you." I accept the glass and take a sip. It bubbles over my tongue, satiny and full-textured, with notes of spruce smoke and citrus. And though I know it's the Liar's magic that makes the drink so effortlessly divine, I can't help but close my eyes as it rolls down my throat. "Now, tell me more about your little game."

His mouth quirks. "My . . . 'little game' . . . is made up of four rounds. The first three will consist of challenges in which each player will be given a portion of my magic to complete a task."

I frown, sitting up straighter. I thought this was going to be a tournament of cards or dice. Not challenges. "What sort of tasks are we talking about?"

His eyes glitter. "Deceit."

"I should have guessed."

"Each round," he continues, amused, "you'll receive a supply of seven magical dice to aid you in making a specific person believe an assigned lie within forty-eight hours."

"I see." I swirl my drink. The thought of crafting magical glamours the way he does makes me quiver with anticipation, but something about the idea of lying to people—especially in a cutthroat tournament like this one—makes my blood run cold. I'm not opposed to lying in general, but the last thing I want to do is hurt anybody.

As though sensing my trepidation, the Liar's jewel eye glints. "Is that going to be a problem?"

"Not at all," I retort. "What is the final round?"

"A surprise." He winks.

"Of course it is."

"However many magical dice remain in your possession at the conclusion of the third round will be all you are permitted to take with you into the final one, so be careful how you use them."

"How ominous."

He plucks up one of the strawberries and bites into its chocolate tip. "To enter the tournament now, you must wager a secret. If you lose—by failing to meet a challenge or by running out of dice—your secret becomes mine. It is at that point that the contents of your secret will become property of the House, to either be revealed to the public immediately or stashed in my vault."

"And if I win?"

He grins, licking chocolate slowly from the corner of his lower lip. "If you win, you'll get that secret back unrevealed and be awarded one Unbreakable Lie."

"And you'll leave me alone?" I raise a pointed brow.

"That was the bargain."

I drain the last of my drink and set the flute on the table as he drops his strawberry's stem into a napkin.

"For the duration of the tournament, you will be housed in the finest accommodations my resort has to offer, complete with meals, complimentary spa service, and a fully stocked wardrobe free of charge. Our only rule is that you do not leave the premises during the tournament or harm any of the other players. Doing so will result in immediate disqualification, which would include forfeiture of your secret."

DEN OF LIARS

"Duly noted."

He leans forward, retrieving the contract and pen once more and holding them out to me. "So, do we have ourselves a deal?"

I scan his face, the glittering scar, the lock of bluish-white in his ebony hair. He smiles, and my body tenses as though run through with an electric current.

Holding his gaze, I slide the pen from his hand. I do not hesitate, do not even flinch as I sign with a flourish, dotting the *i* so hard the pen nearly punctures through. *Astra Tremaine.*

His eyes glint. "The contract stands even if you use a pseudonym."

"I figured," I retort, handing the pen and contract back. They vanish as soon as they touch his fingertips.

The Liar rises. "Now, to extract your secret."

My palms go slick as he takes the place next to me on the couch.

"Hold still," he says. "This shouldn't hurt."

"How comforting."

He retrieves a small, polished piece of raw voratium in the shape of an eight-sided die from his pocket and presses it over my heart just above my neckline. His skin is warm, and the gentle touch surges through me like a tide until I can feel it everywhere.

"Focus on the secret you'll bargain," he says softly.

I think of my name—my true name. My father. The identity I left behind.

But the Liar shakes his head, his eyes hypnotic on mine, and it's as though that gaze is inside me, trailing fingertips along my soul.

"Not that one," he says.

I focus on the memory of the night I was kidnapped. The faces of my kidnappers and their voices. Again, he shakes his head.

"You know which one I want," he whispers.

My thoughts slip to Enzo before I can stop them, and the Liar's lips curl. Something unspools in me, as though he's caught hold of the image of his brother, of our heart beating in a voratium pendant between our clasped hands, of the deal we whispered in the dark. I try to think of something—anything—else, but that night grows brighter, crisper in my mind, as though the Liar's grasp on it has brought it to the forefront.

Panic bolts through me.

No. Not that secret. Not Enzo.

"Yes," the Liar breathes, drawing his fingers together along the skin at my sternum until they come to a point. I shove away, trembling.

But the voratium die in the Liar's palm is already full of flickering soullight, as violet and ethereal as my heart in Enzo's pendant. I gape at it, feeling suddenly quite faint.

"What delicious secrets you keep." The Liar's eyes glitter like a serpent's.

"I—I didn't want to b-bargain that one," I stammer, trying to unscramble my thoughts and steady my quaking limbs.

"It's either this secret, or you do not enter the tournament."

"I . . ." Fury boils under my skin. "You tricked me."

He twitches as though I slapped him, then holds out the die. "Take it back if you prefer. There are other methods of finding out what I need to know."

His jaw has gone tight. Something about his threat feels . . . tired. Like it's lost its edges.

Frowning, I fist my hands in my tutu. This tournament is my ticket inside this casino, my ticket to finding the vault, my ticket to the secret Enzo and I need.

All I have to do is stay in the tournament long enough to find the vault. Then I'll be able to steal back my secret alongside the Liar's.

I can still get what I came here for.

So I level him with a glare I wish would incinerate him. "Fine. It's yours. Until I win."

He lets out a slow breath, then reaches into his inner-jacket pocket and produces a gleaming box made of what appears to be ebony glass. It glows as though lit from within, and when he lifts the lid, I see why.

DEN OF LIARS

Inside sits an array of sparkling voratium dice glimmering like tiny stars.

"Each color holds a different kind of magic." He selects one like a multifaceted ruby, its numbers marked in gold.

As stunning as it is, as mesmerized as I am by the idea of wielding magic, those dice are a symbol of everything I hate, and I do not bother to disguise my distrust as I inspect it.

"Red," he explains, "makes the truth feel false." Next, he lifts out a pale aquamarine one with numbers scratched in silver. "Blue is for creating a visual glamour, while green"—he holds up an emerald one with rose-gold detailing—"is for sounds, scents, feelings, and tastes." Finally, he shows me a die like a citrine, so bright and vivid it seems to glow. "Yellow is for softening emotions to your will."

My stomach flips. He has such power? Has he used it on me?

As though sensing my thoughts, one corner of his mouth quirks in a devilish grin.

I nod at the last die in his palm, a white one with multicolored flecks like an opal. "What about that one?"

"This," he says, looking at the die adoringly, "is the one people fear the most. It gives you the power to sense their lies."

Goose bumps ripple down my arms. Before he notices my fear, I ask, "How much magic do they hold?"

"Each has enough for a glamour to last around ten minutes, give or take a bit depending on the complexity." He extends the box to me. "Choose wisely."

Pondering, I run my fingers over their cool, glassy surfaces. Visual glamours seem like they'd be the most useful, so I lift three blues from the supply. I add a green to my palm, just in case one of the glamours I attempt needs to be rounded out with the other senses, then pause on the yellows flaring like tiny suns. Softening emotions seems like it would come in handy, so I grab one, and then a red for making the truth feel false.

"One more," he says.

My glance snags on the white.

This is the one people fear the most.

Chills rake through me. I don't even want to touch it. Something about it feels dangerous, feels threatening.

Feels like the Liar.

But if I'm going to stay in this game, I need to play like the game maker himself. Holding my breath, I snatch the white die and shove it and the others into my pocket.

He meets my gaze with a knowing smile as he closes the box, tucking it away and extracting a shiny black envelope with glittering purple trim.

"Why don't you take a look at your challenge?"

Ignoring the heat rising up my neck, I accept the envelope and pull out a thin piece of parchment soft as velvet, dark as night. Tiny flecks of what can only be diamonds glint across it like the trails of a fallen star, white, then violet, then blue as I shift the paper side to side.

At the center, in curling golden script, is my challenge.

Mark: Olivia Legrand

I look at the Liar, raising a brow. "Is this some kind of joke?" Surely he knows that giving me the name of a person I have already researched, whose suite I've already seen, gives me an advantage over other players. Not that I'm complaining.

His smile deepens. "Perhaps it'll be a fun challenge for you to see the repercussions of your actions."

"Oh, so not a joke. A punishment." I scoff. "I thought you had no morals."

"Just because some people lack them doesn't mean you should."

"I don't."

"Oh?" He leans in. "You've never made a choice you knew would hurt someone?"

DEN OF LIARS

Enzo's face flickers across my mind, and I jut out my jaw, glaring. I may have deceived Enzo tonight, but that was necessary to break his curse. "Never."

"How saintly of you." The Liar leans back and raises a brow. "Perhaps someone so truly sinless will have a constellation made of them someday. The *good* little thief, whose cons only *helped* the people she stole from. Oh, how zenithics shall fawn."

I scowl and read the rest of my assignment.

> Challenge: Make her believe she performed a surgery on a man named Alzat Lopai in the Hartsmouth District this past spring. The patient died from complications.

My stomach ties itself in a knot as I blink up at the Liar.

His mouth curls as though he knows something I don't, and dread tangles through me.

He rises, pocketing my secret and extending his arm once more. "Allow me," he says, "to be the first to welcome you to the Liar's Den Casino Resort for this year's Liar's Dice Tournament." As I take his proffered arm, he draws me close.

I should pull away, or at the very least remain still, but I find myself leaning in, like he's some kind of moon and I've been unwillingly lured into his orbit.

His lips skate millimeters from my ear as he breathes, "Be wary of my deceits, little thief, for at the Liar's Den, even your heart may make a glamour of truth."

And with that, the Liar whisks me into his world of radiance and ruin.

CHAPTER ELEVEN

LOLA

The Liar's Den is a fever dream.

Mirrored archways usher us through spangled doors. Lights flash from slot machines under ceilings blazing with purple sunsets. Card tables settle like seductive strangers in intricate marble alcoves illuminated by deep-hued candlelight. Playing cards glimmer with gold inlay, dice sparkle across felt, and neon drinks swirl in glasses topped with pink sugars and blue crystal salts.

But what truly catches my attention is a man spinning effortlessly in ribbons of silk overhead. I pause, squinting as my left eye continues to ache.

He twirls through the air, arms and legs weaving in and out of the fabric, and I can almost feel the air rushing past my face, the sensation of arcing and spinning and halting, the thunder of my heart alongside the heave of my lungs.

Stars, I miss dancing.

DEN OF LIARS

Forcing my gaze away, I keep pace with the Liar. I can't be distracted by the finery. I'm here to steal a secret. So, in spite of my fatigue and blurry vision, I turn on my inner con artist, looking past the shining satins and the diamond chandeliers to the shadows and the corners, past the glamorous patrons in their gowns and tuxedos to the waitstaff and the dealers. What can I glean about the Liar from the world he inhabits? What can I learn of his magic? How will I best him?

Shirley LaCour's voice echoes from the nearest room accompanied by the cheers of a crowd, and the Liar steers me through a set of curtains like woven stars into the main gambling hall.

Thousands of people sway to the music, and they are unlike anything I've ever seen. Gossamer wings glint from one woman's bare back, and sparkling scales sprout from another's shoulders. Someone's hair is a twist of ice-blue fire, while the man next to them walks ten feet tall in a silken green cloak that sweeps in curls like snakes around his impossibly long legs.

My heart stutters.

I've stolen through casinos in the night before, hidden among shadows after hours with Enzo, but they were nothing like this. The sheer, thrilling power of the Liar's magic, the way it transforms the ordinary into the mythical, the fantastic, the impossible . . .

I cannot seem to catch my breath.

"You look lovely," the Liar murmurs.

I jump, giving him a quizzical look. "I beg your pardon?"

He nods at my clothing, and I glance down. My tutu has become a cascade of sparkling ebony water down my legs, hugging my curves with tailored precision. It's stunning. I wish I could hate it.

"Is that supposed to flatter me?" I raise a brow at him. "Considering it's *your* magic?"

"My glamours only enhance what already exists." His whisper is a caress along the hollow of my throat, tipping my chin, angling my face so he can watch me bite my lip, watch me tremble.

A dozen retorts bubble up, but I've already let my tongue run away with me too many times tonight. I force a smile and a simple thank-you.

"Don't hurt yourself with that politeness." He smirks, tipping his fedora. "You're not nearly a good enough liar to pull it off yet."

I throw him a glare before I can stop myself, and he laughs. "There it is."

Someone nearby notices us. An excited hush ripples through the crowd.

"It's *him*," they whisper, staring.

I extricate my hand from his elbow. The last thing I need is for people to be looking my way.

"Make yourself at home." The Liar winks and strides through the crowd, which parts for him like a waterfall for a rock. Climbing to the stage, he kisses Shirley LaCour's cheeks, and squeals emanate from the front of the audience as she slinks away. I roll my eyes so hard pain stabs through my injured one.

The way he's glamoured these people into loving him is disgusting.

The spotlight embraces him like a lover, limning him in gold and amber, illuminating his scar like an aurora. Lit from above, he is tall and broad and dangerous, and no matter how much I want to, I cannot look away.

"So sorry to have kept you waiting," he says, and his voice strums music along the particles of the air. "But the time for truth has passed!" That predator's grin cuts across his face as he raises his palms. Light blazes out of them and slams into the chandeliers, igniting them with a sound like a bomb detonating. Sparks plummet around us, a meteor shower fizzing against skin and hair, pooling at our feet.

The crowd screams so loudly it vibrates in my chest.

"Standing among you are fifty anonymous players," the Liar says when the cheers subside. "Over the next week, they will gamble with you, dance with you, dine with you. They will design delights to

DEN OF LIARS

deceive and spin stories to seduce. Can you decipher truth from their lies? Can you unravel fact from their fiction?"

Another round of cheers, and excitement crests through the air like a drug.

"Before we officially begin, I'd like to make a few things clear!" the Liar cries. "First and foremost: no violence. From contestants, their friends, or anyone."

Chills rake over my skin. I'd forgotten about the newspaper headlines during last year's tournament. Two men were murdered and a third was injured. To this day, the perpetrators are unknown, but the police believe they were likely competitors in the game.

"Second!" the Liar continues. "If you wish to play slots, Solstice, Qasar, or any of the other games, you can trade secrets for chips in the Exchange Room." He gestures to a door at the back of the gambling hall. "It opens for two hours at nine o'clock in the morning and again at nine in the evening."

As the Liar outlines rules of conduct, I scan the faces around me, unease rippling under my skin. Which might be my competitors? How dangerous might they be?

"And finally, to the contestants, there is only one more thing to say." The Liar's eyes land on mine, and shivers dance hot through me as every light in the room extinguishes. The crowd goes deathly still.

A deep-throated, haunting murmur breaks through the quiet from behind, like he's right there, mouth pressed to my ear. A growl, a melody, a whisper. "May guile guard your secrets."

A drum pounds a slow, steady heartbeat.

Thump-thump . . .

. . . *Thump-thump* . . .

. . . *Thump-thump* . . .

My own heart rate slows to match it. I feel the casino, the people around me, the magic of it all in my blood, flushing through me.

The beat accelerates.

Thump-thump . . . thump-thump . . . thump-thump . . .
I wonder if Enzo feels it, too, as it climbs even faster.

Thump-thump, thump-thump, thump-thump . . .

My blood drums like a live wire and the world spins—and every thought, every fear, every pain dissipates until there is only this moment, this place, this feeling. A thousand hearts beating quadruple-time as one.

Until everything slams to a halt.

"Let the Liar's Dice Tournament begin." The Liar's voice echoes in the sudden held-breath quiet.

And then the world explodes.

CHAPTER TWELVE

LOLA

Slot machines blaze to life trilling music. Dealers materialize juggling cards like shards of glass. Waiters float by as though on a current, twirling silver platters.

The Liar has vanished. In his place, Shirley LaCour reclaims the microphone and, with a seductive wiggle of her hips, breaks into song.

My head whirls, blood still throbbing through my skull from my injury. The Liar's magic is beyond anything I imagined. If I'm not careful, I might lose myself in it.

So I straighten my glasses, clear my head. First order of business: get my bearings. Map this place out. Assess the most likely locations for a secret vault.

As I shove toward the edge of the crowd, I catch sight of a familiar-looking woman around my age at the bar. I take in her warm brown skin and perfectly rouged cheeks, the tightly coiled dark curls dusting her shoulders, her striking umber eyes. She wears a gold circle dress cinched tight with a red belt that perfectly matches the stain on her lips.

As she waves down the bartender, I realize where I've seen her before. Those eyes and that knowing grin looked down from every newspaper and magazine stand for months.

Estelle Monroe, victor of last year's tournament.

I elbow toward her. If there's anyone who can teach me how to win this game, it's her.

She's perched on a stool, her shiny red pumps curled around one of its legs as she talks animatedly with the bartender, and I take the seat next to her. She glances my way, and an amused smile curls her perfectly shaped lips.

"Astra Tremaine." I hold out my hand, which she shakes politely.

"You've got style, I'll give you that."

"Oh." I look down at the glamoured gown still pooling like liquid midnight around my legs. "This is the Liar's doing. You don't want to see what I'm actually wearing. It would probably burn your eyeballs."

She stares at me for a second before bursting into a bright laugh, tipping her head back so her pearl earrings twinkle. "Not your dress, darling, I meant earlier with the Liar." She nods at the doorway where she must have seen me come in on his arm. "Most people fawn all over him. It was nice to see someone dish back some of his own petulance."

I purse my lips, trying to decide whether my nausea is from the magic of this place or from being so easily read by a stranger. I brace my hands against the counter, trying to force my whirling mind to focus. "You know the Liar well?" I ask. "From last year?"

Estelle's eyes stray to a corner where the Liar lounges at a table near the elevator, legs spread, grin lazy. As he tosses a pair of dice, he rests one hand on the ample hip of a young woman in glittering fringe draped along his side. A second young woman plays with his fedora, twining her fingers through the silver lock of hair beneath it.

"He loves attention, I'll tell you that." Estelle drops an olive into her mouth, biting off the stem. "Obsessed with power. Thrives on

DEN OF LIARS

worship. Believes himself the stars' gift to humankind." She drains her glass and waves down the bartender. "Valen, can I get another?"

The bartender approaches, the picture of opulence in a deep blue tuxedo. Their aquamarine hair is cropped close to their head on one side and spills to their shoulder on the other. Their eyes shimmer the deep gray of clouds before a storm when they take Estelle's glass. "Of course. Anything for your friend?"

"Whatever she's having," I mumble as my headache intensifies. My swollen eye throbs so intensely I can barely think.

"Have you ever had one?" Estelle asks when Valen hands us our drinks.

I stare at the thin neon-yellow liquid. The dancing bubbles on its surface seem to glow as though with starlight. "I don't think so."

"Oh, you'll like it," she says with a smile. "It's a YesterFizz. A magical drink that'll show you an illusion of your fondest memory."

Acid rises in my stomach as my headache sharpens, but I focus my blurry eye on the glass and comb through my mind for what the drink might show me. I tip the glass to my lips, and the liquid buzzes over my tongue with a sharp lemony bite. As I set it back on the counter, the gambling hall goes misty, the sounds filtering as though from far away. I breathe in, and instead of the casino, I smell my father's cigars, his cologne, his orange-and-spice-infused coffee. In the distant drumbeat of music, I hear the rumble of his laugh.

I blink, and the casino fades into my periphery. In its place is a scene that played over and over throughout my childhood. My father, big and warm beside me, his massive hand wrapped tight around mine as we lay on the roof of my childhood home. Constellations unfurling overhead like a field of wild diamonds, and him pointing them out one by one, tracing my small, six-year-old finger along each, telling me which star belonged to which zenithic myth.

When the illusion fades, my cheeks are wet and my heart is aching.

"You all right, Astra?" Estelle asks, her voice soft.

"I'm fine," I croak.

She offers a sad smile that tells me she sees right through the lie and asks Valen for a glass of water, which she hands over in exchange for the rest of my YesterFizz.

My gaze lifts to the Liar in the corner. He's watching me, cocky grin faded. I want to scrub his magic out of my system, purge myself of the pain it's awakened.

My father's betrayal isn't the Liar's fault; I know this. And yet the Liar's games were the jagged edge that lanced my false reality. If I could go back there, unknow what my father's betrayal taught me, and live in the delusion that he meant all the treasures he gave me and the promises he made me, I would. A thousand times, I would.

I would live forever in that lie.

But the Liar unraveled it all, and I will never forgive him for that.

"So," Estelle says, "got a plan in mind for your first mark?"

I almost choke.

She laughs at the look on my face. "Yes, I know you're in the tournament."

"How?" I scour my memory for what might have given me away. Maybe she figured it out because I entered the room on the Liar's arm?

"You came straight for me." She gives me a sardonic grin. "I'm an obvious target if you're wanting a leg up."

My cheeks heat. "I didn't—I mean . . ."

"See those tables over there?" She nods to the other side of the room.

I follow her gaze, squinting with my weak eye to make out several gambling tables with piles of chips spread at regular intervals. Chalkboards gleam behind them with names written in glowing ink. As I study it, I notice a petite woman with long silver-blond hair studying me over her drink.

"Those are where people place bets on the tournament. Guessing which patrons here are competitors, whether they'll make it to the next round, things like that." She leans in, pulling my gaze back to hers with the seriousness of her voice. "You want my advice, Astra Tremaine? Keep your head down. As soon as your name ends up on one of those

DEN OF LIARS

boards, you will be a target. Avoid doing the obvious thing. Like asking last year's winner for advice where everyone can see."

The burn in my cheeks intensifies, magnified by my whirling head and flip-flopping gut. "Thanks for the tip."

"Anytime."

"That blond—you know who she is?" I nod in the direction of the woman I saw watching me before, but her table is suddenly empty, her drink abandoned.

Estelle glances toward the betting rings. "Which one?"

Nerves fizz under my skin, but I shake them away. "Never mind."

"Well, take care." She gets to her feet. "May guile guard your secrets and all that." Leaving a pile of plats on the counter for Valen, she disappears into the crowd.

I glance around to see if anyone saw me with her, but my left eye's vision has gone splotchy, and the movement makes my head spin.

I try to stand, but the world tips. My limbs are weak, and the ache in my skull is so intense my vision shards.

"Are you all right?" Valen asks, reaching for me. "Maybe you should go lie down?"

"I'm fine," I mumble, mopping sweat from my brow. "Thank you."

Valen tips their head and turns to help another customer.

I need to start my search of the casino, but when I step forward again, the room tilts. Maybe I should get away from all the lights and noise until my headache subsides. I could go to Legrand's room, complete my first challenge so I can focus on the vault tomorrow. I stumble toward the elevator, trying my best to keep my composure as I pass the Liar.

"Ms. Tremaine?" He rises, a smear in my peripheral vision.

I aim for the button to call the elevator, but I cannot seem to reach it.

The Liar's voice echoes like it's somewhere far away. "Ms. Tremaine!"

He lunges for me as the world winks out.

CHAPTER THIRTEEN

NIC

Astra slumps into my arms, her unbruised eye rolling back into her head.

Several people nearby shriek, and one of my waitresses rushes toward me.

I hoist the thief against my chest, slipping an arm under her knees so I can carry her. "Get some of Emmeline's healing salve up to suite 2508 as soon as possible," I tell the waitress as I rush to the elevator.

A shutter clicks behind me, followed by a bright flash of light, and I whirl. "No photographs," I snap at the reporters converging on me. "She's fine. Tripped and hit her head. No story here."

"But Mr. Liar, sir—" one man pipes up.

I shoot a blast of illusionary fear into all of them at once. "No photographs unless you'd like to be banned from the casino. Understood?"

Their faces pale and their heads bob as they disperse.

DEN OF LIARS

"Ms. Tremaine." I jostle the young woman in my arms as I step inside the elevator.

Her head lolls. She does not wake.

"Astra?" I try again, but she is out cold.

When the elevator stops at the twenty-fifth floor, I hurry to room 2508, propping her strategically so I can unlock the door with my master key. She's still sopping wet from the rain, the sparkly jacket over her leotard sticking to her skin as I lay her on the bed. I press the back of my hand to her forehead. Her skin is clammy. Sweat beads on her temples. Her hair slicks like glue to her cheeks.

My gut twists.

I didn't hurt her eye or break her glasses or assign her to steal from Legrand, but I did plant the clues that led her to that pocket watch. I ordered my men to chase her. I left her wheezing in the rain on my roof.

This is my fault.

Gritting my teeth, I slide the jacket from her arms and discover fresh wounds on her forearms, mostly scabbed over. "What happened here?" I mutter, pulling a tiny shard of metal from the end of one.

A knock sounds on the door. "Yes?" I say, tossing the jacket onto a settee.

The waitress from downstairs pokes her head in. "I brought up the salve, sir. And a medical kit, just in case."

"Ah yes, thank you." I nod at the bedside table, and she sets the small black bag on it.

"Anything else?"

"Not right now." I sort through the bag for the healing salve Emmeline, the casino's emergency medicine practitioner, swears by. "Keep the media preoccupied. Tell them they'll be able to interview me in half an hour."

"Yes, sir." She pulls the door shut, and the echo of her heels on the floor outside fades.

"You've made quite the spectacle of yourself, little thief," I mutter as I smear the salve on Astra's frigid skin. "Might be front-page news tomorrow: WOMAN NEARLY DIES AT LIAR'S DEN TOURNAMENT PARTY. What a mess."

As I tie a measure of gauze around the wounds, my fingers brush along the veins in her wrist. Her heartbeat flutters like frantic moth wings.

Frowning, I pull off her glasses and fold them next to the medical kit before lifting one of her eyelids and then the other. Her heart shouldn't be beating this fast. She's still fully unconscious. I press two fingers to the artery on the right side of her neck. It gallops against my touch, and she gasps for air like she's sprinting.

Something is off here.

I retrieve the salve and smear some around her injured eye. Could she be dreaming? I've woken from nightmares before with my heart pounding like that, though I'm not sure if people who lose consciousness like this dream the way sleeping people do.

I shouldn't care. I don't have time for this. I need to get back downstairs, field the reporters, manage the party.

But I can't tear my eyes away from her face, so pale, so gray, and the rapid rise and fall of her chest.

"Stars damn it," I growl, curling a hand around her upper arm.

I'm not sure if my illusionary magic will penetrate her nightmare, but the least I can do is send her a feeling of calm. I close my eyes and pull forward the ice in my chest, bracing myself. Magic splinters inside me like shards of ice, and my vision goes white. Power burns through my palm like frostbite.

I grind my teeth as my ears fill with the cries of the girl I loved and the brother I broke. A symphony of torture. A requiem to the people we were.

It's a good thing the Gods Above aren't real. A good thing the stars are no more than burning orbs of gas and not the beings of virtue I once believed they were, who might have writhed in an identical pain, screamed identical screams every time they cast their light.

DEN OF LIARS

My magic purrs between my skin and hers, yearning toward her, and as soon as it makes contact with her blood, it yanks out of me, as though being sucked into some kind of vortex.

Panicking, I rip my hand away, stumbling back from the bed. What the depths was that?

Her heart rate hasn't slowed. If anything, it's gotten worse. It pounds visibly in her neck, the skin twitching with every beat.

A scrape sounds behind me, and I whirl. "Hello?" I scan the suite for the source of the noise, but there is nothing. My gaze lands on the balcony doors, and I shove them open. "Someone out here?"

But the balcony is empty, too. I lean over the railing to peer into the darkness, tasting the air for secrets.

Nothing.

"Mr. Liar, sir?" My security chief's voice breaks through the quiet from the radio at my belt, and I jump. Pinching the bridge of my nose, I stalk back into the suite and yank the door shut behind me.

"Yes, Paol?" I say. "Any word from Taru? Did he search Lioni?"

"I'm afraid it's bad news. He said there was no trace of Laurel or the moonshard."

I spit out a curse, squeezing my eyes shut.

Five years I've been searching for her while trying to simultaneously keep Enzo off her trail, and I don't know how much longer I can keep this up.

I should never have told her what Enzo and I planned to do that night. My carelessly wielded honesty destroyed everything.

"Thank you, Paol," I say. "Have Taru move on to the next location. Keep me posted."

Latching the radio back onto my belt, I return to the bed, inspecting the thief girl. "Who are you?" I whisper, searching her features for the answers I so desperately need. "How do you know my brother?"

But of course there is no reply.

Sighing, I slip off her sodden shoes, dropping them near the wardrobe, and pull the duvet up to her chin.

"Sleep well. And please . . . wake up."

Her heartbeat continues to pound under her skin. A thousand questions swirl through me alongside the sludge of guilt in my gut. Why does my magic react to her like this? Could it have something to do with why my brother hired her? Why didn't he have her join his Tentacles? Where is he now?

As I slip into the hallway and ride the elevator back down, the noise of the party swells, mounting to a fever pitch. When the doors open, I glimpse the zenithic temple through the window at the end of the first floor's hall, a tiny, glowing speck on the horizon beyond the rest of the city, proud and unfeeling as it haunts me. Judges me. Mourns me.

I taste acid.

A symbol of purity and belief, of familiarity and comfort, of another lifetime when truth was simple and straightforward. When I didn't have to manipulate or deceive in order to protect the people I loved.

I stalk into the gambling hall, forcing the image of the temple out of my mind, paste on a cocky grin, sling my arms around a pair of ladies in slinky silver dresses. I am the triumphant casino lord, wealthy beyond imagining, influential to the ends of Celestia.

But when Shirley LaCour's song ends and the audience breaks into applause, it isn't the sound of success I hear. Not the sound of triumph, of money, of influence.

It is the sound of stars screaming.

CHAPTER FOURTEEN

LOLA

*B*ang! Bang! Bang!

I bolt upright. Where am I? What's that noise?

I squint around, but my glasses are missing. My right eye is still swollen shut, and with my other I can barely make out the blankets wrapped around my legs, the spread of a massive bed beneath me, and the hulk of a bedside table. Silver dawn light filters in through a window. A shadow lurches in front of it, and I lean forward, straining to see. That profile looks awfully familiar . . .

And then the pounding of my heart breaks through the confusion like a bull ramming against my rib cage.

Enzo.

I search for my glasses and find them folded neatly on the bedside table. Shoving them on, I stumble to a pair of windowed balcony doors, where Enzo is pounding his fist on the glass hard enough to shatter it.

I fumble with the lock, my limbs still heavy with sleep. Finally, the door pops open, and I fall against him.

"Lola!" he gasps, catching me. "Thank the stars. I've been panicking out here for hours."

Our heart stutters as I squeeze him, leaning my head on his shoulder.

"I couldn't feel you," he murmurs into my neck. "I thought . . . depths, I thought . . . But you're okay."

"That's one word for it." Pain still radiates through my skull from where I struck my face in the vent, and my body is stiff. But at least the dizziness is gone.

Enzo pulls back enough to look at me, keeping his hands on my arms as though afraid I'll disappear. His face is haggard, his eyes bloodshot. "What happened?"

"Apparently spending the night running from police, slamming my head against a metal wall, climbing twelve floors in the rain, and drinking alcohol on an empty stomach doesn't actually agree with my body." I comb through the haze of memories from the party last night. "I think I passed out."

Enzo's grip tightens. "Why was he in your room?"

I step back. "He?"

"My brother."

I frown. "I think he caught me when I went down." I glance down at my arms, now bandaged. Did the Liar do that?

"You were supposed to keep a low profile." Enzo's voice is calm, but his frustration simmers in our heart.

"I'm sorry. I didn't exactly pass out on purpose."

He mops his forearm over his face, and Septavia crawls out of his sleeve to his shoulder, her tentacles popping along the side of his neck in a motherly way. She may not share a heart with him, but she senses his agitation as acutely as I do, it seems.

"I got you something." He crosses the balcony to a set of chairs and a table in the corner, upon which a bulky bag sits. He tosses it several feet away from his shoes, a tentative grin breaking through the tightness in his jaw. "Which is closer, me or this ridiculously heavy sack?" I laugh, letting it loosen the anxiety in our heart. Enzo invented this game years ago, which he lovingly entitled "Which Is Closer, Me or This Thing?" after he learned that my eye condition makes it difficult for me to judge distances. I feign irritation, but we both know this inside joke is one of my favorites. I love that instead of pretending my lazy eye doesn't exist, he is comfortable enough to laugh with me.

"The bag. Definitely," I say.

"Aw, what gave it away?"

"The floor tiles." I point at his feet. "Twelve to it, fifteen to you. Easy."

"Blasted tiles," he grumbles.

"They'll get you every time." I yawn. "What's in it? The snazzatazzles you owe me?"

He blinks. "Snazzatazzles?"

"You promised if I got you that pocket watch, you'd bring me snazzatazzles from the pier!" I feign horror. "You forgot?"

"Oh, *those* snazzatazzles." He raises his hands. "I would never forget. I was just testing you. You'll get them next time, I swear."

"I'd better," I harrumph as he unzips the main pouch, pulls out a massive stack of folders, and spreads them on the table. I move to his side, squinting to make out the text in the meager light.

"These," he says, "are files on every single person staying at the Liar's Den right now. Also blueprints and diagrams of the building. Security protocols and routes, schedules, even info on all the staff members."

"Depths," I mutter. "You're good."

"I know."

I snort. "So humble, too."

"What can I say?"

Rolling my eyes, I gather up the files. "I'd better get to work." I put the papers back into the sack and cinch it closed. "Thanks for the help."

Enzo's jaw tightens. "Please—"

"I know. Be careful."

He sighs. "I'm sorry. I know I'm overprotective." He shakes his head slowly. "I just keep thinking about the night I found you. The utter luck that I happened to be walking down that particular street at the exact moment Salazar's underlings pulled you out of that motorcar . . ." He shakes his head. "I don't believe in gods, but I do believe in fate, and finding you was exactly that."

He's told me a thousand times about that night. Seeing me smuggled into a warehouse at gunpoint, overhearing my captors' conversations, realizing I might be desperate enough to agree to give up my heart.

"This all might have started because I wanted your soullight," he says, "but now it's about *you*. My best friend. The stakes are higher."

"You don't need to worry about me."

"Yes, I do." He climbs onto the railing. "Every second of every day."

I open my mouth to reply, but he swings over the edge before I can, vanishing into nothingness. I stare after him for several long moments, wrapping my arms around myself in the cool dawn air and wondering why his parting words feel so heavy.

"Who was that?" a voice jerks me from my thoughts.

I whirl to see Estelle leaning over the balcony diagonally above me. She raises a perfectly arched brow. "Was that the Thief?"

"The . . . what?" I try to give a lighthearted chuckle. "No. That was . . ."

She snorts. "How you expect to win this tournament is a mystery. You're a terrible liar."

I glare. "That was a friend getting me intel."

"A friend." She straightens, crossing her arms over her chest. "Who wears his hair like the Thief. Who's pierced and bejeweled like the Thief. Who struts around in a leather jacket and disappears at will like the Thief."

"He . . . is a Thief fan. Likes to dress up like him."

"Uh-huh."

"The Thief is dead," I try.

She widens her eyes in a sarcastic smirk. "Didn't look dead to me."

I search my mind for a reply, even consider rolling one of the magical dice in my pocket, but before I do, the light in the suite behind her flashes on.

"Vito's balls." Estelle curses the god of misfortune and leaps off the balcony, barreling into me and yanking me under the table. As we duck out of sight, I spot the Liar's familiar profile in the window above.

"Is that the *Liar's* room?" I ask.

She presses her finger to my lips. "Shhhh!"

"Why are we hiding?" I whisper.

"No reason," she hisses back, leaning sideways to peek up at him.

"Oh, and *I'm* the bad liar." I spy the corner of a small notebook sticking out of her pocket as she glares over her shoulder at me. "Why are you snooping around?"

"Why is the Liar so obsessed with you?" she counters.

I blink. "He's not—"

"He's got double security on your floor reporting to him."

"He does?"

"Do you want to know how many times he checked on you after you passed out?"

"I—"

"Six." She jabs a finger at me. "I want to know why."

I adjust Enzo's sack on my shoulder. "Why does it matter?"

"Why are you having clandestine meetings with his brother?"

I nod at her pocket. "What's in the notebook?"

"What's in the bag?"

We glare at each other for several long seconds.

"I don't have time for this." I shove past her to climb out from under the table.

"Yes, you do." She scrambles after me, grabbing my arm. I fake a stumble, snatching the notebook from her as I go down.

Estelle gasps. "Give that back!"

I lurch through the balcony doors as she darts forward, and we topple into the sitting area. Her notebook slips out of my grasp, flopping open and baring a page of notes just readable in the faint light.

— *Twenty-six floors total: Bottom five are public casino floors. Twelve restaurants, two candy shops, six cabarets, four bars...*

My eyes skip down to another line.

— *Threads of voratium in the walls*

But before I can read more, Estelle snatches it.

"Wait." I scramble to my feet. "Is that true? The threads of metal aren't decoration . . . they're voratium?" I look around, following the shining trails around us. Now that I'm inspecting them, I see they give off an ever-so-faint glow.

"Possibly," she says, lips tight.

My thoughts stray to Enzo's gems. He cannot use his magic without them. Could the Liar's work the same way? But why would it, if he's got the moonshard?

"You don't think," I muse aloud, "they're the source of his power?"

"He never leaves the casino," Estelle replies quietly. "Ever. My current theory is that he must not be able to access the magic outside. Not unless he brings along voratium like his brother does." Her eyes sharpen on me.

DEN OF LIARS

I ponder that until my head starts to ache again. The Liar isn't limited by a curse the way Enzo is, so what could the metal be for? Is this how he keeps his illusions in place?

But why doesn't he leave, then, if that's all it is?

"So," I say, eyeing her. "You're taking notes on him. His magic. His casino."

Estelle purses her lips, her expression utterly unreadable.

An idea strikes me. I slide the sack from my shoulder and pull out the file marked BLUEPRINTS. Shuffling through, I select the page with a detailed design of the first floor and hold it out to Estelle. "Would this help with whatever you're doing?"

She eyes it. "Is this a trap?"

"No."

"A bribe?"

I shake my head. "An offer."

"What's your price?"

I step closer so the page is within her reach. "We share notes. Help each other. Be friends."

She narrows her eyes. "I don't make friends with people I don't trust."

"Fine. Careful allies, then. I give you my notes, you let me see yours. We stay out of each other's way and don't ask questions. How does that sound?"

She studies me, then, finally, takes the paper and replicates the diagram over several sheets in her notebook. With a guarded look, she hands both to me. "You can look at the first page."

I dig in my sack for a spare sheet of parchment and write down the notes she indicated.

— *Exchange Room: First floor, accessed on the east side of the main gambling hall. Open nine a.m. and nine p.m. Chips can be played throughout the casino and exchanged when* the patron exits either for their monetary value or for the secrets they hold.

— Games available: Solstice, Qasar, billiards, Lass, Harpette, various dice games, and slots

— Bars and restaurants offering specialty fare for tournament duration

— Drinks mixed with voratium dust infused with the Liar's magic:

- YesterFizz: gin, fresh-squeezed lemon juice, simple syrup, egg whites, club soda, voratium dust—said to give drinker an illusion of their fondest memory

- Brier Rosé: sparkling wine, lychee syrup, rosewater, voratium dust—said to give drinker an illusion of their most forbidden desire

Once I've finished, I return the notebook. "Thank you." I glance at the clock on the mantelpiece. It's almost seven. "I've got to run. I really need to finish my challenge."

She nods, taking a few steps toward the door, then pausing and looking back at me as though considering. "As an ally . . . I should probably let you know it isn't only the Liar who's been watching your room. A woman called Ostena Vesnes seems to have taken an interest in you."

My stomach sinks. "Is she in the tournament?"

She shakes her head. "I'm not sure. She might have been the blond you mentioned before—she matches that description anyway. She followed when the Liar brought you up here. Waited in the hall for a long time. Even tried to pick the lock on your door."

I swallow. How delightful. "I appreciate the warning."

"Be careful," she says before slipping into the hallway.

I stare at the door for several moments after it clicks shut. I've never prayed in my life, but as my room glows pink with the dawn, I find myself pleading with Vivaris, the supposed goddess of luck, that trusting Estelle won't prove a lethal mistake.

CHAPTER FIFTEEN

LOLA

Shoving aside my dread, I sling Enzo's bag onto a couch and shove my hair out of my eyes. Perhaps the best course of action would be to get my round-one challenge out of the way as soon as possible, that way I can focus on searching for the vault. But before I can do either of those things, I'm going to need a good bath and a change of clothes.

Yawning, I flip a switch near the doorframe, and dangling blue shards of coral on the wall flare to life, illuminating a massive bed with an oak headboard carved in ornate, oceanic curls and piles of turquoise pillows stitched with silver thread. The sitting area hugs a coral fireplace, and a massive wardrobe commands the wall opposite, featuring silver designs along its border. I reach out a finger to trace them.

Scales and teeth, flippers and fins.

A shiver rolls down my spine.

These are elaborate renderings of the zenithic Gods of the Deep.

DEN OF LIARS

I've only ever seen them illustrated in shadows and dark inks, but here they feel almost whimsical.

I think of the lion covered in scales on the front of the casino. The church often speaks out against the Liar, decrying him as a fraud, as seaspawn, as Ivian, the god of lies, made flesh. It seems he wears those claims as an honor. Mocks them, even.

It's cheeky and, considering the influence the Zenithic Church has over the people in this city, brave.

Turning away from the wardrobe, I trail my hand along the walls papered in textured blue and green and cross to the attached washroom, trying to figure out why the suite is at once so unsettling and yet so familiar.

And then it strikes me. It looks how I've always imagined the Tentacles' hideout would.

Enzo and his gang of thieves live in an underwater cave somewhere offshore. They call it the Brig. *It was a ship once,* Enzo explained when I asked about it. *Behemoth of a vessel that crashed into this extinct volcano. If you swim into the hull, you find where it punched a hole in the side of that volcano. There's an entire network of old lava ducts full of air in there.*

I've always wanted to go, but of course Enzo deemed it too dangerous to chance one of his Tentacles recognizing me. Instead, I've spent years imagining the underwater grottos, the treasure sparkling in filtered blue light, the ship's cracked hull surrounded by darting fish. A wicked and wonderful and utterly forbidden place I wish desperately could be my home, too.

It's like this suite plucked its decor right out of my dreams.

A soft knock on the door makes me jump.

Scrubbing gooseflesh from my skin, I open it. The Liar, still clad in the pristine tuxedo he was wearing last night, holds aloft a silver tray spilling assorted breakfast pastries, bowls of fruit, and a steaming pot of coffee.

"You're awake," he says.

"You're observant," I counter.

"May I?" He nods toward the coffee table, and I step aside.

He strides past, all elegance and sharp angles. I follow and sit carefully on the edge of the settee, suddenly keenly aware I'm still wearing the fusty tutu from last night, now glamourless and limp. I pour myself a mug of coffee, trying to hide the way my hands shake, and divide an orange, dropping its peel into my coffee the way my father always did. The familiar combination of bitter and citrus aromas settles my nerves as I eye him over the rim of my mug. "Why are you doing this?"

He seems almost startled by the question. "Why wouldn't I?"

"You're a fancy casino lord with more money than the gods. Surely you have people to deliver room service."

"It's not good press when patrons faint. Any casino lord would want to make sure you were all right."

I sip at my coffee. "I suppose I owe you my gratitude for not letting me hit my head."

"You don't owe anyone anything." He approaches me and tilts my chin up with a thumb. "Does it hurt?"

"Hmm?" I hold his gaze with a stony one, resisting the urge to jerk out of his grasp.

"Your eye," he clarifies.

"It's not so bad."

The Liar chuckles, and I wonder how he senses the dishonesty. Is it a scent? A feeling?

"Did you hurt the other eye, too?" He backs away, settling into the armchair across from me.

"What do you mean?"

"You're making a face."

Stars, his stare is unnerving. "I'm blinded by the sheer brilliance of your magnificence."

He waits, the ghost of a smile hovering behind his lips.

I sigh. "Fine. These glasses aren't as good as my usual pair."

DEN OF LIARS

"What happened to your usual pair?"

"Smashed on my way out with that pocket watch, actually."

"Ah," he says. "Nearsighted or far?"

"Is this supposed to be friendly conversation?"

He does not miss a beat. "It's not friendly if every word you sling is a jab."

"So the casino lord thinks he's witty, does he?" I narrow my eyes. "I know exactly what you're doing."

"Enlighten me."

"You're trying to lull me into a sense of security so I'll give you more secrets." I snatch a pastry and jab it at him. "Don't confuse me with one of the fawning young ladies ready to drop grapes into your mouth at your bidding."

His eyes glint. "Oh, rest assured *no one* would make that particular mistake."

I should not be having this much fun talking to him. He's the villain. And I hate him.

But I smile in spite of myself.

"Which is it, then?" he prompts. "Near- or farsighted?"

"The left one is nearsighted, the other far. But my eyes are a bit more complicated than only that."

He cocks his head, the perfect picture of a curiosity I don't trust. "Complicated how?"

He does not deserve to know more about me. In fact, it would be wise to keep as many of my secrets from him as possible. But the way he's looking at me now—with an expression almost like thirst—seems more than idle curiosity and more even than dangerous scrutiny. I may not share a heart with him, but I do share one with his brother, and the lines around his mouth and the tentative stroke of his gaze along my face remind me of how Enzo looks when he is desperate to feel alive. To feel known.

What if I could use the Liar's curiosity to my advantage? Maybe if

I share a little, he'll be more inclined to reciprocate with information I could use to find the vault.

So I give him an unfiltered truth. "My eyes have been misaligned my whole life, so my brain had to adapt. In order to not have double vision, it learned to shut off the input from one or the other. Doing so constantly meant that my brain never truly developed the ability to compile the vision coming in from both eyes at the same time, something that most people's brains do automatically. It defaults to my right, so my left's muscles are a good deal weaker, and the vision is worse. Having to use it so much is giving me a headache."

His expression softens into something too kind, too human. I don't like it.

"See?" he says. "That wasn't so hard."

"Oh, but it was." I glare and stuff a bite of pastry in my mouth.

"A little thief *and* a little liar."

"Are you calling my bluff?"

His eyes dance. "Maybe."

"How boringly predictable of you."

He gets to his feet. "Let me know if you need more salve for your injuries."

I set down my coffee and the remnants of my pastry and trail him to the door. He's not fooling me with this kindness, but I force a nod and say, "Thank you."

"Thank you?" He lets out a silken chocolate laugh.

"Yes, *thank you*." I cross my arms over my chest. "It's what people say when others do nice things for them."

He shakes his head, still grinning. "You are not going to last long in this tournament."

"Why? Because I thank people for kind deeds?"

"Because you wear your heart on your sleeve."

"I do not."

He reaches up, traces my brow with a slowness so deliberate an ache builds in my center. "You expressed gratitude with your words, yes," he says softly, "but your brow is furrowed." His gaze drops to my eyes, and he runs a thumb along the lower rim of my unbruised one. "And you're scowling."

I want to slap his hand away, but something holds me back. No one has touched me like this—with a gentleness not borne of worry for my safety or protectiveness for my vulnerability, but rather one of hushed awe and quiet intrigue. Perhaps even a bit of reverence.

Like I'm someone to watch, to study, to learn.

It's disconcerting.

"I'm scowling," I snap, feeling suddenly wobbly. "Because my left eye is terrible at its job. Also, you're obnoxious."

He smirks as his fingers skim to my jaw, tilting my face up. "Your teeth have been clenched since I got here." He disentangles my hand from my tutu. "And you've been tying knots in this for the past five minutes." He meets my gaze and cocks his head. "You're worried. You don't trust me. Your thoughts are a neon marquee across your face."

"So being honest is a fault now, is it?" I yank my hand out of his as goose bumps ripple up my arms.

He opens his mouth as though to say something, then pauses. A momentary flash of frustration darkens his expression, but it's gone so quickly I might have imagined it. "Enjoy the freedom you have, little thief."

"The freedom I have? To what, not ruin people's lives?"

He purses his lips, and the gilded light bleeding in through the window shafts across the rim of his fedora, casting his violet eyes into shadow. "Humans like to be fooled."

"Do they? Or is that what you tell yourself to feel better?"

"To live is to lie, little thief. We all do it. But a performer, at least, doesn't pretend his deception is anything else."

"But you do pretend it's a game," I retort as anger flashes in me alongside memories of my nursemaid, my butler, my tutor dead on cobblestoned steps. "And it is not. It has hurt people."

"*Lies* hurt people," he growls back. "Because they imprison them."

"Better imprisoned than dead."

His eyes flash. "Spoken like someone who has never been imprisoned."

"Spoken like someone," I retort, "who has never watched someone die."

His nostrils flare as he draws a slow, steady breath. "Life may be easier in pretty fantasies, little thief, but that doesn't make them true."

I step up close enough to taste the cinnamon-whiskey of his breath, fists clenched at my sides. "Why do *you* get to determine whether we live in pretty fantasies or horrible truths? Last time I checked, you were no more god than I."

His lips thin. "Careful with that tongue."

"Afraid of my venom, Liar?"

He narrows his eyes and dips his hand into his jacket, pulling out a heavy gold key. "This is the key to your suite. Please don't hesitate to contact the front desk if anything about your accommodations is not to your liking."

Then without another word, he opens the door, but instead of crossing over the threshold like a mere plebian such as myself, the damn braggart vanishes.

I roll my eyes and kick the door shut behind him.

CHAPTER SIXTEEN

LOLA

By the time the sun has peeled itself from the horizon, I've bathed away the blood and the rain and the muck of last night and cleaned off the ointment under the gauze. My right eye's swelling has gone down significantly, and the cuts on my arms have lost their angry red color.

I frown as the flash of humanity I detected in the Liar's face filters through my mind and the ghost of his gentle touch skates across my skin. My mouth twists, and I stalk out of the washroom.

Glamour and illusion, misdirection and manipulation. That's all any of this is. He wants me to trust him, but I am far too smart for that.

Shaking away the doubt, I push on my glasses and shimmy into a blood-red satin dress from the wardrobe. It hangs from a beaded black halter top with a neckline that plunges into a deep *V* below my breasts, and shadowy tulle the color of midnight pools like smoke over the form-fitting skirt.

I try to focus on my first challenge. The sooner I convince Legrand of my assigned lie, the sooner I'll be free to search the casino for signs of the vault.

But as I pile my wet curls atop my head and dab red stain onto my lips, the Liar's words chase through my thoughts. *Enjoy the freedom you have, little thief,* over and over like a puzzle. I cannot make sense of it.

I drop my lockpicks into my pockets along with a small notebook and my handful of magical dice, then steal into the hallway. The hairs on the back of my neck prickle as I lock my suite, and I glance around. Is someone there? Watching my door? Waiting for me?

The blond woman I saw at the betting rings last night . . . could she be here? Estelle's warning that she followed me filters through my mind, and I hurry my pace toward the elevator, darting looks over my shoulder. Could she be using one of her magical dice to appear invisible?

Footsteps whisper behind me. I whirl, facing the empty hallway as I jab the button to call the elevator.

But there's no one. Just ornate marble walls decorated in threads of silver and black.

I'm still anxious by the time the elevator delivers me to the fifteenth landing, and I all but dash to Legrand's suite. I press my ear to her door. At first, I hear nothing, but after several moments, I catch a rustle like someone rolling over in bed.

She must still be asleep.

I step back, considering. I could wait for her to awaken, but I need to finish this challenge as quickly as I can. Preferably before whoever was following me upstairs makes an appearance.

Fishing in my pocket, I pull out a blue die and a green one. If Legrand is a doctor, then odds are she'll respond to an injury. I toss the dice and concentrate on the gashes in my left wrist, imagining them fresh and jagged, still weeping blood.

The dice roll to a stop, and cold bursts in my veins. I watch, mesmerized, as one of my scabbed wounds painlessly unknits itself, tearing wider. Blood trails thick down my arm. I probe at the puckered lips of the cut to make sure the green die's tactile illusion is in place as well. The blood coats my fingers, hot and sticky.

I lean against the wall, suddenly breathless. The wound is garish, but the magic is impeccable. I try not to think of the Liar's glittering, pleased eyes, the curve of a devil's grin on his mouth, or how easily he could fool me with such magic as I stumble forward, slamming into Legrand's door.

"Help!" I screech. "I need a doctor! Please!"

Something thuds inside.

I pitch my voice higher, threading panic through every syllable. "Someone call a hospital!"

There's a crash in Legrand's suite. Footsteps shuffle.

I let out another wail. "Help me!"

The lock is thrown back, and a pinched face framed in iron-gray hair peers out at me with pale blue eyes under thick brows like silver caterpillars.

It takes a moment for Legrand's pupils to adjust to the brightness, but once they do, she spots my wounds and frowns, extending a hand. "Let me take a look at that."

"Are you a doctor?" I sway as though on unsteady feet. "I—I tripped, slashed myself on that vase." I wave my arm down the hallway at an intricate glass decoration that certainly doesn't have any edges sharp enough to cause this kind of injury.

"I'm a doctor, yes," she slurs as she lifts my arm to inspect the gash. "Better come inside and let me patch you up."

She leads me into her suite, letting the door fall shut behind us. I stop short, staring. The suite is almost unrecognizable from how it looked last night. A half-empty shot glass stands precariously on an open book on the nightstand, and another lies smashed on the floor next to the bed, which must have been the source of the crash I heard a few moments ago. Plates of half-eaten food are stacked haphazardly next to a partially drunk bottle of whiskey on the coffee table. The curtains have been drawn tight over the windows, casting the space in murky shadow.

"This way." Legrand tugs on my wrist, her voice kind but obviously thick with intoxication. I follow her into the washroom, which is just as cluttered as the bedroom, and perch on the only clear section on the side of the tub.

She riffles through a black medical bag, pulling out a thread. "Where is that damn needle?"

"Oh, no, I don't think stitches will be necessary," I say quickly. "Just a bandage maybe?"

"You'll scar."

I nod. "I just . . . you seem a little . . . well. Like you've had a bit to drink."

Her shoulders fall. "Only had one or two . . ." She sniffs, dropping the thread back into her bag. "You're right. Wouldn't be safe."

Relieved, I give her a tentative smile. "Is everything all right, Dr.—?"

"Legrand." Her hands quake as she elbows empty toiletry bottles out of the way and sets out an array of gauze and ointments. "I'm fine."

Her voice quavers on that last word.

"Thank you for your help, Dr. Legrand," I say as she scrubs her hands in the sink and turns to dab a towel on my wound.

I channel some of the magic to make blood soak into the material, staining it dark crimson.

"Do you have someone I could call for you?" I ask, faking a wince as though the brush of the cloth is painful. "A spouse or a sibling or something? I'd like to get you some help if I can."

She shakes her head. "No one."

"A friend maybe?"

"There's nobody," she repeats, voice strained.

I watch her work for a moment before admitting, "Me too."

"Eh?" she grunts, applying a brownish substance to my arm.

DEN OF LIARS

"My mother died in childbirth, and my father abandoned me when I was fifteen. I only have one friend, but he's . . ." I stop, fingers clenching reflexively.

He's what?

"He's complicated," I conclude lamely and swallow the chalky residue those words leave on my tongue.

"Lonely is an awfully quiet place to be," she says.

"I like the quiet."

"No one likes this kind of quiet." She meets my eyes and frowns, looking at one and then the other with careful focus. "Strabismic amblyopia," she says, naming my eye condition with a snap of the fingers. "Childhood onset, I presume?"

I nod.

"Did you have surgery to correct the muscle issue?"

"No. Like I said, my mother died."

"You also said your father didn't leave until you were fifteen."

I give her a sad smile. "He wasn't very . . . present."

Legrand's mouth purses into a tight line. She raises a finger and moves it slowly from right to left, up to down, just like my nursemaid used to do. I follow its path with my eyes only, keeping my head still. The movement makes the space around my weak eye burn.

"The rectus muscles here should have been loosened." She taps my left temple. "How is the vision in this one?"

"Very poor," I admit.

"Surgery would have helped with that, had it been done when you were still young, though it wouldn't have fixed it completely."

"My nursemaid patched my dominant eye almost every day," I offer, remembering just how deeply I detested wearing that thing. All I knew was I'd never seen anyone with one, and different was something that could get a St. James killed.

"That probably saved the left one from losing its vision entirely. Forced your brain to keep using it when it otherwise wouldn't have."

She presses a clean cloth over the wound on my arm. The glamour is beginning to go fuzzy at the edges, but she seems distracted enough not to notice.

"Are you an eye surgeon?" I ask.

She shakes her head. "Emergency medicine. For fifty years now. But my late wife worked as a nurse for a doctor who specialized in children's eye issues."

"I'm sorry for your loss."

She knots the cloth around my wrist and lets out a slow breath. "Cardiac arrest. I deal with it all the time at the hospital, but for her it happened when I was asleep. She was gone by the time I woke up in the morning."

"I'm so sorry," I whisper. "This was recent?"

Legrand shakes her head. "No, Zora passed ten years ago, but grief like that doesn't go away. You just learn how to manage with it." Tears dribble over her lower lashes, catching along the soft folds on her jaw before dropping onto her stained nightdress.

I should be trying to work in my lie, should be developing the falsehoods I'll sow to complete the challenge, but instead I stride back into her room and pull open the curtains.

"Won't you have some tea with me on the balcony? I'd love to hear more about Zora."

Legrand's brows rise. "You—you would?"

"She must have been an incredible person to leave such a mark on the people she loved."

Legrand nods, sniffing. "She was." Then she straightens and follows me out into the sun. I ring down to the service station for some tea, and we settle into the chairs overlooking the bay.

"Tell me how you met her," I say. "Was it at the hospital?"

A faint smile tugs the corners of Legrand's lips. "No, we met at the training hospital when we were both in school. She was the most frustrating woman I'd ever met, and I loved her instantly."

DEN OF LIARS

She describes a series of petty arguments in the nurse's station that led to elaborate pranks in the operating room. An epic rivalry turned romance. A story of hope, of family, of love, and I find myself entirely enraptured. She tells me of how Zora played basic piano and how she would often come up with little jingles about the most mundane parts of their lives: socks left on the floor, being late for the train, the antics of their pet cat.

As she goes on, her pale, sad eyes brighten. The morning swells into afternoon as the tide comes in and then recedes. Kites bob like colorful birds, boats skim past, and as Legrand's stories progress, she becomes animated, her cheeks going rosy.

I should be watching for opportunities to weave in my lie, but somehow it never feels right. As the hours pass, I push away thoughts of Enzo, of the vault, of the tournament, and I just listen.

Soon the sun dips below the horizon, bathing the world in fire, and Legrand comes to the end of her tale. With misty eyes, she describes what it was like to find Zora cold and lifeless, blue and gone. Tears pool on my lashes, streak down my skin, drop into my lap, and I make no move to wipe them away.

"Loving her broke me," Legrand whispers when she finishes. "But I would never erase what we had. If pain is the cost of having her, I'd pay it over and over again."

"Have you been hurting like this for ten whole years?" I grasp her fingers.

She squeezes back, her hand bony and strong under stretched-leather skin, and shakes her head. "The first year was hard, but after that I was able to grow around the grief. But something happened recently that brought it all back to the surface."

"What?"

"Over the years, different things of Zora's have broken or gone missing, but there was this pocket watch she had—"

My stomach drops.

"—it had been a gift from her father, one of the best watchmakers in Celestia. Worth two million plats, it was, because it was made of raw voratium. It was the last thing I had that felt like her."

The ocean swims before my eyes. I cannot breathe.

"It was stolen last night." Legrand's voice breaks. "And being without it is like losing her all over again."

Bile rises in my throat.

"Are you all right, dear?" Legrand asks. "You're dreadfully pale all of a sudden."

"I'm—I'm fine," I mumble.

But I'm shaking. My stomach hurts, head hurts, heart hurts.

I did this. I ripped open her wound. I rebroke what this poor old woman spent the last decade mending. And I didn't even consider her for one second as I did it.

"Perhaps you need some water?" she says, but her words sound far away.

I shake my head, pushing to my feet so quickly the world tilts. "I'm just tired. I should turn in."

"Are you sure? I could walk you to your room."

"It's not—it's not far . . ." I stumble back through her suite, crunching on the broken glass as I go.

Concern furrows her brow into deep lines. "If you're certain . . ."

I swallow my shame and hold out a hand for her to shake. "Thank you so much for sharing your stories with me." I hold her gaze so she can see how much I mean it. "Would it be all right if I come tomorrow? I'd like to hear more."

A smile breaks across her face. "Really?"

"Yes. Please."

Legrand wraps her arms around me. The hug is awkward, her bony limbs jutting out like broken wings, but I lean into the alcohol-and-sweat smell of her, into the tear-stained pajamas and the messy hair as she whispers, "Thank you, dear. Thank you."

Pressure builds behind my ribs, aching and stretching until I'm sure I will explode. I pull away and duck into the hallway, dragging the door shut behind me.

Then I lean back against it and weep.

I should tamp down these emotions so Enzo will not worry. But Legrand's words keep swirling in my head like a record spinning around and around. *It felt like losing her all over again.*

My sobs choke out, wet and noisy, and I stuff my hand over my mouth so Legrand won't hear me through the door.

"Little thief." The words on an exhale ripple like a caress down my skin.

I raise my head, scrubbing at the tears on my cheeks. The Liar leans against the wall a few doors down, expression unreadable, gemstone eye glittering. He wears a deep emerald tuxedo with silvery stitching that catches the light when he moves. A black orchid flutters in his button hole tonight, sparkling with silver dust along its petals.

A sea serpent in the shadows like Ivian, the god of lies, himself.

Heat floods me. Hot, biting, raging fire. I stalk straight up to him. "You did this on purpose."

"You'll have to be more specific."

I jab a finger into his chest, seething. "You knew what was going on in that room. How my theft had affected her. What that watch meant. And still you sent me in there."

He raises a brow. "Your point?"

"My *point*?" I spit. "You dance everyone around on magical little puppet strings, but it's not our secrets you treasure. Not our lies or even our truths. What you crave is our pain."

He does not blink, does not even twitch, and that makes me want to scream.

I glare daggers at him, wishing I could sear through those emotionless eyes with all the fury in my soul. Enzo can probably feel this, but I'm too angry to care. "You sent me in there knowing exactly what I would find and how it would affect me."

"Did I?"

I cross my arms. "You cannot claim ignorance on this one. I won't let you."

"Let me rephrase," he breathes, stepping in close enough that I have to tip my head back to meet his gaze. "Did I know how it would affect you?"

I clench my jaw so tight my head pounds.

"Did I know you would care? Did I know it would break you?"

"You knew," I whisper.

"Claiming you haven't hurt anyone just because you haven't allowed yourself to see that hurt is humankind's favorite self-deception." His words strike me hard, making me step back and gulp for air.

How many people have I hurt as I've plundered homes and hearts, snatched prized possessions, sacrificed minds and bodies and lives on the altar of what *I* want?

"And you've deluded yourself into thinking you aren't doing the same?" I whisper. "At least I care about the people I've hurt."

His eyes flash with something I cannot name. Pain? Anger? Sadness? It's gone before I can identify it.

"You stand there," I continue, voice gaining strength, "trying to teach me truth and morality like you're some sort of zenithic priest, and yet you simultaneously hoard your own secrets like treasure, lie through your teeth to keep the world on its knees at your feet, and destroy lives one by one with your sparkly little games."

"You know nothing about me."

"But I do, Liar," I whisper.

His gaze smolders, intoxicating and maddening.

"What's the use of having forever," I ask, "if you're nothing but ice?"

I turn on my heel and stalk away. He does not follow.

CHAPTER SEVENTEEN

LOLA

I toss and turn all night and, a few hours before dawn, finally give up trying to sleep. In a vain attempt to distract myself from all that happened yesterday, I paw through Enzo's folders until I find the file for the woman Estelle warned me followed the Liar and I to my room—Ostena Vesnes. A photograph in muted grayscale falls onto my bedspread, and I lift it, angling it to the lamplight.

I recognize her immediately as the one who was watching me the first night. The photo seems to have been taken from a window as she strolls along the sidewalk somewhere downtown. Her pale hair streams out behind her, framing her high cheekbones and sharp eyes.

Prickles race down my spine as I imagine those same eyes watching me, invisible, in the hallway yesterday. I scan through the accompanying notes about her. It appears she's some kind of government official in Moraille, a city in the mountainous northern part of Celestia. A position like that likely gives her a lot of secrets worth bargaining in the tournament, and I imagine the Unbreakable Lie would be incredibly useful to her.

My attention snags on the final few notes: *Runner-up in last year's tournament. Primary stratagem: sabotage.*

Chills race under my skin as I reread that final word over and over.

What a fool I was to approach Estelle the other night where everyone could see me. I might as well have scribbled *Contestant* on my forehead. Staying in this tournament is going to be difficult enough, but with another player actively seeking to undermine my efforts?

I try to steady my breathing as I stow the file back in the bag and get to organizing the others according to which are most likely to be in the tournament. Then as the sun rises, I turn to scouring the blueprints for any areas that look like they might hide a vault.

But I can only keep the memories of my day yesterday with Legrand at bay for so long. Even with the threat of Ostena looming, Legrand's broken smile filters through my mind, and guilt stings like poison in my stomach.

Enzo would be upset I spent so many hours talking to her. Truly, my time would have been better spent focusing on completing my challenge. I have a job to do, and listening to her stories doesn't help me with that. But I cannot find it in myself to feel bad about it. I want to hear more, hear everything. As if listening to her speak about Zora might make up for the pain I caused.

Once the clock chimes a decent hour, I stow the bag back in my wardrobe before dressing and heading to Legrand's floor. When the elevator opens, however, someone is already at her door.

Me.

An exact replica of how I appeared yesterday, complete with the crimson-and-black dress, raises her hand to knock.

Could this be Ostena? Or another competitor in the game, here to botch my challenge? My hand darts to my waist, but I left my dagger upstairs.

Nerves snap under my skin. Enzo only ever trained me for stealth, not combat. Thanks to his magic, we never had a need.

But my father, on the other hand . . . Magnus St. James spared no expense in teaching his heiress how to defend herself. It may not have helped me when half a dozen Salazar goons had guns pointed at my head, but against one unsuspecting gambler? I just might have a shot.

I hurtle down the corridor, channeling not Lola the thief but Magnolia St. James, daughter of the most hated man in Aethera.

My twin twists, eyebrows rising as she raises her fists and charges my way.

Use misdirection when you can, comes the memory of Father's voice. I fling my second blue die. Ice floods me, and I blast it out to my opponent, channeling fireworks across her field of vision. She stumbles, hitting the floor so hard her nose cracks.

She howls, and her illusionary mask melts away. Silver-blond hair flares as blood trickles over her mouth, staining her cream-white chin. I tackle her, pinning her with my knees at the precise pressure points in her arms my father taught me about. She writhes, wrenching one hand free to drag fingernails down my cheek, but I yank her wrist back down, digging my knee into her bicep. Sweat beads across her brow as she squirms. "Get off me!" she snaps.

A massive black fabric rose on her shoulder sparkles in the light, and I rip the flower easily from its seam and stuff it into her mouth, stifling her cries. Then I wrench off a strip of gauzy material from the bottom of her gown and bind her hands tight. She kicks, so I yank the sash from around my waist and cinch her ankles together.

"Valiant effort, ma'am," I say, dragging her inside the nearest supply closet, pulling a length of cord from the head of a mop and using it to fasten her wrists to a pipe over her head.

I grab a hefty metal wrench from one of the shelves and exit the closet, locking the door before whacking the handle with the wrench until it twists into the doorframe.

Tossing the wrench into a nearby vase, I wipe at the raised mark on my cheek with shaking hands.

Father would be proud.

Trying to quell the pang that thought jabs through me, I approach Legrand's door quickly, straightening the bandage on my arm and praying no one comes to investigate all the noise Ostena and I just made.

"Good morning!" Legrand says cheerily when she catches sight of me. "I thought we might go down to the dining hall for breakfast."

I force a grin as my guilt intensifies. "That sounds lovely."

We take our meal in an airy café that backs up to the beach, where the waves crashing against the shore play a soothing background melody to our conversation. When we finish, I challenge her to a game of billiards, something she has confided in me has been a hobby since she was a girl, and make sure we pass through the main gambling hall so I can get a look at the boards in the betting rings.

Astra Tremaine is scrawled out in looping, glittery letters near the bottom of the list. Thankfully, the current bet on it is pretty low, but my stomach sinks all the same.

I've been too conspicuous. First arriving on the Liar's arm, then immediately approaching Estelle. I'm sure my fainting episode in the middle of the party didn't help, either, considering the Liar personally carried me upstairs.

I'm going to need to be more discreet.

As Legrand chatters animatedly about a trip she and Zora once took to Solada, my round-one challenge filters like dread through my thoughts. *Make her believe she performed a surgery on a man named Alzat Lopai in the Hartsmouth District this past spring. The patient died from complications.*

Based on the way she seems to remember every patient she's lost, I know planting a memory of another death will be devastating for her.

DEN OF LIARS

After the pain my theft caused, I don't know how much more she can take.

We play game after game, hour after hour. At several points, our conversations lull, and the trepidation in my gut rears its head. *Now*, I think. *Get it over with so you can focus on the vault.* But then Legrand launches into another joke, another tale from her childhood, another fun fact about the human endocrine system, and I let the conversation continue, promising myself I'll complete the challenge after this game, after this topic. The smack of the sticks against the balls and the *thunk* when they drop into the baskets echo in my ears like staccato dance steps, a thundering accelerando toward some terrible finale I cannot bear to see.

The billiards room is in the center of the casino, so there are no exterior windows, but I still somehow sense when the sun sets. The air thickens, and the conversations around us murmur deeper and gentler.

I am running out of time.

As I lean across the felt to knock a ball into one of the baskets, I catch sight of the Liar sitting at a booth in the corner. People flock around him, moths to a mesmerizing flame. He smiles, answers their questions, even allows a woman to mold to his side and whisper with crimson lips into his ear, but his eyes never leave me.

I try to focus on the billiards stick in my hands, but I slip, knocking the ball against the side of the table. Legrand gives a whoop of triumph, hitting her last ball into its basket. I feign a smile as the Liar's gaze trails static down my arms.

Steeling my nerves, I face Legrand. I've put this off long enough.

"I just realized where I recognized you from," I say.

"You recognized me?"

I dig into my dress, extracting my yellow die and tossing it under the billiards table so she won't notice. The now-familiar flood of ice unspools inside me. I push it toward her, softening her emotions into a deeper trust, a willingness to believe.

JESSICA S. OLSON

"You performed a surgery on my friend Alzat Lopai. This past spring. In the Hartsmouth District."

She frowns. "I don't perform surgeries there. I work in the hospital on 17th."

"It was an emergency," I say. "They sent you with the ambulance, but you said he wasn't going to make it to the hospital in time, and you performed the surgery in his kitchen. On the table."

As the words tumble out of my mouth, I realize how preposterous they sound, how terribly ridiculous it will be for Legrand to take them seriously. Surely she would remember something so out of the ordinary.

"It must have been someone else." She shrugs.

"No, I'm certain," I say, mind racing as I run my fingers along the dice in my pocket. My hand curls around the red—the one meant to make the truth feel false. That's the one I need to convince her she's wrong about never having left the hospital for a medical visit.

"Are you sure you haven't done a surgery like that? Maybe it was so traumatic you've repressed the memory." I slip the die out of my pocket, trying to ignore the guilt simmering inside me. This is wrong.

"Traumatic?" She glances at me and tips the stick against the table. "What on earth happened?"

"Alzat was in a fight." I scramble for any sort of medical knowledge I can use to make my story more plausible. "Hit in the stomach pretty hard. He was vomiting blood."

"Oh dear."

"He passed out, and the medics feared he might also have a head injury, so they didn't want to move him."

"Perforated bowel, sounds like. Or trauma to one of the organs. Liver. Spleen." Her eyebrows furrow together like a pair of arguing caterpillars, and I try not to ache with fondness at the way she seems so studiously bent on puzzling out this fictional injury.

"You were going to remove his spleen," I say. "I know it was you."

DEN OF LIARS

She shakes her head. "I'm sorry, but I never perform surgeries in the field."

Holding my breath, I toss the red die behind me. When its magic fills me, it's slow and lazy like molasses, laughing and wicked like the Liar's steady gaze on me now.

"Maybe you don't routinely leave the hospital," I say, "but this time you did."

"Well, I don't think . . ." She pauses, eyes cloudy with confusion.

"You were wearing the pocket watch," I add, hating myself as the words leave my mouth. "A big, titanium thing. Silver hands, deep blue sapphire face ringed with black voratium shards cut to look like diamonds?"

She stares at me, her certainty fading. She never described the appearance of the pocket watch to me in that much detail, and after our time together, she seems fairly certain I'm a trustworthy, innocent, sweet young woman with no ulterior motives.

"It was awful," I say, hoping she takes the unsteadiness in my words as a sign of grief and not deception. "He was bleeding internally, so you opened him up to remove the damaged organ, but it was too late. He bled out before you could cauterize the artery."

Legrand braces a hand against the table. "I can't . . . I don't . . . I would . . ."

I squeeze my eyes shut, breathing slowly to keep my shame at bay. I don't want to have to use more dice—I only have two left—but I need her to believe me. So I pull out my last blue and stitch together flashes of a man's face, blood spurting from his mouth, the gaping maw of an open abdomen full of medical instruments. I flash them faintly in front of Legrand's eyes, push them into her mind like a memory.

She blinks. "Did you see . . ."

"See what?"

With the tiny bit of magic that remains from the yellow die I rolled earlier, I imagine the deep fear, the shock, the anger, and the despair that Legrand would have felt from such a moment, and I direct those emotions into her. Her face contorts, and tears gather in her eyes.

"Oh . . ." she whispers. "Maybe I . . . maybe I did repress . . ."

With a lump burning in my throat, I press a hand to her arm. "It wasn't your fault."

Legrand sniffs, straightening her jacket. "I'm sorry," she whispers. "I think I need to turn in for the night."

She moves toward the exit, but I grasp her elbow. "Dr. Legrand," I say. "Please don't blame yourself. You did the best you could, and I am grateful to have met you so I can relay how much the Lopai family appreciated your attempts to save the unsavable that day."

Legrand cups my cheek in her leathery hand and smiles softly. "Thank you, dear."

Then she rushes away. I want to follow her, to take it back.

But I can't. Not if I want to stay in the tournament long enough to get to the vault.

So I watch her go, tears stinging in my eyes. I will find her once this is all over. I'll tell her it wasn't true. Make it right.

A question feathers in my heart. A quiet, curious *Are you all right?* rippling through me from Enzo. A balm steadying the tightness in my lungs.

I lean on my billiards stick and breathe slowly through my nose to quell the ache in my gut. *I'm fine*, I try to reply as I force my body calm.

His question fades, but the worry remains, an ever-present echo to my pulse.

A clock begins to chime, and I swivel until I find it—a massive one spangled in stars on the far wall.

It's midnight.

Time for the first-round eliminations.

CHAPTER EIGHTEEN

☾

NIC

I augment the clock's toll, thread it through the air so it thrums in the heart of every patron in my casino.

It's time, the chime trills to them. *It's time.*

By the twelfth strike, I'm center stage, cloaked in darkness, rendered invisible by the ice in my veins. A ghost, watching and waiting as people stream in through the doorways like fluttering moths.

I build upon the anticipation already sparking in the air. Eliminations are the most attended, most celebrated parts of the tournament, when hearts are broken and lies crumble, when bets are lost and gambles won. Newscasters and journalists set up their cameras, pull out their notebooks, ready their recording devices. Spectators whisper excitedly to one another. The live band weaves an accelerating refrain.

But I can't seem to keep my mind on the magic.

You dance everyone around on magical little puppet strings, but it's not our secrets you treasure. Not our lies or even our truths. What you crave is our pain. The thief girl's words ripple through me, harsher and colder than any power.

She's wrong about me, just as thousands have been before her. When all you can do is lie, you lose the privilege of ever being understood, and I've made my peace with that. They can believe me to be the villain all they want; it doesn't make it true.

So why do her words *irk* me so?

If only she had revealed more about herself during the first round. I selected Legrand thinking the girl might slip up, mention something about the watch or why she stole it, but she did not.

I think of her tears last night, her anger when she shouted at me.

At least she felt shame for what she'd done. It's more than most people would manage.

My magic lurches toward the east doorway, a blizzard in my rib cage nearly dragging me off the stage. Planting my feet, I find her in the crowd. She's scowling, as usual, but her eyes are rimmed in red, her cheeks stained with traces of smeared cosmetics, the faint scrape from her altercation outside Legrand's door this morning accentuated by her flushed skin.

The memory of watching her get that mark niggles at me. There's something familiar about the way she twisted Ostena into submission, but I can't put my finger on what. Perhaps Enzo taught her how to do that maneuver; perhaps I've seen his Tentacles use it before.

Dragging my attention away from her, I square my shoulders and face the audience. Time to make a little magic.

"The hour is upon us!" I sing, still invisible as I make my voice dance across the air, echo along the walls.

The audience instantly hushes, turning to the stage in wild anticipation.

On cue, the spotlight blazes to life, and I rain a glamour of stars

DEN OF LIARS

along its beam, coalescing into a whirling figure with my profile. Faster and faster I make it spin, giving off purple, blue, and white sparks. The crowd holds its breath.

And though the magic sears inside me, though the echoes of screams play like a siren song in my skull, my cold heart quickens.

Because here, with the lights and the stars, the beauty and the drama, it is all about the thrill, the excitement, the glamour. No one is getting hurt.

The sparks swirl, so fast and so bright that many people shade their eyes with their hands. Drums crescendo, thundering to a climax.

And then, all at once, I blaze into view.

The crowd cries out as one, applauding madly.

"Round one is officially over!" I spread my arms wide. "What sorts of secrets will we reveal tonight? Which empires shall we topple?" I lower my voice to a dramatic hush. "Who's got blood on their hands?"

At that signal, Paol approaches, cloaked in an invisibility glamour, and sets an equally glamoured silver platter bearing the eliminated players' dice into my palm. I sweep my free hand around and relinquish the illusion cloaking the platter with an explosion of violet smoke.

The audience cheers.

"Twelve dice, twelve secrets!" I say. "Twelve players will be going home tonight!"

Whispers ripple through the throng. The people packed in near the betting rings lean forward, gripping their purses. The boards behind them are already full of names, amounts bet on each one written neatly in sparkling chalk.

My pulse quickens as I select one of the dice.

This is the moment where the thief girl will finally understand. I'm not a liar at all. I am trying to wake the world up.

If I have to lie in order to keep my own secrets, to keep my magic flowing, to prevent my brother from finding the shard, the least I can do is try to free a few people from the deceptions binding them.

I am telling truths in the only way I can.

The die in my palm belongs to a man called Piton Lonen, a prominent zenithic priest from Opalton, a lakeside town in eastern Celestia. I pull off my glove with my teeth and curl my bare palm around the cold burgundy gem.

Instantly, the man's secret unfurls in my mind. My jaw tightens as the scene plays out on the inside of my eyelids—Mr. Lonen taking the stand in a court of law, lying to the judge to protect the governor from embezzlement charges.

My eyes flash open. "I think we'll reveal this one tonight."

"No!" Piton shouts from somewhere in the crowd.

I toss the die. It rolls once, twice, three times before coming to a stop. Burgundy stardust explodes from it, forming into an illusionary recounting of the secret, played out like a theatrical production on the stage.

I try not to see my father in Piton Lonen's form, but the flowing blue zenithic priest's robes are identical to the ones Father used to wear, the gentle way he speaks so similar in cadence to the way Father preached.

I would have donned a similar robe had I stayed in my mental prison, would have taken up a similar post. I once wanted it more than anything. My love for the Gods Above was as real as my love for my father and brother.

Until the night I saw the moonshard break. Saw its magic pour. Felt its power in me.

I'd been taught my whole life it could not exist, and yet there it was, beautiful and terrible. And hidden by the very priests who had said it was a lie.

Now, watching Piton Lonen's secret unfold, the agony of that discovery floods me, as sharp as if it happened yesterday. I can scarcely breathe, scarcely see. It's all I can do to keep my illusions flowing, prevent the audience from seeing the sweat beading on my brow.

If I can help someone avoid this pain with my tournament, if I can break them out of their prisons before their prisons break them, then it will be worth it.

I turn my eyes on Astra as Lonen's secret fades. She's rigid, every muscle in her body coiled as though ready to spring. She's not seeing my purpose. She still thinks this vile.

My mouth twists.

She'll see, soon enough.

A shout echoes from the back of the room as the governor in the secret pelts through the crowd, heading straight for Lonen.

"Piton Lonen," I say smoothly. "You have gambled, you have lied, and you have been eliminated. Goodbye."

Shutters click as the governor tackles Lonen to the floor.

I cast a sharp glance at Paol, who already has three security guards heading to escort the brawling men outside.

Without a pause, I grasp a second die, this one light teal. "Who's next?" There's a sharp intake of breath in the front row from Warka Lanada, one of St. James's main assassins. As her secret filters like a film in my mind's eye, my attention snags on a moment where she tackles another woman to the floor, pinning her in the exact maneuver Astra used this morning.

Of *course*. No wonder it looked so familiar when Astra did it. It's one of Magnus St. James's signature moves, one he teaches all his lackeys.

My eyes rise to Astra's as I pocket Warka's die. "This one will keep nicely for later," I say as adrenaline rushes through me like fire. Boos echo throughout the crowd, as they always do whenever I choose to keep a secret to myself. I silence the jibes with a smile. "Warka Lanada. You have gambled, you have lied, and you have been eliminated. Goodbye."

Several whoops ring out from the betting tables in the corner as Warka glares at me. Then she turns on her heel and stalks out the door.

But I'm already scanning the platter for the next reveal, pulse racing. Surely another of these secrets could be related to St. James, something that might get Astra to reveal more about herself—where she is in his ring of influence, who she works with, whether she's loyal...

I touch each die, searching for flashes of something that might work, until an indigo one gives me just what I need. A man named Victor Vance being contracted to fashion a corpse to look like St. James's only child, Magnolia, after her death four years ago.

It's an intriguing secret. I wasn't aware decoy bodies had been made for St. James's daughter, but among his circles it's a common enough practice to avoid being targets for grave desecration. Perhaps Astra's reaction to this secret will tell me more about who she is and how far back her ties to the gang lord go.

I keep my eyes on her as I roll the die.

In the corner, its owner stiffens, his jaw going hard as the die flicks into the air, arcing out across the stage and landing with a sharp crack. One second passes, then two, and the room holds its breath. Then—

Light erupts from the die, and the world dims. In the space between one blink and the next, Aetheran buildings rise along the stage. Warehouses belch fat gobs of smoke into a cloudy sky. Fog curls in from the nearby river, plunging chilled, wet air down everyone's throats.

Victor's wiry frame slinks into view, striding quickly along a sidewalk.

Astra straightens, pushing her glasses up her nose.

The shrill peal of a telephone pierces the air like a scream, and Victor whirls, searching for its source. A public telephone booth stands alone under a flickering streetlight at center stage. Victor scans the area, brow furrowed. Then, tentatively, he approaches the booth. The audience holds its breath, and so does Astra.

With a quaking hand, he opens the door and lifts the earpiece from its cradle.

"Hello?"

DEN OF LIARS

"Mr. Vance," a garbled male voice says.

Victor whirls, peering through the glass at the street, at the buildings nearby, at all the windows watching him like gaping black eyes.

"Who—who is this?" he demands, a panicked note in his voice. "What do you want?"

"I want to make a deal," the voice says. "You are a cosmetics artist for several television studios, correct?"

"That's right."

"You come very highly recommended. But what I want to know is this: Can you keep your mouth shut?"

Victor wets his lips. "What about?"

"I've got a body I'd like you to dress up."

"A body . . ." he repeats. "A person?"

"A corpse." The word is cold and hard, eliciting a ripple of murmurs from the audience. Astra's brow furrows, and her hands knot in her lap.

"I'm sorry, I don't do that sort of business," Victor says. "Good day to you, sir."

He makes to hang up, but the voice says, "You'd be paid handsomely."

Once again, Victor's eyes dart to the shadows outside. He considers for one shaky breath. Two. Then he whispers, "How much?"

"Four million plats."

Victor leans his head against the rotary and swears under his breath. "What do you need me to do?"

The voice is sharp on the other end of the line. "Do we have a deal?"

Victor swallows hard. "We do."

"Good." The man's voice is satisfied. "Reach beneath the table. Taped to the underside, you'll find a photograph of a young woman."

Victor does as he's told, ducking to see the snapshot attached to the wood. He pulls it out and angles it so the streetlight illuminates the details.

Astra goes rigid, eyes sharp, jaw agape.

It's a photograph of Magnus St. James's daughter, Magnolia. She's clad in a dancer's leotard and pointe shoes, her arms extended over her head with her foot poised against a dance studio barre. The flush in her cheeks is apparent, as is the vibrance of life in her pale eyes and the sunlit glow of her blond hair swept up in a bun.

I don't dare blink lest I miss something. Every line of Astra's silhouette is sharp. Her hands curl into fists in her skirt. Her lips purse.

Yes, Magnolia St. James's death affected her somehow. There's no doubt.

"When you arrive home, you'll find the body," the garbled voice on the phone explains to Victor. "Make it identical to this photograph and drop it off at the address printed on the back of the photo. We need it by two."

"Two?" Victor pulls up his sleeve to check his wristwatch. "But it's already midnight!"

"Better work quickly." The voice laughs. "Oh, and by the way, if you fail to deliver, you will be exterminated. Good night."

"Wait—" Victor splutters, but the line goes dead.

The memory dissipates, the colors fading out like smoke. The lights come back on, illuminating Astra's face, which has gone slightly green.

Yes, she works for St. James. Closely, it seems, if she is familiar with Magnolia's death.

Which means I have the perfect mark for her next challenge.

CHAPTER NINETEEN

LOLA

As Victor Vance's memory fades, the world fades with it. The Liar continues with the dramatics, rolling dice, revealing secrets, but my whole body is quivering and I'm clutching my skirt so hard my knuckles ache. All I hear is that muffled voice on the telephone. All I see is my own face in that photo, so naive, so young, so hopeful.

When Enzo rescued me from Salazar, he told me he would have a corpse planted to make everyone believe I had died. To get Salazar off my trail and keep my father's other enemies from trying to pursue me. The fact that he had the false body made is not new information.

What doesn't make sense is the timing.

Over and over, Enzo has recounted the night he rescued me, just as he did yesterday. How he stumbled upon my predicament. It was luck, he always says. He did not know me, could not possibly have taken that photo of me from outside my dance studio.

That alone had me thinking perhaps the man on the telephone wasn't Enzo at all, but rather my father, commissioning a decoy corpse to keep his rivals from finding what he believed were my true remains.

But my mind keeps zeroing in on the newspaper stand next to the telephone booth with the date prominently displayed.

The day *before* my kidnapping.

Did my father plan to lose me? Or did Enzo plan to find me?

Which would be worse?

As the Liar finishes his demonstration with more stars and sparks and theatrical illusions, I squeeze my eyes shut.

I think back to my conversation with Enzo yesterday, trying to remember if I felt anything in our heart when he spoke of our fortuitous beginning. But I hadn't been paying attention. All I can remember is his worry, thick like a tide.

Could he have been lying?

Did he know I was going to be kidnapped? How?

And why wouldn't he have told me?

My stomach churns. The lights are too bright, the sounds too loud. I push through the crowd, dizzy, sick, and rush to my bedroom.

Slamming the door shut behind me, I press the heels of my hands to my eyes, leaning back against the wood.

"No," I whisper. "This is Enzo. My best friend in the world. My home. He wouldn't lie to me."

But if he didn't, then my father did, and that makes even less sense.

I knot my fingers together, drawing inward to my heart, focusing on Enzo's emotions. Has he sensed my distress? Is he coming?

But it's a gentle, steady thrum. Quiet and restful.

He must have fallen asleep before things got bad.

I want to feel distraught that he's not on his way here, but I sag with a quiet relief that just for tonight, I can mull this over by myself. Just for tonight, I can be alone.

As though to spite me, someone raps on the door behind my head,

DEN OF LIARS

and I close my eyes. Taking a deep breath and not even bothering to paste on a smile, I open it.

The Liar stands in the hallway, as dazzling as he was downstairs in his crimson suit and black cravat, his fedora quirked to one side and a debonair grin on his face.

This is the last thing I need right now.

"Oh. It's you." I cross my arms.

"Don't look so pleased to see me. I might get the wrong idea."

I shake my head. "Don't. Not tonight."

His smirk fades. "You all right?"

"I just don't have the energy to hate you right now."

"Then don't," he says, voice quiet. "You could drop grapes into my mouth with the fawning young ladies you so despise. They say it's quite fun."

I roll my eyes. "Why are you here?"

The Liar pulls another black envelope from his jacket. "Your round-two challenge," he says, which I take as he extracts his glowing glass box and clicks open the lid. "You may select your seven new dice."

My hand strays to my pocket, where the six empty dice I used in round one weigh heavy against the single remaining white one. Considering carefully, I pick up two yellows, three blues, one green, and one red.

"Excellent choices," the Liar murmurs.

Footsteps echo nearby, and I shove the dice into my pocket as Estelle comes around the corner carrying a glass of some kind of cocktail. She pauses, glancing between the Liar and me.

The Liar tips two fingers to the brim of his fedora and gives me a soft smile. "May guile guard your secrets, little thief."

He ripples into nothing.

I roll my eyes. "That trick loses its effectiveness if you do it literally every time you leave," I call out. "Maybe you could try exploding into a sparkly firework next time. Mix things up."

A faint laugh echoes through the air, a wisp and then gone.

Estelle waits a few seconds before approaching. "Are you all right?" she asks quietly. "I saw you leave the party. You looked upset."

"Just tired." I'd very much like to go to bed and pretend today never happened, but Estelle is my one ally here. Glancing up the corridor for where the Liar might still be, I push the door open wider. The last thing we need is for him to overhear us. "Why don't you come in?"

She enters and holds out the glass. The drink inside swirls, a bubbly pink concoction dancing with what looks like golden stardust. "I thought you might need something to help you relax."

I meet her eye cautiously. Her face is smooth, careful, tentative. Honest.

"Thank you," I say. "I'll drink it in a moment."

She smiles, setting the glass on the nightstand next to my bed. "What was that about?"

"Hmm?" I tuck my round-two challenge into my dress and shut the door.

"You were looking at him like you wanted to stab him. Why?"

"Something to do with him being an immoral pig. Though I didn't actually say that to him, which was an oversight on my part. I'll add it to my agenda."

She frowns. "You're playing with fire, Astra."

"What do you mean?"

"The Liar is not someone to be amicable with. He's dangerous."

I shake my head. "Don't worry. I'm aware. And *amicable* is not the word I'd use to describe my feelings for him. *Disgust* would be a much more accurate term. Or *abhorrence*."

She narrows her eyes, searching my expression for several moments before sighing. "If you say so."

I drop into the chair next to my wardrobe to unstrap my heels. "Stars, my feet are killing me."

DEN OF LIARS

"Does he know you're friends with his brother?" Estelle asks abruptly.

I pause, lifting my eyes to meet hers, weighing my options. I could deny again that I know Enzo, but it's clear she doesn't buy that. "Please," I say slowly, "don't say anything about that. To anyone." I swallow. "It would be really bad."

"What kind of ally do you think I am?" She raises a slender brow, a tiny smile curving one corner of her mouth.

"You swear it?"

"I'm good at keeping my mouth shut," she says. "So is your relationship with the Thief why the Liar is so obsessed with you?"

"The Liar doesn't know," I say, trying to piece through what I can share and what I should keep to myself. "He sensed I had a secret he wanted, but as long as I don't lose this tournament, he's not going to find out what it is."

"I see." She perches on the edge of my bed.

"So," I say, "I shared something with you. Will you tell me now why you care?"

She ponders for a moment before finally saying, "He hurt someone important to me."

"Ah. Perfect catalyst for becoming a stalker," I tease.

She breaks out in a grin, picks up one of my pillows, and tosses it at me. Thanks to my poor depth perception, my defensive swipe is too early, and it hits me square in the face. We stare at each other for a moment, and she snorts. "Nice catch."

"Nice aim."

"I'm keeping an eye on him," she says. "To make sure he doesn't do it again."

"That is incredibly cryptic and vague," I point out.

"And your explanation wasn't?"

I laugh. "Okay, fair point. Can I copy down some more of your notes?"

"Depends on if you have more blueprints."

"It's your lucky day." I push to my feet and turn to the wardrobe, then pause, my smile fading. I could have sworn I closed and latched it this morning as a precaution to keep my sack safe, but the doors are slightly ajar. Frowning, I pull them open. My sack is in its place, but the zipper is open, the files haphazardly stuffed inside.

I whirl, scanning the room. "Someone's been in here."

Estelle's face goes stony. "I had a competitor break into my room last year," she whispers. "Was waiting under my bed with a knife."

Both our eyes dart to the dark space behind her ankles. We crouch, bracing ourselves.

But there's nothing beneath the bed, not even dust. We search the washroom, but there's no one hiding there, either.

"Astra." Estelle points to a smudge of mud in front of the balcony door.

My pulse skitters so wildly I'm afraid it might wake Enzo. I press my finger to my lips. Estelle nods, unplugging the lamp from the nightstand and holding it aloft like a weapon.

Silent as cats, we creep to the door. I settle my hand on the knob, take a deep breath, then swing it open and charge onto the balcony.

But no one is there. Whoever it was is long gone.

Estelle peers over the edge of the railing, then squints and tugs at something caught in the wrought-iron decor.

A single, long silver-blond hair.

"Ostena," I whisper.

"I'm staying with you tonight," Estelle says. "You can't be here alone, not when she clearly found a way into your locked suite."

I want to tell her no, that I'm fine, that I can handle myself, but after everything that happened with the first round, the Victor Vance secret, and now this, the idea of being alone has me on edge.

"Thank you."

I drag extra blankets and pillows to the bed for her to use—it's

DEN OF LIARS

more than large enough for both of us—while she runs to her suite for sleepwear, which she takes into the washroom when she returns to prepare for bed.

Nerves still rattling, I slide onto my side of the mattress. My attention drifts to the drink Estelle left on my table. Praying it will help calm me down enough to sleep, I lift it to my lips and sink back against the pillows, taking one swallow, then two. It's a wine-based drink with a sweet, floral tang that fizzes over my tongue. It's delicious.

I close my eyes, and a sleepy warmth fills my limbs. A weight settles onto the bed next to me, and when I open my eyes, it's not Estelle I see, but the Liar. He stretches out next to me barely an inch away, dark hair tousled, fedora and jacket missing, the top of his shirt unbuttoned to reveal more of the sparkling scar on his chest. His eyes are intent on my face, tracing every curve and dip with his pupils blown wide and wanting. He wets his lips, and I find myself staring at them, turning onto my side to face him, drinking in his scent.

Distantly, I wonder why I do not panic, why I don't shove him off the bed at once and scold him for his impropriety. But the thought breezes away, chased by something desperate and warm in my core.

He rests a hand on my hip, hot and heavy, and all I can think is that I need more. More weight, more heat, more him.

As though reading my thoughts, he dips closer, his mouth hovering over mine. "So many secrets, little thief," he breathes, his lips teasing my skin like a dare. "Shall we make one more?"

I have never been with a boy, never even kissed one. My life has been nothing but isolation, the closest thing to physical intimacy the brotherly hugs Enzo gives me. I always imagined I would feel nervous to be touched like this. To be desired like this.

Instead, my hands curl in the fabric of his shirt. Because I am not afraid. I am hungry.

He drags my mouth to his, and it is delicious as dreaming. I press against him as his hand trails down to the hem of my skirt seeking skin, as his other arm curls under me, as he pulls me flush against him.

Then all at once, he's gone. I'm twisted in my sheets, fingers grasping at my pillow, the bed suddenly cold.

What the depths was that?

My chest heaves, and I ache, full of so much want, so much need that my body trembles. I roll onto my back, staring up at the ceiling, sparks trailing under my skin, the memory of his mouth, his scent, his taste still tingling through me like magic.

Magic.

My gaze darts to the half-finished glass on my nightstand. "Estelle?" I call out, praying she doesn't hear the hitch in my voice. "What is this drink you brought me?"

"Oh that! It's one of the Liar's specialties, served only during the tournament. It's called a Brier Rosé!"

One of the cocktails from her notebook. I search my memory for what it was meant to do and then squeeze my eyes shut when I remember . . . *Said to give drinker an illusion of their most forbidden desire.*

"Oh, stars, no." I groan and roll out of bed, snatching the glass from the table and crossing to the potted plant in the corner. "That sparkly braggart *wishes*," I snap as I dump the rest of it into the soil.

But long after I've returned to my bed, long after Estelle has curled up next to me, long after the lights are out and the effects of the drink have subsided, the taste of him lingers, tremulous and wicked, on my mouth.

CHAPTER TWENTY

LOLA

I sleep restlessly, dreams plagued with visions of Victor Vance painting corpses in various states of decay to look like me with both Enzo and my father leering over his shoulders. Finally, when the barest hints of silver dawn light have begun to streak the sky, I fling my blankets aside and creep quietly to the wardrobe so as not to wake Estelle. Retrieving my unopened round-two challenge and gathering Enzo's sack of files, I slip into the washroom and close the door before flipping on the light and perching on the toilet.

I set aside the challenge for a moment and open the sack with quivering hands. "Vance, Vance, Vance . . ." I whisper, shuffling through the files until I come to Victor's. I open the folder across my knees.

A photograph stares up at me, all sharp brow bone and watchful eyes like he was in the memory onstage last night. Chills raise goose bumps on my arms, and I shudder, flipping past to scan through the documents beneath.

JESSICA S. OLSON

Double Loualter's Degree in Stage Makeup and Lumenoring, 8442

Certified Voratium Cosmetic Specialist

Certified Lumenor, Level G, Honors

Vance is a highly sought-after artist known for his impeccable use of voratium-infused cosmetics. Television producers and motion picture directors pay upward of a thousand plats per hour for his services.

While he keeps his techniques confidential, many sources claim he infuses his voratium cosmetics himself with light from Aurie (star of beauty), Loton (health and vitality), and Lex (strength), and has even pulled starlight filtered through seawater for lies and disguise. As such, his voratium cosmetics have been said to alter people's faces and bodies to be utterly unidentifiable as long as the starlight in the cosmetics lasts.

There are several newspaper clippings with articles about awards he won for picture shows and stage productions, as well as transcriptions of interviews with him about his work, but nothing that gives me any indication whether he might have known Enzo or my father.

Sighing, I toss the file aside. There's no way to be sure until I get a chance to speak to Enzo about it. I force myself to focus on the casino blueprints instead, and for the next two hours, I comb through, marking in pencil any places where it seems like the walls don't quite match up or where there might be a space missing that could indicate a hidden room large enough to house a vault.

Finally, once the sun has fully risen and Estelle is beginning to stir, my gaze strays to the black envelope with my next challenge still hidden inside. Sighing, I pick it up, praying it'll be a simple one so I can get it over with quickly. I slip out a bejeweled piece of black paper identical to the one from the first round and read the Liar's looping silver writing.

Mark: Callum Astley

Challenge: Make him believe he conducted a secret funerary service for Alzat Lopai.

Who the depths is Callum Astley? I dig in my sack until I find a thick folder marked with that name. I flip it open.

A pair of deep-set eyes framed by straw-coarse brows and a sparse, greasy hairline stares up from a black-and-white photograph. My whole body goes still.

I know that pockmarked, leering face.

It is one from my nightmares, one I've tried desperately to forget. A face I see when I'm scared and it's dark, when I'm hurt and alone.

Shaking, I shove the photograph beneath the rest of the papers in the stack.

But it's too late.

Memories slam into me, dragging me under like a riptide. My suite washroom vanishes, replaced by my childhood bedroom. My silky pajamas melt into the white cotton nightie I was wearing the night I was stolen from my bed. Details blur as the sensation of being wrenched from my sheets takes over, and I glimpse that face in the moonlight all over again, as though I'm back there in that horrible moment I've tried so hard to forget. His meaty hands clamp down on my arms. His sour breath curdles in my nose. His rasping voice elicits tremors through my entire body.

I squeeze my eyes shut, but the images and sensations pummel me one after the other. A swinging fist. Cracking bone. White-hot pain. Blood pouring down my front. My bare feet scraping on flagstones. The crumpled corpses of my butler, my nursemaid, my dance tutor, blurred by tears. The stick of leather automobile seats. The barrel of a gun cold against my throat. Tears scalding my cheeks.

I press my fingers to my temples and focus on the present, on the here, on the now.

I'm nineteen, not fifteen. I'm in a washroom, not a gang lord's vehicle. I'm alone, not trapped by a man thrice my size.

My body quakes, but soon reality comes back into faint focus and the echoes of gunshots fade.

Callum Astley, my mark for the second round of the Liar's Dice Tournament, was the man who kidnapped me on Moratin Salazar's order four years ago.

I pull off my glasses and rub my eyes with clammy hands, trying to force air through my nose.

What if he recognizes me? What if he hurts me?

I steady myself. Gasp for air. I'm not Magnolia St. James anymore. I don't look like her, don't act like her. I'm a young woman now, not a child. As long as I keep my wits about me, perhaps put on extra cosmetics to enhance my disguise, I will be fine.

I can do this. I have to do this.

But before I can get my heart rate back to a normal pace, an echo of my panic swells from Enzo.

Damn it. He woke up.

Blankets rustle in the other room, ratcheting my pulse even wilder.

The last thing I need is for Enzo to come here right now. If he finds out about my alliance with Estelle, he'll have a conniption.

DEN OF LIARS

I soothe my emotions with every single trick I know. Deep, grounding breaths, closed eyes, envisioning myself on the roof of my childhood home with my hand in my father's.

But Enzo's emotions swell. It's hard to tell for sure, but they seem to be growing in intensity.

He's coming.

I'm fine, I try to tell him through our heart as I pile the files in one arm and rush into the bedroom to pull the curtains closed over the balcony windows. *Everything is fine.*

"Oh, you're already up," Estelle says, rubbing her eyes.

Thinking quickly, I fish the blueprints of the casino out from beneath Astley's file and hand them to her. "I have a deal for you."

Her eyes brighten at the sight of the blueprints. She pushes the duvet off and approaches, adjusting her nightcap. "What sort of deal?"

"These are yours if you go through the casino to mark any discrepancies between the diagrams and the real thing."

"What should I look for?"

"Anything that seems secretive. Like hallways that go nowhere or hidden doors or something. I'd do it myself, but"—I make a face—"I've got to get cracking on locating my round-two challenge."

She cocks her head, taking the blueprints from me. "You're looking for the vault, aren't you?"

I sigh. There's no use denying it, and at this point, I'm not sure I need to. She's made it clear her goals don't interfere with mine, and she's proven she's willing to help. As long as she doesn't find out *what* exactly I need from the vault, I don't see the harm in her knowing I'm after it. Besides, if Enzo is on his way here, there's no time to come up with anything else.

I give a noncommittal shrug. "I'm a thief."

"I knew it." Her eyes dance.

"So will you help me?" I cross to my wardrobe to pick out something to wear.

"You have yourself a deal," she says, "on the condition that under no circumstances do you wear that abomination of a dress." She looks pointedly at the one I'm examining.

"What's wrong with it?"

She shakes her head. "Take it from an expert. Green is not your color." She sets aside the blueprints and joins me, flicking through the fabrics, and I try not to panic as my tether with Enzo grows stronger. "I'm studying to become a costumer with a specialty in voratium-infused cosmetics. I know what I'm talking about."

"Voratium-infused cosmetics?" I need her to leave, but her words stoke the desperate, curious spark still burning in me. "Like what that Vance fellow the Liar eliminated last night did?"

Estelle examines a deep blue gown with black lace detailing on the bodice and strands of black diamonds draping along the shoulders. "Yes, actually. He's one of the best in the business." She holds out the hanger. "This is the one."

"Thank you," I say, slipping into the gown as she changes out of her own sleepwear.

"Oh, is that your mark?" Estelle points at Astley's photograph, which must have fallen out of the folder when I stood and lies face-up on the threshold of the washroom. Estelle retrieves it and holds it up to the light. "I've seen him. In the VIP rooms downstairs."

"Really?" I cross to her, sifting through the papers in his folder, scanning quickly. Enzo's emotions have crescendoed significantly. I'd guess he's maybe only a mile away now, which means I need to get Estelle out of here. But if she has information that could help me with my next challenge . . .

I scan the front sheet in the folder.

ASTLEY, CALLUM

Age: 53

Profession: Zenithic priest at parish on 89 East Wartle Ave. in Aethera

DEN OF LIARS

```
Special notes: Loves to gamble. Has won
several tournaments at various casinos
throughout Aethera. Very wealthy.

Likely works for Moratin Salazar. Attends
the Liar's Dice Tournament every year,
possibly to report back to Salazar.
```

I scan through newspaper clippings and magazine articles about the construction of his parish two decades ago, the renovations it's undergone, and the sort of community outreach it does. There are even records of his more popular sermons and several dozen pages that appear to have been torn out of a theological book he wrote.

"Which VIP lounge did you say he was in?" I ask as Enzo's feelings intensify. He's likely just outside now, climbing the wall.

"He basically lives in the card room. Solstice seems to be his game of choice."

Relief washes through me. Solstice is one my father taught me to play well. Perhaps I could challenge Astley to a few rounds. I'd just need some chips.

Remembering how the chips used must be bought with secrets in the Exchange Room downstairs, I check the clock on the mantel. The Liar should be heading there soon.

I just have to get rid of Enzo first.

"Perfect," I say, getting to my feet. "I'm going to annihilate this challenge."

"And I," she says with a laugh, "am going to annihilate these blueprints."

A footstep scrapes on the balcony.

"Thank you, Estelle." I rush forward, squeezing her fingers and steering her to the hall door. "I've got to run, but I really appreciate you staying with me."

She smiles, grabbing her shoes and slipping out into the corridor. "I'm starting to not totally hate you."

"Likewise," I say, giving what I hope comes off as a casual smile before I fling the door shut and rush to the balcony.

I unlatch the lock and push into the sunlight. Enzo stands, leaning against the railing, forearms braced on either side. His curls dust his shoulders as he tips his head back, and the many gems and rings on his face glitter.

He throws me a grin, but it is not a happy one. "Greetings, Lobster." He nods at the door behind me. "Mind telling me who the depths that was?"

CHAPTER TWENTY-ONE

LOLA

Enzo waits for my answer, his heart growling inside me. He doesn't like that I made a friend, just as I knew he wouldn't. But instead of rushing to apologize or explain, I find myself grinding my teeth as my own anger spits back.

Why should he get a say in who I talk to and how? This is *my* job. Sure, it affects both of us, but *I'm* the one in here. If the roles were reversed, I certainly wouldn't be micromanaging him.

"Who was she?" he asks, voice measured.

I jut out my jaw. "Her name is Estelle."

"You aren't here to make friends."

"Even you have allies."

"No one in this casino is safe to ally with." Enzo's words are curt.

"According to you, no one in the whole country is safe for me to ally with," I snap before I can help myself.

His nostrils flare, a zap of hurt zinging through us as though I slapped him. "Anyone in there," he says, jabbing a finger at the building, "could be working for my brother."

"She isn't."

"And you know this how?"

I cross my arms. "I'm not a fool, Enzo."

His jaw flexes, and he runs his long fingers through his curls, turning away and staring hard out at the sea. "I've never been barred from you like this before."

Septavia emerges from his sleeve and crawls onto his hand, curling two tentacles around his thumb and peering at me with her wide black eyes. A stray he saved from a shark near the Brig once, she's become an extension of him.

Not unlike me.

"How can I protect you if I can't reach you?" Enzo asks through gritted teeth, avoiding my eyes.

"Just think of me like one of your Tentacles. You aren't always with them, and you trust them to make good judgments." I approach, settling a hand on his forearm. "Trust me, too."

He stares hard at my hand, then slowly lifts his free one and settles it heavy on top of mine. Septavia curls a tentacle around my wrist, binding us together like a breathing knot. "You aren't a Tentacle."

That hits me like a kick in the gut. I jerk away, Septavia's suckers popping off my skin like punctuation. "I should be."

"Don't take it like that." He looks at me, eyes tight. "You're—"

"Too valuable, I'm aware," I snap. "I'm not a team member; I'm a tool."

He reaches for me, but I step back, heat flaming in my cheeks as the memory of how the Liar looked at me—not like glass but like a force to be reckoned with—churns an ache like poison in me.

"No," Enzo says. "You're my best friend. Your heart may be important, but I would survive without it." He shakes his head, blowing out a breath. "Like it or not, I care about *you*. Not because of our deal, not because of our heart. Because it's *you*."

I close my eyes, the anguish of both of our hearts like a torrent in my blood. "I care about you, too."

He breathes in slowly through his nose and closes his eyes, turning to brace against the railing and dropping his head. "What if this Estelle person has ulterior motives? What if she's trying to trick you into feeling safe with her because she wants something from you?"

"Or what if," I retort, "I know what the depths I'm doing, Enzo?"

"I just . . . I remember the last time someone you trusted turned out to be lying," he says.

The months after Enzo rescued me swim along the inside of my eyelids. Nights of crying myself to sleep, of missing my father, of scanning the newspapers Enzo brought me for any sign that Magnus St. James was upset his daughter had been taken and killed. Was he angry enough to start a war in the streets? Angry enough to hunt down her killer? Angry enough to retaliate and take Salazar's loved ones hostage?

But every day when there was nothing, every day when Enzo filled me in on Aethera gossip that was decidedly absent of any reaction from my father whatsoever, the cracks in my heart splintered deeper and deeper.

Enzo felt just how much it hurt. He cried with me. Raged with me. Our friendship was forged with bonds that went deeper than love or care. Bonds that came from literally knowing the intricacies of the other's trauma and heartbreak in a way no one else could.

Enzo lifts his head, meeting my eyes with tears in his own. "How could a father lose his daughter . . ." He presses his palm to my cheek. "How could anyone lose *you* and not care?"

I lean into Enzo's hand, trying not to think of my father's laugh or his coffee-and-oranges scent or the way his hand had been so big and warm around mine. Trying not to think of the nights we spent talking about the adventures we would one day have when I was older and things were safer. Trying not to think of how much it hurt every time his visits would end and he would have to return to his home in the city.

Does my father think of me ever? Does he miss those nights, too? Does he wish he could go back to them, the way I do?

"I never want you to hurt like that ever again," Enzo says.

"I know."

And I do know. His honesty is the cement that fused my broken pieces into something solid, something whole.

"I'm being careful," I tell him.

He looks at me for a long moment, then sighs. "All right, Lobotomy."

A guffaw bursts out of me at the ridiculous nickname, and I slug him on the shoulder. "I made it through the first round, you know," I tell him. "How impressive am I?"

"Astronomically." A ghost of a smile flits at the corners of his mouth. "Think we could order in some room service to celebrate?"

I give him a devilish grin. "Pastries?"

"Pastries." His eyes dance.

I dart inside to telephone downstairs. Twenty minutes later, a platter of steaming vegetable soups and pheasant and crusty bread arrives accompanied by twenty different kinds of pastries. I push the cart over to the table on the balcony.

"Cream puffs!" Enzo cries, snatching four off the top of a small pile and shoving all of them into his mouth at once.

"Slow down, son, or you'll make a mess of my floor," I tease, quoting one of his favorite picture shows.

"Are you judging me?" He picks up another two cream puffs. "I think you're judging me."

"I am absolutely judging you."

He glares, stuffing more into his mouth. "Cream puffs are delicious."

"You are disgusting."

"You know you want one." He tosses one at me, but thanks to my lack of depth perception, I miss the catch and it smacks me right in the face, leaving a smear of whipped cream on my nose.

I give him a mock glare, and he raises his hands as though in self-defense. "I didn't mean to! I'll do anything!"

Septavia, now perched on his elbow, squirts a stream of water directly in his face, and we burst into simultaneous laughter.

"See? Tavy's on my side!" I snort.

She makes a tiny popping noise as though in assent, which only makes us laugh harder.

This is what I've been needing.

Being with Enzo is like coming home. It's familiar, it's safe, it doesn't keep secrets. He's the family I never knew I was craving until I found him.

We devour as much food as we can while Enzo asks about the tournament and how I've fared so far. I fill him in, but just as I get to the part about who I was challenged to deceive for my first task, I pause. He doesn't know the Liar caught me on the roof with Legrand's watch, doesn't know the Liar was the one who requested I enter the tournament in the first place with the intent of learning my secrets. I still don't think Enzo needs to know. But if I tell him I was assigned to trick Legrand, he might get suspicious about how much his brother knows and fear I'm being manipulated.

I don't even allow myself the time to second-guess whether I'm making the right choice. I forge through the story quickly, inventing a name and altering details, keeping my eyes on my pastries so I won't feel horrible about lying to him yet again.

"You're doing better than I hoped," Enzo says when I finish.

"Sounds like you should have had a little more faith in me." I pour a glass of orange juice, but when I taste the fresh citrus, likely harvested near where I grew up, my stomach sinks. The familiar flavors drag up memories of golden summer afternoons slurping down glasses of fresh-squeezed drinks between ballet lessons.

The photograph taken of me through the window of my private dance studio—the one Enzo shouldn't have been able to capture because he did not know me when I lived there—flashes across my mind.

I glance at Enzo, stomach twisting. "I actually have a question for you." I dart inside, retrieving Victor Vance's file from my stash, and bring it back to the table, opening it.

"What is it?" Enzo asks, stroking Septavia's shining ebony head with his pinkie finger. "You all right?"

I hold up the photograph of Vance for Enzo to look at. "Do you know this man?"

He studies it. "Should I?"

"He was just eliminated at the end of round one."

"That's good, right?"

I pause, gauging his reaction. "Did you hire him?"

"A makeup artist?" He gives me a mockery of a smoldering, come-hither glance, arching a brow. "I'm already beautiful."

I try to laugh, but it comes out strained. "He apparently was paid an exorbitant amount of money to doctor up a corpse to look like me."

Enzo's brow furrows, and he examines the photograph again. "Ah! Yes, I did hire him. I never met the bloke in person, sorry."

A pit gnaws hard in my stomach.

So the man who bribed Vance in that secret wasn't my father, after all. Should I be relieved? Or is it worse that it was Enzo?

"You were the one on the payphone who called him?" I ask, voice tight as I try to breathe through the dread clenching a fist around my lungs.

"I forgot about that." He chuckles. "The poor fellow seemed about ready to piss himself."

"The funny thing was," I say, hoping he's too proud to feel my heart pounding, "he had a photograph. Of me. Where'd you get it?"

He shrugs, moving his hand upside down and back upright as

DEN OF LIARS

Septavia crawls around and around, her tentacles shining, slick and silky. "What's with the interrogation, here, Lampshade?"

"It was taken before you and I met."

He purses his lips, meets my gaze. "I lifted it off one of your dad's lackeys."

"When?" I ask. "None of my dad's lackeys were at that warehouse where you found me."

Enzo shrugs. "It was after. I took you somewhere safe, then went and got the photo and ordered the corpse."

"Oh." I blink. That makes sense.

Of course it does.

"The only thing is . . . there was a newspaper rack with the date on it in the memory I saw," I say faintly, hoping desperately he has an explanation for this last shard of glass digging into my side. "It was from the day before my kidnapping."

"They probably just hadn't changed over the papers or something; I don't know." He looks at me, pursing his lips. "Why do I all of a sudden feel like I'm on trial? You know me. You know us. None of that stuff matters. It happened four years ago."

I close my eyes. "You're right. It was just . . . This place is . . ."

He pulls me in, resting his chin on the top of my head as his arms wrap warm around my shoulders. "I know. As soon as you get my brother's secret, you'll be out of here."

We breathe together, quiet and steady, and my panic dissipates. The fear fades.

But even once he's vanished over the railing and I've slipped back inside, that pit in my stomach continues to gnaw, a question like an ulcer.

CHAPTER TWENTY-TWO

LOLA

At nine o'clock, once I've strapped on a pair of midnight-blue heels and piled my hair in an extravagant updo, I head down to the Exchange Room. If I'm going to challenge Callum Astley to a game or two of Solstice, I'm going to need chips.

The Liar looks up from his desk when I enter. The lighting is so low I can barely make out his expression, but the faint glow of his scar twitches when he meets my gaze, and my thoughts go unbidden to the image of him leaning over me in my bed last night, his buttons open to display more of that scar. The room feels suddenly too hot.

"Ms. Tremaine," he says with a tip of his fedora.

"Your Royal Liar-ness."

His mouth quirks. "You are far less polite than most guests who sit in that chair."

"I'm far less impressed than they are."

"Why is that?" He leans back, regarding me with his arms crossed over his chest.

"The rest of the world sees you as one of three things." I tick them off on my fingers. "A god, a human blessed by the gods, or seaspawn."

"But you don't."

"I see a bloke who stole power that did not belong to him." I shrug. "Something men have been doing for centuries. Funny, isn't it, how that power always causes their downfall?"

His smile deepens, but I catch the slightest tightening in the corners of his eyes. "If all of this"—he spreads his arms as though to take in the whole resort—"is my downfall, tell me, what would success be?"

"Freedom," I say like a challenge.

The Liar leans forward, interlacing his hands so a massive silver ring on his right middle finger glitters, its stone a snake's eye watching my every move. "Are *you* free, little thief? Or are you as imprisoned by your secrets as the rest of us?"

I purse my lips as Enzo's stress beats an incessant drum against my ribs.

Some might consider my heart in Enzo's necklace imprisonment. The Liar probably would.

But it isn't. I'm freer with Enzo than I ever was before him.

"I hate metaphors," I say, "almost as much as I hate riddles."

"No. You hate when someone who isn't you is right."

I glare. "You're *not* right."

He smirks, and I find myself staring at his lips, remembering how they tasted in that stars-damned hallucination.

Curse him to the Deep for that sparkly drink.

"Can we just . . . get on with the chips and the magic?" I slash my hand in his direction, thankful the light is dim enough to obscure the flush in my cheeks. "I've got a tournament to win."

His laugh fades, but he nods and pulls out a raw voratium gambling chip. "All you'll do is envision the secrets you'd like to exchange, and the voratium will pull it out. Just like last time. Nothing to worry about."

"I'm not worried; I just don't like you."

His eyes glint. "Not yet, you don't."

"You are entirely too self-obsessed."

"And you use sarcasm as a coping mechanism."

I huff. "I do not."

"If you say so." He extends a raw chip, presses it just below my collarbone. I glare, trying desperately not to focus on the brush of his fingers or to remember the way they'd felt against my thigh. Instead, I think of secrets I could stand to lose, like when I broke a vase as a child and told my nursemaid the plumber had done it. Or when I cheated on one of the exams my tutor gave me.

Chip after chip comes away glowing, and the Liar doesn't break eye contact. I find myself wondering whether his eyes were always the color of distant galaxies, or if the violet hue came from the moonshard. Wondering whether the cockiness has always been part of him, or if the magic changed him. Wondering how many lies he had to tell for the moonshard to register that as his defining talent.

The Liar presses another chip to my chest as a memory of Enzo recounting their escapades unfurls in my mind. The magic radiates into my skin, reaching for the image of Enzo's fond smile in my mind's eye. With a cry, I yank the Liar's hand away. "Not that one," I gasp. Even if he isn't seeing the secrets as he extracts them, allowing even a single hint at my relationship with Enzo onto the gambling tables is too much of a risk.

The chip is still dull and lightless. I stopped him just in time.

The Liar cocks his head, searching my face in a way that feels much too intimate. His hand is rough in mine, and the edge of one of his callouses scrapes against my palm. I find myself wondering new things about him. Like where the callouses come from, and what they might feel like against other parts of my body.

DEN OF LIARS

His gaze slides slowly to my mouth. My chest tightens, but I can't tell if it's because of my panic, because of his stare, or because of the thoughts slinking like shadows in my periphery. Forbidden thoughts. Dangerous thoughts.

"I . . . I have to go." I jerk out of his grasp and push to my feet, knocking over the chair in my haste. I stumble out of the room carrying my small pouch of glowing chips and ease into the crowd. It's time now to do what I came here for. Find Astley, lie through my teeth, and show the Liar he has exactly zero effect on me.

Cocky, sparkly bastard.

CHAPTER TWENTY-THREE

LOLA

Clutching my pouch of voratium chips to my chest, I weave between slot machines and tables, down hallways, through a restaurant, and into a more secluded, ritzy part of the casino.

The doorway marked VIP features a swirling fabric curtain made of a thousand winking lights. When I reach out, my fingers pass through, scattering the particles in the material like tiny fireflies. In the gap, I pick out Astley, and my throat closes as though his hand is clamped around my windpipe all over again.

I stumble backward until my spine presses against the opposite wall.

I can't do this.

"Astra?" Estelle comes around the corner with her notebook out and pencil in hand. Glancing around to make sure no one is listening, she rushes to my side, hissing, "There's this closet I want to check with you. It's not marked on the—" She catches sight of my face and stops midsentence. "Are you all right?"

"I'm fine," I reply, but my voice quavers.

"I'm not your mark, Astra; you don't need to lie to me."

I let out my air in a rush. "All right, I'm not fine. I'm . . . kind of terrified actually."

"That Astley will call your bluff?"

"That he'll hurt me." It comes out a squeak.

"Why would he hurt you? The Liar strictly forbids . . ."

"I know. It doesn't make sense." I try to brush it away. "Paranoia, I guess."

She studies me, then straightens. "I could come with you. Be your backup. If that'll help you feel better."

"It . . . it would. But you don't need to. You already spent the night in my room."

"I'm not done with your blueprints yet." She stows the papers in question inside a glittering gold bag and straightens her matching gown. "If you get kicked out of the tournament, then I'll be out of luck."

I smile in spite of myself.

"Go ahead," she says. "I'll be at the table right next to you."

I take a deep breath and steel my nerves. "Thank you." With a final desperate look at Estelle, I plunge through the curtain.

Astley lounges at a Solstice table with a pair of other men, tossing glowing chips and smoking a cigar. He's short and burly, clad in a tuxedo version of zenithic priest robes trimmed in silver buttons that bulge over his thick muscles. I sidle over to the bar along the nearest side of the room and order a glass of water with lemon, which I sip on, pretending to be interested in the acrobat show happening on a stage in the corner. I watch Astley's game progress out of the corner of my eye, taking note of tics and tells, how he sits when he's bluffing, how he always seems to puff on the cigar when he's telling the truth.

Soon, his game is over, and his opponents are grumbling, tossing their cards as they stand. Astley smiles, cigar hanging from his lower lip as he pulls the glowing pile of chips his way. "You sure you don't want another shot?" he asks them.

They scoff and sling on their jackets, muttering curses under their breath.

Now is my chance.

I stand, setting my empty glass on the bar. Every inch of me is trembling, but I set my jaw and approach. "Hello, Mr. Astley?" My voice comes out an octave higher than normal.

He raises his gaze to me, then frowns and glances behind him to see who I'm looking at.

Silently cursing my lazy eye, I focus it in and hope it's pointing the right direction by the time he turns back. His smile is exactly the way I remember, wolfish and yellowed, and it makes my skin crawl.

"What can I do for you?" he grunts, returning his attention to his chips and sorting them by color.

"I'd like to challenge you to a game."

"My secrets are not your affair." His voice is sharp as knives.

"That's not—"

"Piss off, kid." He glances up, blowing a ring of smoke into my face, and adrenaline zings through my body. My legs ache to bolt, but I force them still, chase away the memories of the sound of my nose breaking and the taste of iron on my tongue.

His eyes narrow. "Have we met?"

"Not that I'm aware." Sweat slicks my palms.

He scans my face, still wary. "Who do you work for?"

"I'm a . . . secretary at an office downtown."

"What's your surname?" He eyes the sparkling diamond necklace at my throat. "A family with a pretty bit of money, I'd wager, to be wearing something like that at your age."

I draw myself to my full height. I need to give him a name he'll respect. And since I can't use my real one, I utter the only other name that might give him pause, the only name that might incentivize him to play a game with me. The name of his own employer. "Salazar."

His eyes narrow. "Got a lot of nerve making a claim like that in a place like this. You don't look a thing like Moratin Salazar."

My mind flicks through what I was taught about the Salazar family tree, settling on one branch I know moved out of the city long ago, with whom Astley might be less familiar. "I'm his cousin's daughter."

His brow ticks upward. "Louis?"

I nod once. If I'm right, Callum Astley isn't as high up in the ranks of Salazar's group as he'd like to be. Secrets from his employer's family would get him a long way.

I watch as that thought seems to dawn on him. What would he stand to gain if he won a game against a Salazar? What could he do with those secrets?

He twirls his cigar, considering, then tips his head. "One game." He gestures for me to sit.

My shaking knees buckle, and I channel my inner dancer to roll with the movement so it doesn't look accidental, sliding into my chair with a flourish.

Astley nods at the dealer, who shuffles a black deck with iridescent purple ink. The sun, moon, star, and comet suits glitter as though encrusted in amethysts.

I handle the cards with ease, piling my chips with every wager I make in spite of my nerves. The magical dice in my purse press against my thigh, a heavy reminder of the challenge I'm supposed to complete, but I do not attempt to engage Mr. Astley in conversation yet. If I've learned anything from Enzo, it's to get my marks comfortable before I pick their pockets.

I make sure the first game is close, finessing my wagers to manage a win at the last second so he'll be motivated to request a second game. As I hoped, he grinds his teeth and nods at the dealer to start another.

When I win again, he tosses his cigar, leaning back in his chair and shaking his head. "Well, I'll be damned. You're pretty good, kid."

"Thank you," I say, trying to ignore the way his approval makes me nauseous. "Care for a third round?"

"Why the depths not?" He signals the dealer.

Lunch approaches as we play, and waiters bring us platters of sandwiches on crusty breads accompanied by various cocktails. Once he's had a whiskey, I choke down the nerves in my throat and strike up a conversation between plays. He responds in kind, and when I push a glass of rum his way, he downs it, too. Soon, with a full belly and a mind lazy on alcohol, he visibly relaxes, commenting on the food and asking my opinion about the latest political scandals. I've put him at ease.

Which means it's time to strike.

"I think I know why you recognized me," I say, pretending to slur my words so he thinks I'm as inebriated as he is. "You performed a funerary service for a friend of mine."

"Ah." He peeks at the corners of his cards, lips pursing. "Someone notable?"

"His name was Alzat Lopai," I say, keeping my expression smooth as I inspect my new hand. A six, a seven, and a nine of stars. Not bad. I toss a few chips into the pot. "A few months ago."

He matches my bet. "That name isn't ringing any bells."

I slip my hand into the discreet pouch strapped to my leg and pull out one of my yellow dice under the table. Holding his gaze, I toss it between my feet. Focusing on how it feels to be unsure, pensive, more willing to listen, I push those sensations toward him with the die's magic. "He was only maybe twenty-one? Died from complications during an emergency at-home surgery."

He frowns as the dealer sets out a communal card. A five of stars. If he sets down an eight, it'll give me a nice run. I pretend to deliberate, then sigh and toss a few more chips.

"This was a service done at my parish?" Astley stacks and restacks his chips before raising the bet, which I match.

My stomach is in knots. Though drunk, he seems to have enough of his wits about him that my first yellow die's magic wasn't enough. I force a smile as I roll my remaining yellow die under the table, strengthening the openness to suggestion I've already sent him, along with a red to make the truth feel less sure.

"Yes, the little chapel on East Wartle Avenue," I say, recalling the articles I read about him. "With the stained-glass depiction of Vivaris above the door."

He leans back in his chair, swirling his whiskey. "I'm sorry. My congregation has gotten so large the past few years, it can be difficult to keep track."

The game continues as we trade bets, as cards are placed, as the pot grows. Soon, a small pile of glittering, multicolor chips illuminates Astley's face. He seems to be getting more agitated the higher the bets go, and if I wasn't so scared of him, I'd probably find amusement in how tightly he's clenching his jaw.

As he considers the newest communal card, I toss a blue die under the table and craft an image of the same face I sent to Legrand yesterday. A flicker, a ghost, a memory. A gleaming white casket inside the chapel from the photos in my file upstairs.

He frowns, setting a stack of chips onto the table. "Was it . . . did this Alzat fellow have dark hair? Thick eyebrows? An earring in one ear?"

Hope blooms in me. "He did. You remember? The service was lovely. I liked what you said about our souls going to rest among the stars when we pass away." I regurgitate the sentiments from his documented sermons in the file. "It really helped the family to feel like their son lives on somewhere in the heavens."

"Oh, he does. I have no doubts." Astley downs the last of his drink. "Was this service done quietly? A private affair? I'm trying to place it."

JESSICA S. OLSON

"Yes, only the immediate family and a few friends."

With the magic from one of my two remaining blue dice, I cobble together an image of a small group of mourners seated in his chapel.

He nods once, eyes clearing. "Oh yes, absolutely. Alzat Lopai. It's coming back to me."

Relief twists through my panic, making me lightheaded. "Do you raise? Or have you had enough?" I nod at our cards.

He eyes me. "Confident little card shark, aren't you? I'm calling your bluff." He dumps a handful more chips into the pot.

I should let him have it. Get out of here while I'm ahead.

Yet I find myself staring at my purple chips on the pile. None of the secrets there would be bad for him to know, but what if he recognizes the child version of me? What if he knew my tutor or my nursemaid? What if he puts together who I am?

Feeling suddenly faint, I push my entire pile of chips to the center of the table. I have to win.

"Stars." Astley counts them, then digs in his own pile, and my stomach sinks. It takes every single chip he has left to match my bet. He pauses on one, a brighter, more vibrant chip than any of the others—clearly a more valuable secret. Turning it over and over in his hand, he studies my face. "Damn it, I think you're bluffing." He slams the chip into the pot.

We flip our cards in unison. My eight-card run easily beats his three-of-a-kind. He stares at the table for several long seconds, and I scoop the pile of chips toward me, so relieved I can barely see.

I'm almost done.

"You cheated." Astley's eyes flick to my face. "Nobody gets an eight-card run."

I try to keep my voice light. "I guess Vivaris is favoring me today." Getting to my feet, I extend a hand, catching sight of the Liar watching from the bar. "So lovely to meet you."

Astley grasps my hand, but instead of shaking it, he pulls me closer. "Lovely, yes," he growls, and my stomach drops. "Won't you join me for a drink? I'd love to know more about your strategy."

"No, thank you. I've got some things to attend to." I try to let go, but his fingers tighten.

"Oh, just one drink, Ms. Salazar."

Alarm bells scream in my head, sending electricity through my limbs and fuzzing the corners of my vision. The scrape of his rough palm pulls up the sharp memory of it pressed against my mouth. "It r-really sounds n-nice," I wheeze, "but I have to g-go."

He jerks me into the booth next to him. "I insist."

My heart gargles into my throat. "You're hurting my hand."

"I'm so sorry," he says, but instead of releasing me, he twists my arm so I'm facing him and lifts one of the glasses. "Have a drink, kid, and tell me how you won."

"It was just luck!" I gasp, trying to wrench my other arm to push him off, but the way he's pinned me against the table, I cannot get free.

I am trapped.

All of a sudden, it's four years ago, and I'm back in that basement. It is dark as pitch, the stars are gone, and I am covered in my own blood. The shouts of Astley and his men blare in my ears, the pain of my broken nose hammers into my skull, and the cold of the night scrapes ice along my skin.

And my father isn't coming.

But as my heart rams against my rib cage, something else bleeds through me. A soothing quiet curling around my chest like a cocoon of warmth.

Breathe, Enzo's heart seems to say. *I'm here.*

I may have been alone and defenseless with Astley four years ago, but this time, I'm not alone, and I'm certainly not defenseless.

Astley's attention flicks behind me for an instant, and it's all I need. I steady myself on Enzo's strength and yank my arm out from behind me, snatch the glass from his hand, and slam it against the table. It shatters, leaving only the stem in my fist, which I press a hair's breadth away from the pulsing artery in his throat. The sharp tip digs in just enough to make him wince.

"Let go of me," I growl.

"Or what?" he asks, eyes glinting.

I tighten my grip on the glass, but adrenaline roots me in place. I stare at that pulse in his neck, trying not to imagine the way his blood would spill just like my nursemaid's. Hot and sticky and crimson.

"Hands off of her." The words are sharp behind me.

Astley glances above my head and pales, eyes going wide. "Mr. St. James, s-sir," he stammers. "I didn't—I wasn't expecting—"

St. James.

My heartbeat whooshes in my ears like a hurricane. My limbs go leaden. My head spins.

He can't be here. He's not supposed to know I'm alive. He—

"Do not make me repeat myself," the voice behind me spits, and though it is lethal and full of venom, it does not belong to my father.

Trembling, I peek over my shoulder. Estelle bears down behind me, glaring at Astley with eyes like flint, her fists clenched around something glowing, and it dawns on me. She's using one of the Liar's dice to cast an illusion that only Astley can see.

"So sorry, sir," the priest mumbles, releasing me, "I wasn't aware she was yours."

I tumble out of the booth, and Estelle catches me, bracing me around the shoulders.

"Get out of here, Astley." Estelle's words are low, measured, the calm on the edge of oblivion.

"I'm so sorry, sir, I—"

"OUT!" Estelle shouts. The room falls silent. Even the music halts.

Finally, the priest slinks away, his footfalls thunderous in the quiet.

My knees give out.

CHAPTER TWENTY-FOUR

LOLA

"Let's get you out of here." Estelle braces her arm around my shoulders and leads me across the room.

Every eye at every table tracks us. Even the performers stare. The Liar's gaze is a trickle of frostbite along my skin. If I wasn't so shaken up, I'd shoot a glare to tell him exactly what I think of his horrible game. Instead, it's all I can do to put one foot in front of the other until we've left the VIP area, crossed the hall, and slipped into a secluded, open-air courtyard.

Clouds are thick and heavy overhead, but the faint glimmer of sunset spangles them in orange and purple. The courtyard is strung with lights that dart about like the fairies of the storybooks my nursemaid used to read to me. Trees sway in the crisp breeze funneling in from above as Estelle directs me to a stone bench surrounded by flowering bushes and flanked by seductive marble statues of sirens midsong.

"Where," I ask quietly, "did you get that magic die?"

She gives me a sideways grin. "You're not the only thief here."

"Oh really? Who'd you steal it from?"

"Some bloke downstairs who was trying to get handsy with me. I figured if he wasn't going to respect my 'no,' then he deserved it."

"Must have been one of the players. Did you catch his name?"

"Hildebard, I think? Not entirely sure."

I take a deep breath, letting the fresh air calm the warmth of my still-racing pulse. "How did you know Astley would react that way to seeing St. James?"

She shrugs. "I didn't choose to be St. James, actually. I mimicked how the Liar glamours the decor here. Instead of picking exactly what he wants us to see, he directs the magic to build on whatever would make us feel the way he wants us to."

"So you channeled the magic to create whatever image Astley would most fear?"

She nods. "And I coupled it with a green die to give him the auditory illusion of the voice needed to complete the effect."

I shake my head. "That's . . . kind of brilliant."

"I have my moments."

My heart rate has slowed considerably, but now that the immediate danger is past, Enzo's earlier calming influence has given way once more to concern. He's nearby, tugging on me, clearly desperate for me to reassure him I'm all right. I wish I could shut him out so I could breathe.

As soon as that thought crosses my mind, guilt jolts through me.

Enzo is only trying to keep me safe, as always, and he literally just helped me through an ordeal. Of course he's panicking.

I'll go to him soon, I reassure myself, hoping he'll get the message as well. *I just need a moment.*

As though sensing my inner turmoil, Estelle places a comforting hand on my knee and sighs. "It's different, being here as a spectator instead of a player. The stakes were so high last year, I couldn't really appreciate all the razzle-dazzle."

DEN OF LIARS

"The razzle-dazzle?" I repeat with a snort.

She grins. "Say what you will about the Liar, the man's a prodigy."

"I thought you didn't like him."

"I don't have to like him to acknowledge he knows how to put on a show."

"I imagine as a costume artist, you have a lot of experience with shows."

"Yes, well." She picks at a loose thread in her gown. "I told you I was studying to be a costumer, but that wasn't entirely true. I plan to go to school to study it formally soon, but so far, I've only been an apprentice."

"Oh?" This is the first time Estelle has willingly told me anything about her personal life, and my curiosity is instantly piqued. "Family business?"

"Definitely not." She grimaces. "My parents abhor that sort of thing. Not dignified enough for them. My mother is a senator in Solada, actually, so I was kept pretty isolated as a child. They were trying to protect me."

"Sounds familiar," I say.

"I started sneaking out when I was around twelve, and I came across this traveling theater troupe setting up in town one night." Her voice goes soft, as though carried away on YesterFizz bubbles. "It was so glamorous . . . During a show, I didn't have to be the senator's daughter anymore. I could be a pirate making soul bargains with seaspawn or a princess escaping an arranged marriage in the middle of a siege. I could be a sword fighter or a lion tamer or a bandit on the run.

"But the thing I loved most was hiding out in the tent before the show began so I could watch the costumes and makeup transform people. Watch their faces become palettes for the most incredible metamorphoses. It was like magic."

I tug on the ends of my hair, so different from how it was when I was Magnolia St. James. A transformation from naive dancer to jaded thief, one deeper than makeup or hair dye.

"Once, instead of watching the play, I stayed behind in the dressing room until it was empty," Estelle continues. "I perched on one of their little stools and tried my hand at some of what I'd seen them do. I fashioned myself a nice black eye complete with a gash through my brow right here." She points to her left eye with a laugh. "The stage manager walked in on me, but instead of telling me off, he just sort of . . . stared. 'You did that yourself?' he asked me."

"That must have been an impressive shiner." I laugh.

"I begged him to teach me. Luckily he was from out of town, so he didn't recognize me, otherwise I'm sure he never would have agreed to it. When the troupe moved on to the next city in the fall, I went with them," she goes on. "Sometimes I wonder how long it took my parents to realize I was gone. If they were relieved to not have to deal with me anymore." Her voice quiets, and I can't tell if there are tears in her eyes or if it's only the reflection of the fairy lights. "I wonder if they even tried looking for me."

I grasp her hand. "The similarity of our stories is staggering. I was raised cloistered away for my own protection, too."

"Did you run away from home as well?"

"No. I was kidnapped." I swallow, nodding back the way we came. "Callum Astley was involved. But my family did not care. They never tried to find me, either."

"Depths," Estelle whispers. "So that's why . . ."

I nod. "That's why." I probably shouldn't have told her that much. As far as I'm aware, it isn't common knowledge Astley was the one Salazar ordered to kidnap Magnolia St. James, but Estelle has already proven sharper than most.

But something about her guarded trust, her cleverness, her care is reassuring. She protects me but doesn't underestimate me. Treats me as an equal, not someone to fear or to control.

I like her, and for a moment, I don't care if trusting her is a risk. It's nice to have a friend without strings.

"Are you still with the theater troupe?" I ask.

She shakes her head.

"Why'd you stop?"

"I found a reason to stay in one place."

"Ah. Duty?"

"No." She tips her chin to the sky and closes her eyes. "Belonging."

I smile faintly. "Me too." But Enzo's worry and panic as he paces outside waiting make it hard to breathe, and my smile fades.

"Have you told the Thief you have feelings for his brother yet?" Estelle asks softly.

My cheeks warm. "There is nothing going on between his brother and me."

"I saw his face just now. He was about ready to tear Astley's arms off with his bare hands." She shakes her head. "His interest in you is far beyond curiosity."

"He wasn't—"

"And you," she continues. "You gravitate toward him whenever he's near. Like magnets."

"It's not what you think."

"See, the fact that you know what I'm thinking," she says, "is a giant clue there's *something* there."

"There isn't, though. Unless you count a massive desire to punch his annoying face."

She purses her lips, and when she speaks, her voice is measured. "Have you ever taken a moment to consider the reasons you don't tell the Thief everything?"

"He's a worrier. I don't want to give him things to obsess over when there's nothing he can do about it."

"I've done a massive amount of research." Estelle folds her hands in her lap. "Moonshards don't give powers willy-nilly; they draw on what's in a person's heart. That young man was a thief long before he stole that stone. His magic only amplifies that. And he lives for it."

"So he steals things." I shrug. "I do, too. Doesn't make me a bad person."

"No, but if that moonshard cursed you, I doubt it would latch onto that aspect of your soul."

My cheeks heat. "You did research, you say, but have you met him? Spoken with him?"

"No, but—"

"People believe what they want to believe, Estelle. Are you sure there isn't something making you *want* to distrust him? Something that makes you seek only the facts that confirm what you already think?"

Her voice is quiet. "Maybe you're the one believing what you want to."

"Take it from me: unlike the Liar, the Thief's magic is no blessing."

"How can you be so sure?"

"Because we share a heart," I say before I can stop myself. And then somehow the story comes tumbling out, and I cannot stop it, and I know it is foolish, know I should be careful, but somehow, with Enzo's fear roaring through my system like wildfire, I need someone to see the Thief the way I see him. Need someone else to tell me no, Lola, you aren't foolish for trusting him. For giving him your everything. For relinquishing your father and your life and your ballet in the name of the life he promised you. He was worth it. He *is* worth it.

Estelle listens with rapt attention, eyes wide.

"And that's why I'm here," I tell her, trembling. "Because in order to save Enzo, I need to get the Liar's secret."

Estelle considers me, and I find myself waiting, hoping that the next words out of her mouth will be ones of understanding. Of validation. But when she finally speaks, she asks, "If the Thief ever lied to you, would you know it?"

"We share a heart." My defenses rise again. "I just told you."

"That hasn't stopped you from lying to him."

I frown, biting my lip. "Well, no. But he doesn't have reasons to lie to me."

"That you know of."

"He saved my life. He's never done anything but care for me."

"Why did the Thief save *you*, though? Why you, and no one else?"

"Chance. Luck."

"Do you believe that because it's true?" she asks, her voice gentle as she settles her hand over mine. "Or because you need to?"

"I promise you, Estelle, the Thief is good and real and exactly who he says he is. I know it because I feel it in every inch of my soul, and those feelings didn't come from nowhere."

Estelle stares at me, concern furrowing her brow, softness in her whisper. "Do you really think your feelings are reliable, considering?"

"He's my best friend," I say, emotion choking in my throat. "I would trust him with my life."

She looks at me for several long moments before finally nodding. "Okay, Astra." Then she squeezes my hand. "I just . . . I knew someone like you once. I don't want to see you hurt like she was. But if you trust him, then I trust him." She gives me a gentle smile.

"Thank you," I say.

Enzo tugs at me, his emotions pleading with me to come to him, growing more and more frantic with each passing moment. As much as I don't want this conversation with Estelle to end, I should probably go to him before he bursts a blood vessel.

"I'd better turn in." I get to my feet. "Thank you for your help."

"Of course. And, by the way, I've requested to be moved to the suite next to yours, so if anyone tries anything tonight, just bang on the wall."

"You didn't have to do that."

She smiles. "I know. I just wish I'd had someone watching my back last year."

I lean in, giving her a hug. Her arms twine tightly around my shoulders.

"I'll see you later, then," I say, releasing her and retreating into the hall.

When I reach my suite, Enzo's tugs on my heart have become full-on yanks. I sigh and cross to unlock the balcony.

"What happened in there?" he asks as soon as I pull open the door. "Are you all right?"

"You can't come running every time I have a feeling, Enz," I say, rubbing my eyes. After all the events today and the poor night's sleep I got last night, I simply don't have the energy to placate him. "And could you do some breathing exercises or something? Your incessant worry is going to give me a heart episode."

He stares at me, mouth slightly open. "What?" Hurt flares from him.

I sigh. "Look, I'm sorr—" But before I finish, something creaks overhead. I dart a glance up to see the Liar's balcony door swing wide. Panicked, I turn back to Enzo, who vanishes into incorporeality at once. I retreat silently into my own room.

"Thank you for your help earlier. Really. I do appreciate what you did," I whisper quietly enough the Liar shouldn't be able to hear me. "But also . . . Could you just let me do the damn job? I need a partner, not a nanny."

There is no response. The only sound I hear are the Liar's footsteps above on his balcony, the scrape of a chair, the clink of ice in a glass.

I wait, closing my eyes. Enzo's heart simmers. Anger, hurt, indignation.

Instinct nearly pulls an apology out of me. My mouth wants to tell him I don't mean it.

But I do mean it. And I'm tired of minimizing my feelings in favor of his.

So I hold my tongue.

Finally, resignation settles, bitter and full of sharp edges.

"Sure, okay, Lola," he whispers, brusque and brutal and betrayed.

I open my mouth to reply, but he's already gone, the tether between our hearts pulling taut as he climbs back down the side of the building.

DEN OF LIARS

Pinching the bridge of my nose, I slide the balcony door shut as silently as I can and crawl onto my bed.

I should feel guilty for what I just did. After all, he's trying to help. But I'm too tired to feel how I should.

So instead, I curl up, still fully clothed, and squeeze my eyes shut, thinking maybe if I try hard enough, I can block out both our emotions long enough to get some rest.

CHAPTER TWENTY-FIVE

LOLA

When I awaken, it's pitch-dark. I roll over and flip on the lamp, squinting at the clock. It's nearly four in the morning. I sigh, leaning back into my pillows, straightening the straps of my gown. I hadn't meant to sleep straight through dinner and most of the night. What I should have done was allowed myself a short nap and then spent a few hours combing through the casino. Hadn't Estelle mentioned a closet that wasn't marked on the blueprints?

At least I got the Astley challenge out of the way, which means I have all of today to focus on finding the vault.

My empty stomach gnaws on my ribs. I need food. Perhaps I could start in one of the restaurants downstairs. Get a plate and then search the place until Estelle wakes up and I can ask her about the closet.

I clamber out of bed and strip off the evening gown, snorting at the sight of the sequin-shaped marks in my skin from sleeping in it. I bathe quickly and towel-dry my hair, then pin half of it up, letting the other half spill in curls over one shoulder. This time, I opt for a silky, floor-length deep purple gown with a slit up to my hip on one side. Draping fabric accentuates my curves on top, and off-the-shoulder straps show off my strong arms. I slide a necklace of lavender opals around my throat and put in a set of matching earrings before taking a step back to survey my appearance in the mirror.

I haven't ever been one to assess my beauty. As isolated as I've been my whole life, it didn't matter much to me whether others thought me attractive. But I find myself tracking the outline of my curves, dabbing on some rouge and lipstick, lining my eyes in shadow, and wondering what the Liar thinks when he sees me.

Whether he'd imagine me if he drank a Brier Rosé.

"No, Lola, don't do that," I scold my reflection. "Don't even go there."

I chuck the cosmetics onto the counter and stalk out of the washroom to strap the pouch of Astley's chips and my remaining magic dice onto my leg once more. Then I tuck a sheathed dagger into it as well. It's been a while since I saw Ostena, and I'm not taking any chances.

Locking my suite behind me, I make my way downstairs to a café, where I devour several plates of food. Once my stomach is full, I head for the service hallways to search for the closet Estelle mentioned.

The casino is still surprisingly busy, as though the patrons have forgotten they need to sleep. I pass restaurants teeming with people, cabarets with full audiences, and several rows of slot machines with a patron at each.

When I slip into the service hallway, a familiar silhouette stalks past in the distance, and my stomach flips over.

The Liar.

Where is he headed? How does he spend his time when he's not putting on a show?

Dodging past a bellhop pushing a cart of luggage, I dart after him.

He comes to a stop at an elevator and jabs the button, and I hang back where he won't notice me among the waitstaff, fishing in my pouch for my final blue die. As the bell over the elevator dings, I toss it. It rolls across the marble floor, erupting with stardust. I imagine myself invisible, blending in with my surroundings, and a ripple of ice flows through me.

Once the glamour has taken, I retrieve the used die and dart up the hallway, nearly knocking over a server in my haste. He yelps, looking around for who stomped on his toe. The Liar glances back, eyes landing on me. He frowns.

Blast. Does he see through his own glamours?

Panic floods me as the Liar takes a step in my direction. The lights in this hallway are dim enough he might not recognize me from this distance, but I don't want to give him reason to think I'm following him.

I focus on that chilled electricity in my body from the Liar's die. But as I do, I catch a flash of something from Enzo. He's awake, somewhere, aware of me, and guilt over what I said to him earlier stings alongside my adrenaline.

What would he do if he were here? I think of all the times he has rendered me invisible by capturing my corporeality into his voratium.

I squeeze the die hard, pretending that Enzo is next to me, siphoning my body into shadow.

The Liar furrows his brow, eyes sliding away from mine. Frowning, he turns slowly back to the elevator, ducking inside.

Keeping my grip on my glamour, I sprint after him and slink soundlessly through the door as it closes. I hover silent as a bat in the corner, holding my breath. After a moment, the Liar sighs and leans against the wall, pressing fingers to his brows and kneading the space between them.

He breathes in deep, then goes rigid as though catching a scent in the air, his head jerking in my direction.

My heart shoots to my throat.

He takes in another slow breath and cocks his head. "Hello?" he says, taking a step toward me.

I should have known better than to think the Liar's magic could be used against him. Even if the glamour works on his eyes, he can sense lies. And I'm deceiving him now, trying to make him believe he's alone.

He lifts a hand, but the elevator comes to a halt, and the doors fling open. A crowd enters and immediately swarms him. His lips thin as he answers their questions, autographs their cabaret playbills, and laughs at their remarks, but his eyes never leave my corner.

Perhaps he might lose the scent of my deceit among the secrets these people carry? I slide sideways, getting as near to him as possible without risking him feeling me there. From this proximity, I catch his scent—cigar smoke and cinnamon—and I'm brought back to the moment in the Exchange Room when I caught his hand. The memory of his fingers on my skin makes my breath catch, and I squeeze my eyes shut, trying to ignore the sudden rush of tingles down my arms.

That Brier Rosé drink really meddled with my brain. The sooner I find that vault, the sooner I can get out of this maddening place.

When the crowd disperses on the twentieth floor and the Liar bids them goodnight, I hold as still as I can. The doors slide shut, and the Liar's gaze returns to that place in the corner where I stood before.

I wait for him to speak, to act, but the only sound is the gentle chiming of the floors passing, the only movement the upward thrust of the elevator.

We come to a stop at the twenty-sixth floor, and the doors glide open. The Liar pauses, breathing in slowly as though sifting the air for its secrets. Finally, he steps onto the landing.

I trail him to a simple door in a back corner, where he pulls a key from his jacket and fits it into the lock. As soon as he shoves the door open, a voice calls urgently behind us.

"Sir!"

The Liar and I whirl to see an elderly woman hobbling toward us. She wears a nurse's uniform, and her iron-gray hair is swept up in what must have been an elegant bun but has since become as frizzy as a swab of cotton.

"Emmeline." The Liar steps forward to greet her.

"I've been meaning to speak with you, sir," she says breathlessly, a smile rounding her cheeks like wrinkled apples when he grasps her hands between his. "It's about my granddaughter."

"Lizette?" His voice is one of tenderness. "Is something wrong? What can I do?"

I stare, open-mouthed. Is the concern in his eyes a lie, or does he really care about this person? Why should he?

"Yes, that's the one," the old woman replies in a rush. "She's fallen ill, and we can't pay—"

The Liar shakes his head. "None of that. I'll have some plats sent down to the front desk for you to pick up after your shift. Would ten thousand be enough?"

She blinks at him, eyes filling with tears. "That's far too generous, sir. We'd only need four or five thousand . . ."

"Think of it as a bonus," he says. "You work too hard."

He's giving away money? Just because this old lady needs it? What kind of casino lord is he?

Rattled, I back up to his door. Well, if he's going to be weirdly generous, I'm going to take advantage of his distraction. With a final glance in his direction, I slip into his suite.

CHAPTER TWENTY-SIX

LOLA

I freeze just inside the Liar's door, gaping at the decor. It's like I've entered another world.

Periwinkle coals flicker in a black marble fireplace, illuminating a forest of orchids and stars. The flowers nod in the dark, glowing faintly purple and blue, their roots snaking like vines up the walls and dangling deep emerald leaves from vaulted ceilings. A massive bed of dark wood commands one corner, its charcoal hangings sweeping over a silky black duvet. Elaborate iron chandeliers drip dark purple gemstones overhead. At the hearth stands a fully stocked drink cart next to a leather armchair and a matching footstool.

My eyes are drawn to the corner by the balcony where the vaulting in the ceiling is highest. Mounted to one of the beams twined with vines hangs a set of black, shimmery silks like the ones I saw the dancers suspended from downstairs. Its ends pool on the floor like an invitation, and I can't help myself. I run my hands over the slippery fabric.

A large hoop with a set of ropes attached to it stands propped against the wall. What I wouldn't give to see him dance among the silks or on that hoop. What I wouldn't give to try it myself.

The Liar's and Emmeline's voices murmur through the open door, still deep in conversation, and I drop the silks, which land with a faint poof at my feet that sets the nearby orchids swaying. Hands shaking, I scurry through the room, searching for anything that could give me more insight into the Liar, more knowledge of who he is, what he might be planning, and where he might hide a vault full of his most valuable secrets.

On his bedside table sits a book propped open face down. Trying to predict whether it's some dry text on business strategy or a complex tome outlining game theory, I lean in to scan the title. *Lethal Liaison*. My brows rise. I bought a copy of the same book at the corner shop a few months ago. If I remember correctly, it was a cozy women's mystery complete with a few tantalizing romance scenes that had left my cheeks hot.

The conversation outside begins the downward tilt of wrapping up. Quickly, I tug open the drawer. Inside is an old deck of cards bound by a length of leather. A linen pouch full of simple black-and-white dice, worn smooth by years of use. A tawdry copy of the Odelion marked with so many notes it's nearly impossible to read. A set of ballpoint pens. Then, in the back, I catch sight of what looks to be a plain gold ring at the end of a matching chain.

With a glance toward the open door, I lift the jewelry. It is dull and scratched, at odds with the finery of the Liar's Den. And there, engraved tiny along one side of the band, is a name. *Laurel*. I try to slip it onto my fingers, but it only fits my pinkie. This ring was clearly meant for a person much smaller than I.

His voice approaches the door, bidding farewell to Emmeline, and

DEN OF LIARS

I return the jewelry to its place, shove the drawer closed, and duck under the bed.

His gleaming, two-toned shoes enter the room. I stuff a hand over my mouth to muffle the sound of my breathing as the lights snap on and the door snicks shut. His feet click over to the drink cart, and from this angle, I can make out most of him as he tugs off his suit jacket, draping it on his leather chair before loosening his tie and undoing his buttons.

The scarring on his chest catches the light as he shrugs out of his shirt, a mesmerizing extension of the stardust trails across his face. Its center glitters over the left side of his chest like a galaxy swirling. Another trail arches out across his left shoulder and around his biceps to his wrist, a third curls along his side, and a fourth slashes the other side of his chest and wraps around to his shoulder blade, twining around his arm three times to his elbow. Every time he shifts, it glitters, casting otherworldly shards of light against the vines on the walls.

Tossing his fedora onto a couch, the Liar disappears into his washroom.

As quietly as I can, I shimmy out from beneath the bed. Where the suite's layout is a near mirror image of mine, there is an extra door in the wall where my wardrobe is downstairs. I tiptoe to it and ease it open. It swings silently on well-oiled hinges, revealing a massive study.

Pulling the door almost shut, I dig into my pouch, extracting a few chips to use for light in lieu of switching on the desk lamp, which might leave a visible crack of light under the door that the Liar could see.

The orange glow of Astley's golden chips illuminates a room creaking with wall-to-wall shelving on all sides. Thousands upon thousands of books wink gilded titles, and I run my fingers along their spines, breathing in deep that comforting scent of old pages, of leather, of ink and glue. Mysteries and adventures, children's tales and romances make up two walls, and the others are stocked with textbooks on lumenoring, physics, astronomy. Books on human psychology, on the science of thought and belief, on social function. And dozens on the many religions and cultures of the world, myths and legends from every country I can think of. All of them marked with the Liar's looping cursive notes in the margins. Questions scrawled in corners and cross-references marked between columns. Drawings and diagrams, his notes darting among the lines like ever-circling footprints.

I would have expected books about illusion or theatrics, perhaps even art. This, however . . . it's like he's obsessed with understanding everything about people, about culture, about thought and religion and science.

I pull down several tomes, flipping through them, squinting to make out his notes in the meager light.

In one titled *Starblessed: A History of Myths and Men*, I find a ribbon marking a page about halfway through. Frowning, I adjust my glasses and pull the book nearly to my nose to read the small print:

STARBLESSED: EXPERT TRICKSTERS?

Many have made the claim that the people throughout history believed to be blessed with power from the stars are no more than illusionists wielding well-practiced sleight-of-hand. Others guess they might carry magicked voratium and are simply experts at hiding it.

However, I theorize that the genetic makeup of these people, whether through some cataclysmic event or contact with unstable starlight, has been altered such that the starblessed person is, for all intents and purposes, a miniature star. Studies comparing the lightwaves of starlight against those of a starblessed person's soullight find that the two are virtually identical, suggesting that a starblessed's soullight could be infused into voratium and that the resulting voratium could be used exactly the same as any other infused voratium.

This also explains the extended lifespan of starblessed

persons. The chemical reactions taking place at the cellular level of their soullight staunches the progression of aging and speeds up healing, making them nearly unkillable.

A handful of studies were performed on Nell Lightsworn, who supposedly crafted a moonshard and was thus exposed to undiluted starlight in great quantities. Those reports show an increase in soullight, an excitement of particles at the atomic level, and lumonic decay consistent with my hypotheses. The subject, however, has long been missing, and many presume Lightsworn dead. I, however, purport that if she is starblessed, her death is not a possibility until the moonshard she created is destroyed, which, at the time of the writing of this text, has not yet occurred.

Is this the Liar's research on his own magic? Was this Lightsworn woman the one who created the moonshard the Liar wields? And if the Liar is starblessed, what does that make Enzo, since he was cursed?

Before I can think too deeply on that, the Liar's footsteps click into the bedroom, startling me enough that I drop a few of Astley's chips. I freeze, blood rushing in my ears as I listen for signs he heard me and is coming to investigate.

Instead, music wafts in from the other room accompanied by the scratch of a phonograph needle.

Letting out a relieved breath and returning the Liar's book to its place, I scramble on all fours to retrieve the glowing golden chips. As I push upright, my eyes catch on a massive map spread across the desk like a tablecloth. The entire country of Celestia in black-and-white with a second map of its capital city, Aethera, marked with a dozen red X's and lines of handwriting. I lean closer, scanning the writing for a clue as to what this is all for.

A name jumps out at me. *Josef Bell, professor* is written with a line pointing to North Aethera University, exactly where Enzo and I did our heist and discovered the letter that led us to Legrand's pocket watch. Frowning, I recognize another name. *Olivia Legrand, surgeon.* The line next to her name points straight at the coast. The casino district. The Liar's Den Casino Resort itself.

My stomach sinks as I read each name, check each location. These are all of the marks Enzo and I have staked out for information about the moonshard's location.

Every single one.

Is the Liar tracking us? Or, worse, leading us from clue to clue?

I dodge a glance at the clock and drop Astley's chips into my pouch. I'll find a way to return to read more of that book and review these maps, but for now I am out of time—the illusion of invisibility I cast with that die is sure to run out any second. I prowl to the door and ease it open.

The Liar is airborne, eyes closed as he hoists himself to the top of the silks and wraps them around his waist. He tips back, arms arcing, feet pointing, perfectly in sync with the music playing on the phonograph next to the fireplace. I flit to the hallway door, turning the knob slowly so he won't hear the click of the mechanisms inside. Just before I make my escape, I pause and tip my head against the doorframe, watching through the crack.

His dance reaches for me, pulls me, makes an ache rise in my throat. His legs split wide as he drops several feet, twirling, sending the silks spiraling outward. In spite of myself, I imagine how I would dance beneath him, twisting between the fluttering arms of the fabric. My hands arcing above my head toward him. Arabesque, up en pointe, pirouette, pirouette, pirouette . . . I imagine him grasping my wrists, spinning me faster and faster, silks cocooning around us.

Enjoy the freedom you have, little thief.

His words from the other day filter through my memory as I imagine him dancing with me like that. I think of the way he always seems to be on guard, the way he considers everything he says for several seconds before he speaks, the way he watches me—and all the other patrons here—with careful, intentional eyes.

DEN OF LIARS

What an odd thing for him to say. Unless . . . Could he have meant that *he* wasn't free?

The pace of the music slows, deepening toward a lower register. I watch his face break, his brow furrow. An aching expression like he's looking for something. Someone. Some place, some time too far away to see. His hands stretch for a memory just out of his grasp. His legs strain for a world they cannot reach.

It is hypnotic. No matter the danger, I cannot look away.

This Liar is not the showman I saw on the stage downstairs, nor is it the cocky charmer or even the wicked casino lord. This Liar is vulnerable. Quiet. Troubled. Tired.

I frown as he knots his feet in each silk and spreads his legs in a deep split, muscles straining, toes pointing.

If he is not free, what binds him? Could it have something to do with why he lost his hold on the truth, like Enzo told me before? Why he had to put his secrets into dice to keep track of reality?

This Liar, dancing in the fabric, seems far more honest than he ever is with his words. Could it be that he *has to* lie?

Could he be just as cursed as Enzo?

I fist my hands in my skirt, following every movement with my eyes.

It's not that he cannot tell *any* truths, for he was certainly able to explain the rules of the tournament and how to use the magical dice.

No. Perhaps it is only truths about himself he cannot tell.

As that thought registers, so many of his riddling comments slot into a sensical pattern.

Do keep in mind, he warned me that night on the roof, *attempted murder would be a waste of your time.* Instead of simply saying, *You can't kill me.*

It is not necessary for you to play for the House to get what it desires, instead of *I don't need you to play in order to get what I want.*

I've assumed his riddling, pompous manner of speech was something he did specifically to irk me, but perhaps it's the only way he can speak.

If he has the moonshard, how could he be cursed? Wouldn't he be able to undo it?

I step back, stomach roiling. None of this makes sense. I twist the doorknob so the latch won't catch as I close it, then shuffle to the elevator. I cannot seem to get the ghost of the Liar's melancholic performance out of my head. His facial expressions. His pain.

What happened to him to make him move that way? What does a man like that long so desperately for?

And the last niggling thought I cannot seem to hush away: Is dance the only way for him to express the truth of his soul?

CHAPTER TWENTY-SEVEN

☾

NIC

I can almost forget I'm cursed when I'm airborne. Hanging from silks by only my hands, twisting upward, winding my legs through, dropping until knots catch hard around my body—it feels just like it always did. My shoulders ache and legs fatigue as much as when I was a child and my father bought me my first aerial hoop.

But as soon as I'm back on the ground, the bruises fade too fast, the tenderness eases too early, the silk burns heal too soon. In an hour or two, it'll be like it never happened. My body will forget it's a dancer, forget it knows how to fly.

So I remind it as often as I can.

I climb halfway to the ceiling and knot each foot in one of the silk poles. Sweat makes my hands clammy, and my grip slips ever so slightly as I split my legs, balancing with toes pointed.

My magic has finally calmed down. Lately, it's begun acting up more and more, to the point where I'm beginning to feel the thief girl near even when she isn't. Just now, riding the elevator, I could have sworn she was next to me. And again, in my room, it was like she was here, my magic yearning so intensely I was vibrating with it.

I slice an arm between the silks to cross them behind me, then straddle backward so I go upside down. I hang there for several moments, letting the blood rush to my head, trying to get the image of the thief girl's pale face during that game with Callum Astley out of my mind. But even the rush of my heartbeat in my ears isn't enough to drown out the echo of her trembling voice begging him to let her go or the memory of how violently she was shaking when she stumbled away.

In the days since she came here to steal Legrand's watch, I have never seen her like that. If I hadn't witnessed it with my own eyes, I would not have believed that kind of terror lived inside her.

And, once again, her pain was my doing.

I've won many secrets from Astley over the past couple years, the kinds of secrets that could land him in prison with very little effort. I haven't reported his crimes because I wanted to have blackmail power against Moratin Salazar's forces.

But today, something about that feels less like a strategy and more like an excuse.

You stand there, Astra's voice ripples through me as though I'm back in Legrand's hallway watching her blaze, *trying to teach me truth and morality like you're some sort of zenithic priest, and yet you simultaneously hoard your own secrets like treasure, lie through your teeth to keep the world on its knees at your feet.*

Shame's a sharp sting behind my sternum, and I want to resent her for it.

Except she's not wrong.

A knock on the door breaks through my thoughts, and I pull myself upright. "Yes?"

"It's me, sir," Paol's voice filters through the wood.

DEN OF LIARS

"Ah, perfect." I disentangle my footlocks and climb down. Wringing my aching fingers, I open the door.

Paol enters and follows me into my office. "A couple things," he says, his face grim as he holds out a folder.

Slumping into my chair, I roll up my maps, setting them aside so I can spread Paol's file across the desktop. I switch on the lamp, which illuminates several sheets of graphs and charts. "What do you have for me?"

He leans over, jabbing a finger at one of the top sheets. "I've compiled the records from your lumonic radiation detectors, and you are still getting a significant amount of activity near Moraille."

I frown, inspecting the steep line. "It's increased a lot."

"The flares are getting more frequent and less stable." Paol pulls out several newspaper clippings. "And there have been more reports of destruction. Even a death this time."

"No." The word is small, no more than a choked gasp. I lift the article he indicates and scan through the information.

We've been tracking lumonic radiation for about a year to try to pinpoint the moonshard's location. However, the technology is fairly new and imprecise, so we've only been able to narrow down the increased levels to a certain sector of the country.

If the moonshard is acting up, if it is getting worse and causing actual destruction, who knows what it could be doing to a person whose hands are stained with its light . . .

I pull out the photograph of the deceased, and relief cools my panic. It isn't Laurel. She is still safe, whatever happened.

For now.

"Any word from Taru?" I ask, sifting through the charts.

"He and his team are still scouring all the places you listed as possibilities. No sign of the shard, sir, but at least we've narrowed down the list."

I sigh, stacking the papers and closing the file. "Anything else?"

"Actually . . ." Paol pauses, clearing his throat. "I wanted to talk to you about getting time off in the spring. It's . . . I . . . well . . . I'm getting married."

I stare at him, my mind going utterly blank. "Married?" I repeat.

His cheeks go pink, and he smooths a hand through his shiny black hair. "I just asked her last night, and, well . . . she said yes."

"I—" I straighten, force a smile. "Congratulations. Of course! Whatever time you need."

Paol's smile widens, eyes dancing. "Thank you, sir. Good day to you, sir."

"Good day," I echo as he exits, a bob in his step.

I stare at the door, my entire body suddenly heavy and numb.

Married.

I didn't realize he was seeing anyone. Don't even know her name. I pinch the bridge of my nose and slump into my chair.

Paol has been my head of security since the Liar's Den first opened. The early days were difficult and chaotic, as I was still reeling from the collapse of my worldview and the loss of my brother and Laurel alongside the demands of my new magic and its curse. Then my father died, and Paol was the one who embraced me when I wept, who asked me questions I could not answer about why my brother and I couldn't console each other for our shared loss.

I clung to Paol, desperate to have someone, anyone. I tried to ask him about his life, tried to be a support and a confidant, but whenever he attempted to reciprocate, my magic would halt the words in my throat, keep me from speaking about my past, my present, my dreams.

Paol must have been able to feel me holding him at arm's length, because after a while, he stopped trying, and I stopped, too.

I lean forward, tipping my head against the folder on my desk.

Stars, I miss Laurel. Not as a lover, but as a friend. We used to talk about everything.

I met her when I was twelve. She and her family had moved into my father's congregation, and I noticed her the first day she walked through the parish door. Petite and lovely even then, with dark hair to her waist and dancing green eyes. It took me months to work up the nerve to talk to her, and when I did, she laughed and said, "See? That wasn't so bad, was it?"

She read me in a way my own brother never could, and we spent nights out on the beach under the stars talking about everything. And though she was a devout believer in the faith, she did not look down on me for loving the sea in spite of what the Odelion said about the demons who lived there, and she did not begrudge me for asking questions.

She watched Enzo and me become the Devious. Stood by as we snuck out to raid homes and steal treasures from safes in the middle of the night. Never asked me to explain myself because she could see my guilt and shame were eating me alive bad enough as it was.

But the night before the moonshard job was different, and she knew me well enough to be able to tell. We were sitting on the rocky cliffs that overlooked the northern curve of the bay, and I was so nervous I was sweating in spite of the cool ocean breeze.

"What are you going after this time?" she finally asked.

"It's better if you don't know."

She pursed her lips. "You could stop, you know."

"Stop what?"

She waved her hand toward the city. "Stealing."

"Enzo is never going to stop."

"Sure, but that's Enzo. You don't have to help him."

I laughed, but she didn't join in. I peered at her. "You're serious?"

"Never been more serious in my life, Nic. You hate this. You are not a criminal."

I stared at her, swallowed hard, then said, "I can't."

"Of course you can."

"If I don't help, he'll get himself caught, arrested, or killed."

"Sounds like that's his problem. And if you keep helping him," she snapped, jabbing a finger at me, "you're *both* going to get caught, arrested, or killed. You know if the roles were reversed, Enzo would not put his neck on the line for you."

Anger rippled through me, and I ground my teeth. "He is my brother." I pushed to my feet. "This conversation is done."

She didn't follow suit. Instead, she whispered, "Do you know how hard it is, loving someone who could be thrown in prison or murdered every single day? How impossible it is to sleep when I know you're out there risking your life for a pile of gold or a string of voratium? How terrified I am *all the time*?"

Her words sliced deep, and I crouched next to her. "I'm sorry."

She looked up at me with tears rimming her eyes. "At least tell me where you'll be tomorrow night. What you're doing."

"I . . ." I shook my head. "I shouldn't."

"Please." Her voice broke. "The not knowing is the worst part."

I studied her face, running my thumbs along her cheeks, smoothing her hair behind her ears as I considered.

I shouldn't have told her. But I did.

As soon as she heard the word *moonshard*, she pulled out of my grasp.

"But there's no such thing."

"Enzo thinks there is. And you know how stubborn he can be."

"You can't break into a temple," she whispered, eyes wide. "That's sacrilege."

"Now you know why I'm sick about it." I dropped my hands to my sides. "And why I didn't want to tell you."

"Whether you get caught or not, *they* will punish you." She glanced up at the stars and shrank back, as though they might strike us down for discussing it.

"Enzo won't change his mind."

"What's Enzo going to do when you get in there and there's nothing to steal? Moonshards aren't real! Magic is a myth sown by seaspawn!"

"I know." I mopped a hand over my face. "He's determined. And I can't let him go in there alone."

She grasped my arm as a tear rolled down her cheek. "Please, Nic. Don't do it."

"I'm sorry." I got to my feet, tugging her hand.

But she held her ground. "Choose." Her voice was hard and quiet.

"Choose?"

She leveled my gaze. "Enzo or me."

"What?" I rocked back on my haunches. "Laurel."

Launching to her feet, she stalked toward the city. "I can't live like this anymore."

"You've known who I am for a long time," I said, charging after her. "My brother and I have been 'the Devious' for years now."

"Yes, but I thought you'd grow out of it."

I grasped her arm, yanked her around to look at me. "Love isn't something you grow out of, Laurel."

"And sometimes love is saying no," she snapped. "So say no for me, Nic. Please."

My chest was so tight I could scarcely breathe. "I can't."

Her expression hardened. "Fine. You can make your choice, but I'm making mine. I will not love a thief anymore." She pulled off the ring I'd made for her using Enzo's metalworking tools and tossed it at my feet.

"Laurel, please . . ." I called after her.

But she did not turn back.

The next time I saw her was when she tried to stop me at the temple. When everything went wrong.

She only came because she believed the gods cared. If not for her faith, she would not have been there. None of this would have happened.

The truth—of what the stars really are, of what magic truly is—would have saved us all.

I rub my palms against my eyes as the guilt over the thief girl's interaction with Callum Astley niggles at me. I've been hiding that bastard's truth for far too long, truth that if I had revealed sooner might have spared her whatever pain I saw in her face last night.

Leaning across my desk, I pick up the phone and jab my finger into the rotary to dial the number for the police department.

Protecting Enzo and Laurel from each other is my top priority, and keeping Salazar under my thumb is part of that. But allowing his lackey to walk free just so I have a potential bargaining chip for later isn't worth what I saw last night on the thief girl's face.

"Hello, Aethera Police Department," a voice squawks over the line.

"Yes, this is the Liar," I say. "You're going to need to send a team to 104 Ortona Street to pick up a Mr. Callum Astley."

CHAPTER TWENTY-EIGHT

LOLA

I spend most of the rest of the morning combing through the halls and rooms on the main floor, searching for signs of the vault. As I work, noting odd corners I want to inspect more closely when there are fewer people around and hallways I'll need a disguise to get into, my thoughts keep straying back upstairs to the Liar's office and that map spread across his desk.

Has he been tracking Enzo? Marking down every place we steal from, every clue we find? Or, I wonder, a pit opening deep in my stomach, could the Liar have set us up? Is that map evidence he's been planting false clues?

It would make sense for him to do that if he's trying to keep us from getting to the moonshard. But every time my mind goes down that path, I catch a flash of the pain on his face as he twirled on those silks, the realization that maybe he's just as cursed as Enzo is.

And if he is, then perhaps the Liar doesn't have the moonshard at all.

Perhaps he's trying to find it, just like we are.

But then why would he be setting up clues to keep us from finding it?

Around and around my thoughts go until I'm too dizzy to focus on finding the vault. I need a breather.

Drawn by the lilt of ethereal music, I slip through a translucent curtain into a ballroom and lean against a wall draped in black satin, watching couples twirl as I try to settle my thoughts. Tiny firefly candles float overhead like faraway stars. The dance floor is a spangled ebony that swirls like the tails of a galaxy.

I close my eyes, tipping my head back, letting the music soothe the chaos inside me.

"Would you care for a dance?" a silky voice murmurs to my right.

I turn to face the Liar, and my turmoil heightens.

Because his smile is not the charmer smirk he flashes at diamond-dusted dainties, and it's not the showman's grin he wears onstage. It is like the expression I saw on him when he danced upstairs. Raw and vulnerable and full of questions.

And damn him, it was easier to hate him when I knew he was vile. What do I make of the Liar when the pieces no longer fit?

He extends a hand, brow raised. "Please?"

I want to spin on my heel and run. Could this, too, be a performance meant to knock me off-kilter? "Why?" I ask. "So you can torment me with more of your riddles?"

"No," he replies in a rumbling breath. "So your body can tell me the truths your mouth keeps locked away."

I eye him. I don't want to make a scene. Already, I feel the weight of people's stares. My name has made it up a few lines on the betting rings this morning, I noticed, and turning him away now would make me memorable. Everyone loves the Liar. I need to pretend I do, too.

So I swallow my misgivings and meet the Liar's eye, forcing a smile that likely looks little better than a grimace.

"One dance," I say, settling my fingers in his grasp.

His eyes glitter. "Very well."

He lifts my hand over our heads, twirling me so my dress flares around my legs.

Most of my training was in ballet, but my instructor made it a priority for me to learn as many forms of dance as possible. Ballroom was always my second favorite. Something about moving with a partner, legs weaving and breath syncing, was mesmerizing to me. And though it has been four years since I last danced like *this*, my body moves instinctually as the Liar spins me into the center of the dance floor.

It's clear he knows what he's doing. He grips the middle of my back, solid and steady, holding my right hand aloft with his other. I rest my remaining palm on his biceps and try not to notice the taut swell of muscle under his jacket sleeve. Grinning wickedly, he pulls me around in time to the music, our feet braiding their way across the floor, my dress whipping his legs.

The rest of the world falls away. Legrand and her pain, my worries about Enzo, and the run-in with Astley fade into the background, and all that is left is the feeling of soaring, my body moving in a way it hasn't in so long. Too long.

It feels like freedom.

Our bodies ripple to and fro. He twirls me, pulls me to him, thrusts me away, his eyes never leaving mine. As the pace of the music accelerates, so does the heave of our lungs and the intensity in our gazes, until I am drunk on the scent of him and high on the feel of my body, alive after years of slumber.

It's dizzying. It's electric. It's ecstasy.

As though sensing my thoughts, the Liar cocks a grin, clearly amused at my simple joy. I suck in a breath, and I'm not sure if my heart is beating so fast because of that smile, his hands on me, the dance, or my confusion.

...*His illusions are so powerful you will lose all sense of reality if he wants you to,* Enzo's warnings swirl in my head as fast as we do across the floor . . . *You cannot believe anything you see, hear, taste . . . and especially not anything you feel.*

That devil's smile, the new-money tuxedo, the glittering eye, the absurd purple fedora tipped diagonally across his brow. Does it matter if the Liar has feelings when he dances alone in his room? Would that make up for the games he's played? The pain he's caused?

If this is an illusion—the care, the questions, the vulnerability—perhaps the only way to find out is to play a little game of my own.

"I loathe you," I say when he pulls me close.

"Do you, now?" His smirk is cunning, that scarred eye sharp as knives.

I do loathe him, loathe everything he's done, everything he stands for. But when he looks at me like that, something hot ripples through me, and I find it difficult to breathe.

I try to focus on the memory of my dance tutor dead on the cobblestones. On the agony of losing the only family I had. On the desperation Enzo and I have shared chasing what the Liar holds just out of our reach.

"I don't think you understand how deeply I loathe you," I continue, arching as he dips me, closing my eyes, tipping my head to the floor. "Depths of the seas, height of the heavens, and to the ends of the galaxies."

"Has anyone ever told you," he says, lips brushing like moth wings against my exposed throat, "that you're a tad dramatic?"

I should be disgusted.

Instead, hunger blooms along my skin where his mouth touches me, and I gasp. He pulls me up, spins me out so hard my skirt flares open at the slit. I drag a pointed toe along the floor in a slow, fluid arc.

"*I'm* dramatic?" I say as he whips me back against him, my right breast flush against the right side of his body. "*Your* whole life is a farce." I tip my chin around at the firefly candles, the extravagant satin, the midnight sky beneath our feet. "Tell me, is there anything real about you?"

"Reality . . ." He tastes the word with a sensuality that makes heat pool in my core. "Such a fascinating concept."

We sway, hips pressed together, and stars this feels good in a way dance never has before. Wicked and wild and wanting.

And I want to hurt him like he's hurt me. Punish him for giving me this moment, so wonderful after so long and so tainted with *him*.

But to do that, I need to know what his play is. I need to incite more of a reaction, bluff him to see where his tells hide.

"You know what?" I ask as the music crescendos. His hands brace at my waist, and he tosses me firmly away. I fling my arms out, wide like wings, and land on one foot, extending my other high and back.

"Tell me," he breathes, chest rising and falling with exertion as we sway right and then left. He draws me into a tight spin, our hands braced on each other's waists.

"You believe yourself invulnerable because you guard your truths like a fortress, but you are not as mysterious as you pretend to be."

"Fascinating." He twirls me away from him, fingertips skating around my ribs. Then he stops me, our right hands joined over our heads, our noses inches apart. "Do continue."

My mind races. What might provoke him? What might break through his careful glamours? "I think you can tell a lot about a person from which lies they choose to tell," I say as he backs me along the floor. "You give off an aura of charisma, which tells me you crave outside approval. You feed us whatever appearance will win you our admiration."

We twist and arc, muscles burning, and I'm intimately aware of everywhere our bodies touch. His hard, muscular torso anchors my softer curves as we steal fluidly among crowds that seem as though they're in a separate world. His hands grip mine, long fingers curved around my knuckles, calloused palms scraping my skin, while his arm braces my waist like an embrace.

"I've seen the way you survey the people in your casino. The way you've watched me." I cock my head, lean in close so he can taste my breath. "You thrive on our secrets because having them gives you intimacy without the risk of ruin."

He does not speak, does not even blink, but his pupils are blown wide and hungry as they search my face.

I watch each of my words hit its mark, and a thrill rolls through me.

Maybe, unlike his brother, he does have a heart. And maybe, if I throw the right barbs, I can make him hurt like his game did my father. Like it killed my nursemaid and my tutor. Like it wrecked me.

"We do not give you our secrets out of trust or affection, but out of greed and desperation." I lean in even closer, so close our cheeks touch as I murmur into his ear, "And that tortures the depths out of you, doesn't it?"

The Liar jerks me back as the music blares a staccato, angry line. "You think," he says, his words tinged with an almost-laugh, "because you've watched me for a few days that you suddenly have my heart and soul puzzled out?" His lips curl. "You have so much to learn about deception, little thief. Lies aren't only told with words."

We whirl, and he holds my gaze as his cheekbones soften, his brows furrow, his lips swell ever so slightly. The line of his jaw loses its dagger point, and his eyes ache with a pain that fills me with the need to apologize, to discover what might have broken him, to find a way to fix it.

"Pity me, darling," he says.

"I—" I begin, but he twirls us, and his features sharpen. Eyes glitter wicked and dark, brows arch, and his grin becomes a slash of angry teeth. My heart rate increases, my legs twist away from him.

"Fear me," he growls.

And I do.

Then his face turns gleeful. Facetious. A sumptuous smirk, cheekbones like glass and so maddening I want to slap them.

His laugh is high-pitched and full of scorn. "Hate me."

My stomach sinks.

My body reacts exactly the way he wants it to. My emotions change according to the images he shows me, the way he touches me, the sound of his voice.

How have I allowed myself to think I know anything about him at all? He is a shapeshifter of the wickedest kind.

He pulls me flush against him, and my body molds to his in spite of the horror and awe twisting in my gut. His expression eases, his features soften, and his eyes wait and watch.

"Trust me." His breath skates across my face, a gentle lover's caress that leaves me trembling. I cannot breathe and I cannot look away.

And then the music is roaring louder and wilder and faster, and we spin and we spin, and the world falls away. The other people in the room vanish entirely, and as we whirl, the violet of my dress bleeds around us like a hurricane of sparkling orchid petals cocooning us in its eye.

The Liar's scar glows white-hot, and his stare smolders as he drinks in every inch of me. His hands encircle me like a possession, snaking deliciously up my back, and I want more of it. More of him. His skin and his body and his hands all over me. A desire so intense it has me trembling.

He dips me low against his knee, and my leg instinctually lifts to a point through the slit in my dress, every inch of me alive. Hyperaware. Desperate.

His lips are inches from mine, and I can already taste them.

Whiskey and cigars, ecstasy and abandon, sin and seduction, and I want it all. I want his mouth and his hands, his tongue and his teeth, crave them so deeply I can scarcely breathe.

The petals slow their torrent and drift lazily through the air like snow, igniting at once. The purple of my dress sparks to a violet-blue fire. Smoke twines around us as the music trills into silence.

We are alone among glowing embers in the dark. His lips graze mine, and I gasp.

"Worship me," he breathes.

He does not have to command it. I already do. This prince of deception, this god of lies. I arch into him, desperate to close the final breath of space between our mouths.

Instead, he drags those lips slowly, tantalizingly, torturously along my jaw. I am dizzy by the time his teeth catch on my ear. One of his hands slides up to cradle my chin with feather-soft fingers. "Be wary of what your fickle heart wants to believe, my dear, for it is the most cunning liar of all."

And with that, he pulls me upright. The cinders in the air dissolve. The smoke trailing like lace from my gown vanishes. Sound and light and people materialize exactly as they were before.

The Liar nods, brisk and formal as though we did not just share a dance that felt like sin. My heart roars like fire in my ears, and heat flushes my cheeks and neck. He grasps my hand and brushes a kiss along my knuckles.

"Thank you for the dance, Ms. Tremaine," he says with a knowing smile, plucking the orchid from his lapel and handing it to me.

I take it, blinking as the world comes roaring back to rights, and the heat of desire boils first into humiliation and then into a wild, raging fury hotter than any inferno.

That cocky, sparkly, wretched, conniving, seaspawned *demon*.

I charge at him, but he ripples into smoke, dissipates to nothing.

"Argh!" I growl, whirling to see where he went.

DEN OF LIARS

People watch me from every side, whispering behind cupped hands. I force a steady breath and fake a smile.

Then I whirl and stalk out of the room, crumpling the orchid in my fist and slinging it into the trash can where it belongs.

At least my confusion is gone. The Liar is as much a villain as I ever knew.

But I'll be damned if I let him get away with it.

CHAPTER TWENTY-NINE

LOLA

For the rest of the morning, I search the casino for the Liar and even resort to pounding on the door to his suite, but he is nowhere to be seen. Either he left the building, which I find very unlikely considering his magic is housed in the walls, or he's avoiding me.

The man may be vile, but he's got survival instincts, I'll give him that.

When I've exhausted all my options around noon, I ride the elevator to my own floor, grinding my teeth. If nothing else, I can confront him tonight after the round-two eliminations. The bell dings, and I sigh as I step into the hallway. The window at the far end of the landing looks out over the ocean, where the sun has reached its zenith, and its light reflects purple along the voratium marbling in the decor.

As I approach the door to my suite, a quiet exhalation behind me makes me halt. I glance over my shoulder, but there is no one there. Pursing my lips, I turn back to the doorknob, fitting my key into the lock.

My thief's senses pick up a shift in the air. Slight movement.

The hairs on my arms rise.

I whirl, flinging a forearm up to protect myself as an invisible force rams into me. I see nothing but empty air, but I swing my leg into the invisible person's side, eliciting a grunt from them.

The sound is familiar. An echo of the sound Ostena made when I stuffed a fabric rose into her mouth.

My frustration with the Liar feeds the adrenaline pumping through me as I wrench the dagger I stowed earlier out of the strap on my thigh.

"I was wondering when you'd show up again."

There's a rustle of fabric, and I hook my leg around what feels like her knee. She slams to the floor, rattling the chandeliers overhead, and something hits the tile nearby, shattering.

A clear liquid pools out from what appears to be the remnants of a syringe. Holding my dagger toward the sound of Ostena struggling to her feet, I approach the puddle and take a whiff. A faint, almost indistinguishable odor emanates from it, a twinge in my nostrils I wouldn't notice if I wasn't paying attention.

Ostena's feet scrape, and I whirl to meet her, brandishing my dagger, but her invisibility has me aiming slightly too far to the left, and I'm not quick enough. She wrenches me against the wall, crushing one forearm to my windpipe and slamming my hand so hard above my head the dagger slips from my fingers. I wheeze, kicking my legs, lungs burning. Stars burst in my vision as I claw at her arms.

"Not so clever now, are you?" There's a smirk in her voice, like she's already won.

With one hand, I scratch at her fingers, drawing her attention there while my other hand slips into her pocket and closes around a die.

I glimpse only a green glimmer before I toss it behind her. The icy spread of magic floods my veins, and as blood rushes in my ears, I cast an illusion of pain. Blinding, white, all-consuming.

She screams, ripping away from me. I collapse to the floor, coughing hard as she flickers into view sprinting through the stairwell door.

I retrieve my dagger, stumble to my suite, and spill inside, locking it firmly behind me before mopping the tears and snot from my face and yanking off my pumps. Then I unclip my pouch of chips and dice, unzipping the top to glance inside.

A pit drops in my stomach, and I paw through the chips.

The biggest, brightest chip—the one Astley specifically did not want to part with at the end of our game—is missing. Where is it?

I duck out into the hall to see if I might have dropped it during the altercation with Ostena, but all I see are the shattered remains of the syringe.

A sharp tug thuds in my chest, and I startle, realizing that in my panic I didn't notice the increase in Enzo's emotions.

He's here.

Tossing the pouch onto my nightstand and smoothing my ruffled gown, I cross to the balcony and open the door, staying inside the threshold where he cannot reach me.

"So we're clear," he says before I can greet him, "I'm not checking on you, even though I nearly just suffocated to death. I am definitely not here because of that. Nor am I even going to ask you what happened. Because I'm not checking on you."

"Then why are you here?"

"I have two things to say."

I dart a glance up at the Liar's balcony, but the door is shut tight. "I'm listening."

"First: I'm sorry. I shouldn't be criticizing all your choices and trying to micromanage you on this job. I've been unfair."

"Apology only accepted if you brought me my snazzatazzles."

His eyes widen. "I mean three things! The second one being

DEN OF LIARS

that your snazzatazzles are . . . en route. Held up at the border. Or something."

"Held up at the border? The pier is a mile from here." I plant my hands on my hips. "I can't believe you forgot *again*."

"I told you, they're en route!" He holds up his hands in protest.

"I seriously doubt that," I grumble. "What's the third thing?"

"I—" He frowns. "Actually there was only the apology. I thought you'd bite my head off, so I was giving myself a viable segue into groveling."

"I'm not going to bite your head off," I snort. "It's a bit too full of hot air for my taste."

He scowls. "I'm going to pretend you didn't say that."

"Fine." I finally step onto the balcony. "I forgive you. Sort of."

"You forgive me?" His arms come around me in the tight, bear-hug squeeze that has always made everything all right. He spins me around a few times, laughing.

"I said 'sort of.'" I kick my legs. "You're still on trial, Entropy."

"You *have* to forgive me," he says smugly. "I am clinically undetestable. According to scientists and . . . data analysts."

"You are certainly un-something," I retort as he sets me down, but before I can finish my joke, my eyes catch on the purse I just left on my nightstand, where Astley's chips spill out the top. One of my magical dice glimmers blue on the pile. I frown.

I shouldn't have any blues left—I used the final one this morning to glamour myself invisible for the entirety of my trek into the Liar's bedroom and office. There shouldn't be any magic in that die, and yet it's still glowing.

"Everything all right?" Enzo asks.

"If I used one of your brother's dice to cast a glamour, would it fool him?"

Enzo shakes his head. "No."

"Are you sure?"

"You think he'd let people run around with those dice if he wasn't safe from their antics?" He snorts. "He may be dramatic and pompous, but he's no fool."

"Ah." Confusion rises like a tide in me. If that die didn't work, then how did I sneak into the Liar's room unseen?

"Why?" Enzo asks, ducking to catch my eye. "Did something happen? Did he hurt you?"

I draw in a quick breath, forcing my thoughts away from all of it so my heart won't betray my true feelings when I say, "Just curious."

The map in the Liar's study flashes across my mind, but I shove that down, too. I don't need to cause Enzo concern until I'm sure what it means. Besides, if he knew I'd taken such a risk by sneaking into the Liar's suite, he'd be upset. No matter how he may claim otherwise, I don't think he's at a point where he will fully trust me.

Or maybe it's I who cannot trust him?

That thought makes me feel suddenly ill.

"Is there something else?" Enzo asks. "You seem rattled."

"Are you sure," I begin slowly, "the Liar's magic has no cost to him?"

Enzo's emotions turn wary. "Positive. What's with all these questions?"

I purse my lips, watching sunlight dance like diamonds across the sea. "It almost seems like he cannot say anything about himself. What he thinks or wants or remembers."

Enzo's gaze is intent on me, and though I'm not watching his expression, I know exactly what it must be based on his emotions as they pass through our heart. He's likely frowning, the creases by his eyes deepening, his brow ticking downward ever so slightly.

"Remember what I told you before you came here," he says. "He is going to do whatever he needs to do to make you doubt your reality."

Oh, don't worry, I think but do not say, imagining the Liar's changing face on the dance floor. *You have no idea how aware I am of that.*

Enzo's hand curls around mine. "I am your reality, Lola. *This* is real."

"You're right." I try to give him a reassuring smile.

Enzo is my brother, my best friend, my family, and though his words remind me how little I understand this dangerous game I've been thrust into, they also remind me why I'm here and what matters most. And after that dance with the Liar, I should be certain of what's true here, certain of who's good, who's honest.

So why do I still feel sick?

"I'm really tired," I say truthfully. "I think I need a nap."

"All right, I can take a hint." He squeezes my hand once more. "Good luck, Larynx. Try not to give me any more heart episodes."

I snort. "I'm starting to wonder if you stole a dictionary and made a list of all of the *l* words in it just to annoy me."

"You don't think I could come up with these nicknames on my own?" He presses his hand to his heart in mock affront. "Lockjaw, I'm offended."

"Off with you. Before I change my mind about forgiving you."

He climbs onto the railing, eyes dancing. "Okay, Loincloth."

I laugh, but all this talk of names tugs sharply at another piece of the puzzle, and a question blurts out of me before I can stop it.

"What's the Liar's name?"

Enzo stiffens, smile dropping.

I never cared before what the Liar's name was. He was a wraith in the dark, a monster under the bed. Scary, horrible, inhuman.

Now he's real, and his powers are terrifying, and I'm suddenly desperate to know, desperate to humanize him so his shadows don't seem so dreadful.

Enzo turns away. "He has no name."

"Of course he has a name."

"The name he once had," Enzo says, voice distant as the sky, "is the name of a brother. That brother was a lie."

With that, Enzo ripples into nothing, and I am left alone with the echo of his hurt.

CHAPTER THIRTY

LOLA

A sharp rap on my door pulls me out of my thoughts, and I take a few deep breaths to settle my nerves before crossing to open it.

The Liar tips his head in a slight bow. His fedora, as always, is cocked over his forehead, and his scar glitters as his mouth curves. "Good evening, little thief."

I glare, crossing my arms over my chest. "Come to apologize?"

He raises a brow. "Actually . . ." But he trails off, jaw working.

"That dance downstairs?" I charge on. "Was that meant to intimidate me? Scare me? Make me fawn? You blatantly manipulated me *to my starsdamned face*, and no, it's not okay."

"Yes. That was—"

"Oh no. I'm not even close to finished yet," I snap. "You want to know what makes you a villain? It's this kind of behavior." I jab a finger at his chest. "I am not a puppet on your strings, nor am I a pawn in your little games. I am a person. And people deserve respect. All of them."

"Even the ones who vex me?" The faintest sparkle glints in his jewel eye.

"I only vex you because you're a pompous ass who wants everything handed to him on a silver platter and I don't do that for you."

He stares at me, his mouth slightly parted as though I've slapped him. Perhaps no one has ever called him out like this before.

Someone needed to.

Finally, he nods once. "You're right."

"That you're a pompous ass?"

"That you're not a puppet. That people deserve respect. That manipulation is vile." He swallows. "I—" The words die in his throat, as though held captive. He tries again. "I—" But again, nothing else comes out.

"You . . . ?" I prompt, softening in spite of myself.

"An apology is appropriate," he finally says, defeated.

I sigh and lean against the doorframe. "Just . . . don't do it again."

His throat bobs. "Of course."

"That's it? No pretentious riddles? No dramatic stardust explosions?"

"Not unless that's how you prefer your apologies." He tips his head.

"Thank you." I watch his jaw clench, his eyes tighten, and my anger simmers back.

This could be another act meant to draw out my pity. Enzo would claim it is.

But I'm not so sure.

"Why are you here?" I ask after a moment. "Surely you have, I don't know, an interview with a radio show or some kind of lunch party you're supposed to be at?"

"Actually . . ." He pulls a rectangular wooden box from his jacket, which he holds out tentatively toward me. "This is for you."

"A gift?"

"That's usually what it's called when someone gives you something, yes."

I frown, glancing at his earnest expression. It almost seems like he came *to* apologize. Is this gift some sort of peace offering? But why would he do that?

I take the box, trying to ignore when his fingers brush mine, and open the lid. Nestled inside is the pair of glasses I lost down the ventilation shaft, entirely repaired. I gasp. "You fixed them!"

"They were found when housekeeping cleaned up your—ah—*mess*."

The distant echoes of the gunshots in that vent punch through my memory, as does the scream of the man I sent plummeting to his death.

Shoving down a sudden sting of guilt, I yank off my spare glasses and set the repaired ones in place. The world filters into total focus for the first time in days. "Thank you," I say. "You wouldn't believe the difference these make."

He opens his mouth as though to speak, but the words seem to get lodged once more. He swallows, and a muscle twitches in his jaw as he says, "You were squinting a lot."

Enzo's words earlier, the ones that swirled in my thoughts all day long, repeat, slow and distant in my mind . . . *you will lose all sense of reality if he wants you to* . . .

I stare at the Liar, remembering how his face changed during our dance, how his voice transformed, how his eyes glinted. Obvious magic, powerful and terrifying.

Meant to intimidate, sure. But manipulate?

If he truly meant to trick me, why would he have shown his hand like that? Demonstrated precisely what he is capable of where I could see and scrutinize it?

And then I think of all I said to provoke him. Accusations of weakness, barbs meant to sting, to hurt, to incense.

DEN OF LIARS

I was the one who was manipulating *him*.

My stomach sours as I think through every interaction where he's played a part, told a lie, elicited a desired reaction from me. Every single time, he's done so openly. Made sure everyone involved knew it was a performance.

Always the actor, the magician, the showman.

If he is cursed to lie, perhaps he bows to that curse in the most honest way he can: by making sure we always know that's exactly what it is.

Of the two of us, who has done more real lying?

I swallow the guilt tying a knot in my throat.

It's not the same thing. He's hurting people. I, on the other hand, am trying to save someone.

My lies have purpose, have meaning.

"Are you—" the Liar begins, but his eyes catch on my throat, and his body goes rigid. He lifts a hand, fingers brushing the bruised skin. "Someone hurt you." The words are clipped and hard through clenched teeth. "Tell me who."

"Ostena Vesnes," I say. "One of the tournament competitors."

"Did anyone else witness this?"

I shake my head.

He curses, yanking his radio from his belt. "Paol, get eyes on room 2519. There's been a report the competitor has broken the nonviolence rule."

"Yes, sir," comes the garbled reply.

"Unfortunately," the Liar says to me, "the contract only deems that in order for a player to be disqualified for violence, it must be corroborated by multiple witnesses or seen by my security team directly."

"I understand."

"But if she tries anything again, Paol will catch it."

I nod.

His eyes are so intent a shiver rolls up my spine, and the memory of the Brier Rosé illusion flits through me yet again. The press of his mouth on mine, the heat of his hand slipping down my hip . . .

Who is he, really?

"Would you like to come inside for a drink?" I ask, trying to convince myself this is part of my great scheme to find his vault, and that it has nothing to do with the glasses he repaired or the apology he tried so hard to give or the way his hackles rose when he saw my bruises.

His eyes flick from me to the room beyond as he considers. He nods once. "Thank you."

I step aside to allow him entry, and for a moment, he doesn't seem so big and wicked and untouchable. For a moment, he seems like a young man whose secrets make him vulnerable, just like the rest of us. And something about that is disconcerting. Like seeing what the stars really look like after a lifetime of cloudy nights.

I shut the door before trailing the Liar to the sitting area. He sorts through the glasses on my untouched drink cart.

"A bartender now, are you?" I ask.

"You seem like you'd enjoy a cocktail." He raises a bottle to inspect the label.

"Sure, but I'm warning you." I give him a mock glare. "If I end up dead, you're getting a screwdriver through your hand again."

He smirks, pouring two fingers of whiskey into a glass for himself. "And how exactly are you going to manage that if you're dead?"

"Wouldn't *you* like to know?"

"It's likely the whole world would be interested to know if you've discovered the art of self-resurrection."

"A magician never reveals her secrets."

He lifts his glass. "Doesn't she?"

I narrow my eyes, the memory of him extracting my darkest secret sharp in the back of my mind. "No. Because she's going to win the damn tournament, and how dare you have so little faith in her."

"Then tell me, little thief," he says, settling into the chair across from me, "what deception will you craft with my Unbreakable Lie?"

I let out a single laugh. "I don't share my secrets for free."

"What about for a price?" He nods at the coffee table between us,

DEN OF LIARS

where a small glass bowl holds a handful of playing dice. "Are you up for a little game of Candor or Con?"

I've heard of the game—one children often play, where each person either has to complete an embarrassing challenge of some sort or reveal a secret. It always sounded exciting to me growing up, but since I never had any playmates, I've never tried it.

"You seem a bit older than twelve," I hedge, scanning his face for a motive. What does he want from me? Why? And can I use his curiosity to my advantage?

"If it's a game only for children, then you should have nothing to worry about."

I think of the pile of secrets he extracted from himself, truths he immortalized in voratium so he would not forget reality.

I cannot ask for the secret of the moonshard's location—or even that of his vault—without giving myself away, but perhaps there are other secrets I could win from him that could get me there.

I sip my drink. It's sweet but tart, like pink lemonade. "Good stars, this is delicious," I say before I can stop myself. "What's in it?"

His eyes dance as he swirls his whiskey. "A magician never reveals his secrets."

"He could, though. If he wasn't a coward."

He laughs. "You've just been offered a chance to win my secrets, and you're hesitating. Which one of us is the coward?"

I contemplate him. "You can't even tell me the truth. How would this game work?"

"Paol can bring up a stash of my secrets."

I down the last of my drink and set the glass on the table. "This is a horrible idea."

"All the fun ones are." He pulls an olive out of a jar on the cart and pops it into his mouth, yanking off the stem. "What do you say?"

I shouldn't. He's already uncovered enough of my secrets as it is. And what would Enzo say if he knew?

But the map on his desk, the books in his office, the pain on his face when he twirled through the silks . . . there is so much more to him than I know. And even though I do not trust him, I cannot help but wonder.

His fingers drum slowly on his thigh. "You want my secrets, little thief. Why not win them?"

I sigh. "I'm going to regret this, aren't I?"

His mouth curls upward. "Is that a yes?"

"Stars damn me, I think it is."

CHAPTER THIRTY-ONE

LOLA

The Liar nods at the dice. "Ladies first."

"Happily." I pick them up and roll a set of twos.

"Con right off the mark, eh? You don't mess around." The Liar rubs his chin, pondering.

"Have mercy on me," I tease with my lower lip jutted out and my hands clasped in prayer. "I am but a humble peasant."

His eyes glint. "Not a chance, thief girl."

Pouting, I think of the cons I've heard of, like snatching a pastry from the local bakery or letting hot wax from a candle drip onto skin. What sort of challenges might the Liar come up with? What truths could I pull from him?

He settles back with a self-satisfied smile. "Swallow a shot of Sunflare Sauce."

"With pleasure."

I call up a bottle of the spicy pepper topping from room service while the Liar radios his security guard to bring him a pouch of his secrets. Both arrive ten minutes later, and the Liar pours the burgundy sauce into a shot glass for me.

Keeping fierce eye contact, I raise it in a toast. "Cheers." Then I down the whole thing in one go. The heat is instant and intense, and tears stream from my eyes as I gag, but I hand him the shot glass with a triumphant "Ha" before rushing to the washroom to stick my mouth under the faucet.

He's still chuckling when I return.

"Wipe the self-satisfied smirk off that pretty face," I say. "It's your turn."

"You think I'm pretty?" He gives me a devil's grin.

"If I say yes, can I set your fedora on fire?"

He gives me a look of mock affront. "You wouldn't dare."

"Oh, you know I would."

Scowling dramatically, he tosses the dice with a flick of his wrist. They settle on an odd number seven.

"All right. Candor." I rub my hands together.

"Ask away."

I could dive right into what I really want to know—why he betrayed Enzo, what the maps in his study are about, what his tournament challenges have to do with Enzo's cons—but he's starting to seem more at ease, lounging there on the chair like he hasn't a worry in the world. Asking questions like that would not only put him on edge, but also likely reveal more than I want him to know about me.

No, I've got to start simple and innocuous.

I steeple my fingers. "What was the first lie you ever told?"

He frowns, studying me for a heartbeat. Two. Then he dips his fingers inside his pouch, letting his eyes fall shut as he sorts through the dice, and hands one to me. "Here."

I hold my breath and take it from him. It is as frigid as his magic, as smooth as polished marble. Sparks of light swirl inside, a hurricane of bluish-violet stardust in glittering ebony. There are only six sides like a standard die, but it is shaped like a diamond rather than a cube, and the numbers etched on each face are in an elegant, silver script that catches the light.

I roll it across the table. A cloud of stardust flurries out, and the room ripples into warm shades of amber as a cottage sitting room sprouts before us. Flames flicker in a stone fireplace, a homespun rug spreads across the floor, and a wicker chair slumps in the corner. Windows open to the night, their tawdry curtains fluttering, revealing snatches of molten orange sky.

I glance to my left and spot a younger, softer version of the Liar—maybe nine years old—reading a storybook on the rug with his back against the arm of a couch. A second boy dashes into the room.

I gasp, but the sound is muffled, somewhere outside the realm of this memory world. Warmth floods me at the sight of eight-year-old Enzo parading around with some kind of brass contraption. I marvel at the round cheeks and mussed hair, so different from the sharp features and perfectly tousled curls I'm used to. But just like the Enzo I know, this one sports a dozen rings and bracelets, a fashionable leather jacket, and a mischievous grin.

"What is that?" the Liar asks.

"It's a scale!" Enzo announces, setting the object on the floor between them. A brass pole protrudes from a wooden platform. A moveable crossbeam perches perpendicular at the top, with tiny chains dangling from either end to hold small bowls.

"A scale for what?" The Liar's childlike voice is skeptical. "Bugs?"

"No, nullhead. Diamonds." Enzo says the last word in a hushed whisper. "You measure their exact size with these." He pulls out a small drawer in the wooden platform and extracts a few metal beads, then drops one into one bowl, causing the other to rise up. "A quarter karat." He tosses another bead in. "Half a karat."

"Where are you going to get diamo—" the Liar begins, but he's cut off by a door slamming somewhere in the house and a voice bellowing up the hall.

"Lorenzo!"

The Liar vaults to his feet, yanking the ratty blanket off the couch and folding it, then rushing to straighten the bookcase, gathering the stories he was reading and shoving them into place.

Enzo stows the scale under the couch and sits, angling his legs so they hide the glimmer of brass from view.

"Lorenzo Sinclair!" the voice booms again, and a tall, bony man dressed in zenithic priest's robes stalks into the room, face drawn, eyes tired.

"Yes, sir?" Enzo says, his cherubic face the picture of innocence. "Did you have a nice day at the parish?"

"Why," the man says, holding out a long, knobby finger, "is Mr. Gerard saying he saw one of my boys snooping in the back rooms of his shop this afternoon?"

"It wasn't me!" Enzo bursts to his feet, and the way the words blurt out of him sound like they've been said exactly this way a hundred times before.

Their father unbuckles his belt in one slow pull. "Don't lie to me, son."

"I didn't trespass, and I'm not lying!"

Their father mops a hand over his face. "I'm trying to help you, son."

"You're trying to whip me."

"A whipping is far less damning than drowning in the Deep for eternity." He grips Enzo's shoulder, forces him over the chair. "You made a choice, and that choice has consequences."

The belt strikes Enzo's backside with a sound like a gunshot, and I cry out, covering my mouth. The Liar in the memory likewise clamps his hands over the sides of his head to block it out.

Another thwack, another shriek, and I cringe as the young Liar bows in on himself, eyes squeezing shut, tears rolling down his cheeks. Then, in one shaky movement, he darts to the couch and yanks out the scale.

"Here you go, Father," he says, holding it up.

The priest's belt falters as he glances at the Liar. "What is it?"

"I . . . I took it from Mr. Gerard's shop." The Liar's whole body is quivering, but his eyes blaze with certainty.

Their father releases Enzo's shoulder, and the younger boy scrambles away without another glance, slamming the door behind him.

The Liar clenches his small fists as the older man approaches.

"You didn't steal that."

"Yes, I did."

"Don't lie, son." The priest's face is drawn. Tired. His belt drags on the floor with every plodding step.

The Liar swallows, cheeks flushing, but he does not back down. "I'm not lying. I snuck in on a dare."

His father stares at him for a long time, and my stomach sinks so low I start to feel queasy. Is the old man going to strike him like he did Enzo?

I cannot breathe, cannot blink as my anxiety mounts.

"Not you, too," their father finally says, his mouth twitching downward. He drops the belt, which hits the floor with a resounding thump that makes the Liar jump. Then he turns and walks out of the room.

The Liar stares after him, face pale, hands quaking, and though I do not share a heart with this brother, I feel his pain as though it were my own. He crumples to his knees, sobs hiccupping through his small frame, and in the silence that remains is the harsh slap of utter rejection, the sharp sting of love withdrawn, the soul-breaking strike of stone-cold silence.

My hands are clenched hard around the die as the scene fades and my suite filters back into place around me. I hold the die out toward the Liar, tears burning in my eyes.

"I'm sorry," I whisper. "That was cruel, what he did."

He stares at the die in my palm. "He was scared. Thought that was the only way to help us."

"Yes, but you were little . . ."

He lifts his eyes to mine. "People who have been hurt all their lives sometimes don't know that's not love."

Something heavy settles on my chest as I remember Enzo dashing from the room, cheeks red, eyes swollen with tears. He's mentioned their father was a strict zenithic priest but never told me how brutal he was at ensuring his children stayed in line. I shudder as both boys' sobs echo through my mind.

How could the Liar in that memory—kind, loyal, and willing to take stripes in his brother's place—have become the young man who cursed him to an eternity of oblivion? It doesn't make sense.

"Your turn," the Liar says, exchanging his die in my palm with the pair of regular ones.

I toss them onto the coffee table. A three and a two. The Liar rubs his hands together, a mischievous gleam in his eye.

"What is your greatest regret?" he asks.

The memory of Enzo pressing a voratium gem to my heart flashes across my mind.

I swallow hard. That is not a regret, least of all my greatest one. So why is it sticking in my head?

Shoving away the trepidation coiling like a snake in my gut, I slouch into the sofa. "You ask hard questions."

"Take your time." The Liar pours himself another drink.

I search my mind, back and back, sifting through my memories like Enzo might when he scours people's soullight. Then I meet the Liar's gaze and say, "Believing my father."

"Oh?"

DEN OF LIARS

"He was a ... very important person. Traveled a lot, lived far away." I pick at a thread in my skirt, trying to decide how to tell the Liar the truth without telling him The Truth. "I was raised by a nursemaid, but he visited sometimes, and he always told me he'd take me with him one day. Told me I was the most important thing in the world. That he loved me."

I don't tell the Liar how discovering these things had been lies nearly broke me, but somehow he seems to understand what I don't say. A thousand words pass between us, unspoken.

The Liar knows betrayal. I see it deep and sure as the set in his jaw.

"I should have known it wasn't true." I sniff.

"You were a child desperate for love," he replies, voice low and steady. "Of course you believed him."

A lump rises in my throat at the tenderness in his words. I search his face for the mistruths.

And find only my own pain mirrored back to me.

It could be a lie. Probably is one, in fact. But just for a moment, I allow myself to be seen.

"Your turn again," I say, pushing the dice toward him.

CHAPTER THIRTY-TWO

LOLA

"My favorite physical feature is my lazy eye," I say four hours later. We've migrated from the chairs to lying side by side on my balcony staring up at the clouds stained orange with dusk. The remnants of a dinner brought up by room service litter the space around us.

"Really?" the Liar asks.

"Yes." I roll onto my side, propping my head on my elbow and watching as the ocean breeze ruffles silver strands of hair across his face. "But actually I hate the term *lazy eye*. I wish they'd come up with something else to call it."

"Why's that?"

"*Lazy* is such a negative word. Makes it sound like my eye didn't work hard enough and that's why it points the wrong way. In reality, it has worked far harder than the average eye to actually function."

"A 'diligent' eye," he suggests. "Or maybe a 'persevering' eye."

I cackle. "Do you read thesauruses in your spare time, too?"

"What if I do?"

"It might tarnish your fearsome reputation."

"Ah well, we certainly wouldn't want that to happen." He winks at me, lacing his hands behind his head.

I smile in spite of myself. This has been fun. Too much fun. He's revealed more about himself this afternoon than I ever hoped. I've learned his favorite color is purple (not really surprising) and that his favorite book is an obscure tome of fairy tales his mother used to read to him when he was a child. I got to see the first con he and Enzo ran—to steal the crown of a visiting prince. The Liar had originally refused to do the heist but, seemingly worried for his brother's safety, decided to shadow him. When Enzo got caught by a constable, the Liar leaped in and saved him, and thus they became the infamous duo the world came to call the Devious. An ambitious thief and his reluctant protector.

Though it's been an hour since that memory faded, I can't seem to get the guilt in the Liar's eyes out of my head. Even as he saved his brother's skin, he seemed plagued with horror at his own actions. Was it his religious upbringing that caused that? Or something else?

And how again did the Liar in these secrets become the villain before me now? When did he change? Why?

I've shared things with him, too, though I've been careful not to reveal anything dangerous. I've told him about my dreams for a ballet career and about the first time I ever stole something. He listens, face unreadable, as I weave together my stories, and I wonder what he makes of them. Wonder if he has any idea who I am or why I'm here. Wonder if he, too, dreads the game ending.

His next roll is another odd number.

"Such luck," I tease. "Because I was going to challenge you to run down the hall in your knickers."

"If you want me to undress, you only have to ask," he teases silkily as he props himself onto his elbows.

Heat ripples through me. He's so close I could reach out and trace his scar. So close I can smell his whiskey-and-cinnamon scent. So close it's hard to stop myself from hearing his illusory question, *So many secrets, little thief. Shall we make one more?*

I roll onto my back, trying and failing to steady the uneven lilt in my pulse. "Your first kiss. Who was she?"

The Liar goes still. "Next question."

"That's not how the game works, captain. You have to answer. Unless . . . do you fold?"

"Fine." He digs into his bag and hands over a glittering die. "Enjoy."

"Oh, I will." I snatch it with glee and roll.

Stardust coalesces into the form of a young woman. She sits next to a midteenage Liar, their backs against what seems to be a rock wall. She's petite and elegant, with rosy cheeks, freckled light skin, and amber eyes framed by thick lashes.

"How did you find this place?" she asks, tipping her head to look up at what must have been the ceiling wherever they were. Or the stars. I cannot tell because the magic only reveals what's immediately around them. He's not looking upward, though. Instead, he stares at her like she's the most exquisite thing he's ever seen.

"I was exploring the beach and found an odd fissure in that boulder outside. Got a chisel and chipped at it till I fit through."

"Does Enzo know about this?"

"I've only shown you." He grabs her hand, intertwines their fingers.

"It's beautiful," she says.

He takes a deep, shaky breath. "You are."

"Nice line," I remark to the real Liar.

"Laugh all you want," he retorts with a chuckle. "It worked."

DEN OF LIARS

The young woman looks up at the Liar, her eyes bright. He leans in and brushes his lips against hers, gentle as a whisper, as her hand slides into his hair.

Something sticky wraps around my heart as I watch his arms come around her and their legs intertwine. Heat ripples up my neck and into my cheeks, but it's different than a few moments ago. Sour.

Am I . . . am I *jealous*?

Oh, stars no. I am not jealous. Sure, the Liar is attractive. And all right, yes, the way his hands slip around that girl's waist is pulling up memories of what it felt like to have those hands on my own waist on the dance floor. But I don't care who he kisses or why.

I don't.

As the memory fades, the illusion Liar whispers, "I love you, Laurel."

Laurel. Wasn't that the name carved into the ring I found in his drawer?

I return the die to the Liar. "She seems nice."

He nods, but his eyes are sad, his voice far away. "She was."

"You were quite the charmer," I say. "I'm impressed."

"Were?"

"Fair, you're a charmer now, too, judging by how many people fainted last time you went downstairs." I laugh. "But at least your charm back then wasn't a lie."

"Ah. Well." His smile fades. "There is that." He stashes the secret, then hands over the playing dice for me to roll. "Your go."

"Where was that place?" I ask. "What was she looking at?"

The Liar shakes his head. "It's your turn, not mine."

Rolling my eyes, I toss the dice. "You're no fun."

When it lands even, he pushes up to a seated position. "Dance for me."

"What? No."

"You said you were a ballerina. Show me."

My stomach sours. "I'm sorely out of practice."

"Why? Too much thieving?"

My eyes snap to his, but there's a glint in his expression. This isn't an interrogation. He's teasing me. "Yes, actually, if you must know."

"Why do you steal, then, if dancing is what you love?"

The question hits like a slap, and I find myself suddenly irked. "Not all of us are wealthy casino lords," I retort. "Sometimes people don't get to live their dreams no matter how much they want them."

The Liar's mirth fades. "I—" He tries to speak, but the words seem lodged in his throat. He clenches his fists, knuckling them over his eyes.

"You're sorry," I whisper.

He stills, opens his eyes, looks at me with an expression I cannot read. Wide and raw.

"It's all right," I say.

We hold each other's stare, neither of us breathing, and I wonder for a moment what his heartbeat would feel like next to mine instead of Enzo's.

Breaking the line of electricity between us, I push to my feet and move into the suite, shoving the sofa against the wall and clearing enough space in the center of the room to dance. He swivels to lean his back against the balcony's railing.

Stomach fluttering, I turn away so he won't see my cheeks flush. It's not that I haven't done ballet since Enzo saved me—I've spent many nights leaping across my apartment, imagining an audience on my dilapidated couch—but no one was actually watching. Not even Enzo has witnessed those solo performances.

Taking a deep breath, I begin. At first, my movements are stiff, my arms awkward. There is no music, and all I can hear is the rapid-fire beat of my heart. But then the Liar starts to hum softly. A distant, faraway melody I recognize as the one playing when I watched him twirl among the aerial silks. I sink into the feel of his voice, allow my body to move along its timbre, to roll and prance, to spin and stop.

DEN OF LIARS

And suddenly, I'm not in a suite in a resort dancing for a man with a secret I need more than air. I'm on a stage in front of an audience. Hundreds of people watch me from plush, velvet seats. I'm not wearing an evening gown. Instead, I'm in a costume of sparkle and tulle, and my hair is swept up in a ballerina's bun.

My muscles burn, and there's a stiffness in them that wasn't there when I was young and I danced like this all the time.

And yet somehow it still feels like coming home.

I come to a stop at the center of my imagined stage, arms spread wide as the audience thunders to its feet, applauding. But unlike the moments in my apartment, this time there is real applause. The Liar jumps to his feet, clapping wildly.

"That was exquisite," he says.

He's probably lying, but the words take my breath away anyway.

I point at the dice with a quaking hand. "Your turn."

He rolls a four. I sip at a glass of water, letting my heart rate and breathing return to normal as I ponder what con to give him. He waits, those fathomless eyes never leaving my face.

And, damn him, I want to know the person behind those eyes. Not for the job, not for Enzo.

For me.

Maybe it's reckless. Maybe it's too much, too soon, too fast. But the curiosity burning in me is wild, and it takes over. "I dare you to take me there," I blurt. "Where you took Laurel."

His jaw tightens at the sound of her name, and he studies me for what feels like an eternity. I can barely breathe, desperate for a yes for all the wrong reasons.

Then he stands, tucking his pouch of secrets into his jacket, and extends his arm. "Come."

I do not need to be told twice. I cinch my pouch of dice and chips back onto my thigh just in case and loop my elbow through his, allowing him to pull me out into the hallway. It's nearing seven, and the casino is teeming with people. Many notice the Liar and whisper among themselves, pointing fingers, some blushing, some admiring, some glaring. But then their eyes inevitably trail down to me on his arm, and they keep a respectful distance. A thrill rolls through me, a pride, to be held close to his side like this.

We pass through the main gambling hall, and I catch sight of the betting ring boards. My name has climbed the list, sitting near the top with a pretty sum scrawled next to it.

It seems the dance the Liar and I shared this morning—and my rage afterward—were enough to make me memorable.

I pull my arm out of his and pretend to fix my hair. His brow furrows, but he does not speak as he steers me to the staff halls. Waiters, dealers, and bartenders nod deferentially at the Liar as we pass, giving me curious glances.

He comes to a stop at a nondescript closet door. Is this the one Estelle said wasn't in the blueprints? I try not to let him see my curiosity as he pulls a ring of keys from his belt and slides one into the keyhole. The bolt throws easily, but before the Liar twists the knob, he presses his hand flat against the wood. Something inside gives a quiet scrape, and he pushes the door open. I think of the panel in Dr. Legrand's suite that detected my lie when I tried to steal the watch. Is there a similar charm on this door, too?

Thousands of voratium gambling chips overflow from an array of shelves inside—some glimmering with bargained secrets, others dull and ready to be refilled. The Liar leads me inside, letting the door fall shut without turning on the light. Flares of red, blue, green, and gold illuminate the outline of his broad shoulders, his angular jaw, his wavy hair with its streak of bluish-white. He throws the lock behind us.

I should fear being alone in the dark room with a seaspawn casino lord, but like the starsdamned fool I am, I feel heady. Reckless. Emboldened.

"This way." He grasps my hand. His fingers are thick and warm, and I'm wildly aware of every contour of his palm as he draws me deeper into the closet, past several sets of shelves until we reach the back.

"What you're about to see is something you must keep secret," he says, and though it's too dark to make out the details of his face, I sense the intensity of his gaze. "Please."

"'Please'? Does His Royal Liar-ness have manners, after all?"

The faint glow of his scar crinkles into what must be a soft smile. "Don't tell anybody."

"I promise."

He pauses for just a beat before pulling the shelving forward. It swings easily on well-oiled hinges, revealing a nondescript door behind it. Another key, another latch, and the door opens, a hole like a mouth gaping in the wall.

"So, little thief," he whispers. "Would you like to see the stars?"

"Stars?"

Smile flashing, he pulls me into the dark.

CHAPTER THIRTY-THREE

LOLA

The Liar grips my fingers tight, keeping me close, and I press my second hand to the wall, which turns rocky and wet as we descend. The air chills.

A hundred more steps into what feels like the center of the earth, and a faint bluish glow filters up from the bottom of the stairs. We pass through the opening, and I gasp.

It's a wide cavern teeming with deep violet and turquoise orchids. Their petals, vines, and leaves are dusted with bright blue bioluminescent algae, which also climbs the walls and speckles the ceiling like galaxies. Roots unfurl into a still black lagoon, which reflects the lights from beneath like a mirror.

"What do you think?" the Liar asks, his eyes tracking every inch of my face like he's worried I'll tell him I hate it.

"It's breathtaking," I whisper. "You found this?"

He doesn't respond. Because that would be to share a truth, and of course he cannot.

I find myself moving closer, as though my proximity might heal the fact that he'll never tell a story about his childhood, never state his opinion or express how he feels in words. Yes, he was able to reveal a few secrets to me, but what are a handful of memories when it comes to sharing your life, your soul, your heart with someone?

I think of his body, arcing among the silks, reaching for someplace far away, telling a truth he has no words for.

"I imagine you walking back from a heist with your brother," I whisper, and the curvature of the stone walls spangled in ivy makes my words echo like a haunted lullaby. "He rushes on ahead, but you stay behind. You catch a glimpse of something. A crack in the face of a stone, maybe, with an orchid sprouting from it."

He's utterly still, his face unreadable in the dark. I may be getting the details of his story wrong, but I forge on, desperate for him to hear at least part of his truth spoken aloud, even if it's just one thing, one sentence, one description.

"You worked your way in and found . . . a tunnel? Maybe it was the remnant of some kind of channel of water, worn smooth by time."

He steps closer, and his fingers meet mine like a question, the barest of touches as they drag to my palm. His thumb strokes a slow line from the tip of mine to the center of my wrist.

"I'm probably getting it all wrong . . ." I mumble, feeling suddenly warm in spite of the chill in the air.

He angles his head so our eyes meet in the dark. His scar glitters. "Don't stop."

My chest flutters as tingles erupt in my hand where he's touching me. "Maybe this became your refuge," I say. "Maybe you would come here when you needed a moment to think, when you wanted to get away. When the guilt and shame for the lies you were telling and the crimes you were committing became too much."

"Maybe." He releases my hand to continue his thumb's slow trail up my inner forearm, and tremors shake through my whole body. I can scarcely breathe.

"And maybe," I continue as his hand finds the sensitive inside of my elbow, "when your magic stole away all the relationships you ever had, when it turned your very soul into a secret that could never be shared, this was the one place you could come. The orchids growing here the only living things that would hear what you could never say."

His hand encircles my arm, warm and soft, skin against skin.

"Because they knew you before," I say, shivering and yet somehow warm, "back when you weren't a liar or a casino lord, but a boy."

"Maybe," he says again, quiet as a wish.

"So when it came time to build your casino, you built it right on top of the one place that didn't—couldn't—believe your lies."

He doesn't speak, doesn't even seem to be breathing. His hand is tight around my elbow, and every inch of me wants to pull him into me. To feel him closer. To taste him.

"How did I do?" I ask.

"You have quite the imagination." He holds on for a heartbeat longer, then draws his hand back down to mine, pulling it palm up. With a slow, steadying breath, he presses something into the center. The pair of dice from my bedroom. "Your turn."

When I roll an even four, he nods at the water.

"Jump in."

"Is it cold?" I eye it warily.

"Why don't you find out?"

"I hate being cold."

"Are you scared?" He smirks.

"Never." I slip out of my dress, fold it on a rock, and set my glasses on top. Standing in nothing but my underthings, I plant my hands on my hips. "If this was all some ploy to get me out of my clothes . . ."

"Let the record show, your honor, that the con was to jump in the water, not to disrobe. The lady did that entirely on her own."

DEN OF LIARS

Sticking my tongue out at him, I leap into the lagoon.

The water is frigid, and it sends a shock wave through my entire body as I go under. I thrash up for air, and when my face breaks the surface, the Liar's laughter echoes against the cavern walls.

"You b-b-bastard," I growl, teeth chattering.

"I'm sorry," he says through chuckles.

The fact he can say that means it's a lie, and he knows I realize this, because he only laughs harder.

"Ha, ha, ha." I shudder. "Very hilarious."

"If the casino gig doesn't work out, perhaps I could become a comedian." He extends a hand to help me climb out.

"Yeah, maybe." I grasp his forearm, dig my heels against a gnarled wall of orchid roots, and yank.

He splashes into the water beside me, fully clothed. When he comes up spluttering, I'm the one laughing.

"That'll teach you," I tease, treading water toward him.

He wipes his face, pure, unfiltered mirth in his eyes, and I wonder if this is the first time I've ever seen him. Just him. No illusions, no glamours, no lies.

He's beautiful.

"You had better watch yourself, little thief."

"Yeah, yeah, terrible magic, much intimidation." I nod at him. "Your turn."

"The dice are over there." He points to the lip of the lagoon where I rolled them before.

"Then let's assume it rolls odd, and you owe me a truth."

"Truths are difficult to come by."

"Fine, con then."

He treads closer, and his hands brush so close to mine the water rushes over my skin, sending new shivers rippling through me. "What's your con?"

"I dare you to tell me your name."

He laughs. "Sounds like a truth, not a con."

"A truth *in glamour*," I tease. "You know all about those."

His smile fades, and questions flicker like ghosts in his eyes. He ponders me for a moment before resolve settles his shoulders, and he moves closer, brings a fingertip to my chin. His touch is impossibly hot in contrast to the frigid ice, and I find myself gasping at the sensation, tipping my head back instinctively.

"What do you see?" he asks.

I blink. Without my glasses, all I make out is a fuzzy smear of otherworldly blue overhead. "What am I supposed to be looking for?"

"Do you know your constellations?"

I follow the blurred lines of bioluminescent algae weaving among orchid buds, its light rippling from the reflection of the water around us. And then, all at once, I recognize the shape. It's an exact replica of one of my favorite constellations in the winter sky. Father told me its story a dozen times. The hated star god of trials, Larsus, fell from the sky with such velocity he got stuck in the earth. He pleaded for help from all who passed him, but the people were happy to see him trapped. They'd longed for freedom from adversity all their lives, so they left him to starve.

Until a young boy, struggling to make ends meet in the aftermath of his father's death, heard Larsus weeping and, though he blamed the god for his misfortune, took compassion on him. The boy was weak, and digging blistered his hands. At the end of every day, he went home trembling with fatigue, his palms bleeding from the exertion. But every morning, he returned.

It took a month to free the god, and by the time he finished, the boy's muscles had grown and his hands had become calloused. Larsus returned to the skies, leaving the boy strong enough to provide for his impoverished family.

"Donnic." I whisper the name of the boy in the story.

The Liar stills and takes a shaky breath.

I grasp either side of his head and tilt it so his eyes meet mine. They flicker in the blue-green light, pupils blown wide.

"Donnic," I repeat, tracing his features with a finger, pausing on the stardust swirl through his brow. I wonder if he ever shortened his name, the way Enzo shortened Lorenzo or the way I always went by Lola instead of the full Magnolia. I lick my lips. "Nic?"

He tenses, eyes closing. "Again," he rasps.

"Nic," I repeat, and he tips his forehead against my shoulder. Warm against my frigid skin, solid against my softness.

We stay like that for a long time, not moving, not even daring to breathe. The two of us, silent as the stars, alone but together in this underground horizon.

I find myself looking at the constellation again, wondering how he made it. Is it merely another illusion meant for my eyes alone? Would another person see it just the same way?

And then, as the water settles and the ripples slow, as the reflective light cast on the stone twitches to a stop, I notice the subtle shadows of parts of the stone carved away, purposeful and sharp along the lines of the constellation.

He must have come down here with a chisel of some sort and carved the ceiling so the algae and the orchids' roots would grow in just this pattern. But why? Could this be another way he has told his truth to the world? The only way his magic allows?

No one knows his name, but this cave, who loved him before he became a liar, who cradled him before he was powerful, keeps that secret forever told in glowing blue stars.

The Liar—no, *Nic*—in spite of all his bravado and charm, simply wants to be known.

And suddenly it's not enough for me to know him. I want him to know me, too. Not as a little thief or as Astra Tremaine. Not as Enzo's sidekick or Magnus St. James's daughter.

Just me.

So I take a deep breath and do something I shouldn't.

"My name is Lola," I whisper against his neck.

He lifts his head. "Lola," he repeats.

My name on his mouth shoots a bolt of electricity through me. Like he's the first person to ever say it and *mean* it.

He pushes my hair out of my face and brings his mouth to my forehead. "Lola," he murmurs against my skin, his breath tracing hot spirals along my brow. His lips drag to my ear. "Lola." They skate to my mouth, hovering over mine. "Lola."

Every part of me is quivering, on fire in the cold, aching to wrap around him. My hands slide around his neck, elbows resting on his shoulders as my eyes flutter closed.

"Nic," I breathe, our lips grazing.

His hands circle my bare waist, molten.

I could kiss him now. Let him devour me just as I imagined it before. I could give in to the want, give in to the way I cannot seem to breathe or think, give in to the sound of my name on his tongue.

My heart thunders. And beneath it, a question. A curiosity that does not belong to me. A wariness.

Enzo.

I jerk back, zeroing in on the emotions in our heart. Does he feel the tingles racing under my skin? The heat in my neck? The desperation and lust roaring like a tide? Does he realize these emotions are about the brother who cursed and imprisoned him, who has kept the secret to his freedom locked away for years?

"I—I have to go." I push away from Nic and clamber out of the lagoon, excitement turning to panic, heat turning to ice.

"Is something wrong?" He follows, water dripping from his tuxedo like rain.

"I just . . . I shouldn't be here." I wring my hair, yank my dress over my head, and shove my glasses on. My cheeks are so hot the lenses blur.

Nic doesn't respond. He stands there, sopping and shivering, limned in a pale blue glow, nothing like the liar I was convinced he was before today. Nothing like the scoundrel Enzo always told me he was.

DEN OF LIARS

His expression is unreadable. A mask of neither pride nor hurt, as though none of this happened, as though I didn't feel the beat of his heart against my own just a moment ago.

He loosens his tie, undoing the top button of his shirt so his collar spreads just a touch, and I watch a drip of water slide along his throat and pool against what appears to be a gold chain at his throat. Something glitters on the chain, but in the dark I cannot make it out.

My heart somersaults, Enzo's attention sharpening, scrutinizing, suspecting.

"I'm so sorry," I say.

And then I run.

CHAPTER THIRTY-FOUR

☾

NIC

Lola disappears up the stairs, leaving me with nothing but the lapping of the water behind me and the stars overhead. Just like another night, another sky, another rush of waves as a girl I cared for took the truths I gave her and ran away with them.

And then those truths destroyed her. Destroyed everything.

I am a fool. Five years later, and apparently I haven't learned a damn thing.

When I proposed the game of Candor or Con, it was with the intent of learning more about the little thief who guards her secrets while wearing her heart on her sleeve. Discovering who she is and why she came here and how she knows my brother.

But somehow I got swept up in the game and in the way she seemed to actually *see* me. Listen for the words I could not say. Understand the thoughts I haven't been able to share with anyone since the night that moonshard shattered.

DEN OF LIARS

It was foolish to show her my secrets, foolish to let her glimpse any of my past or my present, foolish to tell her my name.

Letting Lola in means losing control, and losing control means disaster.

The Gods Above may not be real, but fate has a way of punishing us for our mistakes anyway. I betrayed my father's expectations for me, and fate punished me with his death months later. I was careless with Laurel's heart, and fate took her from me, too. I embraced the thing the moonshard made me—an evil I was raised from birth to abhor—and fate made sure I could never be anything else.

What will fate do to me when the truths I've shared with Lola tonight unravel the careful narrative I've constructed?

My vision tunnels.

What will it do to Lola?

With Laurel and with Enzo, I did not know how dangerous my truths were, but this time, I can stop it. I can save her.

I sprint up the stairs. Shove into the storage room. Bolt down the hallway.

She's heading toward the elevator, water sluicing down her back and leaving a trail of sparkling puddles in her wake. I grasp her elbow as she reaches for the elevator button.

"Wait."

She glances up at me, that panic I glimpsed in her before she ran still twitching in her jaw. "I can't, Nic," she whispers.

I look at her, at the curve of her jaw and the chatter of her teeth, at the way her glasses magnify the size of her right eye and make her left one seem ever so slightly smaller, at the way her freckles stand out stark against her pale skin. How do I deceive a girl who knows I'm lying?

The answer surfaces, slow and quiet, and I hate myself as soon as I see it.

I have to make her doubt her reality. Second-guess what she's seen. Wonder which lies were lies and which ones weren't.

Every part of me recoils.

But I have no choice.

So I settle my showman's mask in place, curl my mouth in the charming grin I know incenses her, and throw my shoulders back, leaning casually against the wall next to the elevator.

Ever a liar, ever a monster, because that's always what it takes.

"Allow me to escort you to your room," I say as though I'm nothing more than a casino lord taking care of a contestant. I even let my eyes dance with a smugness I've perfected.

I've got you right where I want you, my mask tells her. *You walked right into my trap and revealed everything.*

She eyes me. "I'm fine."

"Don't make me insist." I infuse my face with the cool, relaxed visage I've worn a hundred times. The one that sets people at ease, makes them like me. "It's bad business if guests catch hypothermia."

Her lips thin. "Bad business?" She turns away, jabbing her thumb into the button. "It is late, and I am tired."

"Very well," I say, slinking backward with a tip of my head. "But don't hesitate to contact the front desk should you need spare towels."

She whirls and incinerates me with a scowl. "Don't do that."

"Do what?"

"I see exactly what you're trying to do, and it's not going to work on me. Not anymore."

I feign innocence, panic rising. "What am I trying to do?"

"That"—she flings her arm back the way we came—"was real. All of it. And now you're scared, so you're trying to undo it."

"I—" Stars *damn* this girl.

"You took a risk, and now you're terrified of what I'm going to do with what I've learned. So you do the only thing you know how: make me think everything was a lie so you don't have to be vulnerable."

"That's not—" I protest, but she interrupts me.

"It is! And you know what? I've had it with people trying to control me." The elevator dings as it reaches our floor. "Relationships are not about supervision or regulation; they're about trust. But you wouldn't know the first thing about that, would you?"

I swallow, her words biting through me sharper than my magic ever has.

"If I did," I croak, "would I be able to tell you?"

She backs over the threshold into the elevator. "No," she says, the word final and hard. "But you wouldn't even try, either."

"You don't know that."

"I do." She clenches her jaw. "I told you; I am not a pawn in your game anymore. I refuse to be. So don't bother trying to construct another illusory world for me. I deserve the truth—the actual truth—and I deserve to make whatever choice that truth leads me to, regardless of what you want."

I swallow as the door begins to close, my mind raw, my hands quaking. She's wrong about me.

And yet . . . she's not.

"Good night, Donnic Sinclair," she says softly. "Come find me when you're ready to stop hiding behind pretty glamours."

CHAPTER THIRTY-FIVE

LOLA

Nic's hand slams between the door and the wall. He pries it open and stalks into the elevator with me. Apparently something I said hit a nerve.

Good.

His eyes flash. "You seem to think I enjoy lying."

"You do." I've had it with these brothers and their games. I just want one of them to be straight with me for once in their lives. I elbow past him to jab the button for my floor.

"You think I enjoy forcing secrets out of people? Seeing the horrible things they've done? Knowing exactly how treacherous humankind is at its core?"

"I think you do not care."

"If you believe that—after *everything*—then you are being willfully obstinate."

DEN OF LIARS

"Fine, I recognize that you care." I grit my teeth. "But feeling bad doesn't absolve you of the lives you've destroyed."

"These people destroyed their own damn lives!" His voice is brusque, on the edge of cracking, his whole body vibrating. "This is about *their* lies, *their* secrets, *their* sins. All my game does is bring them out of the shadows."

I stalk close. "At what cost?"

He stares at me, jaw working.

"You do not see what happens after they leave your casino because *you* never leave. But I have seen it. People kidnapped. Betrayed." I swallow. "Killed."

Shadows flicker in his gaze.

"You think yourself benevolent, don't you?" I whisper. "You think you're saving us."

"And you," he says, voice low, "think you aren't doing the same thing I am."

I raise my brows. "I'm not!"

"Everyone in the world does it. They lie a little here, pretend a little there in order to get the people around them to do what they want, think what they want, believe what they want. Is that not deception?"

Every lie I've told Enzo over the past week—in order to soothe, protect, get him on board with my heist—flits through my mind in quick succession, dragging with it a shame hot enough to burn me.

I seethe. "You and I are on completely different levels. I'm trying to survive. You are a villain."

"And all villains are wicked?"

I think of Enzo glaring daggers at the casino that bars him entry, the symbol of his imprisonment and his curse. I think of the map upstairs on the Liar's desk, its list of planted clues that might mean we've been chasing our tails. I think of the lie I told Legrand and how Alzat Lopai's family might have been our next lead if I hadn't been the one to plant it.

"If they didn't want to be wicked," I say, "they'd stop."

Nic steps closer, bracing his arm over me on the doorframe.

My stomach drops, and I cannot say whether it is because of the elevator's movement or because of the embers burning in those violet eyes.

"Do you want me to stop?" he asks, his voice low and deep in his throat.

It's a question heavier than voratium, heavier than lies or truth or hurt or freedom. And in a breath, I know he's no longer talking about his villainy. He's talking about his mouth on my forehead, his name on my lips, his secrets dropped into my hands like promises.

He's talking about us.

The elevator comes to a stop at my floor, and the bell dings. The door slides open, but Nic does not move. He watches me, unblinking, those eyes piercing to my very soul.

And, stars damn him, I don't know if I want him to stop. Because yes, he is a villain and he is dangerous and he is oblivious to the hurt he causes.

But he's also so much more than that. Calamitous yet kind, chaotic yet achingly careful. And because of him, what once made so much sense now makes none at all.

"I loathe you," I say, voice quivering.

The words hover between us, charged with electricity, and we realize at the same instant that they have changed since the last time I spoke them.

They are no longer true.

His eyes ignite. Slowly, he reaches behind him and pushes the button to close the door. Then he twists the emergency key that locks the elevator in place.

I cannot breathe under that stare, vibrating with an intensity that has me weak. Static courses hot and delicious through me.

He approaches, deliberate, intentional, until his hips press against mine, his hands brace on either side of my head, his lips hover so close I can taste them.

"Say it again," he growls.

I do not know what any of this means, do not know how I feel about him or how I've allowed myself to crack. I do not—*cannot*—desire him. Not a villain, not a liar, not a ghost in a mask I can never know.

But my body does not care whether I want to feel things for him, does not care whether it makes sense or whether it'll ruin me. It doesn't care that I've never done this before. All it knows is the whiskey-and-cinnamon scent of him, the taste of his breath, the heat of his body, the wildness in his eyes.

And it *craves* it.

"I loathe you," I breathe, "and I'm not thinking about how desperately I want you to kiss me."

The lies hit their mark.

His mouth comes down hard on mine. Urgent. Angry. Reckless.

I should not be here, compromising my job, betraying Enzo. I should not kiss him back.

But his tongue parts my lips, and all at once, the girl I was—the quiet daughter, the acquiescent friend, the obedient protégé who never ventured outside the safety of her fences—is gone. With the heat in his touch, he burns all those "shoulds" to the ground.

I tangle my fists in his hair as his hands trail down my hips to wrap around my thighs and lift me off the floor. Bracing my spine against the wall, I slide my legs around his waist, and he groans into my mouth.

He kisses me with a wildness I've never felt, never seen, and it *unmakes* me. I am desperate, ravenous. I cannot breathe, cannot think, and I will not stop until I have all of him against all of me.

He tears away to set the elevator moving again, and I press my lips to his neck, whispering, "I haven't imagined your hands on my skin."

He takes a quivering breath, testing the air. I wonder how my lies taste, what they do to his body.

Perhaps I should find out.

"Down in the lagoon," I whisper, nipping at his ear, "I wasn't thinking about what your mouth tasted like. I wasn't craving your touch."

He drags my mouth to his, palms hot on my back, body solid against mine.

The bell dings again, and the elevator door slides open.

I disentangle my legs as he sets me down, and we stumble, still kissing, into the hall. I yank at his buttons, pulling them apart one by one as he barrels me up the corridor to press my body against the wall next to his suite door.

He traces the subtle jut of my hip bones, and then one hand dips lower to caress the bare skin exposed by the slit on my thigh, just as he did that night in my dream. I whimper at how much better it feels in real life.

Grinning, he leans in as he fumbles in his jacket pocket for his key. The stubble around his mouth scrapes along my jaw and down my neck. His teeth graze my collarbone, and I'm dizzy. Intoxicated.

Faintly I realize how erratic my heart is beating, how my body floods with lust as my hands slide up his bare torso over his scintillating scar, but the thought does not register.

I'm too far gone.

My fingers knot in the chain hanging from his neck, and I drag him closer as he finally locates his key and slides it into the lock.

"I haven't imagined you taking me here," I lie. "I haven't wanted it once."

"You . . ." He pulls my face up so our mouths meet again. "Deceitful little creature . . ." The kisses slow, turn from a roiling boil to a soft, molten spread. Languorous and deliberate. Quiet and questioning.

As his hands skate up to my bare back, my own snag on what feels like a key hanging from the end of his necklace. I peek one eye open. It looks like a simple pendant. A stone with smooth edges. An image that does not match its reality.

A glamour.

It's enough to pull me out of the moment for a breath.

What's so special about this key that he would glamour it?

Nic doesn't seem to have noticed I've found the pendant. He works the pins out of my sodden hair one by one, tossing them behind us. My curls spill around my shoulders, and he cups the base of my skull, angling my head to drag a tongue along my ear.

I gasp, arching into him, struggling to focus on the pendant as I turn to putty in his hands. He laughs, a gravelly sound into my neck as I break the link holding the pendant to the necklace and tuck the key carefully into the pouch on my thigh. Then I abandon myself to him entirely.

Kissing him is like dancing with him. We move together, synchronized on a level that feels almost like instinct. My body turns when his does, melts when he strokes my skin, shudders when his tongue feathers against mine.

Just when I'm ready to drag him into his suite myself, a loud cough breaks through the fever.

One of his security guards stands a few yards away, hands clasped behind his back, eyes trained on the ceiling. "Pardon me, sir, but there's a disturbance downstairs."

"Paol," Nic groans, tipping his head against the wall next to mine as heat floods my cheeks. I straighten my dress, suddenly very aware of how high Nic had hiked it up my hip.

"I'm sorry, sir," Paol says.

Nic's hands tighten on my waist. "What kind of disturbance?"

"Card counting. Table twelve. That Collings man we've been keeping an eye on. He's already raked in over a thousand chips tonight."

Nic swears under his breath and releases me, rebuttoning his shirt and knotting his tie. "All right. I'll be down in a moment." He dismisses Paol with a wave of his hand and waits until the security guard has disappeared into the elevator before turning to me. He lifts his thumb to my chin and angles my face so he can breathe a kiss on my lower jaw. "Let's get you to your room."

My body is still quivering, but I force a steadying inhale, trying not to glance at the door to his suite so he won't remember he unlocked it. "No, it's all right. You go ahead. I can get there on my own."

"You sure?"

"Absolutely." I offer him a smile. "Don't worry about me."

"All right." He drags me in for a last lingering kiss. "Until the round-two eliminations, then," he says, brushing his lips against my cheekbone. Then he grins, presses a finger to the side of his nose, and explodes into a shower of sparkles.

I laugh in spite of myself. "I told you it would be more dramatic!"

His invisible fingers whisper across my lips like a promise, and then he is gone.

I slump against the wall, heart thumping in my ears, my skin hot and tingling in all the places he touched it. With trembling hands, I pull off my glasses to wipe the smudges from the lenses before stooping to pick up the pins at my feet.

Once I'm certain Nic is no longer close by, I shuffle to his door and push it inward. I pull out the glamoured key I stole from his necklace, but as I make to step into the room, I pause.

Legrand's tear-streaked face flickers in the corners of my mind, and I grip the doorframe hard as Nic's words echo back to me from that night. *Claiming you haven't hurt anyone just because you haven't allowed yourself to see that hurt is humankind's favorite self-deception.*

Entering his room isn't hurting him. I'm not stealing his most prized possession the way I did with Legrand. At least not yet.

But I plan to. And when I do, what will that do to him? How will it break him?

And can I live with being the betrayer, knowing what that feels like on the other side?

I throw my shoulders back. I cannot let myself be distracted by

DEN OF LIARS

his kisses or his eyes or the vulnerability I felt in him just now. He *is* the villain, and sometimes people have to get hurt. It's not cruelty, it's justice.

I can reckon with my guilt later.

Steeling my nerves, I slip into the dark.

CHAPTER THIRTY-SIX

LOLA

I flip on the lights, and Nic's suite flares to life. His sheets are twisted in a knot at the foot of his bed, and the silky black duvet is a pile on the floor. Empty glasses litter the coffee table, and a few embers glow in the fireplace.

The balcony door is slightly ajar, and the ocean breeze ruffles the orchids, which dance softly in the quiet. The silks from before have been braided and stashed in the corner with the aerial hoop.

I head straight for the study. But when I turn on the lamp, I groan. The desk is bare.

"Blast it," I mutter, scouring the shelves for the maps. The drawers only hold spare pens and sheaves of paper for the typewriter, and when I sift through the cabinets behind the desk, I find only electrical bills, slot machine repair tickets, and an extensive array of files with incredibly detailed information on thousands of people—perhaps past guests?

DEN OF LIARS

The map is nowhere to be found.

I pull out Nic's key and drag my fingers along its edge, trying to imagine what the teeth must look like since I cannot see them. It's fairly hefty, simple, and unornamented. Perhaps he has a secret cupboard somewhere?

I look around for something that might take a key like this, pushing on various books and items on the shelves, thinking of the times I've read about hidden doors behind bookshelves in novels, but nothing budges.

Returning to the bedroom, I open the wardrobe and riffle through dozens of expensive tuxedos and fish among his shiny black shoes. When that yields nothing, I get on my hands and knees to look under the furniture.

Still nothing.

"What do you go to?" I snap at the key, plopping in frustration on the edge of Nic's bed.

Is this what I've come to? I've been here for several days, and while I have made strides in learning more about Nic, I'm still no closer to figuring out where the moonshard has been taken. There are only a few days left—one challenge, and then the final round.

I glance at the clock on the nightstand and get to my feet, sighing. I have just three and a half hours until the round-two elimination. Maybe my best next shot is to meet up with Estelle and see if she's found any other inconsistencies in the blueprints.

A glass bowl of tawdry playing dice identical to the ones we played with in my suite catch my eye from the drink cart, and I approach, picking up a handful and rolling them slowly around my palm.

When I leave this casino, I'll either have been outed as an ally of the person Nic hates the most, or I will have stolen his most valuable secret. Either way, he will hate me. Either way, there will never be an us, never be a future where I am not the thing he detests the most.

The one who gained his trust and then used it against him.

My traitor heart sinks.

I drop the dice one by one back into the bowl, pausing on the final one. Then, before I can second-guess the decision, I drop it carefully into the sodden pouch on my thigh.

I try to tell myself it's not because I care about him. Not because I desire something of him to keep for when this is all over. Not because part of me, deep down, wants to remember his secrets, the kiss, our game.

But even I can tell I'm lying this time.

"Lola?" a fierce whisper makes me jump. I whirl, but there is no one there.

My heartbeat roars in my ears. Has Nic already returned?

"Over here." The balcony door twitches.

My stomach drops to my shoes as I recognize the voice. "Enzo?" As soon as I key into his emotions, I realize how loud they are. I've been so distracted I didn't realize he was here.

I rush over to the balcony, pulling the door mostly shut behind me, trying not to let him feel my sudden burst of panic.

I should have known he would come. Should have known what transpired with Nic would concern him.

"Why are you here?" Enzo materializes in the corner with his arms crossed over his chest.

"I'm searching his room for clues." I shrug as though that's all there is to it.

But Enzo's glare intensifies. "Has he hurt you?"

"Of course not," I say, trying to calm the raging in my chest, knowing he can feel it anyway.

"Did he capture you? Threaten you?"

"I'm fine."

His eyes narrow, trailing to my mouth, where I'm sure my lip stain is smeared. "I thought we had an understanding. So long as you are in this tournament, you stay away from him."

My hackles rise. "I'm being careful, Enzo."

"Then tell me why you are in *his* bedroom."

I hold my jaw steady as my stomach flops and the ghost of Nic's hands ripple across my skin. "I already told you why."

"I'm not a fool."

"No one said you were."

He glares. "You owe me an answer. A true one."

Anger sparks inside me, and all my frustrations with him over the past few days come roaring to the surface. "We're partners. I don't owe you a damn thing."

He barks a laugh. "Oh really? Because last time I checked, you owe me *your life*."

I stalk toward him, seething. "My debt was paid when I handed over my heart. I don't recall also swearing fealty and obedience."

He holds my glare with one just as cold, his words deliberate as slaps across my face. "We are leaving."

"No, we are not."

"Yes," he bites out, grabbing my wrist. "We are."

I try to yank out of his grasp, but he only pinches his fingers harder into my skin and heaves me to the railing. A flash of Astley dragging me out of bed with the same sort of grip flares panic through me, hot and white and fast.

I dig in my heels. "You take me away from here, and you damn yourself!"

Enzo glares over his shoulder. "What are you talking about?"

"The secret I bargained to enter the tournament?" I lift my chin, wrenching out of his hands. "It was the one about our deal. If I leave, that secret is his."

"You . . ." He stares at me, reddening, then slams his fist into the wall.

I yelp, jumping back as the windows in the doors rattle. His knuckles come away bloody, but he winds up and punches it once more, leaving a crimson smear on the marble.

"As long as you let me do my job, the Liar's not going to find out," I tell him, keeping my voice level as a new sensation ripples through me, one I've never felt around Enzo before. Fear.

He shoots me a glare. "What has he learned about you already?"

"Nothing important."

He barks a laugh cold enough to make me shiver. "If you think he's that clueless, you really are naive."

"Me? He's been playing *you* for *years*, Enzo! We've been pawns since the moment we met!"

"What?"

I explain about the map, about all the heists we've done marked on it, about the way every single one of the challenges I've completed in this tournament has been connected to people he's been tracking.

"You honestly think I'm foolish enough to fall for my brother's little"—he spits at his feet—"party tricks? This is a trap. He knows you're involved with me somehow, and he's trying to misdirect, make you suspect me so you don't notice him puppeteering you right into the palm of his hand."

"I'm telling you," I argue, "none of our leads are real. Winning this tournament is our only shot at finding the moonshard."

He climbs onto the railing, glaring down at the ocean crashing against the shore two dozen stories below. "You disobeyed me. Deliberately."

"Disobeyed?" I see red. "Who the depths do you think you are?"

"I am the one who trained you to be better than this." He swings over the railing, pinning me with a glare. "Just remember when everything goes to shit and I have to come rescue you—again—that you mucked it up yourself. I'm done being responsible for your mess."

He climbs out of sight.

Growling, I slam my hands against the balcony railing so hard the iron bites into my skin. His words thunder in my ears alongside our shared heartbeat.

DEN OF LIARS

Enzo has never spoken to me like that. He has only always protected me, laughed with me, supported me. Loved me.

Then again, I've never gone directly against his will like this.

I double over, retreating to the balcony door and sliding to the floor.

Maybe he only loves the thief he made me into, the sweet, obedient lackey who stays put and waits for his command. Not Magnolia St. James, the girl who was raised to dance and to dream, take risks, fight back.

Is that love, if it is withdrawn the instant I try to think for myself?

Uncurling my fingers, I glance down at the key where it has dug little red welts into my skin. My eyes widen. The glamour has vanished now that I'm outside, leaving behind the key exactly as I imagined it. A dark, iron trinket with jagged teeth. Frowning, I move my hand through the open door into the suite and watch as the glamour of the stone stitches itself into place. When I bring it out into the moonlight, the magic fades, and I can see the key once more.

Pausing to wipe my glasses on the hem of my skirt, I inspect the key. There seems to be something smudged on its top. I run my thumb over it, and the blue substance sloughs off onto my palm, which I tip into the shadows. The blue doesn't darken. If anything, it glows.

"The underground lagoon," I whisper, leaping to my feet and dashing through the suite into the hall.

I do not know what this key opens, but I am not as inept as Enzo thinks. I will prove to him, prove to Nic, prove to *myself* that I am more than a pawn to be used and cast aside as soon as I think for myself.

This is *my* game. *I* make the rules now.

And I will win, no matter the cost.

CHAPTER THIRTY-SEVEN

LOLA

Lights flash and music trills as I rush through the casino, elbowing past crowds, ducking between waiters.

What is Nic hiding in that cavern? Could his vault be somewhere down there?

Desperate hope fills me. If it is, I could snatch his secrets right now. Get out of this tournament, out of this casino, out of this mess. Claim my freedom by the end of the week.

I try not to think about what that betrayal might be like for Nic and instead focus on how triumphant it will feel to hear Enzo apologize.

When I reach the service hall, I pause. There are only a couple of hours until the round-two eliminations, and the party is already in full swing. Waitstaff and performers clog my path forward. I dig out the blue die that should have been empty and toss it, using its magic to disguise myself as one of the servers. It may not fool Nic if he shows up, but at least I'll avoid drawing anyone else's attention.

DEN OF LIARS

I keep my head down as I make my way to the closet. Glancing over my shoulder, I dig into my hair and find one lone pin near my ear. I jam it into the keyhole and soon hear the delicious scrape of the lock mechanism inside loosening. But of course the knob does not turn. I plant my hands on my hips and think back to when Nic opened it. He unlatched the door with his key, but then he also pressed his palm to the door, exactly the way I had tried to do with the false handprint in Legrand's room.

I grind my teeth. How on earth am I supposed to fake having Nic's hand? I don't have any of the fingerprint putty, and besides, that didn't work last time anyway.

If this room is full of gambling chips, then surely Nic isn't the only one permitted by whatever spell guards this door. Several members of the staff probably have access. Either the spell recognizes all their handprints, or something else is at play here.

I chew on the end of the hairpin. Nic's magic can sense lies and unravel secrets. Perhaps what went wrong in Legrand's room wasn't that the panel registered a flaw in the handprint, but rather that it sensed it was a lie. It could be that Nic spelled it so only someone not trying to be anyone but themselves could enter.

I glance down at the illusion I cast over my appearance. It's beginning to waver. A few more minutes, and it'll flicker out completely. I could try pressing my hand to the door now, as a waitress, and pray it will recognize me as staff. But if I do, will an alarm sound just like the one in Legrand's room and alert Nic?

If I let the glamour fade, one of the waiters rushing past is sure to notice I'm trying to break into a room I'm not supposed to be in. I'll be thrown out either way.

I mop my sweaty palms over my thighs. If only I could deceive Nic undetected.

The blue die that was supposed to have been empty is still clutched in my hand. I squeeze it, thinking of the last time I rolled it to cast my glamour of invisibility. Nic looked back and caught sight of me, but then something changed, and he lost me. What did I do to fool him? How did I get his own magic to work against him—and also somehow not draw any of the power out of the die?

And then it hits me.

I thought of Enzo. Imagined myself like him, pushing away my corporeality the way he'd done to me during a hundred heists.

What if I didn't use Nic's magic when I made myself invisible? What if I used *Enzo's*?

Sweat slicks my palms and sparks dance under my skin. That's impossible, right? If I could use Enzo's magic, wouldn't I have figured that out long before now?

I close my eyes, drawing inside to that place where our hearts pump in time with each other, where his anger and frustration simmer like a shadow to my own.

What if I tried to do it again, just to see? Made myself noncorporeal and walked through this door without even using the panel or the knob? Would the door still sense my secrets?

It's worth a try.

I focus in on my body, on the sensations of air on my face and the floor beneath my feet. Of blood pumping and lungs filling. Of scents and tastes and sounds. Tightening my hand on the now-empty shard of voratium, I imagine how it feels when Enzo sucks away my corporeality, and I shove it away myself. Jam it into the metal.

My body flickers into nothingness.

Excitement bolts through me.

I just used Enzo's magic. *I just used Enzo's magic!*

Grinning dazedly, I make to set my palm against the door, and just as I hoped, my fingers pass through like it's nothing but air. Stifling a squeal, I charge forward into the glowing closet of gambling chips.

Somehow, this bond between Enzo and me is far more than I realized. Does he know?

I venture to the corner and forge through the shelving into the entrance to the underground lagoon before letting my body turn solid again.

Breathless, I dash down the stairs into the cold.

The blue light of the algae draws me into the underground cavern. The water is a mirror reflecting the constellation above so that it feels as though I am suspended in the middle of some ethereal universe, surrounded by stars and orchids on every side.

I search the rocky edge of the lagoon for where this key might fit. It's too dark to see very well, so I drop to my hands and knees to run my palms over the stone, push aside flowers and gnarled roots and twitching leaves, reach into the water to feel along the walls. I make my way around the area, scouring every single surface. By the time I return to where I began, my knees are aching and my hands are shaking with the cold.

"Blast," I whisper, slouching against the wall and stretching my legs out in front of me.

Maybe I was wrong. It's possible that whatever this key unlocks is somewhere else entirely, and it only had the algae on it because Nic had it with him one of the times he came down here.

A lump rises in my throat.

I was so sure this was it, that I would be able to prove to Enzo and to myself that I am not foolish, not reckless, not wrong. Even if it isn't the vault that this key unlocks, surely it must lead to something important. Why else would Nic wear it on a chain around his neck?

I should get out of here, return to my room and wash off the makeup that no doubt still looks like I've been thoroughly kissed. If I stay, Nic might find me.

But instead of climbing the stairs, I tip my head against the wall and gaze up at the sharp corners the stars make and the way the algae glows like ethereal specters trapped in the rock.

Nic seems to have a specific interest—and maybe even a passion—for the zenithic religion. The Gods Above and their evil counterparts in the Deep. The lion on the front of his casino, overtaken by scales and flippers. The depictions of seaspawn in my suite, beautiful and whimsical instead of wicked.

I follow the reflection of the bioluminescent constellation along the surface of the water.

At every turn, he subverts expectations, forces people to confront what they think and believe, points out where good is wicked and wicked might be good.

I frown as an idea unfurls in my mind.

What if he's done that here, too?

Most people, whether they are practicing zenithics or not, harbor a fear of the Deep and what might lurk beneath its surface. Could he be, once again, playing with those assumptions? Could he have hidden treasures where people fear monsters?

I scramble to my feet, strip off my dress once more, and fold my glasses on top. Then I tuck the stolen key into the waistband of my undergarments and, steeling myself for the shock, dive into the icy water.

It's dark as pitch beneath the surface and so frigid I can barely move my limbs. As I propel myself deeper, the water presses in around me, colder and heavier than it should be. My lungs scream for air much sooner than I expect them to, and before I even approach the bottom, I'm forced to change directions and barrel for the surface to drag in deep mouthfuls of oxygen.

However, as I tread water, shivering, my lungs suddenly don't seem as starved for air as they did moments ago. Almost like I didn't need it as much as I thought I did.

I glance up at the boy with his spade on the ceiling and roll my eyes. "You tricky bastard, Nic," I mutter. "That was a glamour, wasn't it?"

Taking another gasp of air, I dive again, kicking hard. Sure enough, the deeper I go, the more the water presses in from all sides. Adrenaline zings through my limbs, my lungs scream for air, and my heart thunders in my ears, the silence of the water turning into a roar that sends stars shooting across my vision.

When I feel like I might pass out, my hands brush gravel at the bottom of the lagoon.

I squint, but the combination of the darkness and my poor vision makes it nearly impossible to see anything.

The water above me glitters blue with the algae. If only its light could penetrate this far . . .

And then I remember.

I dig in my waistband for the key. The algae on it glows faintly, just enough to see a few inches around it. I hold it close to the lake bed, scanning the pebbles and roots for a sign of a door, a lock, anything.

After a few more seconds, I go up for more air, then dive back down, scouring the entire lagoon one gulp of breath at a time.

Finally, in the far corner, I see it. An archway carved roughly into the stone and twined with ivy, the faintest bit of algae smeared across the lock. No handle.

I jam the key into place and twist it hard. The water pressure compounds, eliciting spasms in my legs as their instinct to flee threatens to overwhelm me.

The door heaves inward, and I swim forward into an even deeper darkness. I drag my hands along the walls as panic builds in my stomach. How long is this tunnel? Should I have gone up for more air? Just when I'm about to turn back, the tunnel angles upward, and I break through the surface.

It's another chamber. More algae coats the walls and ceiling, but in here it's been allowed to grow wild, collecting in corners and spreading like glimmering mold across the rocks and among more orchids.

I stumble onto the stony bank, gasping for air. In front of me hulks a massive shadow the size of my suite upstairs. I approach, mopping water out of my eyes and wishing I had my glasses. I run my hands along the side of the shadow.

Cold metal, smooth under my hands.

A vault.

"Bleeding stars," I whisper. This is it. The secret to the location of the moonshard is on the other side of this heavy door.

I lean against it to catch my breath and steady my body. Then I feel around the safe until I find the dial and the handle.

It's a standard Cavendish & Coppell lock just like the one in Legrand's room, a style I've cracked dozens of times.

"Thank Odelia." I press my ear to the door and get to work, spinning the dial this way and that, listening carefully for the telltale click when I hit the correct numbers.

Minutes later, I yank on the handle, and the door groans forward.

Inside on shelves stretching high above my head are dice of every shape, color, and size. Small ones with only three sides, massive ones with at least fifty. Glittering like crystals in every hue imaginable.

Scarcely daring to breathe, I search for any ebony dice with galaxies inside like the ones Nic kept in his pouch during our game of Candor or Con.

I sift through thousands of the glittering game pieces, taking care not to accidentally drop any of them. As my fingers trail along their glassy edges, I try not to think of what dark deeds are encased in their depths, if any belong to my father, or whether I'd roll his if I found them.

I come to a small ledge encased in thick glass near the rear. Inside, several dice sit in a row, each a different color. There are empty spaces in between them, as though there used to be others. The last in the line looks familiar. A violet die with silver script.

I gasp, pressing my palm to the glass. That one's mine.

I search for a way inside the case, dragging my fingers along seams, suddenly desperate to have my secret back now that I can see it.

But there's no way to open it that I can find.

Sighing, I resume my search, and my gaze catches on another

smaller glass case nearby. Inside it, a die the size of my palm rests on a pedestal. Every single color imaginable swirls within it, reflecting the light of the other dice in a hypnotic, otherworldly rhythm. Like it's breathing.

The Unbreakable Lie.

My fingers reach instinctively for it, but again, there is no lock, no door, no latch, and soon I give up.

I comb through the rest of the shelves, but it becomes all too clear that what I'm looking for is nowhere to be seen.

Nic's greatest secret is not housed in his vault. None of them are.

CHAPTER THIRTY-EIGHT

NIC

"You're an imbecile," I growl at my reflection in the mirror as I towel water out of my hair after an evening shower. "A stars-damned fool who deserves to be shot."

It's been two hours since I kissed Lola. My quick jaunt downstairs to reprimand the card counter reminded me I still had to make an appearance at the Exchange Room at nine to swap people's secrets for chips. My shift there, however, was cut short by a fistfight among patrons at the tournament's betting rings followed by an impromptu visit from one of Salazar's lackeys making demands. Somehow, even after all that, my head is still out in the hallway where I left her. I taste her lips every time I speak, smell her breath every time I inhale.

I shouldn't have drunk as much as I did. Shouldn't have lost my damn mind and showed her that memory of Laurel. And I certainly shouldn't have taken her down to that cave and let her figure out my name.

DEN OF LIARS

I was a witless lonely fool who let my whole entire brain short-circuit because a pretty girl listened to me.

I groan, crossing through my suite and into my office. I brace my hands on my desk, squeezing my eyes shut as images of her soft smile, her arcing arms, her flawless dance fill my head. My soul aches all over again. Aches to rise, to join her, to trail my hands along her waist as she twirls, to spread my fingers across her ribs, press my mouth to that sloping neck and taste her pulse.

I want desperately to blame my temporary foolishness on my magic, but I know I can't. It yearned for her last night as always, yes, but when she danced like that, eyelashes fluttering against freckled cheeks, dark curls tumbling over her shoulders, her movements telling truths without price, without bargain, without magic . . .

I wasn't drunk on lies or power or even the alcohol. I was drunk on *her*. On the way she shared secrets like she *wanted* to. On the way she listened to mine like they meant something to her.

Slumping into my chair, I drag my list of round-three marks toward me. I pick up a pen to match players to each one, but the names blur as echoes of her reprimands fill my ears.

I've had it with people trying to control me.

I'm not controlling anyone; I'm *protecting* them.

I am not a pawn in your game anymore.

Hours and days and years spent fabricating a trail to keep Enzo from the moonshard. To keep him out, to keep him away.

I deserve the truth—the actual truth—and I deserve to make whatever choice that truth leads me to, regardless of what you want.

I hurl my pen and shove to my feet.

None of what she said should matter. I'm supposed to be figuring out who she is and how she's involved with my brother. Not trusting her, not letting her into my life, and certainly not kissing her.

I let a stream of air out slow and soft, remembering the brush of her lips, the press of her hips.

Something about her refusal to slot into my plans the way everyone else does feels like that loosened breath. Like a binding around my limbs released. Like a weight lifted from my shoulders.

Like maybe, with her, I could just *be*.

I told her the night I caught her on the roof that lies are like tapestries. I've woven so many of them I'm suffocating beneath their weight, tangled in their myriad strands. Every muscle in my body quivers as I try to keep them aloft.

What if I set down just one—hers, and hers alone? Would it be enough to rest? Would it be enough to breathe?

I uncurl my fists, stare down at my shaking hands as the flicker of ice inside them thaws.

I don't know how she is associated with my brother, don't know what their relationship is or what she wants from me. But maybe I don't need to.

The telephone rings, startling me out of the terrifying pull of those thoughts. I swivel in my chair to pluck the earpiece out of its cradle.

"Yes?" I ask.

"Aethera City Prison calling to follow up with you, sir. This is Detective Gaff."

I chew on the end of my thumb. "What's the status on Callum Astley?"

"He was brought in less than an hour ago, sir."

"What charges have you put in his paperwork?"

"Attempted assault is the primary one. Extortion. Embezzlement. Money laundering. Unlicensed possession of a firearm. Any others you'd like to add?"

I mop a hand over my face. There are dozens more charges I could bring against the man, but any more and he would be placed in solitary confinement, and I need him available for my brother to find. After all, the memory Lola planted about Alzat Lopai's funeral is a piece in the multilayered network of false clues I have Enzo chasing for signs of the moonshard.

DEN OF LIARS

The other day, the idea of having Enzo's own thief unknowingly planting the clues that would undermine him gave me a twisted sort of thrill. Now the thought makes me ill.

I sigh, reaching for the pendant at my neck.

But my fingers only wrap through an empty chain. The key I've kept there since the night I set up my vault downstairs is gone. Panic flares through me, and I paw at my pockets, then swivel to scan the floor.

"Sir?" the detective asks.

"Send someone over to pick up a folder tomorrow," I say, taking care to keep my voice calm even as alarm bells jangle in my ears. "It'll contain the information you need to convict him for several crimes he should have been arrested for ages ago."

I prop my phone between my jaw and shoulder in order to move my typewriter aside and shuffle through the papers on my desk. But still, no key. I yank out the drawers and riffle through their contents.

"Thank you, sir."

A yell echoes across the telephone line as I drop to my hands and knees to peer beneath the desk.

"Who's shouting?" I ask, catching sight of a single golden gambling chip on the floor. I pick it up, smoothing a thumb across its face.

"I'm not sure," the detective replies. "Kohstor, what are you going on about?" he calls, his voice muffled as though he's pressed his hand over the receiver.

"He's gone!" comes the panicked response.

"Who's gone?"

"Astley! The door's still locked . . . no sign of anything in there. It's like he walked straight through the wall!"

I grind my teeth, sitting back on my haunches and pinching the bridge of my nose. Enzo wasn't supposed to *rescue* the priest, only search his soullight. Abducting a criminal right out of prison makes things messy, and Enzo knows that. So why did he do it?

And if Astley has already gone missing, it'll only be a matter of hours before Enzo is at the Lopai family's door searching for the next clue. Which means I don't have time for missing keys or mysterious gambling chips. I need to call Paol, make sure my men are tracking Enzo, verify that the next leads are in place.

"I'm sorry, sir." The detective's voice comes clear over the line. "It appears . . ."

"You lost him."

"We'll send out a squad," the detective says quickly.

"You do that." I drop the earpiece into its cradle, frowning at the yellow chip in my palm. There's something familiar about it. I hold it up, angle it so it glitters.

An image flickers across my mind. A memory of Lola stuffing a pile of chips bright as a sun into her purse after her game with Astley.

Is this one of those chips? If so, how did it get into my office?

Curious, I close my eyes, drawing the soullight in it through my skin.

An image explodes across my mind's eye. Astley, rushing to unlock a door. Banging into a room full of shadows. Catching sight of a young girl in a white nightdress stained crimson with blood. Golden hair is matted to her cheeks, and a bright purple bruise blossoms across a swollen nose.

And next to her, my brother grins at Astley, his hands pressed against the girl's sternum, the telltale gems in his eyebrows, ears, and lips glowing.

"Hey! How'd you get in here?" Astley barks, finger curling around the trigger.

Enzo grins. "Magic."

The pair ripple into shadow, and Astley squeezes off shot after shot at the empty place where they stood.

I open my eyes as the images fade.

That was Magnolia St. James; I am sure of it. She may have been bloodstained and beaten, but I saw enough photographs of her in the aftermath of her murder that I'd recognize her anywhere.

DEN OF LIARS

But this time something about her feels familiar in a way it never did before.

I squeeze the chip again, replay the secret, then pause on the moment when the girl turns to meet Astley's glare.

Her left eye, though bruised and swollen, is open enough to see that it is not pointing the same direction as her right.

Magnolia St. James had a lazy eye.

I drop the chip as though it burns.

"No," I breathe, shaking my head. "Magnolia St. James is dead."

Except she's not. I just witnessed her rescue.

Magnolia St. James is alive. Working with the brother who wants me dead. And not only that, but she's here. In my casino. Disguised as Astra Tremaine.

And I just kissed her.

CHAPTER THIRTY-NINE

LOLA

I come around the corner onto my floor's landing and catch sight of Nic at the other end, facing my suite's door, twisting his fedora in his hands. I freeze, then back silently the way I came, ducking out of sight.

He's discovered the missing key. I'm sure of it.

Panicked, I dart onto the elevator and jab the down button. The last thing I need right now is to try to muddle my way through a lie when my hair is a sopping giveaway of where I just was and when the incriminating evidence is in the pouch on my leg. It'll be better if I find somewhere to hide out until the elimination, when he'll be distracted.

I take the elevator all the way to the ground floor and slip down the nearest hallway. A pair of aerial dancers exits their rehearsal space in front of me, so deep in conversation they do not glance my way when they pass.

DEN OF LIARS

Shivering as my hair soaks icy water into the back of my dress, I venture into the rehearsal space, sliding the door shut silently behind me.

The only light filters through from the window in the door, bathing the quiet room in a faint lavender-blue. Several sets of silks hang like specters from above, knotted in braids that keep their tails off the floor. A hoop like the one in Nic's suite revolves slowly in the dark.

I spot a wall of tiny closets overflowing with exercise wear and spare clothing. Breathing a sigh of relief, I clamber through strangers' belongings until I come across a set of clean women's athletic wear that looks like it'll fit me.

Peeling off my wet things, I yank on the stretchy clothing. It's a bit snug around my hips, but it should do. I squeeze out most of the remaining water in my hair and braid it, securing it with a ribbon from someone's bag. Then, gathering my sopping dress and purse, I pause, staring at the hoop.

I really shouldn't touch it. What I need to do is use the remaining time until the elimination to figure out where to look next for Nic's dice and come up with what I'll tell him if he asks about the key I stole. Maybe I could find Estelle, see if she's been able to pin down anywhere else a vault could hide.

But as I cross the rehearsal space, Enzo's anger flares, a sticky, achy stab. Now that the adrenaline of finding Nic's vault has dissipated, the pain of Enzo's rejection threatens to crush me. I rest my hand on the hoop to steady myself. Breathe.

How many nights did I slip out to my dance studio as a child when missing my father made it impossible to sleep? How many hours did I spend twirling to utter exhaustion in order to make sense of the thoughts clamoring for space in my head?

I need to dance.

Stowing my things under a chair nearby, I approach the hoop again. The bottom curve is about as high as my shoulders, and I wrap my hands around it. It's solid and hard, yet somehow more delicate than I expected it to be. It's wrapped with a coarse tape that scrapes nicely against my palms.

I think back to some of the movements I watched the dancers do on this hoop before and try to yank myself up. The hoop wobbles when my feet leave the ground, and I stumble, losing my grip.

This is a lot harder than it looked.

Gritting my teeth, I grasp it again and swing a leg up, hooking my ankle next to my hand. "Hold still," I growl at the hoop. But when I kick off the ground, it spins so fast I lose my balance, nearly falling off the apparatus once more.

"It's incredibly unsafe to practice aerial arts alone," a voice says behind me, and I shriek, nearly jumping out of my skin as I steady myself with the toes of my spare foot.

"Nic," I gasp as he steps out of the shadows. "I didn't know you were there."

He does not smile. Instead, he grasps the side of the hoop. "Would you like a few pointers?"

"I was doing just fine."

He raises a brow.

Looking into his eyes is doing messy things to my heart—things that make me think of lies and betrayals and broken trust. I drop his gaze and swallow hard. "Okay, sure," I say. "How do I get on the damn thing?"

"Easiest isn't from the bottom." He lifts my calf off the ring, then pulls both my hands to the side, one above the other, as high as I can reach. His fingers curl around mine, his arms cocooning me against his chest.

"Now what?" My voice comes out higher pitched than I intended, but I can't seem to breathe.

"Take a giant step forward until you're directly under where the apparatus attaches to the ceiling." He releases one of my hands and trails his fingers up my arm to tip my chin against his collarbone so I can see where the rope loops through a contraption above. Trembling so hard I'm sure he can feel it, I do as he instructs. "Then pull yourself up, chest to hands, and hook a knee over the bottom."

In one movement, I'm hanging diagonally off the hoop, which barely sways this time. "All right."

"Now all you have to do is climb hand over hand to sitting."

The steel digs into the meat of my thigh, and I grimace as I follow his instructions. "This is a lot more painful than it looks," I grit out. But something about the sensation grounds me, pulls my focus away from the hurt and guilt in my chest.

"Now swivel your hips to bring the other foot up and in."

And just like that, I'm sitting in an aerial hoop.

It twirls slightly, and I close my eyes, letting my heart rate slow. Air brushes my face, and a smile curls my lips. This is what I've missed. The feel of my body maneuvering through new movements, the burn of fatigue, the triumph of accomplishment. Because I couldn't control my father or my situation, but I could control me. "Show me more."

Nic obliges, instructing me through a few basic moves, helping me situate myself only when needed, his fingers gentle on my body. But unlike this morning, when his eyes burned with desire, he doesn't smile, doesn't rise to my jabs like he usually does.

Finally, when I'm sitting with my spine braced along one side, toes gripping the other, he says, "Callum Astley was arrested today. Multiple counts of assault and several other charges."

Trying to shove down a ripple of panic, I raise a brow. "Good."

"Funny thing, though," Nic continues, voice still measured and distant. "He disappeared from his jail cell this evening."

"Disappeared? Like he escaped?"

"Yes, but the circumstances were peculiar." He pauses, assessing me as he says the next part. "The door was locked from the outside and didn't appear to have been tampered with at all. There was no other way out, not even a window. Walls several feet thick of solid concrete."

My stomach tightens, but I try to keep my expression unperturbed. "That *is* peculiar."

"It is, especially when you factor in the gambling chip someone left in my office that belonged to him." A bolt of electricity slams through me as one of his hands curls around the hoop between my feet. "The secret of a girl he kidnapped four years ago who vanished without a trace straight through another solid wall."

My heart hammers into my throat. "Oh . . ."

He does not blink, does not twitch. A thousand conversations pass between us in an instant.

"Lola is short for Magnolia, isn't it?" he says, voice low with accusation.

I glare down at him, twisting to sit in the center of the hoop once more. He knows I cannot deny it. He would sense it as soon as I tried.

So instead, I clear my throat. "You think my escape from Astley is somehow related to his escape from prison?"

"It absolutely is. Because both were facilitated by the Thief." His face goes stony. "My brother does not meddle in anyone's affairs unless he feels like he needs to. It's clear why Astley's useful to him, but what about you made you worth the risk?"

"As far as I know, he saw me as an opportunity."

"An opportunity for what?" He twists the hoop, bracing his hands on either side so my knees press against his chest. "Are you one of his Tentacles?"

I sidestep the first question smoothly. "No, I am not."

"But you stole the pocket watch for him."

"I did," I say.

"Are you working with him now?"

My mind whirs. I cannot let Nic know the extent to which my relationship with his brother goes, and I certainly can't reveal that I'm here on Enzo's errand, but I also cannot lie or he'll see through it immediately. "We . . . had a disagreement," I say carefully. "He gave me a set of rules to follow, and when I disobeyed, he left."

Nic's mouth thins. "Why did he help the priest escape?"

I shake my head, combing my mind for possibilities and coming up with very few. Enzo could have just sifted through Astley's soullight like he's always done and left him in his cell. Why he helped him escape makes no sense. "Maybe it has something to do with the lie you had me tell Mr. Astley yesterday?"

He hoists the hoop into a slow twirl. "That shouldn't have been enough to make him assume the risks that kidnapping an alleged criminal will bring upon him."

"You think this was a kidnapping?" I ask, turning my head to keep his gaze as the hoop whirls its lazy way around. "Not a rescue?"

"He typically doesn't bother himself with people. He's much more concerned with their secrets."

"Sounds like someone else I know."

I meant it as a teasing remark, but his jaw tenses. He grasps the hoop, jolting me to a stop, and leans in. Though he is below me, I fight the instinct to cower.

"Did you," he asks, "steal something from me?"

I lick my lips, forcing my eyes not to flick toward the pouch on the floor. "Was something taken?"

"Would I be asking otherwise?"

"You know, I really don't know." My heart is thundering so loudly in my ears I can hardly think, but I try to keep my voice steady as I reach for the top of the hoop and pull myself to standing, arms braced around the rope connecting it to the ceiling. "Sometimes I think I have you figured out"—I hook one leg and then the other around the top where the strap connects to the hoop—"and then other times it's like I'm still that girl on the roof, terrified you're going to let me drop twenty-six stories to my death."

"Did you. Steal something. From me." His voice is a whisper. Undeterred. Cold.

I yank myself to seated on top of the hoop with the rope between my legs and glare at him. The hoop rocks under my unpracticed hands, and something about the risk, about the danger of hanging unsteady eight feet in the air makes me bold. "I'm sorry, but you can't kiss me like you did earlier and then show up a few hours later to treat me like this."

"How exactly am I treating you?"

"Like I'm a criminal." I jab a finger at him, then lose my balance, pitching downward.

Nic catches me against his chest. "Aren't you, little thief?"

Anger bubbles through me, and whether it's solely my own or whether Enzo's rage is still having an effect on me, I do not care.

"You know what?" I say, yanking out of his grasp and stalking to the hoop, hoisting myself back onto it. "You can be the impassive, impartial, impenetrable casino lord if that's what you want. You're good at it. The world fears and lusts after you in equal measure." I come to a seated position, and the hoop twirls faster until I brace a foot against his chest to stop it. "And you can even lie to me and tell me you're saving the world one secret at a time. That the world would be better off if you revealed all their horrible truths for them. But you and I both know that isn't true."

His mouth thins, but he does not reply.

Good. Because I wasn't done yet.

"You soothe your wicked little heart with stories about your grandeur in order to hide from the fact that you're a charlatan. You pretend your lies are justice, that they are a game, that they are freedom"—I level him with a glare—"but the only one here who buys it is you."

"Is that so?" The stardust in his scar glitters, ethereal as the constellation of algae far below our feet. Then he kicks off his shoes and shrugs off his jacket, which he drops next to my clothes on the ground. The black-and-white dice from our game of Candor or Con roll out of the pockets, but he ignores them as he grasps the hoop and yanks himself up with me, curling along its outside, legs braiding expertly through it as he slides in over me, hooking an elbow around the knot.

"You can tell yourself the prettiest lies in the world," I say, holding tight to the hoop as it whirls, "but at the end of the day, when you're alone and cold in that little cave downstairs, they will still be just that: lies."

"And what do you know of it, Magnolia St. James, coddled and protected by her billionaire father until she was coddled and protected by a magical thief?"

I glare hard at him, my body so full of fury and pain it might burst. "Coddled and protected?" I repeat in a lethal tone barely louder than a whisper. "You destroyed my life. My nursemaid, my butler, my dance tutor . . . the only family I had in this whole damn world I watched bleed out on my front porch because of your game."

"Did *I* destroy your life?" he says, voice low and quiet, his expression unreadable as stone. "Did *I* pull the trigger? Did *I* shoot your family?"

"No, but the crooks who did wouldn't have been there if not for you."

"Your father," he says, his jaw tight, "is the one who incited them to do what they did, not me. If he wasn't a killer, if he wasn't a swindler, if he wasn't a criminal bent on controlling everything and everyone in this city, no one would have cared about you."

Rage tears through me. It's like I've been holding this back all week, and now that the dam has broken, the tide has come to destroy everything in its path.

"I was ripped from my bed in the middle of the night by a stranger," I say, the words rushing out of me faster and louder, harder and sharper. "I was beaten up. Thrown in a basement. Forced to listen to a mob of men four times my size debate whether to put a bullet in my head. Can you even imagine—for one infinitesimal second—what sort of damage that does to *a child*?"

"Callum Astley did those things to you," he growls as the hoop spins faster. "Moratin Salazar did those things to you. Your *father* did those things to you."

My hands are so tight on the hoop they burn, and everything in me is burning, and I want Nic to burn, too. I leap off the hoop, yanking him down by the ankle onto the cushioned mat and pinning him there with my father's signature move. Nose to nose, eye to blazing eye.

"My father kept me a secret to protect me," I growl. "He may not have loved me the way I needed him to, but he loved me enough to do that."

Nic's legs cinch around me, and he rolls us over, pressing me down beneath him on the mat, hands ramming my wrists near my head.

"People are vile," the Liar says, violet eyes gone molten. "They lie and they cheat and they destroy, and then they lie to themselves that it wasn't their fault. They find a scapegoat to point their fingers at and say 'It was him!' because they are too afraid and too damn proud to ever consider that they're the liars, the cheaters, or the villains."

"I may mislead people," I retort. "I may pretend to be something I'm not, but it is always with the intent to protect the people I love, just like what my father did for me."

Nic shoves my hands away and stands, disgust and anger tying his mouth in a hard knot. "Your father wasn't protecting you. He was protecting an asset."

I hurtle to my feet, shoving him against the nearest wall so hard the lockers rattle. "Don't you dare," I spit, "call me an asset."

He glares, venom pulsing in the vein in his temple. "That's the problem, Magnolia St. James. You never should have been. How can you look at a man cloistering you away from society, depriving you of friends and love and experience, imprisoning you like a bird in a cage, and believe him when he calls that love?"

The words strike deep and hard, and I can barely breathe. I want to claw his face off. I want to scream.

I want to break down weeping.

"You don't know anything about it," I snap. "The night you sacrificed the secret of my life on your rhinestone altar, you stole my childhood from me. You stole my father from me. You stole my future from me. And you can never, ever give that back."

"And yet you're here." His eyes dart back and forth between mine, that silver lock of hair hanging over his brow, tangling in his eyelashes. "You're dancing. You're climbing buildings and snatching pocket watches. You're winning challenges and besting competitors and," he growls, "confounding a seaspawned charlatan."

The room is so quiet, so still. His body is hard beneath mine, pressed against the wall, and our chests heave against each other, hearts thudding in syncopation.

"I thought I was 'vexing' you," I whisper. "Not 'confounding.'"

"Vexing, confounding . . ." His hand slides up my neck. ". . . Tormenting . . ." His palm comes to the base of my skull. ". . . Tantalizing . . ." He takes in a shaky breath, eyes dropping to my mouth. ". . . Tempting . . ."

"You've been reading your thesaurus again, haven't you?" I choke out.

He leans in, lower lip grazing mine, and I gasp.

All at once, he whips me around by the hand on the back of my neck, ramming me against the wall. Our mouths come down hard on each other, and it is a kiss of fire, a kiss of pain, a kiss of vengeance and betrayal. His hands are frantic, everywhere, rough and wanting, and I cannot get enough of them.

We lie to each other. Lie with our tongues and teeth, with desperate sighs and fingers clutching at hair. Lie that this could be real. Lie that we could be friends, be lovers, be more. Lie that we aren't monsters and villains the both of us.

Because he's right. He wasn't the one who hid me away, wasn't the one who made me a target, wasn't the one who spilled the blood of the ones I loved.

Stars, I wish he had been. Because then I could keep hating him. It was easier to.

I cry out as his mouth trails down my neck, teeth scraping. Tremble as his fingers dig into my ribs. Cling to him as his hips pin mine to the wall.

And just when this angry, desperate hunger is ready to incinerate me, he pauses, his mouth hovering over mine. Our breath tangles as I open my eyes.

"Please, be honest," he says, desperate yet guarded, "are you still working for my brother?"

Panic rocks through me, and I search for some way—any way—to answer him. "You still do not trust me."

"Trust is dangerous. It is all risk for very little gain."

"This isn't about advantages and strategy and bluffing." I smooth his ruffled hair. "This isn't a game."

"It's always a game," he whispers.

"Fine. Then I'm going to give you two options." I hold up a finger like he did the night we met. "Option one, you keep shutting me out and trying to control what I get to know. You interrogate me like I'm some card counter in your casino, another suspect on your list. And when this tournament is over, I will walk out and you'll never see me again."

He waits as I raise my second finger.

"Or option two. You stop sequestering who you are behind steel and stone. Choose to trust me."

"What about option three?" He brushes his lips against mine, and shivers ripple through me, and I know he feels every single one of them.

"What *is* option three?" I ask, planting my hand on his chest and pushing him back enough to meet his eye. "Because if you plan to shut me out again tomorrow, then option three is no different than option one, and I want nothing to do with it."

His hand stills on my waist. "You cannot trust a liar, Magnolia."

"Lola," I whisper.

"Lola," he repeats, and my whole body electrifies at the sound of my name spoken like a prayer, like a plea, like a promise.

"You're not a liar," I tell him. "Not really."

He lets out a pained chuckle. "You just said I ruined your life."

"I said you aren't a liar, not that you aren't a villain," I reply. "Liars are malicious. They want to deceive. They don't care who they hurt, as long as they get what they're after."

"And I'm not?"

I shake my head. "You want to be seen and known as much as I do."

"What if that is a lie, too? How would you know?" His eyes smolder dark and dangerous. "What if you have fallen for a con?"

I hold his gaze with my chin held high. "What if you stop being afraid?" I let go of him and slip past to where his jacket lies in a pile on the floor. I gather up the two dice that fell out of his pocket earlier and hold them up for him to see. "Candor or con?" I toss them, and they roll to a stop on a one and a two. "Con," I say, turning to him. "You may not be able to speak the truth, oh impassive, impenetrable Liar, but you can live it. I dare you to."

He looks at me for a long moment. I watch him wrestle with what I've said, wrestle with the vault he's erected around his heart. Someone hurt him long ago. Broke him. Taught him to be wary of words and even warier of connection.

"Please," he whispers. "Just tell me the truth. No riddles, no evasions. Are you still working with Enzo?"

I stare at him, adrenaline stinging through me.

Stars, how I want to tell him everything. Want to describe the weight of carrying someone else's soul with you everywhere you go. Want to whisper the pain of Enzo's anger, the way our heart is heavy as lead in my chest. I imagine finally being able to put to words how restricted I've felt for months, how all I want is to be truly free, truly alive, truly seen, and how, no matter how much I've tried to believe it, I haven't felt that with Enzo. Not now, not ever.

I'm as tired of secrets as Nic is.

And more than that, I realize I want to share them with *him*. I want to do exactly as I'm asking Nic to do for me. Open up, share, trust, be vulnerable. Forgive.

But even as I open my mouth to form the words, Enzo's pulse thunders, a twin echo of mine.

My heart is not my own to give, my secrets not my own to share. And no matter how much I want to be as honest with Nic as I'm asking him to be with me, my life does not belong to me. What I do, who I trust, where I go, who I care for . . . all of it affects Enzo.

One heart, two souls, until I get that moonshard back.

Guilt floods me, but behind it, quiet resolution.

I have no choice. Not if I want to keep Enzo safe. Not if I want to finish this job once and for all.

I need to lie.

But how do I lie to a boy who will know the instant I do?

I close my eyes, remembering rippling into invisibility using Enzo's magic, and then again later, using it to get through Nic's spells on the closet door.

Magic runs on soullight. When Enzo sneaks through walls, he suppresses the soullight of corporeality. When he needs more strength, he takes on that soullight from someone else.

When Nic tests the air for lies, he must sense the soullight of their secrets.

Could I use Enzo's power to suppress the soullight of *my* secrets exactly the way I suppressed my corporeality earlier?

It may not work. But if it does, if I could lie to the Liar himself, it could protect Enzo. Just long enough to get the moonshard.

And once I do, once my heart and my life are mine and mine alone, I can tell Nic everything.

So, steeling my nerves and choking down the guilt tying my stomach in knots, I gather my things, pretending I'm only getting ready to depart, but letting my fingers brush against one of the empty voratium dice as I meet Nic's gaze, jaw clenching. Focusing on the cold of the metal against my skin, I push my secrets away, thrust them as though pushing water along a pipe. The secrets Nic would be able to sense, I give to the die until there's nothing left.

Then, I lie.

"I'm not working with Enzo anymore." It feels like burning, like splintering, like dying. "You can trust me."

Nic stares at me, nostrils flaring as he tests the air for hints of secrets.

I wait, bile rising in my throat.

After what feels like a year, he lets out a strangled sound, something between a gasp and a cough. A smile breaks across his face, a sunrise that takes my breath away. He plucks my things out of my hands and tosses them aside so he can pull me against his chest. This time, when we collide, it is not stars or explosions or magic. Not fire, not ice, not salvation or sin. It is quiet. A whisper, a wish. Skin against skin, heart against heart.

I should feel triumphant as his hands settle warm at my waist. I lied to the Liar, and he does not know. I fooled the one man no one alive can fool.

But instead, everything hurts. Body, heart, soul, frigid beyond the ice of any magic, aching beyond the hurt of any blow.

What will it cost both of us when I do precisely the thing he fears?

Nic tilts my chin with a thumb and tangles his fingers in my hair, and I wish I could surrender myself completely. Unbolt the stone fortress Enzo and I have built in my chest.

But I do not. Some secrets are best kept locked up.

Too soon, Nic pulls back. "The round-three ceremony . . ."

My eyes burn, and a lump rises in my throat, but I force a smile and say, "I'll see you soon, then. Wouldn't want the Liar to be late to his own party."

He breathes a kiss to the hollow of my throat. "Thank you," he whispers, "little thief."

And then he leaves me alone in the dark where I have nothing to distract me from the cracks spidering along the stone fortress inside me. The wisps of ivy curling through. The tiny orchid buds sprouting within.

CHAPTER FORTY

LOLA

When I enter the gambling hall an hour later clad in a draping white gown cinched with golden ropes, the prickle of watching eyes ripples down my neck. I look toward the betting rings. A broad, bushy-haired man with hands like slabs of meat watches me with ice-blue eyes. His mouth thins, and he leans over to whisper something to the woman at his side.

She turns, flipping long white-blond hair over her shoulder. Ostena. Of course. I shoot her a glare as I stride past, nerves jangling like dice as I search the board behind her where names and bets have been placed.

Astra Tremaine winks out at me near the top of the list in bright chalk with exorbitant sums listed next to it. A few other people in that corner glance my way, muttering to one another.

Estelle's warnings replay over and over in my ears, and I straighten my shoulders. There's only one challenge left to complete before the finale. I have a maximum of three days left. I need to keep my wits about me, focus. No more mistakes.

I locate Estelle at a table near the stage, and I weave through the crowd toward her. She hands me a steaming mug of coffee as soon as I reach her. "Latte?"

"Stars bless you," I say, inhaling its deep aroma to soothe my nerves.

"Did you have a good evening?" Estelle asks.

"Yes, I did."

Her lips purse. "I came by to check on you after dinner but decided not to bother you when I heard the Liar's voice." There's an unspoken question in her tone, and all her warnings about Nic, about avoiding getting close with him, filter through my mind.

"I was careful," I say by way of answer.

She searches my face, then sighs and covers my hand with hers. "All right."

"All right?"

"I trust you." She smiles.

Those words crack through me, sincere and honest, and it's all I can do to blink away the moisture suddenly blurring my vision.

At the sight of my tears, she frowns. "He didn't hurt you, did he?"

I shake my head, sniffing. "No. It's just . . . nice to hear that."

Estelle sighs, her thumb rattling against the side of my hand. "Listen. Do I like the Liar? Not one bit. But I'm not the one living your life. I told you what I think, you've heard it, and now you're doing with that information what you think is right. As you should."

I flip my hand upward to squeeze hers. "Thank you."

She opens her mouth to say more, but the overhead lights flare and then fade, and the room hushes. Lavender-black smoke billows in from the corners, curling like ribbons through the crowd, stroking its fingers along cheeks, twining around arms. It sparkles faintly, multihued like the rainbow of stardust in Nic's dice.

DEN OF LIARS

People gasp as a single violin somewhere sings a mournful melody. The smoke rises above our heads, billowing out like clouds, crackling with static, raining down sparks that settle in our hair like scintillating snowflakes.

The music peaks at a high note in perfect vibrato, and the smoke detonates. A lightning bolt slams into the stage, and Nic explodes into view, violet fire licking along his arms, his shoulders, his fedora.

He raises a hand, grins, and snaps white-gloved fingers. The smoke vanishes, the fire extinguishes, and the audience roars with applause.

Gone is the vulnerable man from the hoop. Gone are his fear and hurt. He is not Nic anymore, but the Liar, all jagged angles and raised brows and smirking smiles.

I miss him.

He has changed into a deep black tuxedo with decorative stitching in shimmery silver thread. The color makes his glinting eyes seem even more fathomless, and I can't help but stare at them, at the way his cheekbones cut sharper, at the gentle swoop of his single lock of white-blue hair.

He catches my eye, and everything softens just a touch. When he smiles, I feel the ghost of it on my mouth.

"Thank you for an exciting second round," he cries, pulling a handful of glowing dice from his jacket. "Let's not waste time. There will be fifteen eliminations tonight."

He lifts one—a gorgeous crimson like a ruby. The man who was watching me near the betting rings stiffens and, before anyone can stop him, launches himself toward the stage.

But Nic vanishes before the player's hands close around his throat, and the man jolts sideways as though smacked, slamming to the floor. A pair of security guards is upon him seconds later, yanking him upright by his arms and hoisting him into the audience.

Nic reappears a few feet away from where he was standing before, his slightly amused expression utterly unchanged. The only difference is his raised fist. He lowers it slowly.

"Tomas Hildebard," he announces, then removes his glove to wrap his palm around the die. He closes his eyes, and as he watches whatever it holds, his smile fades. When his lashes flutter open, he's looking straight at me.

He considers for several moments, and the room holds its breath, waiting. Finally, his throat bobs, his hand tightens around the die, and he nods once—the tiniest movement, so slight nobody but me seems to notice.

I cannot breathe. Panic, fear, and hope tangle inside me. What could Tomas Hildebard's secret be for Nic to look at me like that?

Holding my gaze, he tosses the die.

Ruby stardust spills out of it, and an expensive sitting room sprouts across the stage. Black leather seats face a crackling fire. A white tigerskin rug lies spread-eagle on the floor, its head and paws stuffed, its teeth bared. Bookshelves sporting priceless trinkets, sculptures, and vases line the walls.

Two men coalesce, and I recognize them immediately. Ignalus Price, my father's second-in-command, glares at Hildebard with his hand on his pistol. A third man ripples into view. He studies the fire, back turned, but it takes only a heartbeat for me to place why his silhouette is so familiar.

It's my father.

"He's dead, sir," Hildebard says gruffly, his voice rumbling like a coming storm. He tips his head to my father. "Took care of it myself."

"Did he put up a fight?" my father asks.

"Nothing I couldn't handle."

Father turns, and his eyes meet Hildebard's, beady and gleaming, desperate and hungry. "Show me."

Hildebard glances at Ignalus. "It's right outside the door."

Ignalus nods and bustles into the hall.

"He's not precisely . . . er . . . recognizable, if you catch my meaning," Hildebard says as Ignalus reappears dragging what looks to be a body wrapped in burlap.

DEN OF LIARS

"I'd like to see my daughter's killer with my own eyes," my father growls.

A pang stabs through my chest at the way his voice reverberates. Why is he acting like he cares? Who does he think killed me?

A thousand times I asked Enzo to find out whether my father was looking for me, and a thousand times Enzo came home with tales of an unfeeling man who was continuing about his business as though my disappearance were a blessing. I scoured hundreds of newspapers for signs of St. James retaliating against Salazar, searched every line for mentions of violence motivated by my death. Not one had noted even a minor brawl in my name.

My father pulls away the dirty material draped over the corpse's face. Or what's left of it. Hildebard wasn't exaggerating when he said it wasn't recognizable. All that remains are clumps of blood, shards of bone, and pulpy flesh. I gag as Hildebard returns his attention to my father.

St. James fishes out the corpse's arm. Blood stains the shirtsleeves and flecks across the skin, but dark tattooed circles ring the dead man's wrist.

My mind whirs. I remember when one of the Tentacles went missing soon after Enzo rescued me. Enzo was stoic and edgy for weeks, a sharp contrast to the easiness and mirth I'd been starting to get used to.

"Immortality, my ass," Father mutters through his teeth. Then he leans in close. "May the demons of the Deep punish you. May their icy fire make you scream until your soul comes apart." His voice cracks, and he grits his teeth, blinking hard. "You miserable son of a bitch." Then he slams a fist into the corpse's wrecked face, his whole body shuddering with intensity, shoulders quivering as though keeping something much worse reined in. "Death was a mercy you did not deserve."

I stare at him, unable to breathe.

Why is my father on the brink of tears? Which Tentacle did he think killed me? And why?

A voice calls from somewhere else in the house, and he yanks his hand out of the corpse's skull, mopping the blood from his knuckles with a handkerchief, which he tosses over the Tentacle's face. "Weigh that bastard down and chuck him out to sea," he barks before stalking off and slamming the door behind him.

Ignalus raises his eyes to Hildebard. "This isn't the right man."

"Course it is," Hildebard spits, yanking the material back over the corpse.

"I've seen him," Ignalus says. "He's got darker hair. And he's a bit slenderer."

"I'm telling you, it's him."

Ignalus raises a brow, but before he utters another word, Hildebard rams him against a wall, shoving the barrel of a gun under his chin. "Pretty little daughters you've got at home, don't ya? And a baby boy on the way?"

Ignalus spits in his face, and the mucus slides down his sneer. He makes no move to wipe it away.

"If you utter anything but assertions that this is our guy," Hildebard hisses, "there will be no pretty babies to carry on your stars-forsaken name."

The illusion fades.

I stare straight ahead, an ocean roaring in my ears. I feel Nic's eyes on me, but I cannot meet them, cannot focus.

After a pause, Nic continues, rolling dice across the stage one by one, stardust stitching together tales of deceit that I do not see. Shadows creep in at the edges of my vision. I'm gripping my mug so hard the handle bites into my hand.

I know Enzo spread rumors I had been killed so none of my father's other enemies would come looking for me, but surely he hadn't incriminated one of his own Tentacles. Why would he have done that?

And if Hildebard had gotten the wrong person, as Ignalus said, which of the others had been the target?

DEN OF LIARS

My father's words echo back to me. *Immortality, my ass.*

Had . . . had he meant to kill Enzo?

As the thought registers, so do trickles of conversations I've heard over the years, rumors like the one the dancer shared the night I snuck in to steal Legrand's watch. Rumors of the infamous Thief, caught and slaughtered by one of his victims. I'd never paid them any mind. *If you want to know the truth about the Thief, don't talk to a zenithic or a baker or a journalist,* Enzo said a dozen times over the years. *Talk to the Thief. Everyone else has an agenda.*

But now that I think about it . . . when that Tentacle went missing, Enzo became obsessed with making sure none of our cons could be traced to him and started using that fingerprint putty to incriminate others for his crimes. I always figured he was just being careful, but now . . .

Why would Enzo need people to believe him dead? Just to protect his own hide?

Or was it because my father was hunting him down for my murder?

Chills ripple up my arms.

If my father never cared I'd been abducted, why would his voice crack like that? Why would his hands shake?

Why would Enzo need to hide?

Unless . . . Unless maybe Magnus St. James *did* mourn me. Maybe my disappearance broke him the way his indifference broke me. Maybe my death shattered him to his core.

Bile rises in the back of my throat.

Who told me my father did not care? Who said my father never looked for me? Who brought me the newspapers?

I remember the last time someone you trusted turned out to be lying, Enzo said just the other morning. *How could a father lose his daughter . . . How could anyone lose you and not care?*

I never want you to hurt like that ever again.

Only . . . had I needed to hurt like that?

Four years, I've craved a relationship with a man I thought never loved me.

Could that apathy have been a lie?

Could the agony I've endured, the loneliness, the grief have been for naught?

Could I have had a relationship with my father all this time?

I set down my mug, but my hands are shaking so hard the lukewarm coffee sloshes over the rim onto the tablecloth.

"Are you all right?" Estelle asks, but her voice is far away, as though I'm hearing it through water.

"I'm fine . . ." I glance up to Nic. While the other tournament players have their eyes on whatever secret is being revealed in stardust on the stage next to him, his gaze is directly on me, the memory of his words a death march in my ears. *My brother does not meddle in anyone's affairs unless he feels like he needs to. What about you made you worth the risk?*

Estelle's voice punctures through that melody like percussion. *If the Thief ever lied to you, would you know it?*

I press my hands over my ears as though that might block out the memories of their unanswerable questions.

Enzo has only ever been good, been kind, been safe. It is only because of him I am alive. He would not lie, not to me, not about something this big.

I know it.

But confusion roils deep in my belly.

The audience roars to life, startling me, and I look up to see Nic take center stage. He must have finished revealing all the secrets, because he raises his hands wide to thunderous applause. "To those whose dice have been rolled this night, there is only one thing left to say," he cries over the din. "You have gambled, you have lied, and you have been eliminated. Goodbye." Cheers punctuate the familiar lines, and he raises his hand with a grin. "To the remaining players, whoever you are, be warned: Round three is one of sudden death. Unlike the previous two rounds, this one will only last twenty-four hours. May guile guard your secrets."

"I have to go," I mutter to Estelle as the audience shrieks even louder and the tumult inside my head reaches a fever pitch. I can barely see, let alone stay for the after-party.

She opens her mouth to speak, but then, as though seeing something on my face, she nods. "All right. I'll come find you later."

I squeeze her hand one more time and then elbow my way to the deserted hallway. The elevator seems miles away, but I stumble for it as tears blur across my vision. My stomach lurches, acid climbing violently into my throat, and I dive for a nearby vase and retch into it.

This isn't happening. There is an explanation. The past four years of my life can't have been a lie. They *can't* have.

CHAPTER FORTY-ONE

LOLA

I collapse against the wall next to the elevator door and press my face to the voratium swirls in the marble.

Enzo hovers behind my heartbeat. He has noticed my confusion, and his anger and frustration have simmered in the wake of a gentle concern.

Do you need me? it asks, as it always has.

And though he must hate me now for lying to him, he would never abandon me. I know that deep in my soul.

If I went out to my balcony, he would come. He would wrap me in his arms, give an explanation for every question, tell me his side of the story I saw play out on that stage.

But the idea of seeing him makes me feel sick. How would I know his explanations are true? If he has been lying for four years and I never was able to tell, then what I feel from him in our heart won't be enough to judge his honesty. Can I ever trust him again?

Part of me wishes I could go back to before the tournament. Life was simpler then. It was easy to believe him. Things were straightforward, and there was beauty in that. Enzo's embrace was home, his laugh calming, his supervision safe.

But all of that is gone.

"Are you all right?" Nic's voice asks behind me.

"No," I choke out. "I'm not."

His footsteps clack on the floor, and then his arms slip around me, warm and heavy. I bring my hands up to grip his forearms and turn my head against his chest, pressing my ear to his heart.

It does not beat in sync with mine. It is different, wholly separate, and somehow that is comforting. I close my eyes, let the sound of it drown out the chaos.

"What's wrong?" He rests his cheek on the top of my head.

What do I even say? How do I explain? "It's become . . ." I try, ". . . difficult to keep track of what's real."

He breathes in as though about to speak, but the words seem to get lodged in his throat. I turn in his arms to look at him.

"You know what that's like," I whisper. "Don't you?"

"Pretty fantasies are easier than the truths that subvert them every single time." His throat bobs. "If you've devoted yourself fully to a particular idea, the suggestion it might be false is as terrifying as an attacking assassin. Only the most courageous people are willing to look that in the face and not fear its wielded blades."

"How can you tell if you've landed on what's real?" I whisper. "How can anyone ever be sure of anything?"

"Truth holds up," he replies, running a thumb over my cheek. "You can question it, you can dig at it, and it will continue to be true, no matter how you feel about it."

His eyes are tired, as though they've seen too much. As though the weight of secrets has grown too heavy.

"If what you've been told is a lie," he says softly, "do you want to know?"

That question cracks something in me, something lethal, something deep. It is a question I cannot consider, and yet it's like it's been hurtling at me for weeks.

If Enzo's been lying to me, do I want to know?

I don't. I want to run away, hide, barricade myself from the knowing.

Vomit lurches into my mouth again. I shove out of Nic's arms and barely make it back to the vase before I retch so violently the muscles in my abdomen cramp.

Nic comes behind me, pulling my hair out of my face, steadying me with a quiet, heavy hand on my shoulder. When I'm done, and my stomach is empty, he gathers me into his arms. "Let's get you to your suite."

I let my head fall onto his chest, let him carry me upstairs, let him tuck me into my bed.

His violet eyes are the last thing I see before the refuge of slumber pulls me under.

"Sir!" a crackling voice barks, slicing through my aching head. I awaken with a jolt, and for a moment, I'm blissfully thoughtless.

But then the events of yesterday and the weight of the ceremony last night slam down on me, and I cannot breathe all over again.

I push to sitting, gasping for air, and see Nic, who seems to have fallen asleep watching me. The armchair from my sitting area is next to my bed, and he slouches over one side, eyes closed, chest rising slowly.

"Sir!" the voice comes again, echoing in static.

I frown and clamber across my bedspread toward Nic, who's still so deep in slumber he does not seem to hear the radio at his belt.

"Sir, it's Paol," it barks. "Contestants are waiting for their challenges. Sir! Where are you?!"

DEN OF LIARS

Their challenges . . . I gasp, pulling my glasses from the nightstand where Nic must have set them last night, and stuff them on my nose to check the clock. It's already nearly eight thirty in the morning, which means I—and the other remaining contestants—have already lost several hours in our allotted time.

Carefully, I pull out the lapel of Nic's jacket and dip my hand into his inner pocket. Inside is a bundle of black envelopes. I sort through them quickly, scanning the script on each one until I find my name. Heart pounding in my throat, I flip it over and dump out the parchment inside.

Mark: Lorenzo Sinclair

Challenge: Make him believe the moonshard he seeks has died.

I stare at it, my whole body going numb. A high-pitched ringing buzzes in my ears.

"What is this?" I whisper, pressing a hand to my forehead as though that might be able to settle the way my mind is suddenly spinning.

This isn't happening.

"Nic," I say, and my voice sounds like it's miles away. "Nic . . ." The noise in my ears rises to a fever pitch, and I cannot even hear myself anymore. I squeeze my eyes shut and shout over the din, "Nic!"

He startles, leaping to his feet. "What? What's going on?"

I stare at him, raising the parchment, arm leaden and slow. "What the depths is this?"

He stares at the parchment for a moment, still confused. Then all at once his eyes widen and his face goes ashen.

"That wasn't . . . you weren't . . ." He clears his throat.

I shove off my bed, waving the paper in his face. "Is this some kind of test? To see if I'm being honest?"

He shakes his head. "The challenge was meant to be updated after our conversation last night. There wasn't time before the ceremony, so it was going to happen afterward, but then I . . ." The words get lodged.

"You still don't believe me," I grit out, my fingers clenching around the parchment so it crackles.

I know it's not fair of me to expect him to, considering that the acrid taste of my lies is still sharp on my tongue, but I want to shout at him, want to rage. The dam keeping me together has already splintered beyond repair, and all of my hurt and fear are ready to explode through.

When will someone in this wretched world just *trust* me?

Nic steps forward, grasps the corner of the paper, and tries to pry it from my hand. "The challenge was supposed to be updated. It was meant to be—"

"No." I yank it away from him and stalk to the door, swinging it wide. "Don't baby me. You want proof I can handle myself, you'll get your proof. You don't get to take this back. You don't get to treat me any differently than any other player. I am a St. James, and I fear nothing. Least of all a pair of sniveling, petty, quarreling brothers."

"Lola—" He reaches for me, but I sidestep him, gesturing out the door.

"I have a challenge to complete."

Nic stares at me. "You're not going to let me explain myself, are you?"

"You couldn't even if you tried," I snap, avoiding his eyes as tears bite at the corners of mine. "Because you're a liar."

He stiffens as though I just landed a blow. "You're not the only one," he says, dead quiet, "who has been betrayed, Lola. Not the only one who has been abandoned by people you thought loved you."

"I know," I say, but he holds up a hand and nods at my purse on the nightstand, where glowing gambling chips and magical dice sparkle.

"You're still carrying around that white die."

A stone drops in my gut. *This is the one people fear the most. It gives you the power to sense their lies.*

I sigh, leaning against the doorframe and pretending I haven't thought about that white die since I picked it up. "Oh, that. I haven't had a need for it yet."

"Truly? Or could there be someone outside this casino you'd like to use it on?"

The question is a knife's edge against my throat.

"Consider that challenge," he says, pointing at the parchment in my hand, "the House's white die, played before the House knew for sure you weren't bluffing. Unless"—he steps closer, tipping his head to catch my eye—"the House is mistaken."

I grit my teeth, calling on every ounce of strength in me to keep the tears in my eyes from spilling.

Nic slides a hand into his jacket and pulls out the slender ebony box that has become so familiar. "Time to select your dice," he says, jaw tight.

"How am I supposed to find Enzo if he's barred from entering?"

"He's been invited for a lunch meeting. Spells have been lifted." He opens the box and holds it out to me.

I consider the tiny, glowing gems carefully. How will I lie about something this big to the person who knows me better than anyone? I pick up three yellows—I'll definitely need to be able to soften his emotions. Then two reds to make the truth feel false. I still have a green left over from the last round, so I grab one more and then round out my collection with a blue.

He snaps the box shut, tucking it away and buttoning his jacket.

"Sir!" Paol barks over the radio again.

"You'd better go," I say. "You're late." I cross to the pile of envelopes on my bed and hold them out for him.

He takes them, catching my hand in his. "You're all right?" His voice is sharp, but I hear the concern masked behind the bite.

"Fine." I force a smile.

He searches my face, an unknowable emotion flitting in his eyes, before finally tipping his head. "Very well." He stoops to retrieve his fedora from where it must have fallen to the floor during the night and replaces it strategically atop his head.

I step aside as he passes on his way to the door, but he pauses right next to me, our arms barely touching, and his pinkie finger grazes mine. I turn my head to look at him, but he doesn't meet my gaze.

And though I'm still angry, still upset, still feeling so much guilt it might topple me, I curl my pinkie around his for just an instant. He closes his eyes. Swallows.

"May guile guard your secrets," he whispers, and then he's pulling out of my grasp, walking away, leaving me with far too many secrets and not nearly enough guile to guard them from destroying everyone I care about.

CHAPTER FORTY-TWO

LOLA

I move through the morning in what feels like slow motion. My stomach churns, my body quakes, and I cannot seem to get myself to focus on any one thought. Instead, a thousand plague me all at once, so loud and insistent I cannot make sense of any of them. *Why did my father think Enzo had killed me? Why didn't Enzo tell me? Could Nic be manipulating me? How will I lie to Enzo? Should I? Should I have let Nic switch my challenge like he meant to? How will Enzo react? Where is the vault? I'm running out of time . . .*

Over and under and around and around, a cacophony, a chaos.

I bathe and dress in a black lace, floor-length gown lined in midnight-blue satin. The neckline follows the curves of my chest, and the off-the-shoulder sleeves drape to my elbows. Stars twinkle faintly in the lace, and when I move, they catch the light like a distant galaxy. With shaking hands, I pin my curls atop my head and line my eyes in dark cosmetics to match the gown, then finish the look with a set of dazzling diamond earrings and a coordinating necklace and bracelet.

By the time my purse of chips and dice is stowed on my leg once more, I feel Enzo approaching.

Prickles stab at my extremities, but I steel my nerves and slip out the door, taking care to lock it behind me, then walk on unsteady feet toward the elevator.

"Oh, there you are!" a familiar voice calls.

I glance back to see Estelle rushing to meet me carrying a pair of sparkling drinks.

"Thought we could do a toast!" she says as she reaches me, holding out one of the glasses.

The elevator dings, and I step inside. "A . . . toast?"

"For making it to the third round!" she chortles, following me.

I peer at her, taking the glass. She's behaving so . . . oddly. Like the interaction we had over the table last night when I said I needed to leave never occurred.

The door slides shut, and the elevator lurches downward.

"The eliminations were exciting, weren't they?" she says, too cheery. She raises her glass to me with a smile, then takes a sip and waits for me to do the same.

I lift my own glass to my mouth, but instead of drinking, I sniff. A subtle tang radiates off the cocktail's surface. Faint, but distinct. The exact aroma I smelled on Ostena's syringe the other day.

Could this be Ostena again, using another illusory die?

"Something wrong?" she asks.

"Oh, no, everything's fine." I tip the glass to my lips and pretend to take a sip. "Just tired."

Then I jerk the glass forward, splashing its contents into her nose and partly open mouth.

She screeches, lunging for me, and I dart sideways. She slams into my shoulder, pinning the arm holding my now-empty glass against the elevator door. Grinning, she grabs my hand, tearing my glass out of my grasp. I squirm, trying to wrench away, but she smashes the glass against the wall and points the jagged stem at me.

"Careful," I say. "If you hurt me, you'll be disqualified."

Ostena bares her teeth. "Only if the Liar finds out."

Slipping my hand into my pouch, I pull out one of my empty dice from the earlier rounds and push my corporeality into it, just as I did to sneak into Nic's room.

As my body ripples into thin air, I throw myself through the door. A shout echoes behind me, and I hear her slam her fist against a button. The elevator screeches to a halt.

I take off running down the corridor toward the stairwell, focusing on keeping my body noncorporeal in spite of my panic, but my unpracticed hold on the magic slips, and I reappear.

Enzo's emotions swell nearer—he's almost reached the lobby. Maybe he could help me.

I yank open the door to the stairwell just as the elevator doors slide open, and Ostena comes dashing after me. I barrel down the steps, skipping multiple at a time as Ostena gains on me, her heels clacking as loud as gunshots. I try to fumble in my purse for another empty die, but even as I clench one in my fist, I'm too panicked to focus, running too hard to be able to channel my corporeality into the voratium.

She grabs hold of a section of lace streaming from my dress as I reach the ground floor, and the fabric tears, sending her tumbling backward. I wrench open the door and sprint down the corridor.

But I'm not fast enough.

She slams into me, and we topple.

I thrash, but she yanks my arms behind me.

"Stop!" I shout, desperate for someone in the gambling hall next door to hear me, for Paol or Nic to come running. But music is blaring, and audiences are cheering, and nobody comes to my aid.

I jerk sideways, trying to wrench free as she binds my forearm with a rope she pulled out of her bodice.

My hands are clenched so hard the empty die in my hand cuts into my palm. I try once more to push my corporeality into it the way I did before, but adrenaline is still making it difficult to focus.

Enzo's concern—still tinged with anger—ripples through me, sudden and bright.

He's entered the casino.

Come, I scream at him internally, praying he will feel my desperation. *I'm right here.*

I think of Enzo and his gems, multicolored all over his face and ears and neck. He doesn't just go incorporeal, he also steals others' soullight. Words and memories and . . . and strength.

That's it.

I grasp Ostena's hand and *pull.*

Soullight explodes around me. A thousand colors and sounds and echoes. The sudden appearance of it makes me dizzy. Thinking back to the times Enzo has stolen people's strength, I focus in on what it feels like to be strong, sifting through the flares of light until I find one that feels that way.

Ostena cries out as I drag her soullight into the die, then she tips sideways, every muscle going limp. My voratium glows like a sun, and I draw its power through my skin.

Ecstasy rolls through me. I'm suddenly more alert than I've ever been in my life, each nerve tingling with heightened stamina.

I pull my hands apart, hard, and the rope splits like it's no more than frayed thread.

"Bleeding stars," I marvel, grinning.

And then I dash for the front lobby.

CHAPTER FORTY-THREE

LOLA

My legs pump faster than they ever have. I could climb a thousand Liar's Dens with this kind of power, leap across every roof in Aethera.

I make it to the lobby in seconds, and my heart rate, if anything, has come down. I skid to a halt.

It's empty.

I close my eyes, sink inside myself to my heart. Enzo's emotions are sharp as knives, poignant as fire. Mentally grasping hold of the cord between us, I race to the gambling hall, where Shirley LaCour is belting into the microphone and the audience is screaming along.

Enzo. I need you, I let my heart cry out to him with my desperation and my fear. *I'm here.*

I elbow through the throng, focusing on that tether between us, letting it draw me forward.

His emotions grow wilder and louder until he paws past a group of dancing patrons, barreling into view. The tightness in my chest loosens. He's dressed in his best jacket, a slim-fitted button-down shirt, and a finely tailored set of slacks. His hair is swept back from his face, styled with some kind of mousse. He's even taken out his facial and ear piercings, a tactic that has always been his simplest disguise, since most people don't recognize him without them.

We reach each other at the center of the crowd, and he grasps both my arms, peering into my face. "What happened?"

"I was attacked," I shout over the din.

"Are you hurt?" He inspects me head to toe.

I shake my head, scrambling through my brain for what to say. He can't know I've been assigned him as my challenge, or else lying to him will never work.

"How are you in here?" I ask, feigning surprise. "I thought there were spells . . ."

He presses a finger to my lips, looking around to make sure nobody's listening, then looks sharply back at me, a reprimand in his eyes. "I've got an important lunch appointment."

Now that his fear for my safety has passed, his anger returns in full force, and he releases me, turning away and striding through the crowd.

"Wait!" I shout after him. "Where are you going?"

I follow his trajectory to where Nic stands near the bar, deep in conversation with Valen, the bartender.

Cursing, I hustle past several gamblers to grab hold of Enzo's jacket. "What the depths are you doing?"

"Speaking to my brother," he spits through his teeth, trying to wrench forward.

I tighten my grip. "Do you know how many guards would attack if you tried?"

"They don't scare me."

I resist the urge to roll my eyes. "I'm sure they don't. But they should."

"They can't kill me."

"They can hurt you, though."

He vanishes, and my fingers grasp thin air, making me stumble.

"No, they can't," he declares, materializing so he can cross his arms in front of his chest. "And besides, I was invited."

"Fancy trick, Enz," I snap, then shove him through a curtain of diamonds that scatter like a cloud of fireflies. The dining room on the other side is already bustling with lunch orders, and the sizzling aroma of meat and butter fills my nose. I gesture to an unoccupied booth in the corner. "Let's get coffee before you start a war."

"He asked me to come." He glances at a gold wristwatch. "We're supposed to meet in ten minutes."

"Then you have time for coffee first," I retort, pointing toward a table. "Please?"

He glares, considering, before finally stalking to the booth, grumbling under his breath.

"Now," I say, taking the place across from him. "What did his invitation say?"

"He had something important to discuss with me."

I blink. "That's it?"

"I'm here to get answers," he snaps. "He hasn't reached out to me in four years, Lola. This is finally my chance."

"So you're going to ask him where the shard is?" I almost laugh.

"Yes, actually. And then I'm going to kill him."

"He's just as incapable of dying as you are, dumbass."

He closes his eyes and pinches his nose. "And you're still incapable of understanding just how much I hate him."

"Of course I am." My throat is thick, and every word stings. "You barely told me anything about him. Or about what happened between you two."

"It's not your business."

I slam my fist down on the table. "You made it my business when you stole my heart and locked me up." The words tumble out before I can stop them, and as soon as they're out, guilt slicks oil through me.

His eyes snap to mine. "Locked you up? I freed you."

"Sometimes . . ." I wet my lips. "Sometimes it doesn't feel like freedom."

"The parameters of our life are what keep us alive, Lizard." He sighs. "And to be clear, I didn't steal a thing. You agreed to the deal."

I drop his gaze as the ridiculous nickname—something that would usually make me feel special—sears like a slap. "You didn't tell me everything I was agreeing to."

"There wasn't time," he replies softly, "and you wouldn't have understood."

"You never gave me the chance." I glare at the table, which warps as tears sting hot in the corners of my eyes.

A waitress approaches, clad in what appears to be a cloud of crimson glitter. "What can I get you?"

"I'd like a coffee. One cream, no sugar," I say.

"Get me the sugariest, creamiest concoction on your menu," Enzo says, flashing the waitress his most charming smile.

When she bustles away, he presses his hands flat against the table. "You're right. I should have told you what our deal entailed before you agreed to it. It was unfair of me."

His heart, still full of anger and frustration, cools just a fraction. He's always been stubborn to a fault, but there, in the slight way the emotion flowing from him twists with sorrow, I sense his sincerity.

He means it.

"Thank you for the apology," I say. "Now will you tell me what answers you're planning to beat out of your brother? Because, in my professional opinion, punching him in the face isn't exactly a foolproof tactic."

Enzo mops a hand over his face. "You were right."

"I'm sorry, can I get that in writing?" I allow the slightest of smiles to break the tension between us.

"We'll commemorate it with a holiday." He smirks. "People will celebrate for generations to come."

I stick out my tongue. "What was I right about?"

"While you've been in here," he says, "I found a clue that Legrand might have passed the moonshard to the priest who officiated the funerary service of one of her patients."

"Callum Astley," I whisper.

Enzo nods. "My plan was to raid his voratium supply, but I couldn't get what you'd said out of my head—about my brother planting false leads."

The waitress returns with our coffee, and Enzo drinks deeply from his before setting it down and wiping whipped cream from his upper lip.

The gesture is so familiar it makes my heart ache. Enzo isn't a bad person. He couldn't be. Not the boy with the sweet tooth, not the one who pores over fashion magazines and sings to his pet octopus and comes up with games just to make me laugh.

"So," he continues, "I decided to try a different tactic with the priest than I did with the others. I broke him out of the prison where he was being held. And instead of searching his soullight, I interrogated him."

"Yeah, I heard about that," I murmur. "As soon as the Liar heard a man had vanished from prison without a trace, he knew it was you."

"I don't give a flying damn what my brother thinks."

I roll my eyes. "Could have fooled me."

His eyes glint with the hint of a smile. "Anyway. If you're done criticizing my kidnapping skills . . ."

"Oh, I wasn't. Just your motive." I sip my coffee. "What benefit is there to rescuing criminals who—"

"The benefit," he interrupts, "is that instead of basing all my knowledge about the moonshard's location on the glimpses I would have gotten from his soullight, if I interrogate the person myself, I can poke holes in their story. See where it falls apart."

"And?"

He sighs, dragging a hand through his curls. "It didn't hold up. He seemed to genuinely believe he had done the funeral, but when I asked him for more specific details, he got confused. It was like he was trying to grasp onto a dream and not a real memory."

"If you'd asked me first, I would have told you I'd planted that clue myself," I tell him. "I was assigned to Astley in round two, and the lie I had to tell him was exactly the one meant to fool you."

He sighs again. "I guess I owe you another apology, then."

"Two in one day?"

"I promise it won't happen again."

"Oh, of course not." I shake my head very seriously, and something tight in my chest, like a breath I've been holding in for days, releases. "What did you do with Astley?"

"Dumped him back in his cell an hour ago." He shrugs.

"Is he going to identify you?"

He scowls, offended. "What do you take me for, an amateur?"

I snort, and he winks.

He's forgiven me. We've cleared the air.

Yet my stomach still churns with all the questions I'm not ready to ask.

"So you were planning to, what, march in here and break the Liar's nose repeatedly until he fessed up?" I say to keep him from noticing my turmoil. "Interesting method for getting answers."

"Well, that, and maybe yell some bad words at him. Mess up his perfectly swooped hair."

I snort again. "Sounds like an excellent reason to risk letting the whole world know you're actually not as dead as they think you are."

"Did I ask for your feedback?"

"Maybe you should have."

He steals my cup and gulps down the last few drops of coffee, then makes a face. "Stars, that's vile." The brotherly glint in his eye sends a pang through my heart.

I don't want to lie to him.

But I have to finish this job. And if lying to Enzo is what it takes to get Nic to open up the rest of the way and tell me where his secrets are, then it's in everyone's best interest for me to complete my challenge. I do this now, and Nic's dice are as good as mine.

Enzo will forgive me when he's free.

Nic, on the other hand, likely never will, and I hate myself for that—for being exactly what he fears I am. A liar, a thief, a betrayer. But if he cares about me at all, I hope he'll understand that I need my own life back.

Just like he needs his.

Because, whether he realizes it or not, this will free him, too.

Enzo cocks his head. "What's wrong?"

Damn this shared heart. At this proximity, he doesn't miss even the tiniest emotions.

I slide my hands off the table and knot them on my knees. How do I make him believe the one lie that would devastate him beyond any other? How can I steal the only hope that keeps him going, even for just a day?

"What's going on?" he prompts me again, leaning in.

"It's just that . . ." I lick my lips and forge ahead. "It's gone."

"What's gone?"

"The moonshard."

He blinks. "What?"

"It detonated. We're too late."

I stare at the boy who rescued me, who has given me life, who has made me what I am today, and I hate myself. Because even through everything, lying to him feels like carving out a piece of my soul.

CHAPTER FORTY-FOUR

LOLA

Enzo leans back, twirling one of his voratium rings around his thumb. "That's not funny."

"It's not a joke."

His sleeve rides up, baring the black circles on his wrist where Septavia usually is. He must have left her in the water to feed, and I find myself staring at the marks but seeing a different set of them on a corpse's arm.

"What do you mean, it detonated?"

"We knew it would, Enzo. It's been unstable since the Liar took it. It was only a matter of time."

He stares at me, assessing. "You're not lying?"

"Why would I lie about this?" I want to vomit. My whole body quakes, but I keep my gaze steady, breathe slow to keep my emotions in check.

DEN OF LIARS

"What's . . ." He licks his lips, searching my face, doubt creeping in. Then desperation. Then despair. "What's your evidence?"

I discreetly slip my hand into my pouch and roll one of my yellow dice under the table. Considering how recently I broke his trust, my only hope is that Nic's magic might be enough to soften him to what I'm saying.

"I overheard the Liar speaking on the phone with one of his investors. They were discussing a man who was killed by a moonshard's explosion last night. You know even better than I how rare moonshards are. It has to be ours." I pause, steeling my nerves. "That's probably why he invited you here. To tell you about it."

"If a moonshard exploded," he says slowly as his heart rate climbs and his thumb rattles on the table, "why have I heard nothing about it?"

My mind whirs as the skepticism bleeding through my heart from Enzo grows. This has been his goal, his life, his purpose for years now. He needs to believe what I'm saying isn't true, because if it is, he's lost. He's stuck. He's doomed.

He clings to the possibility I'm wrong, burning fully through the first die's magic in moments as he scrabbles to maintain hope.

But I feel every splinter of that hope like it's cracking my own ribs.

With shaking hands, I pull out a second yellow die as well as one of the reds to help make the truth feel less sure. I toss them together as I tell him, "It happened in"—I scramble for the name of the farthest city I can think of—"Moraille. I'm sure people here will be talking about it by the end of the day."

In spite of the magic from the two dice, Enzo's heart is still resisting, and the power trickles out too quickly. I'm going to have to try something else.

"If it was in Moraille, how did the Liar find out about it already?" Enzo asks, staring through me, fingers knotting so tight his knuckles blanch white.

"He got a telegram. Straight to his room." I dig in my pouch for a blue die, a green one, as well as an empty one from earlier as an idea strikes me. "After we talked yesterday, I found the Liar's vault."

He nearly chokes. "You did?" His voice is small, and in the panicked set of his jaw I see the little boy bracing against the pain of a belt.

Aching, I toss the magical dice and weave together a glamour over the empty one, making it glitter with stars trapped in ebony the way Nic's real secrets looked.

When I pull it out to show him, Enzo stares at it, eyes slowly widening. "This . . . this is it?" His voice is hushed, almost reverent.

"Roll it."

He snatches it from me and obeys, eyes bulging as he waits for it to land.

I grab two more dice—one red, and one green—and try not to panic at how I only have two dice left in my pouch—one yellow and one white. Neither enough to make him believe me if this doesn't work.

With another portion of the magic left in the blue, I craft an illusion of a lanky man carrying a glowing parcel exactly the size of the moonshard. I fashion a glimpse of Nic watching the man steal through the streets of Aethera toward the train. "Run, Rilva." I use the green's power from the previous die to make Nic's voice rumble in time to the illusion. "Quick." Alongside it, I use the red to make the truth—that none of this is plausible, that Enzo would have heard about it—feel false.

I let that illusion fade.

He frowns, staring at the place where the fictional Rilva man just vanished. "Who is this man?"

"Rilva was the one mentioned in the telegram. Who died from the explosion."

He stares at me, mouth working. "No," he whispers.

I feel it coming, the despair like a torrent like a whirlwind like a storm. And I hate myself for it, for everything. Hate myself for causing him this kind of pain, even though I know it's for the best.

"I'm so sorry, Enzo," I choke out, tears filming over my eyes.

But we're not quite there yet. He's still clinging to hope. I need one last push to break his hold.

The magic fades to nothing. I close my fist over the empty die so he won't see the illusion on it fade, but I peek down at it between my fingers. It was one of the blue ones, though now it's dull. I squeeze it tight in my palm, willing it to give me even a scrap of magic.

Come on. A crumb, a wisp. Please.

But of course there's nothing. It's empty.

I grit my teeth as desperation turns my hands clammy, and reach into the chilled place at the die's core that flickers in my mind's eye.

Give me something, I plead. *Anything.*

The tiniest trickle of ice dribbles out, so cold I hiss.

That'll do.

I drag at the magic, and it's like trying to wrench a current through the eye of a needle. Sweat slicks my palms, dampens my back, but I pull and I pull until there's enough to stitch together a glamour of a telegram onto the parchment in my bodice with my challenge on it. Trying not to pant with the effort, I draw out that parchment and hold it up for Enzo to read.

"I stole the telegram from him," I say. "See for yourself."

`Rilva Rastnah found dead. Blast from possible explosive. More soon.`

Lilya Wright

He takes it from me, slow, his hands shaking so hard the paper crackles. He stares at it, reading and rereading as the tidal wave of surrender rears its head.

"I'm sorry, Enzo," I whisper.

He lifts his eyes to meet mine. "It's . . . gone?"

The pain hits us both at once. But instead of a raging storm, it is a weight. A heaviness. A smothering.

There is no breathing, no feeling, no living in this place. Dark and endless.

Enzo slumps forward, dropping his head onto the table, dead weight.

"Enz?" I whisper, barely able to hear my own voice over the thick fog of his numbness.

He does not rage, does not scream, does not cry. Does not even move. I might wonder if he passed out if not for his sudden shallow gasps every few seconds.

"It's going to be all right. We'll get through this. We'll find another moonshard, see if we can't modify the curse with more magic or something," I hear myself saying, the words tumbling out like they might be able to soften the roar of quiet I've never felt from him before. This living, suffocating shadow filling every inch of me with lead. "Or we'll do some more research. Create a moonshard ourselves. We can fix this. Nic has a thousand books about the magic—maybe we could ask him . . ."

Enzo goes rigid.

"Or we could go to the temple, see if we can't find the priest who worked with the moonshard, talk to them . . . maybe there's residual power somewhere . . ."

Enzo lifts his head, his eyes focusing in on my face, sharp and hard, pupils shrunk to tiny pinpricks. "What did you say?"

"I . . ." I blink at him. "Which part?"

"You called him Nic."

"What?"

Enzo sits upright, palms flattening on the table as his nostrils flare. "My brother told you his name."

I backtrack, fumbling through explanations while simultaneously trying to keep myself calm. How could I have made such a careless mistake? We were *nearly there*—I had convinced him. "I—I . . ." I stammer. "I fooled him into trusting me."

"You called him Nic, though. Casually. As though that's how you refer to him in your head." Enzo's eyes flash as his anger boils in my chest. "He is no longer the Liar to you. He's . . . he's *Nic*." He hurls the name like a dagger.

"That's not true," I begin, but he cuts me off as the despair inside us gives way to something with claws and teeth.

"Let me make one thing absolutely clear. The Liar—*Nic*—does not trust you." He stands, his voice lowering to a lethal whisper. "And neither do I."

"Enzo, please."

He shakes his head, digging in his jacket and tossing a pile of plats onto the table next to the empty coffee cups. "We're done here." He stalks away.

With trembling hands, I pull out the yellow die, leaving only the white one behind, and toss it as I dive after him. Magic fills me, and I push out feelings of trust, of friendship, of honesty toward him.

"Enzo," I plead, catching his arm. "You know I wouldn't lie."

"That's where you're wrong." He meets my gaze with a glare of ice rimmed in red. "I want to. Depths, Lola, do I want to." He glances down at the table behind me, and I know without looking that the telegram has vanished, leaving behind only the parchment that carried the illusion.

"Enzo," I whisper.

"How long have you been working for him?" Enzo's voice quivers, and whether he's holding back tears or rage, I cannot tell, the emotions roiling inside me are too vast, too sharp. "How long have you been planting evidence to mislead me?"

"I—"

He shakes his head. "Never mind. I don't want to know." He turns to leave, but a voice breaks the air between us, silken like chocolate.

"Hello, brother."

I whirl as the Liar strides into the restaurant, straight-backed, broad-shouldered, and wearing a smile that could cut glass. He stops before us, wreathed in shadows, a wicked angel of the Deep.

"Seize him," he says to his guards.

They pounce, but Enzo vanishes.

Nic laughs, a sound like raining shards of ice that fills me with both terror and awe.

I back up slowly, retrieving my empty dice as Nic scans the area, eyes dancing. "Lorenzo," he calls in a singsong voice that raises the hairs on my neck. "Come out, come out, wherever you are . . ."

A fist materializes, slamming so hard into his jaw that he pitches straight into our booth. The coffee cups smash to the floor.

Nic laughs, pushing himself upright, rubbing his face. "I missed you, too."

"Shut up, you son of a whore." Enzo appears, a vein pulsing in his temple as he lets his fist fly again.

Nic catches the punch and throws Enzo into a neighboring table. "That's not a very nice thing to say about our mother."

Enzo spits. "You think you're so clever. Mastermind of so many little games. What fun this has been." He hurls himself at Nic, ramming him against the booth by the collar. "But it's over now, and you're going to tell me where the moonshard is."

Nic's smile is cold. "Or what? You'll disappear at me?"

Enzo's rage is hot and so wild my whole body is shaking with it. I should stop this, break up the fight. And yet . . . which brother would I protect? Which side am I on?

I have lost Enzo. Nic may still believe he can trust me for now, but once he sees my secret, I'll lose him, too.

My only chance of preventing that—the only chance that leaves a path open to some kind of freedom—is if I get my secret from the vault and run.

DEN OF LIARS

When Enzo lands another punch to Nic's face, I hike up my dress.

"Fancy trick," Nic says when Enzo vanishes again. "I want to try." He glamours his own body into invisibility.

A game, indeed.

I scan the area, taking stock of the security guards waiting for Nic's command. With them all distracted, now is my best opportunity to get to Nic's vault unnoticed.

When the brothers materialize again, flinging simultaneous punches, I slip through the gathering crowd of onlookers and head for the staff hallway.

This tournament destroyed my childhood, and I'll be damned if I let it destroy my future, too.

CHAPTER FORTY-FIVE

☾

NIC

Enzo's fist slams into my jaw, and my neck cracks as I stumble backward, laughing. Finally, a pain that doesn't come with echoes of screams or memories of betrayal. The good, old-fashioned kind like when we used to wrestle on the kitchen floor as boys.

I mop blood from my lip as Enzo prepares another blow.

"What is she to you?" I ask, slinging my jacket onto a table. The conversation between Enzo and Lola just now clearly showed they had more of a relationship than she let on, and I need tangible, concrete details of how they're connected. And why.

"She?" Enzo asks, feigning ignorance with a smirk.

I roll my eyes, and though I'm sure my face is red and my jaw tight, I keep a gentle stream of illusion going so all he sees is a mask of disinterested curiosity. "Lola."

DEN OF LIARS

Enzo's green eyes spark at the sound of her name. "Just some thief I hired for a job."

I pick my fedora off the floor, dusting its brim before hanging it carefully on the back of a chair. "It doesn't take magic to spot a lie that obvious, Enzo. She's Magnolia St. James. Daughter of the most powerful gang lord in Celestia."

A muscle ticks in Enzo's jaw. "I'm aware."

"You're trying to tell me you rescued the daughter of the most well-known criminal in the world from a whole passel of Salazar soldiers and risked having a target on your back from both sides as well as a warrant out for your arrest . . . just to have her *pick some pockets*?"

He glares, raising his fists. "Yes."

I loosen my tie, keeping my voice measured. Something isn't right about the way she looked at Enzo—with all of her fire tamed, with her eyes pleading, with her shoulders hunched. So very unlike the Lola I've come to know.

Whatever happened between them was not nothing.

"You orchestrated a murder scene," I say through gritted teeth. "Paid millions of plats to have a body fashioned to look like her. Bought off a doctor to do the forensics report for even more money, I'm sure, because no one willingly lies to Magnus St. James."

Enzo lunges, but I dance to the side, swinging a foot into his ribs and sending him toppling into another table. Silverware rains to the floor as he scrambles to his feet.

"And?" Enzo rasps. "You want to claim you've never paid people to lie for you?"

"You fed her." My voice rises, the words coming faster and harder as I stalk toward him. "Housed her. Taught her to fight and to steal. Dyed her hair, created a whole life for her. You even gave her stars-damned *freckles*, for shit's sake."

Enzo's fist flies again, and this time I catch it in my palm.

"Do you think I'm thick?" I ask.

Enzo's eyes flash. "Do you want me to answer that honestly?"

"You like money." I shove his hand away. "You like diamonds and jewelry and fancy clothing. You like eating pastries and taking naps and making pretty trinkets."

"Sounds like you've got me all figured out."

"Tell me why you'd spend that much money," I say as I grasp his collar, "that much time, that much *effort* on her."

Enzo shrugs. "Seemed like a fun idea at the time. Now she's turned into a bit of a thorn in my side, if I'm being honest."

Now.

Now.

Does that mean they're still working together somehow? Does that mean she came here on his errand, just as I thought in the beginning?

But she told me point-blank that none of that was true, and I didn't sense a single lie.

So what is going on?

I grind my teeth and shove him back into the same overturned table. "You'd think after four years with a curse that makes you dependent on other people, you would have, I don't know, learned how not to be such an ass."

Enzo rights himself. "Don't you dare." He holds up a warning finger, his voice dropping to a low whisper. "Don't you *dare* speak of what this curse has made me. Whatever I've become is because of you."

My eyes dart to where Lola was standing to see if she heard that, but she's no longer there. I whirl, searching the restaurant for her.

"Where'd she go?" I ask, then point at Paol in the corner and say it loud enough for him to hear. "Where'd she go?"

Paol jolts to attention, rushing toward the door. "On it, sir." The rest of the guards file after him.

I pay attention to my magic, to the way its gravity shifts to wherever she is. It yanks on my navel, bending me toward . . .

The service hallway.

DEN OF LIARS

My vault.

She's after her secret. A secret I know now more than ever I need. Enzo swings a punch toward me, but I'm already running.

I arrive at my vault the exact instant Lola's hand closes over her die, the broken shards of the glass case it was in littering the floor at her feet next to the rock she used to smash it.

"Lola," I gasp, mopping a sodden orchid petal from my face.

She turns, clutching her secret tight. Water streams off her like stars, eyes flashing behind dripping glasses. An instant later, Enzo appears at my side, dry and seething.

I step forward, holding out my hand to Lola. "You lost, little thief." My voice is quiet, barely a cracked whisper. "We made a bargain."

She glances at Enzo, a war in her gaze. Desperate, terrified.

I want to tell her it's okay, I believe her, I don't need to know.

But I do.

So I watch her fingers clench and unclench around the die. Wait as she looks from me to Enzo and back. Feel her splinter between us, pulling both ways at once.

Finally, her eyes stop on Enzo, flaring as though trying to communicate something as she raises her hand, holding the die out for me.

Something loosens in my chest. I step forward to retrieve it, but then she cranks back her arm and hurls it toward Enzo.

I lunge as it whips past me, but likely thanks to her lack of depth perception, the throw goes wide. Enzo dives for the little violet crystal as it soars out of reach. A cry chokes out of Lola's throat as the die hits the rock and rolls once, twice, three times before coming to rest at the water's edge.

"No!" Her scream echoes as violet stardust explodes into the air. She stumbles forward, grabbing the voratium, trying to block the magic with her hands, but it streams out between her fingers anyway.

The cavern flickers into darkness. A locked, windowless room. A girl weeping in a corner.

And then there he is, my little brother, rippling through a brick wall. I watch the moments that transpired before what I saw in Astley's chip with my mouth going dry.

A voratium pendant clasped between his hand and her chest. A deal struck, a payment made.

One heart, two bodies, for as long as she would live.

There's a glint in past-Enzo's eye, one I know well. One that says he knows exactly what he's doing. That he's got a plan.

But I can't tear my gaze away from fifteen-year-old Lola, clinging to Enzo's hands like a lifeline.

How young she was. How broken, how desperate, how afraid.

Before my eyes, an innocent girl becomes a thief. Present becomes past. One imprisonment becomes another.

Something breaks in me.

She *lied*.

How she did it, I cannot fathom. But as that voratium pendant glows violet in the dark, as two souls become one, I see that Enzo did nothing out of the ordinary. A simple drawing of soullight into a raw shard of the metal, as he and I have both done a thousand times.

So how is she *still* bound to Enzo? How is there *still* the same pendant around his neck? How are they *still* joined?

If my brother did nothing out of the ordinary when he made his deal with her, then it is not Enzo's magic that binds them. At least not entirely.

It's something about *her*. Something different. Something dangerous.

And Enzo knows what it is.

When the illusion vanishes, I stare in silence at her now-empty die, chest heaving like I've run a thousand miles. No matter how hard I try to push it down, all I can see is Lola's face in the aerial rehearsal room when she dared me to trust her, an afterimage like a nightmare burned into my retinas.

If she was lying then, she could have been lying all along.

And somehow, her taking my truths and running with them like this hurts more than when Laurel did it. Because at least with Laurel, it was real.

This—whatever it has been between Lola and me—was nothing more than illusion.

Fury and despair whip through me, and, as though sensing that, Lola scrambles away across the rocks toward the water.

She has been nothing but my enemy from the beginning. Nothing more than a figment of my imagination, a relief from loneliness I wanted so desperately I was willing to ignore the signs.

I revealed too much. Enzo now knows I've orchestrated his clues. My control is crumbling around me.

So I make a decision. If kindness and care won't win her over, if lies and magic won't fool him, then perhaps fear will settle this for both.

I dart after her, flipping her onto her back. Yanking my dagger out of my belt, I jab it against her throat, pinning her body beneath mine on the rock.

"How?" I bark at Enzo.

"I'm going to need you to be more specific," he drawls.

"You've never been able to hold anyone's soullight in permanence like this before. How have you accomplished it with her?"

"Magic."

My jaw clenches so hard it creaks. "Tell me *how*!"

"I took a leaf out of your book, Nicky. Instead of stealing the soullight, I asked first."

"Then why haven't you done the same to win yourself words? Corporeality? Why start and stop with only her?"

"I tire of your questions." Enzo fakes a yawn. "And the dramatics are a little over the top, even for you."

Lola strains against my grasp. "Nic, please."

"I think we're done here, Lola. What about you?" Enzo saunters over.

"Let me talk to him, Enz." She meets my glare with one of her own. "Let me explain."

He scoffs. "Explain? You already mucked up everything. We're leaving."

"Don't talk to her like that," I snap.

He doesn't even look at me. Instead, he holds out his hand for her. "Time to go."

"Please." She grits her teeth. "Let me try."

"Enzo," I warn. "Touch her, and I'll—"

He barks a sharp laugh. "You honestly expect me to believe you'd actually hurt her? I know you far too well for that, big brother." He grabs her arm as she tries to wriggle away from him, pressing a piece of black voratium to her skin.

I slash my dagger toward him at the same instant she snaps, "No!"

They vanish as one, sending me slamming into the rock.

"Enzo!" I shout alongside her echo, whirling toward the water.

But there is no reply. Whether he pulled her through water or stone, she is gone, and so is he, and all I have left are my secrets.

I back up until my spine hits the side of my vault, then tip my head against it. I squeeze my eyes shut and pull out my radio. "Paol?" I say into the speaker.

The response comes through weak and broken. "Yes, sir?"

"Lock down every entrance. Neither my brother nor Astra Tremaine are to be permitted inside again. Got it?"

"Yes, sir."

I sigh, digging into the magic at my core, pushing the spell I've carried for so long—the spell that has kept my brother out for years—back into place.

Fences keep things out just as surely as they keep things in. And in this case, a fence would be better for everyone.

CHAPTER FORTY-SIX

LOLA

Enzo drags me through stone, through walls, through floors, through doors. I wrench against his grasp, desperate to break the contact. If only I could get back to Nic, if only I could explain, I could make this right, somehow, for both of them. For me.

But Enzo's grip is a vise, the voratium clasped between us an anchor, and as long as my corporeality flows into it, we are fused. I try to shout, but without vocal cords, I make no sound.

Fury burns through me, hot and ferocious, and a scream builds in my chest. Like chemicals under pressure, the tension of it mounts until I cannot see anything but my rage and I can't feel anything but Enzo's hand like a shackle.

And then we are outside, and he is still pulling me. Down the street, through traffic that whooshes through us like we are not there, around corners to where apartment buildings stack like blocks, crooked in the wind. The afternoon sky is dark as pitch as clouds gather, thick and heavy and violet, static sparking in the air to fan the flames of my anger.

It isn't until we plunge safely through the locked door of my apartment that Enzo finally releases his hold.

My body rushes back to me, and I round on him. "What the depths is wrong with you?"

Enzo's body is all rigid lines and jerky movements as he pulls his earrings and nose rings out of his pocket and shoves them in place. "I was saving your ass. Again."

"I told you no, and you ignored me!"

"We were finished."

"He wanted to listen. He *would have* listened."

"He wanted to hurt you."

My voice pitches higher. "You said yourself he wasn't going to!"

"Not physically. That's not his style. Emotional and mental manipulation, though? All bets are off there."

I huff a laugh. "That's rich, coming from you."

His eyes sharpen. "What's that supposed to mean?"

"You claim Nic lies to me, but of the two of you, he's the only one who never has!"

Enzo snaps a glowing hoop through his lip, then another and another, his eyes smoldering. "When have I ever lied to you?"

"When *haven't* you?!" I cry, my voice pitching higher.

"Never! I'm telling you; you can't trust him!"

"This isn't about him."

"It's entirely about him." He stalks up to me, jabbing the final bar through his brow. It glows deep emerald, accentuating the color of the inferno in his eyes. "He's made you think he cares, but he does not. He's tricked you into believing he's innocent, but his soul is as stained as they come."

I harden my jaw. "Why do you think he's been planting false leads for us all this time?"

"Because he's a sick bastard, that's why."

I take a deep breath, parsing through the memories Nic shared with me. All the times he did not want to go on heists with Enzo but felt he had to in order to keep his little brother safe.

"Have you ever thought," I say, "that maybe he's keeping you away from the moonshard to protect you?"

"To keep me cursed."

"He's just as cursed as you are."

"No, he isn't."

I stare at him, search his face for hints. There is not a tic in Enzo's jaw, not a flare of shame in our heart.

He truly doesn't know. Truly believes his brother the villain. Truly thinks Nic's willfully keeping the moonshard from him for selfish reasons only.

"What if he's trying to take care of you, the way he always has?" I ask, aching for him even as my rage still simmers hot. "What if you *need* to believe he cursed you and is keeping you captive out of cruelty?"

"Why would I need to believe that?" Enzo snaps.

"Because then you don't have to reckon with the fact that everything that happened that night was because of you."

He stares hard at me, a vein pulsing in his jaw.

"Nic was never the villain. You were," I say, and though my anger is still hot as wildfire, I ache for him and the hurt I know he's running from. "Nic didn't want to go, didn't even believe there was a moonshard to steal, but you wouldn't be dissuaded. So he risked his life to save you, and everything went wrong."

"My brother is a liar."

"Your brother is good."

He shakes his head hard. "No. You weren't there. You don't know. Whatever he told you, he twisted the story to make himself the hero."

I meet his glare. "What, like how you twisted the story of the night you found me?"

"What are you talking about?" He frowns. "I rescued you, and my brother's made you think I was the bad guy in that, too?"

Something balloons in me. A panic, a dread, a rage, swelling like a bomb ready to detonate. I'm running from it as hard as I can and also sprinting toward it, bracing for impact, terrified and yet desperate for it all at once.

I slip my hand into my purse and curl my fingers around the white die I've held on to for so long. I close my eyes as certainty fills me, first like a trickle, then like a flood.

But I do not call forth its magic. I don't need to.

My whole world shatters at once. A physical blow that pummels me in the chest, sending cracks spiderwebbing through every part of me. My body shakes violently, and my knees buckle.

"Lola?" Enzo reaches for me.

I slap his hand away. "You told me," I grind through my teeth, "that you *found* me. Happened upon my kidnapping by mistake. Fate, you called it." I pause, taking in a rattling breath. "But you orchestrated the whole damn thing, didn't you?"

"Your father was keeping you like a prisoner. I got you out. The how and the why are unimportant."

"*Unimportant?*" I shout in his face, jabbing a finger in his chest. "You told me my father did not care! You *felt* how that broke me. You watched me cry myself to sleep for months. That man loved me, and you told me no one did!"

"Your father is a killer and a criminal," Enzo says, voice even and quiet. "You're better off without him."

Tears sting in my eyes, and my voice quavers as I spit, "That was *my* call to make. He was *my* father. It was *my* life. *Mine.*"

Thunder growls outside. Rain slams the window. Neither of us moves, neither of us blinks. Our emotions war within us, anger battling anger, rage pounding against rage.

I drop my gaze deliberately to the pendant glowing purple through his shirt. "You stole my heart."

DEN OF LIARS

"You consented!"

"Was it really consent if I couldn't say no?"

His chest heaves, his guilt and pain twisting through my own, a tragic dance like none our hearts have ever done.

He rubs both hands across his face, eyes glassy and rimmed in red. "I have made mistakes. Horrible ones. But you have to understand I was *dying* inside." His voice is so quiet I almost can't hear it over the sound of the waves, but I feel each word as he says it like a pulse in my soul. "At first, you were just a tool, I'll admit that. Something I needed in order to feel alive. But then you were you, and we became us, and suddenly, you were more important than my curse. Suddenly, your friendship was the thing keeping me alive, not your heart."

A sob chokes through my throat.

"The stakes got too high," he bites out. "I was terrified you'd figure out what I'd done, afraid I'd lose you. So the lies built up. More and more until I didn't know how to claw my way out."

His turmoil licks the inside of my ribs, desperate like starving, pleading like thirst.

I close my eyes. "How do I know," I whisper, "that you're not still lying?"

His regret slices ice through my sternum as he cups a palm to my cheek. "I swear to you, Lollipop."

He's still trying to perform like the curtains aren't on fire. I jerk away from him. "The show's over. You're done."

"Lola . . ."

I shove past him, my hands trembling, a lump choking into my throat. "Please leave."

He follows me. "Come on . . ."

I whirl and cry, "I said *leave*!"

He halts. His throat bobs as he gives a single nod. "All right."

He pauses, as though waiting for me to change my mind, waiting for me to understand and let him have the benefit of the doubt, the way I've always done.

But I hold my ground as tears slide down my cheeks.

Finally, he shuffles to the door, but before he passes through it, he slides a hand into his jacket and pulls out Legrand's pocket watch. It winks in the storm-lit room, and he stares at it for a long moment. "I never deserved you," he whispers. "I think I knew it. You were too good a friend, too good a thief, and I lived in fear one day you'd figure that out." He sets the pocket watch on the small side table. "I should have made you a Tentacle long ago. You more than earned it."

I do not reply. I cannot.

With one final look back at me, he whispers, "I'm sorry." Then he dissolves through the door.

Sucking in a rattling breath, I stride to the window and shove it open. Rain lashes my face, and water speckles the lenses of my glasses as thunder heaves in the iron sky.

Everything hurts.

The sky strikes the sea in the distance with daggers of lightning, plunging deep and fast and hard. The sea roils, taking the pain, accepting it, welcoming it. And I wonder for a moment if maybe the sea was never as wicked as I've been told, either. Maybe it's spent eternity believing it deserves the pain. Maybe it loved the sky too much to ask why.

Enzo's words swirl around in my head, crashing alongside memories of him teaching me to pick locks and crack safes, scale buildings and lasso chimneys. Evenings we spent playing games, telling stories, imagining futures.

Until a few days ago, there was never a doubt in my mind about Enzo. He was my brother, my best friend, my confidant.

And yet.

In the days since I scaled a casino wall, stole a pocket watch, and signed a contract, I've seen a side of Enzo I never knew. One who threatens, who withdraws, who refuses to admit fault until he cannot get away from it. Who's willing to lie to keep me docile.

DEN OF LIARS

I gasp for air. What is there without Enzo, without this life we've built? Without his safety and his answers? Our shared goals?

My sobs are deep, so serrated they make no sound, so thick I cannot breathe. I sink to the floor and hug my arms around my chest as rain continues to hammer through the window, splattering against the chipped tile, soaking me to the skin. I curl my knees up like I can protect myself from the pain.

But I cannot.

It is everywhere.

And so I scream with the waves outside as Enzo's lies strike me like lightning. The sound of it is drowned out by the roar of the wind and the bark of the thunder and the thrash of my bleeding heart.

I hope Enzo feels this. Hope it carves him up, hope it hurts.

CHAPTER FORTY-SEVEN

LOLA

I lie in that puddle on the floor for an eternity. Afternoon wind slaps my skin as the storm recedes, and still I do not move. Eventually, my tears slow, leaving an ache in my throat and a fatigue that drags me into dreamless slumber.

When I finally awaken, night has fallen, and the sky is clear.

Numbly, I push to my feet and strip off my wet clothes. After a quick bath, I yank on a dry set of pants and a loose blouse, pull on a cardigan, and retrieve my purse of dice and chips. As I check through the contents, I notice the bracelet Enzo gave me the night of the Legrand heist, and my stomach wrenches. The voratium is dull and lightless, but I lift it out, squeezing my eyes shut.

I pretend for just a moment that I'm still the same girl who wore it a week ago, that he's the same boy who gave it to me, like a bracelet might put us back together. And even though I shouldn't, I slip it on and wish it made me feel better.

DEN OF LIARS

Sniffing, I pause at my door and glance down at Legrand's watch. It glows faintly, and I remember the way her hands felt grasping mine, the awkward hug, the gentle smiles. The way she made me feel loved and seen and appreciated, simply and wholly and without requirement.

I lift the watch from the table and smooth my palm over its glossy face. I don't know if it's her soullight, still flickering in the voratium, or if it's my own desperation, but a quiet calm filters through me, settling my nerves and slowing my pulse. Clutching it to my chest for comfort, I venture into the night.

I wander for a while, breathing in the clean, after-rain air. Horns blare and sirens warble in the distance as a gentle breeze lifts the hair from my neck.

I let my feet go, allow my body to take me where it wants, and soon I find myself at the sea. The pocket watch seems warmer here, and I kick off my shoes and track through the sand to the salty foam.

As I tread through the waves, the watch seems to hum, and there's the subtlest tug backward, like how Enzo's soullight would pull me sometimes, but much weaker. I frown, looking over my shoulder.

I pick out a figure just outside the Liar's Den half a mile up the shore. Pale silver hair shimmers in the diffused light, and long, knobby limbs drape over pointed knees.

The watch brought me to her, the soullight in it craving its home. Dr. Olivia Legrand.

Taking a deep breath of salt-stained air, I angle toward her. She turns her head when I approach, her gaze tracing the red rims of my puffy eyes. "Good evening."

"Hi," I say weakly.

"Care to join me?" She pats the sand next to her, and I plop down with a heavy sigh. "Why are you out here? Isn't the round-three party starting soon?"

"I've been kicked out," I croak.

"Kicked out? What did you do?"

"I messed up." I scrub my hands across my cheeks. "Lied to some people, stole from others."

"Ah. So generally all the ways people mess up in a casino."

I let out a strangled chuckle. "I need to apologize to you."

"What for?"

"It was me." I roll my head to meet her eye, holding out the watch. "I was the one who took this."

She stares at it for several seconds, then takes a shaky breath and lifts it gently out of my grasp. The tenderness with which she handles it makes guilt pang through me, and I blaze on. "I made this deal once. A foolhardy, desperate deal. I hoped your pocket watch would be enough to meet the terms, but it wasn't, so I entered the Liar's Dice Tournament to see—"

"You were one of the players?" she interrupts.

"Yes. I hoped I'd be able to win my freedom that way, but I failed. Then I found out my friend has been lying to me, and I don't know what to believe anymore."

She rubs her thumb over the face of the watch. "This friend of yours, they're the one you made the deal with?"

I nod. "He's all I've got. Or all I had, anyway."

"So what will you do?"

"I wish I knew."

She ponders. "Why not leave him behind?"

"I don't know how." I shake my head. "I've never lived on my own. As a child, my father and nursemaid gave me structure, gave me security. And then, once my friend and I made our deal, it was the same thing again. He kept me safe, provided what I needed, taught me to survive."

"Sounds like they kept you dependent. No wonder you're scared." She purses her lips, tucking the watch into her jacket. "I think the sooner you break free of your friend, the better."

I bury my face in my hands. "What if I'm wrong, though? Yes, he lied to me, but that was four years ago, and sure, he shouldn't have done what he did, but I understand why. He didn't know me then, and he was desperate."

Legrand listens quietly, digging her fingers into the sand.

"Stars know I've done horrible things to people and regretted it later." I meet her eye. "Like with you. Like with the Liar. What if I'm throwing away a good present and a promising future because of a messy past? What if he's right, and the Liar and his casino and everyone else have muddled my brain and turned this into a bigger deal than it is? Enzo warned me from the start that people would try to paint him as a villain."

She lets out a soft chuckle. "Dear, if anyone ever tells you to distrust everyone but them, they aren't interested in truth. Only control."

I groan, rubbing my hands over my face.

"I want to let you in on a little secret." She drops her voice to an almost-whisper. "None of us knows what we're doing. We're all making things up as we go. And we're all scared. Sure, it's simpler to build a house when you've got someone telling you where to lay every brick, but when it's finished, is that really your house?" She smiles faintly. "The beauty of living is in the discovery. Yes, we make mistakes, we get lost, we have our hearts broken a dozen times . . . but that's the only way to live with your eyes and your arms and your heart wide open." She presses a hand to my shoulder. "If you spend your life hiding from the monsters you think live in the dark, you'll miss the stars every single time."

"What about loyalty?" I whisper. "What about forgiveness?"

"What about truth?" she replies.

"Maybe it doesn't matter. We have a good life. I've been cared for and secure. I know who I am and how to be. I'm happy."

"Are you, though?" Legrand meets my eye. "Or have you been told you're happy for so long you've never stopped to ask yourself if you really are?"

"What if I get hurt?"

"Looks like you already did." Her cheeks wrinkle in a sad, comforting smile. And she isn't my father, doesn't look a thing like him, but something about the way she smooths a raindrop from my cheek with her thumb feels like those nights on the roof so long ago. "It's easier to stay where things feel safe and familiar, I know. But you are too smart to let someone else think for you."

I swallow, tears stinging at my eyes all over again. "Thank you."

"I'd better get back inside. My old bones don't take well to storms." She pats my shoulder. "I'll see you around, Astra."

"It's Lola, actually."

"Lola," she repeats with a smile.

"Before you go . . ." I take a deep breath. "Alzat Lopai . . . the friend I said you did surgery on?"

"The one who died." Her voice is soft.

"He wasn't real. It was my first challenge in the tournament." Shame heats my cheeks.

She lets out a long, slow breath. "I . . . I see . . ."

"I'm so sorry."

"I'm going to have to sit with that one a while," she says after a moment, pushing to her feet.

I nod. "I understand."

She gives my shoulder a squeeze. "Best of luck with your decision, Lola dear."

I watch her disappear up onto the veranda, then reach into my purse to run my hands over the dice within as though the magic that once made them glow might still be there. As though if I can find a trace of Nic inside them, he might tell me what I should do.

One of them feels different, colder and glassier than the others. I pull it out.

Lightning illuminates a glittering ebony die with a multicolor tempest inside.

DEN OF LIARS

"What . . . ?" I whisper, turning it over, rubbing a thumb along the silver-inscribed numbers on its faces. This is not one of the dice I used in the tournament. Where did it come from?

And then it dawns on me. This is the plain playing die I stole from Nic's room. Just like the key on Nic's pendant that lost its glamour when I went outside the perimeter of its magical boundary, so, too, did this die.

This is one of his secrets. Maybe even the one I've been seeking.

Instinct raises my hand to roll it. This is what I've wanted more than anything these past few years, isn't it? To find the answer Enzo craves?

But something stops me. Something faint, there in my chest, hidden beneath the tide of Enzo's betrayal.

Legrand's words fill my ears as though she's still here, repeating them to me once more. Do I really want what I've been told to want? Do I really think what I've been trained to think? Do I really feel what I've been conditioned to feel these past four years with Enzo's fears, his hopes, his dreams literally living inside me?

What do *I* want? What do *I* think? What do *I* feel?

So, though it feels like betrayal, I close my eyes and push aside Enzo's desperation, his shame, his hurt. Push it all to the back of my heart. And then I breathe.

Seagulls caw. Waves crash. Wind rumbles. A symphony of sound.

I stand. My arms arc over my head, rounded into place as I rise to my toes. I quiet the thief I've become. Dampen her worries, her devotion, her protests.

And I set the dancer in me free.

I twirl in the sand. I roll onto the balls of my feet and leap. And though the sodden earth drags and the wind lashes, I listen to each sensation. The fatigue in my limbs. The ache in my head. The hurt in my heart.

My whole life, I've been abiding by rules, hiding from dangers, being what my father and then Enzo needed me to be. But is this life my own, if I'm only building it exactly how I'm told? Is who I've become who I really am?

Who might I be without the structure of someone else's expectations?

Once that question surfaces, dozens tumble after it.

What if there's more to Nic's story than what Enzo has told me? What if there are reasons he wants the moonshard to stay hidden? What if I'd care about those reasons, too?

I could roll Nic's secret right now, yes, but secrets are meant to be shared, not stolen. Just like hearts. I betrayed his trust with my lies, but perhaps he'll still listen. Perhaps handing over the secret unrolled, showing him I did not give it to Enzo, will be enough to prove I'm no longer beholden to the Thief. That I'm sorry. That what happened between us was not just part of my plan to betray him.

That I want to be the one he can trust.

I turn toward the casino. My feet are heavy with sand, with doubts, with fear, but I lift them. One and then the other. And I cradle my pouch with Nic's secret, his key, the empty dice from the game, and the still-glowing white die nestled safe inside.

Maybe all of this isn't about getting my heart back from Enzo. Maybe my heart has been mine all along.

And maybe I am finally ready to choose how to give it.

No matter how much it hurts.

CHAPTER FORTY-EIGHT

LOLA

This time, when I approach the Liar's Den, I wear no armor, harbor no walls. Not like before, when the truths I believed were held together by threads so fragile questions could fray them, digging could stretch them, living could snap them.

Now Nic can throw his sharpest lies my way. The truth does not have to be protected. It simply is.

And the steadiness of that is stronger than any armor or any wall.

I slink along the street. Motorcars slosh past, sirens blare in the distance, and the music of the cabarets on either side tinkle faintly in the thick, wet air. I taste the salt of the sea on the wind, the cleanse of the rain, and the smoke of the city. And beyond that, a faint citrus washing in from the south. A scent like Father, a scent like home.

The gilded front entrance glimmers in the streetlights, and a pair of security guards stands on either side, quiet and watchful. I frown, glancing around. Have there always been security guards posted there?

Trying to act like I belong, I stride up to the doors.

As soon as I get close enough to recognize, both guards' hands go straight to their belts, yanking out their pistols and pointing them at my head.

"Astra Tremaine," one barks. "Stay where you are. Keep your hands where I can see them."

"Wh-what?" I stutter as the second guard pulls out a radio.

"Sergeant Paol, we've got her. Front entrance."

"Turn her away," comes the response.

My stomach twists, but I do not allow the fear to penetrate. I have nothing to hide from these people. Not anymore.

"What is all this about?" I ask sharply.

Neither replies.

"I need to talk to the Liar," I say, holding myself to my fullest height. "You can escort me to him, if you like. Search me. I have no weapons."

"Afraid that's not possible, miss. He's given us strict orders to keep you out."

"Keep me . . ." Frustration roils sticky in my blood. "He doesn't even want to talk to me first?"

The guards' glares are answer enough.

Sirens wail closer. Could Paol have telephoned the police? I lower one hand toward my purse. If I could reach one of my empty dice, I could use Enzo's magic.

"Keep your hands where we can see them!" one guard snaps, brandishing his pistol.

As I raise my arms, the empty voratium bracelet slides up my wrist. Focusing in on the feel of it, icy as lies against my skin, I throw a final defiant smile at the guards and shove my corporeality into one of the beads.

My body ripples into nothingness, and the guards start shouting, barreling for me.

I dive for the door, ready to pass through it like I've seen Enzo do a thousand times. But instead, I slam against it like I'm solid as stone.

DEN OF LIARS

Frowning, I move a few feet and press my palm to the wall. My fingers flicker through just enough to make it clear I am in fact noncorporeal, but then they hit a barrier like the air inside has turned to steel.

I shove my hand as hard as I can, and it passes a centimeter deeper before my whole body seizes. It's as though inside this wall is an intense illusion of the senses. Not a true wall, but one of magic so concrete my body shudders, jerking back involuntarily, an instinct so primal that fighting it is like trying to stop myself from vomiting when my stomach is already heaving.

Gasping, I grit my teeth and jam against it once more. My body convulses, stars exploding across my vision as pain and nausea slam through me, and before I can stop it, survival instinct wrenches me backward.

It seems that whatever barrier Nic had up to keep Enzo from entering the casino has been reerected since we left, and since I'm using Enzo's magic, I am barred as well.

I retreat, scanning the area. Another pair of guards comes around the corner, and the first ones yell at them to fan out to look for me.

I glance at my bracelet. The bead holding my corporeality glows faintly purple with soullight. I have no idea how much more of my corporeality it can hold, so I dash around the corner of the building, pausing at every door and window to check if I can pass through. I even try relinquishing my magic to break in the old-fashioned way, but everything is bolted tight, and with the guards searching for me, there's not nearly enough time to pick the locks.

I come to a stop at the back of the building, tipping my head up and counting the balconies to my suite. The doors are clearly latched closed, the windows dark, but movement flickers in Estelle's neighboring suite, the lights inside glowing yellow.

If I can get up to her balcony, perhaps she'll let me in.

My whole body aches with fatigue. I barely made the climb to the roof a few days ago, and I wasn't nearly as tired or as stiff as I am now.

Shouts come from the guards in the alleyway.

I slip the voratium beads into my palm and stalk forward, pressing my spine to the corner. As they come barreling past, I let my hand go corporeal so I can slam my bracelet against the back of one man's neck, sucking his strength out until he collapses.

The other guard swivels to see what happened to his companion just in time for me to press a second bead against his face until he topples.

Pulling their combined strength into my body, I leap at the wall and climb. After four years of scaling buildings and maneuvering up chimneys without magic, the thrill of darting up a sheer marble wall like this—floors in seconds—thrills me. I can't help it. I laugh.

Of course I've always known Enzo augments his abilities with the soullight he steals, but I never knew how much of a difference it made. How delicious it felt.

For four years, he's spoken as though his curse has little benefit, but it's clear that was another lie, too. Nic's magic may be flashy, but Enzo's is quieter, stealthier, fitting for a thief who works alone in the dark. But it is just as powerful, just as dangerous.

In minutes, I hoist myself onto Estelle's balcony, barely winded. The bead of my corporeality seems to finally have filled, because my body flickers back into solidity as I rap on the window.

She pulls open the door a crack and peers at me. Her eyebrows shoot to her hairline as recognition dawns on her face, and she yanks it all the way open. "Astra? Where the depths have you been? I've been searching for you all day."

"I got kicked out of the tournament," I say as she pulls me into her suite. "It's a long story. But first, what time is it?"

She nods at the clock on her mantel. "Just after midnight."

The third round has officially ended. Which means Nic is downstairs on the stage rolling dice and revealing secrets. Perhaps I can snag him when he retreats backstage, get him where the crowds won't see. That gives me only roughly thirty minutes to figure out how to reach him without being caught.

My eyes stray to an open suitcase on Estelle's bed, stuffed with clothes and cosmetics and shoes. Her wardrobe stands open; all that's left inside is an array of empty hangers.

"Are you leaving?" I ask, crossing to pick up a newspaper on the foot of the bed. It's not one I recognize, and it's open to an obituary page of an older gentleman. I flip to the front page. "*The Moraille Gazette*?"

Estelle folds the last few garments on her bed. "Yes, I've got to go north."

"Did you know this man?"

She shakes her head. "No."

"Then why—"

"I want to tell you, I really do," she says, "but it's a matter of life or death for someone I care about, and the secret isn't mine to share. If that ever changes, I promise I'll tell you."

I meet her eyes, and something softens inside me. She was the first one to see me—not the liability my father hid or the thief Enzo whittled. Something bigger. Stronger. Worth respecting. And though I still know little about her, her words are open and broad, her gaze like a pledge, a hope.

So I nod. "Okay, Estelle."

"Okay, Astra."

I swallow. "Lola."

Her brow furrows.

"Short for Magnolia," I say.

"That's a dangerous name to have in this city." She cocks her head. "St. James's daughter? The one who was murdered?"

"We faked that."

Her eyes widen. "There's a story there."

"There is."

"Does it happen to involve the Devious?"

"It does, in fact." I smile. "Do you have time to hear it? Because I need your help."

She checks the clock on the mantel again. "I need to leave in thirty minutes to catch my train, but if you keep it shorter than that . . ."

"I have one condition."

She smirks. "Oh, we have conditions on honesty, now?"

"Will you help me with a disguise?"

"A disguise, you say?" Her eyes sparkle. "What are careful allies for?"

CHAPTER FORTY-NINE

LOLA

Thirty minutes later, clad in a slim-cut silver gown that pools along the floor behind me like liquid metal, I check my reflection in the mirrored surface of the inside of the elevator doors. Estelle's precision with the cosmetics and finesse with my hair has completely transformed my face. Though we couldn't change my glasses, and I cannot really reliably go without them, she was able to round out my cheeks, plump up the end of my nose, straighten and lighten my hair, and alter the coloring of my eyes with her curious concoctions. It's still me, but less recognizably so. Enough that anyone who doesn't already know me won't look twice.

Now that I'm inside the casino, I'd likely be able to go noncorporeal if I needed to, but since I want to conserve as much of my raw voratium as I can, the disguise will be instrumental in getting me to Nic without his guards noticing.

The elevator settles on the first floor, and the doors slide open. I slip out, trying to channel some of Estelle's poise and confidence. She departed moments ago, and the ache of not knowing when I'll see her again is almost as sharp as the myriad of other pains in my heart.

I angle straight for the main gambling hall, but when I notice the open doors, my stomach sinks. I press forward, going up on tiptoe to squint over gamblers' heads to the empty stage, but Nic is nowhere to be seen.

I whirl, glimpsing a crowd of people filtering out another exit. Could they be following him?

Hiking up my skirt, I dash after them, joining the throng as they file into an elevator in smaller groups. I do my best to look like I know what's going on and lean casually against the wall, angling my ear toward the nearest conversation.

"I was here last year," one man dressed head-to-toe in glittering fish scales is saying. "It's in an amphitheater on the top floor, and you get to look down onto the main stage to watch the whole game. It'll be over in an hour, at the most."

The elevator doors slide open again, and I shuffle inside with the next group. My stomach lurches to my throat as the elevator climbs to the fifteenth floor, and it does not settle even after we step out onto the landing and make our way along what looks to be a glass bridge over a courtyard to a separate section of the casino, one barred by several sets of guards.

I try to look relaxed as I pass the first pair. They glance my way but don't seem to recognize me, continuing their conversation without pause. Once around the corner, another pair searches each member for weapons, patting down arms and legs and checking inside purses. Using one of the voratium beads at my wrist, I render my pouch of dice incorporeal, and they don't look twice at me, ushering me through.

We approach another elevator set into a column that I remember from my investigations earlier this week. It should lead us to several performing areas on higher floors, exclusive and ritzy and barred to the general public. Another pair of guards stands at the entrance to the lift, collecting something from each patron as they enter.

I crane my neck to see what it is, nerves jangling.

Tickets.

I look around frantically and spot one sticking out of the back pocket of the man next to me. Using the oldest trick in Enzo's book, I stumble into him.

"Oh, I am so sorry," I say as I slip my hand into his pocket.

He grumbles but does not seem to notice my theft.

I turn just in time to reach the guard.

"Ticket," he drones dully, eyes flicking to my face as he holds out his hand.

I drop the ticket into his palm.

"Go ahead," he says, and I take a step forward. But then he pauses, sticking out his arm. "Wait."

My heart pumps into my throat. "Is there a problem, sir?" I ask.

He opens his palm again, eyes sharpening on the paper. "What is this?" he grunts. "'Ralton Lee'?"

The blood rushes out of my face. I didn't realize the tickets had names on them.

"I don't know what you mean?" I try to keep from fidgeting as adrenaline bolts through me.

He looks me up and down once. Twice.

"Hey, Garvel," he barks at the other guard. "What color was the Tremaine girl's hair supposed to be?"

"Dark brown," comes the response.

"I'm sorry, what's the problem, sir?" I ask, trying to keep my voice light and airy.

He scrutinizes my face. "What's your name, ma'am? Are you Astra Tremaine?"

"No, sir." I manage a chuckle. "My name is Claire Lowell."

His hand strays to a tie tack on his lapel, and I realize with horror that it's a glowing white shard of voratium, exactly the same color as the die I've been keeping since round one.

The one that senses lies.

As soon as his fingers brush the surface, his jaw hardens, and he goes for the pistol at his belt.

Before he can get it out, I swing a leg around, hooking him behind the knees. He topples, and I plant my foot into the small of his back and kick him into the crowd behind me. I blaze into the elevator, shoving a couple out of my way so hard they go sprawling. "Sorry!" I cry, jabbing the button to force the doors closed.

"Stop!" The second guard runs for me, but the doors snick shut just in time.

I sink against the wall, panting as the elevator rises.

But before it goes even half a floor up, one of the passengers jams the emergency button. "Who are you?" he shouts at me.

"Why are they after you?" another cries.

The elevator jolts, and alarm bells ring. The other passengers shuffle, muttering among themselves, scrutinizing me with fearful or downright contemptuous eyes.

Before I can reply, the elevator drops back to the level we just came from, and the doors screech open.

"All right, everybody against the wall!" the guard I kicked bellows, pointing his pistol into the crowd. "Arms up!"

I snatch a bottle of gin out of the hands of an old man nearby and dart for the security guards, walloping one and then the other so hard they topple and their weapons fling out of their grips. The other passengers scream as the bottle shatters against the second man's shoulder, spraying clear liquid everywhere.

"Sorry about that." I grab the man who was holding the gin. He lets out a panicked squeal as I shove him hard at the guards, pummeling them backward into the hallway. I scan the ceiling, then jab a finger at a young man around my age staring at me like I'm some kind of wild bull. "You, give me a boost or I'll"—I try to come up with a suitable threat, but nothing springs to mind—"punch you in the face?"

He raises his fists like he's ready to duke it out, and I almost laugh. He's not even putting his thumbs in the right spots. "I apologize for this," I say as I wind up and land a hard kick to his groin.

Yowling, he doubles over, and I plant my foot on his back, using it to launch myself at the ceiling, shoving the nearest tile up and hoisting myself through.

"Stop her!" the guard shouts as he rights himself, wiping gin out of his eyes.

I scramble out of reach before he can swipe at my dangling legs.

He retrieves his pistol and aims it at me through the opening. "Stop, or I'll shoot!"

I kick the ceiling tile back in place. Quelling the thunder in my heart, I peer around for a way up.

Cables run up from every corner, and I wrap my hands around one, lodging my feet against the wall. I climb, siphoning what's left of the strength in my bracelet. I just need to get to the next floor, then I can pry open the doors and get out of here before the elevator moves.

But when I reach them, shouts echo from the other side. "Use this! Get it open!"

A metal tool jabs into the shaft.

Swearing, I pull myself above the opening and wait for the guards to crank it wide. Three of them stick their heads into the shaft, looking downward. "You see her?" one asks.

I swing down, slamming into them, sending all four of us sprawling onto the tile in the hallway. One's gun goes off, shattering a nearby vase, and I take off running for the door to the stairwell.

Guards spill out to meet me.

"Come *on*." I slam to the ground and roll behind a statue as bullets scream past my head, scanning the area for an escape. My eyes land on a green door that looks familiar somehow. Gold writing on the paint winks at me. DRESSING ROOM.

This is where I came during the Legrand heist.

The guards hurtle toward me. With a cry, I dive across the hall into the dressing room, slamming the door shut as bodies hit the other side. Gasping, I shove a nearby bureau in front of it, then barrel past a group of shrieking dancers to the changing room where I went the first night.

Pushing a chair over to the newly repaired vent, I locate hairpins and tweezers on a nearby cosmetic table and get to work unscrewing the bolts. Soon, the vent comes free, and I hoist myself through, propping my back against one side and my feet against the other just as I did last time.

If what the people in the elevator said is correct, then I need to climb eleven levels. With the remaining magic in my bracelet, I just might make it. And if I can do so before the guards discover where I've gone, I might stand a chance of finding Nic.

My muscles scream and my lungs burn, but I focus inward, on the steady *thump thump thump* of my heartbeat. Enzo's hurt still simmers there, but it's drowned out by my own determination.

Finally, I reach the twenty-sixth floor. My stolen strength has run out completely, and my legs and arms are quaking with fatigue, but I muster up every ounce of stamina I have to slam my fist against the grate. It takes several tries, but soon the slats bow inward, and I'm able to fit my hand and wrist through to unscrew the bolts and spill into an empty hallway.

Wheezing, I sit against the wall. A familiar voice murmurs nearby.

Taking care to keep my breathing as quiet as possible, I crawl on all fours and chance a glance around the corner.

Ostena Vesnes speaks to what looks like Nic's head guard next to the only door in the hallway, one crafted of glistening obsidian. A silver handle juts out, shaped like a massive spoon instead of a knob.

DEN OF LIARS

"So glad you could join us, Ms. Vesnes," the guard murmurs. "Please, offer your leftover dice from the earlier rounds to the door. They will be your ticket into the final game."

"Thank you," Ostena says, and she digs into her pocket, producing a handful of glittering voratium. It drops into the bowl of the spoon-like door handle with a sound like plats pouring out of a slot machine.

When the door opens, curling bluish-violet smoke twists into the hallway, scintillating with dust that looks strikingly like the stardust in Nic's pores. She scoops her dice back out and slips into the dark beyond, letting the door click shut behind her.

I press my back to the wall. How am I going to get past the guard? I search around me for something to use, but a voice makes me jump.

"Ms. Tremaine."

I whirl. The guard stands before me, arms crossed over his chest.

"Oh, um . . . hi." My thoughts go unbidden to the last time he caught me unawares—with Nic's mouth on my neck and his hand skating up my thigh—and my cheeks burn.

"You're a slippery one, aren't you?" He raises a slender black eyebrow, hand drifting to the radio at his belt. "I'm afraid I'm going to have to ask you to leave."

"It's Paol, right?"

He gives a tight-lipped nod. "It is."

"I need you to let me through that door. Please."

He unclips the radio. "I've got orders."

I sigh, gritting my teeth. A thousand lies spring up. Excuses, reasons, stories. I just need something to get him to help me. But as his deep brown eyes search mine, I know what I need to do this time.

Tell the truth.

"I want to talk to the Liar," I say.

Paol's thumb pauses on the radio button. "If he wanted to talk to you, he wouldn't have given orders to have you barred from entering the casino."

"He doesn't want to, I know, but . . ." I mop a hand over my face. "I need him. And he needs me."

Paol frowns, gaze trailing all over my face as though trying to read me.

"There's something going on here that's bigger than us," I press on, "bigger than this game, bigger than even this casino. But in order to find out what it is, I need to get through that door. Please."

He glances at his radio, then back to me. "Are you . . . like him?"

"I'm not sure," I say, voice small.

He purses his lips. "He's been different this week."

"Different . . . good?"

"It's like he was sleeping before. And now he's not." Paol grimaces, running a hand through his silky black hair. "Ah, blast. He's going to fire me if I do this, you know that, right?"

"He won't." I shake my head. "You know him. He'll listen. He'll understand."

Paol sucks in his cheeks, then shakes his head. "Ugh. Fine. But if you break him again"—he meets my eyes with an intensity I feel to my core—"I swear to the gods, I will hunt you down."

"I'll do my best," I croak, wishing I could promise him more.

That seems to be enough for him, though, because he jams his radio into his belt and stalks to the glittering door. I follow, pulling out my white die.

"Thank you," I say, and drop the die into the basin. A latch inside the door slides back. Retrieving the die, I grasp the handle. "Here goes nothing."

But it doesn't budge.

I rattle it. Still, it does not move.

"It unlocked!" I growl. "I heard it unlock!"

Paol frowns, jiggling the handle himself. "Do you think it knows you're not in the game anymore? That your secret was already revealed?"

Cursing, I drop the die into my purse, where it knocks against the empty dice I used in the earlier rounds. I pull one out, glaring at it, and press it to my chest. "Want a secret?" I hiss through my teeth. "You can have any damn secret you like." An angry lump rises in my throat. "I will bargain all of them. Every memory, every feeling, every dream." Tears burn across my vision. "Just let me *in*."

Though Enzo's magic is not the Liar's, I beg the die to respond to me, beg it to take my secrets.

A flicker of ice trickles into my palm. Just a spark, and then nothing.

Frowning, I pull it away from my chest and open my fingers, squinting at the die. It still looks just as black and dull and empty as before.

I hold it out for Paol. "Do you see anything?"

He frowns. "Should I?"

I lift it to my chest once more, pressing it to the skin over my heart. Closing my eyes, I focus on the feeling of it, the glassy texture, its cool touch.

Nothing happens.

I squeeze it even harder against my sternum. I felt something. I know I did.

And then, *there*. A tiny shard, a slice of cold, a flash and gone. Far away, the way the magic felt when I was trying to create that telegram illusion with Enzo. As though something's damming it up. Like when I was in that hallway, desperate for Nic not to see me, and I was able to pull, pull, pull the magic from somewhere simultaneously outside of me and within.

But different. Like secrets instead of strength. Whispers instead of wildness.

I grasp hard on that tiny flicker with all the mental energy I have left and *yank*.

Frigid magic rushes through me, so hard and so fast I totter backward, crying out. Multicolor light blooms on the inside of my eyelids, refracting like diamonds across my vision as the flow rushes colder,

colder, colder until it burns, shards like daggers along the insides of my veins.

Screams echo in my ears for several seconds before I realize they are my own.

Lights and sounds and colors and whispers flurry around me, a storm of faces and places, and I recognize every single one. Father. Orange trees and summer breezes. Worn-out pointe shoes. Textbooks and lessons. Astley's face in the dark. Terror, blood, tears. Enzo's laughter, his embrace, his gentle presence as familiar as breathing. Nic's amethyst eye winking like a beacon, the press of his lips, the echo of his pain. Love and hate, dreams and nightmares, everything spooling out like threads in a tapestry of brilliant light.

Estelle's voice is like birdsong. *Why did the Thief save you, though? Why you, and no one else?*

Nic's is like a storm. *My brother does not meddle in anyone's affairs unless he feels like he needs to. What about you made you worth the risk?*

Legrand's is like a lullaby. *If you spend your life hiding from the monsters you think live in the dark, you'll miss the stars every single time.*

Whatever I'm doing now, whatever this magic is . . . *this* is why Enzo chose me, why Nic couldn't stay away from me, why I've become so tangled in their magic and their deceit.

It's not only Enzo's magic I can wield. Somehow, I'm wielding *Nic's*, too.

As that realization hits me, a thread blazes out from my heart to braid among the others, making them all tremble.

Some secrets are intricate tapestries impossible to disentangle. But when you do, the world unravels.

This is the secret the door wants, the secret Nic craves, the secret Enzo has guarded since he whisked me into a new life.

I am not just a liar, not just a thief, not just a criminal's daughter.

I am something *more*. Something that can wield both brothers' magic . . . and maybe even others'. And though I do not know what that makes me—whether I am starblessed or seaspawn or something else entirely—I know enough to recognize how valuable, how dangerous this truth is.

I mentally grasp the secret's glowing thread and wind it toward the piece of metal at my chest. It drizzles downward, coiling like a snake into the voratium's heart, pulsing with frigid life.

And then the tapestry vanishes, the light winks out, and I stumble forward, catching myself against the door.

Paol presses a hand to my shoulder. "Astra? Are you all right?"

"Yes," I whisper, holding out my palm, where the die blazes violet and scintillating. I tip my hand, and the secret drops into the basin.

The door swings wide, and darkness swallows me whole.

CHAPTER FIFTY

LOLA

Light flickers ahead, winking along the curling stardust. As I stride forward, my steps echo from close around me, like I'm in some kind of tunnel. Nic's voice filters through the air around me, raising goose bumps on my arms.

My stomach winds tighter with every step. It's not like I'll be able to talk to him now while he's in front of hundreds of spectators, maybe even thousands, but I cannot very well wait until after things are over. He's made it clear he doesn't want to see me.

My mind buzzes, but I press forward, clutching the glittering die with my secret inside to light the way.

Finally, the outline of the end of the tunnel sharpens. Taking a deep breath, I plunge out into the open.

Lights glitter from every side. The floor beneath my feet is an ebony mirror reflecting a galaxy of diamonds above my head. Spectators watch from every side, though they are shrouded in shadow; the only indication they are there is their quiet whispers and hushed movements.

At the center of the amphitheater stage stands a table that looks as though the floor spouted a cascade of glass. Four people stand around it. I recognize Ostena's silver-blond hair immediately, and the two people on either side of her seem vaguely familiar—they must be the other players that made it through to the finale.

And then there's Nic. A deep turquoise tuxedo with glittering black swirls stitched into the fabric stretches taut and snug over his broad shoulders, accented by a silky black shirt and matching blue cravat. His fedora is the same shade with a black rim, and as always, it's tipped just so on his head. His cuff links glitter like stars as he gestures to the crowd.

"—has been a game of magic and spectacle," he's saying, "but this fourth and final—" His eyes catch on me, and the words die in his throat. He blinks once. Twice.

Murmurs erupt among the audience, but I keep my gaze on Nic, squaring my shoulders, holding my head high. The other tournament players glance back at me, and Ostena frowns, as though trying to place my face.

"It appears we have a little thief in our midst," Nic says quietly, and though his mouth curves in that showman's cunning smile, there is a sharpness in his expression. A frigidity.

"Hello, Your Royal Liar-ness." I feign a mock curtsy.

His smile fades, and a few snickers ripple through the crowd.

"How did you get in?" He catches someone's eye behind me and gives a sharp nod. "Take her away."

A guard approaches.

"Wait," I say quickly. "I need to talk to you."

"There is a game happening." He spreads his hands to the audience. "And everyone here is eager to get on with it."

"But," I blurt, mind catching desperately on a foolhardy idea, "I'm one of the players."

The Liar does not pause. "You failed your round-three challenge."

"I did not fail round three. I still had a die left."

"Your mark didn't believe your lie," Nic says, waving a dismissive hand.

"Actually, he did," I snap. "But then you punched him in the face."

Whispers explode around the room, and Nic's mouth thins.

"Even then," I say, "I might have salvaged it, except for the fact that you rudely disqualified me without cause."

"Without cause?" He stalks toward me. "You broke into my vault!"

Gasps filter through the crowd.

"Nowhere in the tournament agreement did it say I was not allowed to break into your vault."

He jabs a finger at me. "That sort of thing absolutely goes without saying."

I jab a finger right back at him. "You breached your own damn contract."

He gestures at his security guard. "Take her to Holding."

"I wonder," I say, raising my voice so it will carry over the crowd, "how the Liar's Den will fare when people hear its owner does not honor his own contracts? That the House stacks its decks against its players?"

The guard pauses at my elbow but doesn't grab me.

Nic stiffens, his glare intensifying. "You stole from me, lied to me, and now you threaten me?" His eyes glitter. "A thief *and* a fool."

"I stole from you. Meant to do it again. And I lied to you, yes," I say, meeting his glower with one of my own. "I made you trust me when I did not deserve it. But that doesn't mean that everything that happened between us was a lie."

More whispers spatter like rain through the crowd. Because, if anything, the Liar's Dice Tournament is all about spectacle, and we are certainly delivering that tonight.

Nic's lips thin. "A secret was required to play in the tournament. Yours was revealed."

I close the distance between us, holding out my hand. "I bargained a new one."

He frowns, plucking the purple die from my palm and inspecting it. "You . . . how?"

"Does it matter how?"

"You can't just bargain any secret." His eyes narrow. "It's supposed to be a valuable one."

"It is." I meet his glare. "Or can't you tell?"

He frowns, nostrils flaring.

"What do you all think?" I cry, turning to face the crowd. "Should he let me play?"

They stamp their feet, holler, cheer, clap.

I turn back to Nic. "Seems unanimous to me."

He considers me for a moment, then his mouth slants in a sideways grin. "Very well." He pockets my secret. "Join us at the table."

"But—" Ostena protests.

"That's hardly fair," another man blurts, but Nic holds up a hand.

"The Liar's Den upholds its contracts," he says, retaking his place at the head of the table as I slide in next to Ostena.

She glares sideways at me, arms crossed, and I give her a sweet smile. All her attempts to sabotage me, and yet here I am.

"Let us continue," Nic says, his voice taking on its theatrical musicality once more. "Up until now, this game has been one of magic and spectacle, but this round will be a test without tricks and without glamour. It hearkens back to games played on board ships under the stars on distant waters." He gestures to his guard, who brings forward four cups and a bag, which Nic upends over the table. Deep blue dice roll out, silver markings glinting. "An old-fashioned game of Liar's Dice."

He continues, explaining the mechanics of the game, one I'm very familiar with. My father worked with many pirates over the years and often played it with me during his visits when we tired of Solstice. Players roll their dice inside their cups and, based only on what they see in their own hands, must make wagers on what the entire table's dice have rolled.

Nic finishes up his explanation of the rules and turns to the player nearest him. "Your remaining dice from the other rounds, please, sir?"

The man holds out four glittering dice, and Nic exchanges them for four of his playing ones.

I open my purse and peer inside. There's only the white one I never used that's still glowing. Not great odds.

I glance at the empty ones.

What if . . . ?

As Nic exchanges the next man's dice, I dip my hand into my purse and curl my fingers around one, closing my eyes. I used Nic's magic to put my secret in a die to get through the door, which means maybe I could fill these myself.

Squeezing the metal in my palm, I reach into it for the ice I've sensed there before. It's distant, but I know it's in there, and once I grasp it, I imagine the sensation of visual illusion and pull on it hard. The magic ripples through me, burning like frostbite. When I open my eyes, the die glows a bright cerulean.

A thrill dances along my spine. Yes, that will do quite nicely.

I manage to fill four more dice before Nic finally turns to me. "Your dice?" He holds out his hand.

With a satisfied smile, I drop the six glowing game pieces into his palm.

He stares at them for a second, then his gaze darts to my face. "Where did you . . . ?" Then, as though remembering I'm a thief and deciding he doesn't have it in him to care anymore, he shakes his head, swiping the glowing dice from my grasp and replacing them with a set of six plain dice.

"And with that, let the final round of the Liar's Dice Tournament commence!" Nic cries before sweeping to face us. "May guile guard your secrets, dear players." He winks, and the stars above us spark like fireworks. The crowd cheers, a thunderous sound loud enough to rattle my bones.

The game progresses quickly and is more intense than any I ever played against my father. With every passing round, we rattle our dice in our cups, slamming them down as one on the tabletop. I watch each player's face carefully for tells, but they're all expressionless. Careful. Clever.

Nic plays the effortless showman and charismatic dealer, announcing bids to the crowd. Cameras flash, and every time a player loses a die, cheers and boos ring out like cacophonous music. The betting rings seem to be in full swing in one section, where gambles climb as each round passes. I try to keep myself from looking at the pot on my own head as it grows.

Though Nic moves around the stage like a dancer, winking at audience members and casting his charms over the masses as always, I feel his focus on my every move, my every breath, and though he never even approaches me, the sensation of his body hovering warm behind me makes me wonder if he's really there and if the man flashing his debonair smile to the crowd is actually an illusion.

By the time the first player is eliminated—one of the men whom I do not know—I've only lost one die. It takes just ten minutes after that for the second player to turn in his final die. When he is banished from the table, shrieks peal from the betting rings. It seems several people had a lot of money riding on him.

I flash a smile at Ostena. "Only the two of us left," I say.

She sniffs. "Appears so."

"Who are you?" I ask as we rattle our dice and slam down the cups.

"I am this year's winner," she replies coldly. "No matter the cost." She tips her cup to peek at her own dice before raising her gaze to meet mine. "Your bid."

As the turns progress and the bids rise, my nerves buzz under my skin. If I lose, I'll be sent out alongside the other eliminated players and likely won't get a chance to talk to Nic. Winning would make having me arrested for trespassing or taken off the premises very difficult, as I know from reading newspapers and magazines from previous years that the press likes to sit the Liar and his winner down together to answer questions for all the articles and puff pieces they'll be putting out in the coming weeks. Surely, somewhere in between all of that, I'll be able to get Nic to a place where I can talk to him, hand over his secret, and prove to him he really can trust me. Convince him I'm sorry.

But Ostena is an exceptional liar. She doesn't bare a single hint on her face, and I lose three dice before she loses another, bringing her total down to five. As the number of dice on the table reduces, it's getting harder and harder to bluff, especially when she has more of the total under her cup.

Another round, and I'm down to my last die.

My gaze snags on Nic. He's twisting the ring on his finger around and around and around, its snake-eye gem catching the light like a wink.

In order to win, I need to be able to call all of Ostena's bluffs. Perhaps I could channel some of his magic, that magic I feared for so long. The magic that helps me sense when I'm being lied to.

Curling my fingers around the voratium of my bracelet, I draw in the ice once more, this time channeling into it what I sensed the moment I knew Enzo was deceiving me. The despair, the certainty, the hurt, the hope. And then, as Ostena makes her bid, I keep my hand there, where the magic burns.

I know the instant she lies by the way the air changes, the way her secrets seem to fill it with an aroma I cannot pinpoint but that smells exactly the way my heart felt just before it broke.

I call her bluff, and she loses her die. And then her next, and her next, and her next.

Soon, we are one-to-one, and the entire room holds its breath.

DEN OF LIARS

She glares hard at me as we roll our dice and slam down our cups, the sound so much louder than before.

But when she makes her bid—"One three!"—my hand slips, and my bracelet drops to the floor. My gut twists. If I bend to retrieve it, someone in the audience might catch on. Or Nic might. None of the beads glow, but if he suspects I can channel his magic through them . . . Swallowing, I meet Ostena's gaze, search her expression, the rigid lines of her neck and shoulders, the white-knuckled grip she has on her cup.

And behind her, Nic watches me, his scar sparkling like a galaxy.

I'm pretty sure she's lying. By the set of her mouth and the crease near her eyes, she looks exactly like she did every other time I successfully called her bluff. But what if I'm wrong?

I take a deep breath. I didn't need magic to tell me Enzo was lying. Maybe I don't need it now, either.

"You're bluffing," I whisper.

"What was that?" Nic asks.

I clear my voice and speak loud enough for everyone in the amphitheater to hear. "You're bluffing!"

Ostena's jaw hardens, nostrils flare. Then she raises her cup.

A five. She *was* bluffing. The wave of relief that crashes through me is so sharp and quick I have to brace myself on the table to keep from toppling.

The audience erupts. Cameras flash. Nic's eyes meet mine.

"Esteemed friends, lawless foes, gentlefolk, and ne'er-do-wells!" His voice booms against every wall as he raises his hand to me. "Give a warm round of applause to the winner of this year's Liar's Dice Tournament!"

CHAPTER FIFTY-ONE

LOLA

The stars flare like spotlights, swiveling around a hundred directions before snapping onto Nic as one, illuminating his spread arms, his iconic tuxedo, his dashing grin. For a moment, I'm back in the instant I first glimpsed him downstairs. And, just like last time, when his eyes meet mine, I cannot breathe.

"But first, there remain three eliminations." He holds out his hands, where a silver platter with three glittering dice unfurls into view.

He plucks up Ostena's first—a silver one rippling with light. Her jaw flexes as she watches him wrap his palm around it and close his eyes.

The room holds its breath.

His mouth twists as he sees the secret's contents, and anticipation builds in my stomach. Will I finally see what she's been so keen to keep hidden? Will her secret reveal why she's tried so hard to sabotage me specifically?

DEN OF LIARS

But when the Liar opens his eyes, a mask slides into place, hiding from me whatever he's feeling.

"This will keep nicely in my vault," he says, glamoured eyes glittering.

Disappointment sinks in me, increasing my curiosity as several audience members hiss.

"Ostena Vesnes. You have gambled, you have lied, and you have been eliminated. Goodbye."

Ostena's shoulders sag, perhaps with relief, as she rises to her feet. Casting one more hateful look my way, she stalks to the tunnel and disappears into the dark.

I track Nic's hand as he drops her secret into his pocket. What I wouldn't give to know the contents of that secret, see what made him need a stronger mask when he viewed it. But I stay in my place, tamping down my curiosity.

Ostena is not important. Not right now.

Boos echo from the betting rings, but Nic appeases them by rolling the dice of the other two eliminated players. The secrets are juicy. One involving an affair among Moratin Salazar's ranks, and the other a financial scheme at the Bank of Aethera.

Nic seems unperturbed. Relaxed, even. Every toss of the die is a show, every smile self-possessed, every movement an illusion.

Or is it?

Does he care for me like he seemed to before? Was everything he said as real as it appeared? Every kiss as sincere as it felt? Or could it all have been just as much a glamour as the show he's putting on now?

Is he the Liar? Villainous? Unfeeling and calculating?

Or is he Nic? Quiet? Broken and cursed?

The Liar would never trust me, but Nic might, and as the show progresses, I cling to the certainty of who I know he is. Who he has to be.

"And now. The winner." His gaze locks on mine, and my breath unspools like it's being whisked out of me and there's no more air in the world. The audience roars as a spotlight finds me. Whistles and shouts echo, and a thousand pairs of eyes follow my trek across the stage. My heart gallops, and I wonder distantly whether Enzo feels it. Whether he knows why, whether he cares.

Nic holds out a velvet box. "Your prize, miss." His voice is formal, as though it's never whispered to me in the dark. His smile distant, as though he's never pressed it to mine.

"Thank you, Your Royal Liar-ness," I say with a saccharine smile, accepting the Unbreakable Lie.

He holds out a hand to shake, and when I take it, he pulls me in close.

"Be careful of the deception you sow with that," he breathes against my ear in a way that sends warmth pooling straight to my toes, "for it cannot be undone."

Too quickly, he withdraws, turning us in a slow circle to view every member of the audience, raising our clasped hands above our heads, and swinging low into a bow once we've made our circuit. I follow suit, clinging to his fingers, ready to pull him through the tunnel to somewhere private as soon as the spectacle is over. I don't know what I will say, I only know I have to try.

The lights wink out when the applause reaches its peak, and Nic tries to yank away, but I grasp hard. Even when his shadow flickers to nothing, even when the sensation of his hand in mine vanishes, I do not loosen my hold.

"I need to talk to you," I say. "And I'm not leaving until I do." Then I drag him to the tunnel. There's a resistance to the air between my fingers, but I only squeeze tighter until finally he gives up trying to magic me into thinking he's not there.

When we get to the end of the hall, cloaked in stardusted shadow next to that magical door, I pull him to face me. His gaze settles on mine, unreadable and cold in a way I've never seen it before. "You," he says, stepping in close so I can smell his cologne, "and my brother can search high and you can search low. You can scour the world to the ends of the horizons. You can dismantle this casino brick by brick, but you will never get your hands on my secret, and you will never find that moonshard."

"That's not why I—"

"Now," Nic says, "if you'll excuse me, there are about a thousand things that need attending to."

"Listen to me, stars damn it!" I cry as he stalks back toward the amphitheater.

He does not so much as pause.

"I didn't come here to try to find your secret or the moonshard," I snap, grasping his elbow. "I came to apologize!"

He turns. "And what makes you think I'd accept any sort of apology from you?"

"I lied to you, and in a way I shouldn't have." I step closer, wishing he could feel my guilt the way Enzo would. "What I did was manipulative. I used your emotions to get you to trust me, weaponized your own secrets and your own shame for my ends. I knew what I was doing would hurt you, and I did it anyway. And no matter how much I hated myself as I was doing it, I should have realized you were right."

"Right about what?" he asks, voice hushed, face unreadable.

"That lying is violence," I say. "Even when the liar thinks the victim needs it, even if they think they're helping, even if they're doing so with the intent to save the whole damn world."

His throat bobs, but his expression is stone. He doesn't even blink.

"I once accused you of thinking yourself a god," I go on, voice quavering, "when really, I was the one who thought myself powerful enough to know what Enzo needed, what Legrand needed, what Estelle needed, and what you needed. I thought I was protecting everyone." I hold his stare as tears flood my vision. "Then I had the audacity to call you a villain for liberating people from their shackles and chains, and

I can never, ever express to you how sorry I am for being so cruel and so utterly wrong."

He nods, jaw working, and slips his elbow out of my grasp. "Thank you for saying that."

"Please. I have questions."

"Trust is earned, little thief, as are secrets."

"But you have questions, too," I say. "You want to know what's so special about me. Why I'm different from the others Enzo has stolen from."

He doesn't reply. But he also doesn't leave.

"I know you don't owe me anything. Not after what I did." I suck in a slow, shaky breath. "I shouldn't have deceived you. But I was under the impression that I needed your secret in order to be free."

"And now?" His voice is measured.

"And now . . . well, that's not the whole story, is it?"

He stares at me for several long seconds, his nostrils flaring, and I wonder what my truths smell like to him, if they are as fragrant and tantalizing as the lies I told him when he kissed me.

"I want to know why you keep the moonshard's location a secret," I try. "Enzo told me you stole it, used it to curse him and bestow yourself with powers. But you are cursed, too. And"—my voice cracks—"he lied to me, and I don't know how far that deception goes. How many of the things I think are facts . . . aren't."

He cannot answer. But he wants to. I see it in the way his eyelashes flutter, the way his hands clench.

"So I asked myself why, if living with this curse is so difficult for you, do you continue to guard that shard? What would really happen if Enzo found it?"

Nic tips my head with a finger on my chin. I meet his eyes unblinking and unafraid. His gaze trails across the planes of my face as though he's searching for something.

"You wield your tongue well, little thief," he whispers in a way that makes me tremble, and the words transport me back to the first time he spoke them, the night I agreed to his game. The words he said next echo through my mind alongside the ones he speaks now. "But do not make the mistake of thinking that because you are quick with words that you are clever enough to outsmart the House. You will lose, in the end."

"Breathe in deep, Donnic Sinclair," I say. "You know I have not spoken a single lie."

"Do I?" he asks, stony. "Because we've already established that you can lie to me undetected."

"Fine. You want lies? I'll give you lies," I snap. "I don't mean a single thing I just said. All of it was exactly what you think it was—twisted manipulation, just like before." He stares at me, and I know he can sense the deceit, know he sees what I'm doing, and it emboldens me. I lift a hand to his jaw. "I came all this way because I still want to hurt you. Betray you. Destroy you." I push up on my tiptoes, brush my lips against his. "I feel no remorse for what I did. I feel no sadness for your pain." I pause, dropping my voice to a whisper. "And I feel nothing for you."

He stiffens under my touch, but he does not retreat, so I grasp his lapels and pull my mouth to his ear. "I loathe you."

His hands jerk to my waist, as though by instinct, and they fist in the silky fabric there as he sucks in a tortured breath. "Deceitful little creature," he says. "I loathe you, too."

My body is a live wire, humming in his hands. But instead of kissing me or saying anything else, he releases me.

"Please," I say, "I want to know the truth. And you want to trust me. So do it."

"In that," he says, his voice thick, "you are mistaken. Trusting you is the last thing I want to do."

"Liar," I retort, breathless. "You *need* to trust me."

"Why would I need to do that?"

"Because you want to be free of your life of lies just as much as I want to be free of mine."

He shakes his head. "Do not think because you have spent a week in my casino that you understand me."

"I have something to show you." I dig into my purse and pull out his secret, now transformed back into the plain die, and push it into his grasp. "I stole this from your room."

His jaw hardens as he inspects it. "All the more reason not to trust you."

"Is it?" I point at his open palm. "I never rolled it."

I can tell he senses the truth in my words because his hand clenches into a fist around it.

"I wanted to. I nearly did." I meet his gaze. "But secrets are meant to be shared, not stolen. And you are more important to me than whatever secret that die holds."

His pupils are dark, his jaw hard. "Be satisfied with your win. Take the Unbreakable Lie, and leave."

"I don't want your prize, and I don't care about your game," I snap. "You said once that facing the truth is as scary as facing an assassin. I'm ready to." I lean in and meet his eye. "The question is whether *you* are."

Frowning, he stares hard at his fist still clenched around his secret. "What gain would I achieve by sharing any more of my secrets with you?"

"I know what a burden they can be," I say.

He scoffs. "You want to alleviate my burden by adding a slew of your own problems to my back?"

"No," I say. "I want to alleviate your burden with my friendship."

He barks a laugh. "You think highly of yourself, little thief."

"Fine. You don't want friendship? We don't need to be friends." I meet his glare head-on. "But your brother rescued me for a reason. Find out why. Dig through every secret of my past." I step so close there's barely an inch of space between us. "Lay me bare."

He licks his lips but does not reply.

"There is something in me your magic craves," I whisper, raising a hand to trace the scar over his cheekbone and eyebrow and into his hair. I twirl the white strands around my fingers. "Find out what it is, and use it to gain the relief you seek."

"How can I find relief," he says, taking a slow, deliberate breath, "in someone so vexing?"

"Confounding, I thought," I say.

"Tormenting." He dips, his lips grazing mine like a secret. "Tantalizing." His tongue slips along my mouth. "Tempting." I arch into him, and his hands slide over my curves, slow and intentional.

"Does this mean you trust me?" I ask when his teeth scrape my bottom lip.

He pivots, dragging slow, maddening kisses along my jaw to my ear. "Why do *you* trust *me*?" he breathes, nipping at my lobe. "Why give me the power to break you?"

Tingles race under my skin where he touches me. "I—"

"The game is over." He gives me one last kiss, then releases me. "May guile guard you, my dear."

And then he's walking away. Again. Only this time, it feels absolute. A closing door, a grand finale.

But I'm not done yet. It cannot be over.

I pull out the die I filled with my new secret. I do not know what it means, what my magic is, or how I got it, but Nic might, and if he finds out about it, he could do just as his brother did. Make me a prize and a pawn all over again.

I should run. Find a way to live with half a heart, tethered to Enzo for better or worse for the rest of my life. Keep searching for the moonshard.

But Nic's question swirls in my mind. Why do I want to trust him? Why do I want to help him? Why do I want to risk vulnerability and ruin?

My secret flares as though in response.

Because I'm listening to my own heart, my own mind, my own judgment, for the first time, and those things tell me he is worth trusting.

"Nic."

He looks back to me. His eyes fall to my fist, where violet light radiates between my fingers.

"You want to know why you should trust me?" I hold up the die. "Because I'm choosing to be vulnerable first."

He swallows, waiting, eyes darting from the die to my face.

Trust was never the thing that gave people the power to hurt me. Abandoning myself was.

I roll the die.

It clatters across the floor, and when it comes to a stop, I close my eyes.

Yes, this opens me to the possibility of being put in another box, just like before. But even if it does, I'll always have myself. My heart, my mind, my questions, my resolve.

And I will never abandon me again.

CHAPTER FIFTY-TWO

NIC

Lola St. James's secret explodes in a chaos of stars and light.

The splinters of ice in my veins warm as her truths unspool around me.

There she is, rendering herself incorporeal just like Enzo, trailing me to my room, watching me dance. And there she is, stealing strength the way he does to escape another player in my casino. And there, using more of his magic to scale the outside of the building.

But also . . . there she is, drawing *my* magic into an empty die to create an illusion of a telegram. And there, digging into the darkest parts of herself to extract a secret and cage it inside a die. And a final time, filling dice at the table in the finale with glamours.

Somehow, this mesmerizing, maddening young woman was able to use not only my brother's magic but mine as well.

The secret swims past her in flecks of stardust, lifting tiny strands of hair away from her face, reflecting in her glasses like a sun flare.

This is how Enzo has managed to compound his power and buy himself time. She's some kind of conduit for magic. A vessel.

My power wrestles inside me, driven wild with her soullight. She meets my gaze, and the corner of her mouth quirks.

She is gravity. A black hole in space. A force of mercurial magnitude like a piece of polished voratium.

I force my feet to stay where they are and not give in to her pull. Force my hands to remain at my sides and not cup her cheeks. Force my lungs to breathe in and out and not drink her in like she's the only oxygen in a universe devoid of it.

And I know as the stardust fades to flickering ashes around our faces that it's not just her effect on my magic that has me desperate. It's *her*. The little thief who wears her heart on her sleeve, who doesn't try to hide what she feels or what she wants. The dancer whose body moved against mine in the most truthful, honest way I've ever known. Whose ears caught every word I did not say, whose eyes caught every gesture I did not make.

The girl who values truth as much as I do.

So when she steps close, when she captures my mouth with hers, I kiss her back. Kiss her with everything I am and everything I wish I were. My hands tangle in her impossible curls, my tongue slips into her impossible mouth, and my heart twists itself into impossible knots trying to figure out how to make this last. How to be what I say I am.

Too soon, she pulls back, breathless. "So that's a yes?" she gasps against my mouth. "You'll help me?"

I pause, hands stilling against the base of her head.

Will I help her? *Can* I?

Suddenly, even surrounded by the delicious scent of her, I cannot breathe. Her secret flashes through my mind over and over, and alongside it, all the memories I have of her and my brother. The way he knew her too well to believe her deceptions in the restaurant—a knowing that seemed deeper than sharing a heart. The way her eyes flickered to him when we found her in my vault, like he was her home.

The way her voice broke when she begged him not to whisk her away. And the way it rasped a few moments ago when she said, *He lied to me.*

He did so many times it broke her. I feel the cracks in her kiss, in the tremble of her lips, in the way she searches my face for reassurance every time I speak.

He took her heart, kept it under false pretenses, and she lived her life according to them. Every choice she must have made, every thought she must have had, everything she must have become was because of what Enzo told her.

And now that she knows he lied, she is shattered.

I know exactly what it feels like to have reality ripped away like that. Stars, I remember the crushing weight of realization that night watching my whole belief system melt with the liquid light all over Laurel's hands. The pain, the terror, the anger.

Have I . . . Have I done the same thing to Enzo?

The thought hits me like a physical force, and I stumble backward, shaking.

The false leads I planted . . . the game board I made of this city . . . the pawn I turned him into as I played him from clue to clue, keeping him in the dark because I was too afraid of what he'd do with the truth.

Cold dread slicks through me, more frigid than any magic.

If Enzo is Lola's captor because he planted lies to keep her under his thumb, then I am his.

A liar as vile as they say.

She peers into my face, clearly waiting for a response, but I cannot speak.

I want to trust her. Stars, how badly I do. And she wants to trust me. She's standing there begging me to let her.

But could I do that when I have already proven to be the very thing I thought I despised?

I've tried to be good in spite of my curse. Finding ways to get consent before I take secrets, fabricating games to help people escape their mental prisons, calculating everything to protect the ones I love.

But I am no better than the priests who hid away that moonshard to keep their influence sure. No better than Enzo, who boxed Lola in with professions of love.

What is my protection worth if it comes at the cost of my brother's freedom? Or Lola's?

Who am I, indeed, to think I have any right to people's secrets?

As Lola says my name, I hear Enzo whispering it, his face illuminated by the moonshard's light in the temple moments before its magic detonated around us.

As she reaches for me, I see Laurel's outstretched hands bleeding soullight, hear her tortured cries, see her eyes wide like moons.

I couldn't explain myself to either of them, just as I cannot explain myself to Lola now. This curse will forever keep her from knowing who I am, from seeing the truth of me, and in that way, no matter what relationship we could ever have, it would be just as much of a lie as the one she's shared with my brother the past four years.

The sound of the crowd is far away, like the distant roar of the ocean. The only light comes from the faint glow of my scar. It traces her in silver, dusts her in night.

She presses her palm to my chest and repeats her question. "Will you help me?"

I settle my hands along the slender sides of her neck and lean in. Her mouth parts as mine hovers just a breath away. Air trembles hot between our tongues.

She tastes of truth. Of vulnerability and trust. Of freedom.

Things too pure for seaspawn like me.

"Lola," I say, so quiet I can barely hear it over the pounding of my heart. "You need to leave."

"No, I don't." She tries to meet my eye.

But I can't look at her. If I do, I might give in to the parts of me begging not to let her go. Those parts will exploit her. Will keep secrets because that's all they can do. Will imprison her with them. Will break her.

And I am done breaking people.

"Please." My voice grates over something thick in my throat.

"Damn it, Nic." Her voice cracks as she pounds a fist on my chest. "Let me in!"

I swallow the lump in my throat. It hurts, just like the magic. "You have your prize. Take it and go."

"I don't want the starsdamned prize!" she cries. "I want *you*, you ridiculous, sparkly, lying, cocky bastard!"

"You do not know me."

"I want to."

"No, you don't." I raise a finger, press it to her lips as I finally meet her eyes in the dark. "Trust *that*."

Her breath trembles against my touch. "Please, Nic."

"Please," I whisper as I come undone. "Lola."

I've been a disappointment from the beginning. I am nothing if not reliable in that.

But it still hurts, to see her lose hope, lose faith, lose trust. Hurts just like it did with Laurel and with Enzo.

It's better like this. Better now, when it will only hurt and not destroy.

So I let the tears roll down her cheeks. Let her glare burn through me until I feel nothing, hear nothing, see nothing. I keep my expression impassive as she quivers molten before me.

As she learns to loathe me all over again.

But she doesn't release her hold on my jacket. Doesn't retreat.

She is not going to let me go, not without an explanation. So perhaps I should give her one. Give her a reason. One final lie to spare her from a lifetime of more.

My heart lurches, my stomach flares, and I back her up until her spine hits the wall, then thread my hands through the hair at the base of her skull. Heat floods me as my thumbs press her jaw upward and to one side. I lean in and breathe against her ear, "You were warned when you arrived."

"Warned of what?" she gasps, trembling in a way that makes me want to kiss her. I let her feel my desire, let her taste it, let the truth twist itself into the lie I need her to hear next.

"Be wary of my deceits, little thief," I hiss, my words an echo from the night we met, "for at the Liar's Den, even your heart may make a glamour of truth." I tip her chin so her eyes meet mine, close enough to devour her. "You do not want my trust, and you do not want my help. You only think you do." I release her. "You have been glamoured."

With that, I yank open the door, forcing myself not to look back when the breath rushes out of her.

I keep my composure until the door has closed behind me. Until I've ventured to my suite and locked myself inside. I cross to my silks where they hang from the ceiling in the corner and run my hand down their length. A growl rises in my throat, bleeding into a roar as I grasp them and pull.

When they tear, the sound is the scream of stars, of a brother who learned to loathe me, of a girl who my love once destroyed.

And another whose trust I will never, ever deserve.

"Sir?" Paol's voice crackles over the radio.

Slamming my thumb on the radio's button, I bark, "What?"

"You'd better come down here."

"Not now, Paol."

"I'm sorry, sir," comes the reply. "It's just . . . Magnus St. James is here. He was at the finale, and he has some questions."

I still, unclipping the radio and gripping it hard. "Questions?"

"About Tremaine, sir."

Dread chills through me, freezing away every other sensation.

Did he recognize her?

Swallowing, I lift the radio to my mouth with a shaking hand. "Send him up to my office. Please."

CHAPTER FIFTY-THREE

LOLA

I walk in a daze through the building, taking the servants' corridors to avoid the journalists and photographers. The casino is loud, but all I hear are whispers. It is bright, but all I see are distant stars cloaked in shadow.

I spill out onto the street, where the night is cool and clear and the air is tinged with sea and citrus.

Shirley LaCour's voice trills behind me, *"Spin me like a tale, one where I'm the one you need . . ."* But it cuts short when the door clicks shut. Automobiles speed past, horns blare, and journalists who have been waiting on the sidewalk rush toward me, cameras shuttering as they clamor from every side. I push past them, not sure where I want to go, only that I need to. The noises rattle around in my ears, a chaos accentuated by the blinding neon lights on every casino down the block.

I slip into a side street until quiet envelopes me and lets me slow my pace. I wait to feel something. Anger? Hurt? Despair? But all that's there is Enzo's heart, contemplative and quiet and full of shame.

My feet turn of their own accord, shuffle down the sidewalk, slosh through the puddles left in the wake of the storm.

Be wary of my deceits, little thief...

I increase my pace. I don't want to hear Nic's voice. Because if I hear it again, I might cry, and I've done enough crying over these brothers. Enough hurting, enough begging, enough chasing.

...for at the Liar's Den...

It was real. I know it was real. His kisses and his secrets and his quiet, watchful hurt.

...even your heart...

I break into a run, but his words are there in my head, echoing louder than the music, than the city, than even my heartbeat.

...may make a glamour of truth.

I was so sure, *so sure*, he would listen, that he was worth trusting. But I was *so sure* Enzo had been telling the truth, too.

Perhaps everything that happened with Nic was just as much of a deception.

I swing around a corner and make a beeline for the ocean, a place forbidden and yet somehow home. Wind whips my curls away from my face and salt stains my tongue. I do not stop running until my feet hit the sand, and it is only then that I glance back at the casino district, bold yellows and crimsons and greens against the sky. The Liar's Den spires high above them all, a glittering seaspawn monster. A masterpiece. A lie.

I kick off my shoes and slog through the heavy sand to the water's edge, plunge my feet ankle-deep in white foam. I close my eyes and beg the fabled demons in the waves for the answers the stars and their spawn refuse to give.

"Hey, Lola. Which is closer, me or this four-pound bag of snazzatazzles?" Enzo's voice is like a blade to my heart.

I blow out a slow breath. "I thought we were done."

"Would it help if I apologized?" The mirth in Enzo's voice fades. "Because I want to."

I shake my head, keeping my back to him. "I don't know."

He doesn't respond for several moments, and when he does, his voice is scratchy. Grief and remorse weigh our shared heart heavy against my ribs. "Can I try anyway?" he asks.

Finally, I turn. He stands several yards away next to a massive burlap sack emblazoned with the bright-purple-and-fuchsia snazzatazzles label. The wind tousles his curls, and the gems in his brows, lips, and ears sparkle in the moonlight. His hands hang limply at his sides. His wrist is bare—Septavia must be frolicking in the waves now, and the black tattoo of her suction cups curls around his wrist in her absence.

"Maybe." The wind and the waves swallow up my whisper, but as always, our heart speaks a language no one else knows, a language that doesn't require words. And as I look at him, I don't see a betrayer, a liar, or a con man. I see only my best friend. My brother. My protector.

I want to sink into that reality. Pretend what has happened the past week never did. Relinquish myself to the story that was so comfortable for so long.

Enzo scoops up the bag and carries it toward me, his steps heavy and slow in the wet sand. "I can't tell you how sorry I am," he says, coming to a stop before me. "I should have been honest with you from the beginning. Shouldn't have treated you like a child or kept you isolated. I understand if you never forgive me for it." He presses the bag into my hands.

I sniff, turning my gaze away from the heartrending vulnerability in his face, and stare at the moon hanging low and blue and shining on the horizon.

"Look . . ." He sighs. "I know that a bag of snazzatazzles isn't going to change your mind, but . . . I want a chance to make things right. To answer your questions."

I hate how his words and his damn bleeding heart make me ache. I nod at the bag of candy. "Did you steal these?"

"Oh, come on, don't tell me you went to a casino and got noble," he teases. "What's the point of having magical thieving powers if you pay for things all honest and pure?"

I snort in spite of myself. "Fair enough."

He takes another step closer. "I heard you won the tournament."

"I didn't get the secret, though."

He purses his lips. "Still . . . an Unbreakable Lie . . . perhaps we could use that."

I suck in a slow breath, holding it until my head pounds and my lungs ache and my chest twitches, ready to burst.

I hate this. Hate that the place that once felt so soothing to me now feels like poison. Hate that the sound of his voice, once a lullaby, has become a warning bell.

What if I'm making a mistake?

"Why did you choose me?" I ask him, my voice small, like I must have sounded the night he found me, bruised and broken.

"What do you mean?"

"When you offered our deal. Why me?" Did he know I was something different? Did he know about my ability to channel magic?

He sighs, running a hand through his hair and studying my face. "I found out you were kept away from others your whole life. I figured you'd be naive enough to believe me." He purses his lips. "Stars, that sounds awful to say out loud."

I wait for that answer to be enough for me to shove down the doubts. Enough to lock them up behind stone walls and reassure myself that the details don't matter. That one day it will make sense, and besides, if I'm happy, who cares if it doesn't add up?

But it's different now. Nic's ivy has split through the stone. Crumbled it. And with that refuge in rubble, Enzo's words are empty. Not enough. Won't ever be enough.

"It didn't have anything to do with what I am?" My voice breaks.

"What you are?" He frowns and takes me into his arms, warm and familiar as breathing, and oh, how it hurts. "It was your vulnerability and isolation that made you my target. That, and nothing more."

My heart sinks.

Because even without my magic, even without rolling a single die, I know now what his lies sound like. And this is another one.

He knows about my magic. He's always known.

I press my face into his shoulder.

"Does this mean"—he pulls back to look at my face—"that you believe me?"

"I—" I begin, but my voice breaks.

He rushes on. "I swear to you, I will never lie to you again."

I want to believe him. How desperately I do.

But as I stare at him, watch his eyes tighten, feel his earnestness pleading inside me, I know. Just like I knew with Ostena in the game of Liar's Dice.

I don't need a die to tell me what's true. I don't need a devious boy or a father or even a careful ally. I don't need stars or magic or a moonshard.

I have a clever mind. I have keen eyes. I have a heart. And though I share it with Enzo, it is mine. Always has been, always will be.

He is lying. And he will lie again and again, for as long as I let him.

That knowledge fills me, not with rage, not with anger, and not even with sadness.

With hope. A swelling, warming, calming sort of strength that steadies my breath, slows my pulse, quiets my fears.

For years, I have been subjected to the games of the Devious, marched around on their pretty game boards, but not anymore. I play my own games, chart my own course.

Me.

Enzo's still waiting, watching every emotion on my face.

DEN OF LIARS

I need answers. About who I am and what I am, about what happened the night that moonshard cursed these brothers, and what it has to do with me. About what my father knows and what exactly Enzo plans to do with the moonshard once he gets his hands on it.

I need the truth. And if neither of the Devious will give it to me, then I will have to become the game master, the ringleader, and the puppeteer myself.

But as long as we share a heart, no matter what I might say or how I might lie, Enzo will know. If I've learned anything about conning people, it's that I need to make sure they won't realize they're being tricked.

Discreetly, I dig in my purse for the Unbreakable Lie.

If I want Enzo to let me in, he needs to believe me naive once more.

So, though danger thrums like vibrating strings in my soul, I toss the die behind him. It flicks across the sand and lands in the foam. The tide swallows it as magic pulses into the air, a mesmerizing twirl of iridescent smoke. It twines lazily to meet my skin, and when it does, power thrums through me more poignant than any of the Liar's dice I have used before.

"I'm so sorry," Enzo says again, worry still apparent in his voice and heart.

I take a deep breath as the words I need to speak carve through me. "I trust you, Enzo."

My lie cements itself, a living, breathing being between us, and the magic rockets out of me, stardust funneling to the sky, filling it with light for an instant before it vanishes.

But Enzo did not see, did not feel any of it. He raises his brows, hopeful. "You do?"

"Yes." I force a smile as tears burn my eyes, imagining my teeth sharpening like Nic's once did, my cheekbones rising hard like glass. "But things are going to be different from now on. No more holding me at arm's length."

"Of course."

"Take me to the Brig. Make me a Tentacle. Show me I'm not as expendable as you treated me today."

Holding my gaze, his stare turns cautious. "Once you become a Tentacle, you are a Tentacle for life. Are you ready for that kind of commitment?"

"I wagered my heart to you already. How much more commitment do you need?" I say. "The secret's already out. Nic knows who I am and what I am to you, so it's truly in your best interest to let me in. Keep me close."

His smile widens, and his eyes spark. "I show you the Brig; you show me that Unbreakable Lie."

"How about you show me the Brig because I earned my spot in it?" I say, keeping the sharpness I feel out of my voice. "No more bargains, no more deals, no more bribes."

The breeze lifts his curls, blows them across the glittering gem in his left dimple as he nods. "All right, Ligament. Let's go." His fingers interlace with mine, a voratium gem clasped between our palms. Our bodies ripple as one into shadow as we stride into the tide.

My heart is aching, my soul breaking, but I hold my head high.

I have another secret to win, but this time I'm the House, and as Nic once told me, the House always gets what it desires in the end.

I slip into the deep a dancer *and* a thief.

And utterly devious.

Acknowledgments

I still remember the first time I uttered this book into existence. I was on the phone with one of my dear critique partners, trying to explain a nebulous concept about "some brothers who are like . . . crimes? And it's sort of a love triangle, but also not? And one of them is basically cursed to lie about everything. But in a sexy way? I promise it sounds a lot cooler in my head."

So here is where I acknowledge the wonderful people who listened to all that babbling and lied to me as skillfully as Nic that it did sound cool. That it totally made sense. That no, I was not speaking gibberish. And that I should absolutely go eat more snacks.

First, to the critique partner in question, Kim Chance. Thank you for nodding and smiling and not telling me how convoluted my plot sounded until later when I'd actually written it and it thankfully was less of a dumpster fire than it initially seemed like it would be. Thank you for being the best cheerleader every step of the way, for listening to me sob over the phone about books and life and everything in between, for fighting for me and always being willing to drop everything to read a draft when I need it. I am endlessly grateful you and Megan made me your third musketeer. You can never get rid of me now.

Speaking of Megan, here's to you, LaCroix! Thank you for being

ACKNOWLEDGMENTS

the best sounding board of all time. For uttering the question I'd been thinking for weeks—"Should the Liar have his own POV?"—and forcing me to actually consider it. For listening to my jumbled brainstorms and combing through my manuscripts at every stage. Your word-cutting skills are unmatched, but your friendship and support are even more so. Hope you like dumb jokes, Taylor Swift memes, and existential crises, because you're stuck with me!

To Jessica Froberg. Sigh. What would I do without you? Probably cry a lot more. Eat my weight in Cheesecake Factory every time I have to do a synopsis. And write significantly less coherent novels. Thank you for squeeing about my characters, fighting me when I say I suck, and listening to my endless rambling messages. Thank the stars for you, my dear.

To Lindsay Puckett, who read the messy first draft and didn't run screaming. And who also is solely responsible for my growing obsession with specialty teas. Thank you for the late-night messages, the midday encouragements, and the fantastic feedback on this book. You are the best.

To J. Elle, for always listening and always reminding me of my worth and my potential. For the hours-long chats about everything under the sun and the encouragement at every step of the way. Thank you, thank you, thank you.

To Holly West, editor extraordinaire, who caught my vision and held me up as I ran with it. Who directed my hands back to the steering wheel whenever the car veered off course. Thank you for seeing the magic in this story, for your brilliant editorial eye, and for your enthusiasm. This book never would have become what it is without you.

To Mary Lusebrink for your fantastic feedback. To Emily Stone for your impeccable copy edits and Lelia Mander for your meticulous notes. To Aurora Parlagreco and Abby Granata for the beautiful book design. To Lorena Lammer for the gorgeous cover art (I'm obsessed). And to everyone else on the team at Feiwel & Friends. Thank you for championing this book from the beginning.

ACKNOWLEDGMENTS

To Christa Heschke and Daniele Hunter. I love how I said, "So I have this idea for a book about some brothers . . ." and you instantly became *Den of Liars*'s biggest fans, even though I hadn't written it yet. You are both so supportive, so kind, and so endlessly enthusiastic about some of my wildest concepts. Thank you for going to bat for this project and finding it such a fantastic home.

To Leslie Alder, whose Marco Polos and constant stream of funny reels have been the flamingo floatie that kept me above water for the past couple years. I quite literally wouldn't have been able to write books if not for your encouragement and your friendship.

To Kylie Lee Baker, Diana Urban, Tricia Levenseller, Rebecca Ross, Shelby Mahurin, and every other person who has encouraged me, listened to me whine, and made me laugh during the writing of this book, I don't deserve you.

To Julie Lochridge for the gorgeous digital art you painted to help me announce this project.

To my parents, who have always supported this dream since my days of crafting picture books as a child.

To badass spinny lady Eré Domínguez for igniting my passion for aerial hoop. I was only going to take ONE CLASS for research, but damn it, you just had to make it too fun. Thank you for helping me fly!

Also, to Frieda Austin and Suzo Blackwood for teaching me all the silks and hammock things I needed for this book, and to the rest of my circus friends for making me laugh and welcoming me with open arms when I decided to try something new and fell in love with it.

To my four brilliant, wild, adorable, wonderful children. I am the luckiest person alive to get to be your mother and watch you grow. Your stories are the most beautiful ones I've ever known, and I can't wait to see what you accomplish, who you become, and how you dazzle the world with your magic. Thank you for being you.

Finally, to Jon. Always to you. For the take-out dinners and the late-night laughs, for the top-of-the-lungs car singing and the mid-morning snuggles, for the long walks hand in hand and the whispered

ACKNOWLEDGMENTS

hopes for the future. You will always be the love interest in every version of my story. The best friend, the confidant, the hero, the rock. Thanks for being my strongest supporter, my loudest cheerleader, and my most brilliant brainstormer. None of these books would be what they are without you.

And now, here at the end, I tip my sparkly fedora to all of you, dear readers. Whether this is the first book of mine you've picked up, or if you've been with me since *Sing Me Forgotten*, thank you. Thank you. Thank you. Stories are meant to be shared, characters meant to be known, magic meant to be wielded, and you are what make those things happen.

May guile guard all of your hopes and dreams and maybe even your secrets, too.

Thank you for reading this Feiwel & Friends book.

The friends who made

DEN OF LIARS

possible are:

JEAN FEIWEL, PUBLISHER
LIZ SZABLA, VP, ASSOCIATE PUBLISHER
RICH DEAS, SENIOR CREATIVE DIRECTOR
ANNA ROBERTO, EXECUTIVE EDITOR
HOLLY WEST, SENIOR EDITOR
KAT BRZOZOWSKI, SENIOR EDITOR
DAWN RYAN, EXECUTIVE MANAGING EDITOR
KIM WAYMER, SENIOR PRODUCTION MANAGER
EMILY SETTLE, EDITOR
RACHEL DIEBEL, EDITOR
FOYINSI ADEGBONMIRE, EDITOR
BRITTANY GROVES, ASSISTANT EDITOR
AURORA PARLAGRECO, ART DIRECTOR
ABBY GRANATA, JUNIOR DESIGNER
LELIA MANDER, PRODUCTION EDITOR

Follow us on Facebook or visit us online at mackids.com.
Our books are friends for life.